MANTLER'S SHACK

MANTLER'S SHACK

A Novel

R G SCHMIDT

SPRING CEDARS®

First edition, 2026

Book cover and design by Spring Cedars

ISBN 978-1-963117-80-6 (paperback)
ISBN 978-1-963117-81-3 (hardback)
ISBN 978-1-963117-82-0 (ebook)

Published by Spring Cedars
Denver, Colorado
www.springcedars.com

TABLE OF CONTENTS

CHAPTER 1

THE BRIDGE

Time has no weak spot, no bargaining moves;
We all carry our pennants, and we all fall down.

Jon Mantler jogged as smoothly and purposefully as he could through the cold drizzle of the early evening. He passed three bridges before turning onto a fourth. It was dark, misting, frigid, and he was getting increasingly wet as he crossed the river toward Budapest's more forested side in Buda.

Puffing and panting, he slowed to examine the area adjacent to the bridge for a sign of human life or any life at all. He was searching for eyes that might be looking back at him on this blustery night, but mostly he was looking for Karl Bircher.

As he neared the farthest side of the bridge, Mantler paused as if to stretch out his legs and elongate his back, but it was to allow him a more focused surveillance of the surroundings. Once satisfied that he was alone, he scurried down a set of steps leading to the water. In years long gone by, there had been a separate pedestrian stairway and an exit from the lower portion of the bridge to the forest that was connected to these steps. Mantler knew this because he had been here before. Over time, however, the lower portion of the stairs was no longer functional, and the trees and shrubs had become overgrown from below, which now made this part of the bridge inaccessible from that side.

As Mantler descended, he saw the shadowed outline of a man standing at this lower level. Karl Bircher. Mantler was assured of this as soon as he saw Karl's signature green toque, which on this cool, dismal evening was pulled down quite low near to his eyes and well over his ears.

"*Guten Abend, alles klar?* (Good evening, everything alright?)," uttered Karl in German. He didn't smile as he stepped forward to greet Mantler.

"*Ja, alles ist in Ordnung, aber das Wetter ist wirklich Scheiss,* (Yeah, everything's fine, but this weather is really shit)," Mantler answered.

Karl Bircher was an easy man to like. He smiled a lot and presented a warmth accompanied by a sly wit. He was uncomplicated and very skilled at sticking to the point of a conversation. He was not a waster of words.

Karl and Mantler were not close friends; however, since they had met on numerous occasions, there existed a respectful connection and camaraderie between them. Mantler was generally pleased to see Karl, and on occasion, once duties were completed, they would foray into conversations of a more casual nature. Karl probably knew more about Mantler than Mantler knew about Karl, but until today, there had been no reason for this to matter to Mantler.

Both men knew that on this foul night, there would be no time to waste on cordial chatter. They had originally intended to meet at this location two days earlier, but Karl had not appeared. It was not particularly unusual for Karl to miss or be late for one of these rendezvous, and there was always a plan in place for such mishaps; a set procedure to follow if one of them was unable to make it. Meetings would only be aborted if they had run out of options and no other choice existed.

Mantler was visiting Budapest for a total of four days; therefore, the backup plan was that they would repeat the same meeting protocols twenty-four hours later. For Mantler, the fact that he had been on this bridge the previous two nights in similar weather added a layer of urgency and tension to an already rushed and unpleasant night. This was the third and last chance for them to engage and exchange information, as Mantler was leaving Hungary on the midnight train to Vienna.

Generally, in these meetings, Mantler would give Karl both handwritten and verbal information about things like military exercise locations, arms purchases, coordinates, protocols, and planning. In turn, Karl would give Mantler a specific series of letters and numbers, which Mantler was not trained to decode and did not understand at all. He was only charged with transporting them to his boss, who presumably could decode them. "Never leave a paper trail" Mantler was so often told, and he abided by this creed. Once the information was delivered, he made sure he retained no shred of evidence from any of the transmissions.

Mantler never knew the actual meaning of these symbols, and for someone who very much liked to know everything, this was not easy to accept. However, he also identified with and respected the importance of these operations and thus was content to stay within his lane of the rules of conduct. He was curious but disciplined. Also, the West German Interior Ministry paid him well for these exchanges. Though it was not in his basic nature to partake in such shady activities, the process was rather simple, and in the nearly three years that Mantler had been involved in these exchanges, it had been a problem-free experience.

Today, under this bridge, it would be immoderately different. Two days late and in this vile weather, Mantler and Karl shook hands, impatiently smiled at each other, then quickly got to the point. The formal aspects of these exchanges generally lasted ten to twenty minutes, but tonight, within the first few minutes, Mantler sensed that something was out of sorts.

Karl, normally unhurried and deliberate, was rushing. He abruptly handed Mantler a few small notecards. Mantler verbally delivered technical information relating to an F-18 aircraft, but he was doubtful that Karl was taking it all in. So he carefully repeated each of the three parts of the message twice. The meeting concluded rather tensely.

As Mantler and Karl shook hands a second time and rendered their goodbyes, they noticed what appeared to be a man walking onto the upper bridge from the forested side.

"*Ich sehe es, Du must aber gehen. Geh jetzt!* (I see him, but you need to go. Go now!)," Karl blurted out.

"*Ja, okay, bleib gut und bis nächstes Mal,* (Yes, okay, stay well and see you next time)," Mantler nervously replied as he promptly ascended the steps to the upper part of the bridge. As he jogged toward the city, he didn't look back until he was more than one hundred meters farther along. Then, curiosity and a sense of duty caused him to stop and feign tying his shoe so he could look back at Karl. The stranger had ambled down the same stairs Mantler had just come up. It was a bit difficult to see because it was raining harder now, and there were too few lights on the old and rarely used bridge.

Mantler stretched his body closer to the edge and looked out over the rail. Just then, he thought he saw Karl and the man engaged in an animated argument. As the light reflected off the water below, Mantler thought he saw the man strike Karl.

The rain was pouring noisily onto the concrete. Mantler instinctively began running back toward the stairs. He did not take the time to pause and carefully consider his next actions. Once he reached the top of the steps, he slowed for a moment, afraid, trying to figure out what was actually happening.

Mantler noticed the third man was quite big and wore a long, brown coat. Then, he saw Karl tumble onto the stairs. As the man ran up after him, Mantler hit him with a body check from his left side, just like an ice hockey defenseman. It propelled the big man down a few steps, where he landed on his knees. But he immediately rushed back up the stairs toward Mantler, yelling loudly. Now it was even clearer that the man was far bigger and probably significantly stronger than Mantler.

Mantler panicked. He had never been in an actual physical fight in his entire life, at least not since he was seven years old. He acted before he reacted; he acted without thinking. He anticipated the moment when the big man was about to mount the last step that separated them, rushed forward, and body-slammed him again, this time like an offensive football lineman. Pure fear and passion ruled him; all rational thought had left.

Acting on impulse was unusual behavior for Mantler. The impact caused most of Mantler's momentum to stop, yet he still fell forward onto the wet concrete and metal a few steps below. Simultaneously, he heard the most agonizing grunt and moan as the big man fell a second time. This time, he fell backward and awkwardly much farther out and toward the metal guardrail. The big man did not sense or see the dilemma of the raging river behind him.

He tripped through the one narrow opening where there was no rail, where there was only a small, knee-high, metal-link chain. Despite the darkness and the rain, Mantler could see the entire tragedy slowly play out before him. Crawling forward on his knees, Mantler watched in astonishment as the big brown lump with a black toque landed in the gray-black (not blue) Danube.

Later, when Mantler would try to remember this in greater detail, he would recall most vividly the sound of the smack and the height of the splash as the big man's body gracelessly hit the water. Time stopped; only the rain continued.

Then, as if controlled by robotic intervention, Mantler looked away. He rushed back up the steps to Karl, shouting his name. There was no reply. Once Mantler got close enough, he realized Karl was never going to reply. The third man was gone, and so was Karl.

Mantler had only seen one other dead man in his life, and that man was his father. Back then, it took him a long time to recognize what death was. This time it did not. He checked Karl for any sign of life and confirmed there was no breathing, no pulse, and no warm blood flowing through his veins. There was no doubt he was dead.

Mantler paused briefly as he tried to stop his arms and shoulders from shaking. He was now glad for the rain, glad it was dark, and glad that there was still no sight of any other people on or near the bridge. He scanned his surroundings again as best he could, hoping no one had witnessed what had just happened.

Thinking a bit more clearly, he surmised that the incident had occurred in merely a minute, maybe two, and he did not want to be on that bridge any longer. He needed to get away. Fast.

Knowing it was only a few steps to that preposterously placed chain in the guardrail, Mantler awkwardly dragged Karl down to the landing. That part was easy; the challenge was rolling Karl's lifeless body underneath the chain.

Mantler peered into the reflecting light of the Danube as it separated Karl from his trademark green toque, the water gobbling them both into the reflecting waves. He checked his surroundings all the way up from the chain to the steps above. Still no one in sight. He did spot thick liquid pooled on the concrete where Karl had fallen. Luckily, the pelting rain was working away at it.

There was nothing else Mantler could do about the blood except plead for more rain. He retraced his path up and down the steps and did not notice anything else. Not knowing what to do next, he chose to rely on the storm and moved on.

Before Mantler was aware of it, he was jogging across the bridge toward the city. The jogging kept him from shaking. He was not thinking anymore; he was in a trance, breathing hard and running fast. Keep moving, he told himself. Keep humming along.

Three years of living in Europe had made Mantler quite used to running in the rain, and he knew how to dress to deal with the elements. His baseball-style hat was sealed with weatherproof spray, and his outer apparel was made of nylon, coated with Gore-Tex protection. This was the third straight night he had made this run and the third straight night he had been drenched with rain. Rain on, thought Jon Mantler.

There were a few pedestrians with umbrellas as he neared the city center, each immersed in their own personal circumstances as they challenged the weather. Once within a few blocks of his hotel, he stopped for a moment under a streetlight in order to survey his body and clothing. He noticed cuts and blood on his right hand and saw his running pants were torn through to the skin on his right knee. Otherwise, there was nothing—no mud, no fuss, only the wetness.

He took in a couple deep breaths and exhaled purposefully, just as he had learned to do in moments of emotion and stress. He fought off, as best he could, the pressure that had built an almighty concrete mass in his head. Mantler knew he needed to stay focused. He needed to stay flexible and agile.

Bit by bit, a story formulated and worked its way into his brain as he stretched his legs and moved under a rooftop overhang to avoid the rain. Right now, he still had choices. He could run to the nearest phone and report a version of what had happened to the local authorities, or he could run to his hotel, connect with his companion, and leave Budapest as scheduled. What he could not do was stand too long at this wall, stretching his groin muscles and deliberating over his options.

He tried to make sense of what had happened, but that was futile; there were too many unknowns to make that work. He knew that Karl was dead; he couldn't be sure about the third man, but it was unlikely that he would survive the fall and the power of the cold water. But why was this stranger on the bridge? What if he did survive? Did he know about their meeting? Even if he lived, he most likely would not have known what or who hit him before he fell in the water. Unless he already knew who Mantler was.

When under stress, Mantler had a tendency to think too much. He knew that thoughts triggered emotions, and emotions caused more thoughts, and he didn't want to fall into that circle. So he continued running.

The rain kept coming down. Mantler turned right and then up a small hill in the direction of his hotel. The hotel was now in sight; his decision had been made.

Waiting for him at the hotel would be his traveling companion and lover, Nora Baker. They had been a common-law couple for about four years and lived together in West Germany, just outside of Heidelberg. As always, Nora would be organized by the time Jon arrived at their hotel. They would need to leave for the train by 11:15 p.m.

It was just after 9:00 p.m. when Jon entered the lobby and hurried to the elevators. He was returning a little later than on the previous evening runs, but there was still ample time to clean up and change clothes to catch the train.

He entered the elevator and pressed the button for the sixth floor, glad to be alone. The ride up gave him a few moments to help him prepare to greet Nora. Since moving to West Germany, Jon had become more and more adept at keeping information from his partner. He didn't technically lie to her, but he was skillfully selective in what he shared with her and what he held exclusively to himself. In this situation, he would keep things as simple as he could.

It was a stupid move he had made earlier, trying to jump up onto a higher curb as he was running. The water had made the cobblestones extremely slippery, and he fell forward onto his right side. He replayed it a few times in his mind in order to make it feel easy. He knew Nora would believe him, as it was not the first time he had come in bloodied after a run. She would be annoyed with him but would buy the story. Focusing on his "running accident" helped Jon deflect any thoughts of the dreadful reality—the two bodies in the Danube.

Nora was dressed and lying on the bed, watching the news on the hotel's new English BBC channel, when Jon knocked on the door. She arose and opened the door without looking at him in any detailed way.

She had expected him to be late and soaking wet, and he was.

"Hi, honey. Sorry, I'm a bit late, but I slipped and fell out there, sort of crashed and burned again. I'm gonna shower right away." He carried on straight past the bed and into the bathroom. Once inside, he shed his wet cap, jacket, and running pants and looked at his bloodied wounds. The physical injuries looked dramatic but in actuality were minuscule.

"I have your clothes out here on the bed, and I packed everything else. Just put your wet running stuff in this plastic bag," Nora said through the bathroom door.

"Thanks, honey, we still have plenty of time. I'll order a taxi when I'm out of here," he replied in as normal a tone as he could muster as he tried to stop his body from shaking.

"I just don't get why you have to run every night in this horrible rain," she answered.

Jon almost found that remark humorous, even under the circumstances. Why indeed, he thought as he took out of his baseball cap the small note cards bearing numbers that Karl had given him. He was pleased to see they had stayed dry. He could make out all the numbers, although this wasn't as important to him now as it had been on other exchanges. He put the cards inside a compartment of his bathroom carry case and turned on the shower.

Under the hot water, he felt a sting on his bruised knee and bloodied hand, but everywhere else it felt remarkably soothing. The noise from the shower was a great relief. He held onto the wall and took his time—he needed time—and he let the tinglingly water pressure hit the back of his neck.

Suddenly, without warning, tears poured from his eyes. He sobbed and gyrated to keep himself from slipping, then lowered himself onto his one good knee near the drain of the tub. He tried to control the sobbing as the water hit his lower back. He let his body feel all his emotions and involuntarily convulsed. He felt like he was being transported to another planet, certainly into an altered state. He cupped his hands to his face, covering his mouth to cage the sounds he feared would escape from within.

The outburst of emotion subsided nearly as quickly as it came. Concocting new emotions was a skill he had perfected bit by bit throughout his young life. As a child, he had been very emotional, but in time and with age, he came to realize that emotions were actually a good thing. They were integral to survival.

The humming was something he had learned as a child from his mother, who taught him how to gain control of his thoughts and emotions. The method used was a simple rhythmic chant. It was not unlike singing, except it consisted of no words, only noises induced by random letters that triggered no actual thought or meaning and thus allowed his mind to go into a trance and relax. He and his mother had called it "humming," but it was much more than that; it was meditation therapy, and he needed to invoke this method now more than ever.

Never had he been tested at this level. His river of emotions was deep and wide, but with the humming, he was able to move his overactive thought patterns away so he could cope. He had to be certain Nora would never suspect anything out of the ordinary had happened to him tonight. Not tonight, and not ever.

Jon knew he had to get out of this tub, out of this bathroom, and, most importantly, he had to get out of Budapest.

He moved more swiftly and purposefully. He dried his body, wrapped himself in a big white towel, gathered all his running gear into a big ball, then opened the bathroom door and entered the room. As he put his wet clothes in the plastic bag, Nora saw his bloodied and bruised knee, but as predicted, she was not surprised by it. She simply shook her head and shrugged. Jon quickly got dressed in the clothes she had left out for him.

He explained the details of his cobblestone fall on the slippery Budapest streets and tried to paint his words in the most natural tones he could muster. He even chuckled at his clumsiness. Simultaneously, he put his wet shoes and running gear into another plastic bag from the hotel room closet and stuffed it into his already packed suitcase. He thought he should dispose of all his running gear but decided this was not the right place to do it. Probably better to get everything out of Budapest, he concluded.

"And how did you like your four days behind the Iron Curtain?" he playfully asked the ready-to-depart Nora. "I'll call the desk and get a taxi." He picked up the phone on the desk. "The reception says they have taxis available all the time, so I guess we can go whenever we're ready."

The train station was ten minutes by car from the hotel, and soon, Jon Mantler and Nora Baker made their way through the hotel lobby, out the front door, and into a waiting taxi that would take them to the main station. The rain was driving down even harder now than it was on the bridge. There was a volley of desperate thoughts intent on pressing into Jon's consciousness. He blocked them out the only way he knew how. Jon hummed.

At the same time, he sought to keep up a chat with Nora about the museums, restaurants, shops, and sights that they had encountered on their mini-vacation. Nora was an eager history buff and easy to engage in such conversations. These small cultural trips always inspired her and were primarily her idea.

This was their first time in Budapest, or so she thought, and she had enjoyed the experience very much. She had a wide variety of views and observations to share with Jon and seemed content to do so.

He feigned interest as he gazed out the window in the direction the river was flowing, which would eventually move Karl and the third man southward toward the center of the city. The rain, the cold, and the darkness were Jon's most valuable friends in this moment.

They boarded the train at 11:40 p.m., entering the first-class cabin that all foreigners traveling to and from Hungary rode in when booking tourist visa journeys such as this. It would be about six hours to Vienna and then another five hours to Munich, then onto Stuttgart and home.

Jon and Nora were escorted to their sleeping cabin by a hefty conductor, who checked their passports and visas. He held onto them until it was time to wake them up near Vienna; passports would be returned once the train crossed from Hungary into Austria.

Soon, the couple was alone in the cabin, where the small bed was already turned down. Nora went first to the washroom to prepare for a short night of sleep while Jon sat on the side of the bed. A few minutes later, Nora joined him, sliding in beside him and kissing him on his cheek.

Another rush of emotion overtook him. He hugged her close and told her that he loved her because he did, but also to help distract him.

He told her how pleased he was that they had this wonderful life together with such opportunities to travel and learn about the world. He hoped he was not talking too much and alerting Nora to the relentless anxiety inside him. But Nora seemed okay with it all, agreeing and smiling as he slipped off the bed and into the bathroom to wash his face, brush his teeth, and complete his pre-bedtime routine.

When he felt the train begin to move out of the station, he relaxed a little and took a softer breath, feeling the first moment of relief since running back from the bridge.

Still, he wasn't sure what he should be feeling, so he tried to make his mind go blank. Nothing but a whole bunch of nothing, he repeated to himself while he hummed and the train wobbled westward.

CHAPTER 2

SCHOOL

I still hear your voice! I hear you calling me!
And I miss you.

At the age of six, John Mantler Jr. finally got to go to school. He was way past ready for this. There was nothing he wanted more in his life than going to school.

Most of his childhood friends were older, and they had been in school for at least a year. Every day, he really wanted to go with them, but alas, it was not allowed because he wasn't yet six, and in his small village, that was when school started. He was bound to stay home and continue being taught by his mother, playing games, reading books, and building things. But he could not wait to go to school.

For years, the school in the Canadian prairie village where he had grown up was his favorite place to play. He loved the gigantic yard with the three small baseball diamonds and the many caragana trees that defined the boundaries. He would often go there on his own just to feel like he was a student and to play with his older pals before and after their classes.

When that official September day finally arrived and he was allowed to attend school, he was ecstatic. John Mantler Jr. crossed the street in front of his house, dashed up the alley to Main Street, and continued into another alley that led behind the village hall. He went across Queen Street and into the schoolyard. It was going to be the perfect day. Except it was also the day his mother left.

That morning, John Mantler Jr.'s young mother dressed him in special clothes, which had been delivered by post from Eaton's catalog a few weeks earlier. She watched him head down the trail to school until he turned left on Main Street and was gone from sight.

She then changed her clothes, took the two packed bags from her bedroom, and walked to the bus depot near the highway. Soon after, she was also gone from sight.

When John Mantler Jr. returned from school later that afternoon, following what he thought was the greatest day in his life, his father told him the news.

"She said she was going to visit her sister, but I don't know for sure, and I don't know when she will be back," was exactly what John Mantler Sr. said in an expressionless state.

John Jr., who throughout his childhood was called JJ by most everyone in the village, asked his father a series of questions. However, after ultimately realizing his questions were being answered with silence, he gave up and went into the other room. JJ had already learned that his father would only reveal information on his terms and on his own anguished timeline.

Once he got into the room that, until this day, was the one he had shared with his mother, he flopped onto his bed, which was near the foot of his mother's bed. He wondered why she hadn't told him she was going on a trip. Maybe she didn't want to bother him on his first day of school, he thought. But that didn't make much sense, not even to a six-year-old.

Time was still a slow-moving measure for this young boy. Most days seemed endless. This day, however, felt like it had no time in it at all. School had started and ended in a flash, and he tried to remember what they had done in class. But he couldn't because real time had abandoned him.

John Mantler Sr. had lived many years in his small, self-built house, which had become known to all in the village as Mantler's shack. The villagers, however, knew little to nothing about John Mantler, primarily because he never spoke to anyone about himself.

He had no known family, no particular friends, and in a town where everyone knew each other and all of them were somehow related to everyone else, this was quite unusual. So to compensate, people who knew only a few elementary things about old John Mantler made up stories about the rest. They said that John had returned from the war and had chosen this village to purchase a small lot on King Street as the site where he would build his three-room shack.

Older residents speculated that John had been a young carpenter and house builder prior to the war in the far north of the province during the drought and recession years.

Times were extremely hard in what became known as the Dirty Thirties. From there, when time transitioned into a dirty war overseas, John enlisted and was soon off on a big boat to a faraway place. The Great Depression and five-plus years of war in a foreign land now lived inside him. He never spoke about the war, which was a common practice for those who had returned from the episode, except to confirm that he would never again go back to such a horrific place.

It seemed like all John Sr. brought home from that war and those faraway nations was a broken-up body and a soulful sadness that caused him to grow more and more reclusive as each year passed. JJ knew only what he had sensed from a very young age, that his dad had experienced something awful in his life and was still suffering through it.

"John! Never go to war and never go to that awful place where I was."

JJ thought that the awful place he meant was France, but he didn't know much else about it.

On this afternoon and for most of the evening, JJ stayed on his small bed and waited for something good to happen, but nothing did. He tried to think about his day at school, but his mind wouldn't let him focus. He thought he remembered being told that his mother had a sister in a far-off place called Toronto. How would she get there from here? He wondered, knowing nothing other than it was far away. His curiosity was being cruel to him. He already missed his mother and wanted to tell her about school, and he wondered how long she would be gone.

"Is this what happens when you go to school, your mother goes away?" JJ muttered out loud.

In the next room, which was sort of a living room but also doubled as the room that John Sr. slept in, there was a sofa and a single bed, where he spread out.

Most days, John rested at about this time of the afternoon. He was an early riser and completed more work before noon than most could accomplish in a week. After lunch and after he had rested for about an hour, he would go back to working either in his garden or his woodshed until suppertime, usually between 6:00 p.m. and 7:00 p.m.

What if she didn't come back? JJ wondered. No, she would be back, he concluded.

The house that John Mantler had built piece by piece with his own hands did, in fact, look like a shack from the outside. It was all unfinished gray and brown wood, intentionally left that way to naturally mature and be weathered by the elements. But on the inside, which few other than JJ and his mother had ever seen, it was no shack at all. It was a masterpiece of beautifully sanded and stained hardwood.

Every inch from floor to ceiling was clean and immaculate. It was warm in the winter from the wood-burning stove that John diligently kept stocked and burning, and it was cool in the summer from the insulation and ventilation systems he had installed. Outside, behind the house, there was a classic two-holer outhouse, which the Mantlers used daily, except in the absolute coldest months of the year. There was also a fully stocked woodpile beside a woodshed where John spent most of his time, and farther down, at the bottom of the long property, there was an old garage beside a no-longer-functioning well. Through the eyes of the six-year-old JJ, living here was paradise.

As the days clicked by and turned into weeks, and then later into months, it became quite apparent to both Johns that JJ's mother, Roxanne Martin, was probably not coming back. JJ's lessons of time were now becoming hard. Life in the shack became long and silent ever since she was gone.

JJ filled his time with school, went eagerly every day, and that became a kind of sanctuary for him. He was young and had no choice but to live the life that lay before him each day. His aging father tried as best he could to support young JJ and provide the basics of what a growing boy needed. John made sure clothes were clean and food was always readily available. Together, they grew older a bit more rapidly than might normally be expected. Though they rarely spoke about Roxanne, they were both sharing and adapting to a dramatic loss.

The drama became much more confusing one day when JJ brought a letter home with him from the post office. Often after school, JJ would pass by the post office to see if he could be of assistance to Mr. Lenton, the postmaster. Before he was old enough to attend school, he would hang out with Mr. Lenton whenever he saw the elderly man pushing the two-wheel mail cart across the open lots that separated the post office from the train station and the tracks that connected through the village. The train did not pass through every day. Sometimes, it didn't stop at all, but a few times each week, there would be enough post and shipments to warrant a stop. On those days, the postmaster would have been informed and ready to meet the train at the station.

JJ eagerly accompanied Mr. Lenton on these missions and felt he was a valued employee of the National Postal Service. Since he now attended school, he had to miss many of these adventure-filled train stops, but he still liked to go to the post office on his way home from school and parlay with his "boss." In doing so, he would also pick up any mail destined for the Mantler shack.

It had been about two months since Roxanne had left the village when JJ carried a letter home to his father. It was in a light blue envelope with a pattern around the edges. JJ had never seen a letter like this before. First, John read it silently, but upon seeing his son staring up at him intently, he decided to read it out loud.

JJ didn't understand what the letter was saying until John put it down on the kitchen table and sat beside him. In reality, neither Mantler understood the letter because it did not make a great deal of sense. It did, however, succeed in one aspect: It confirmed that Roxanne Martin was not going to return to the village.

The blue letter was ostensibly from Roxanne's sister, Elizabeth, and it proclaimed that Roxanne Martin had been killed in a traffic accident near that faraway place known as Toronto. The accident had taken place many weeks earlier, and Elizabeth apologized for not informing John sooner.

She claimed that she had not known whom to contact from the community of friends from Roxanne's time living out west. It was all very sad and shocking, she said. The family had taken care of the required funeral details and buried Roxanne near their home in a town she named in Ontario.

John looked at his son, worried about how this might hurt him. "All this means is that she's not going to come back here. I'm sorry, John, but we'll just have to go on as we have been, without her."

JJ could see pain in his father's eyes, and he didn't want to do any further damage, so he nodded as if he understood.

John knew this letter was a poorly crafted attempt to stop any pursuit that he might have been intending to locate Roxanne Martin. A pursuit he had not at all intended. John knew from the day that Roxanne left that she would not return. He always knew this day would come, but he thought it would be years later. His concern was for the well-being of his son, so he chose his words very carefully. The arrival of the letter, foolish as it was, succeeded in bringing an end to any thoughts JJ might have had of his mother returning.

"This letter doesn't mean anything other than that. You can't believe everything you read," John advised. "I don't think that very much else here is true." John didn't know how to make the news any gentler on his son; he knew it was confusing for him.

JJ's seventh year of life was turning out to be a difficult one. In the ensuing days and weeks, he drew closer to his father, who spoke to him more and more about life and how it came with unwelcome circumstances that you had no choice but to accept.

Roxanne was a vibrant twenty-one-year-young woman when she arrived in the village after tracking her cousin, who was scheduled to marry a farm boy in the region. This cousin was living with the boy and his family on a countryside farm, quite a few kilometers from the village. Roxanne oddly ended up in the village and subsequently met John Mantler on one warm sunny day outside of his shack as she walked the streets of the village, looking for the post office.

John was tending to window repairs on the front of his home when a quite distraught Roxanne passed by. She was stuck and stranded, with nowhere to stay and no place to go. When John became aware of her predicament, he simply provided a place for her to sleep until she could sort out her desperate situation. It turned out that her situation was beyond desperate and beyond simple sorting, and thus her stay in the Mantler shack became extended. A friendship soon developed.

Roxanne felt safe living inside the modest Mantler shack with the town recluse known as John Mantler. It was a kind of safety that she could not recall ever having felt. Time continued to do what time does, and as it did, Roxanne remained a roommate in the shack with old John Mantler.

The talk in town was swift and cruel, but Roxie, as she soon became known to all, didn't seem to care in the least what anyone thought or said. John hadn't ever cared what anyone thought or did. From the outside, these were two people who could not be more different. On the inside, just like on the inside of the shack and on the inside of a lot of things people don't bother to actually look clearly at, no one really knew anything.

Roxanne came to life in the secure confines of the shack. Her hidden character shone. She was intelligent, and as her confidence grew, she embraced life outside the shack and in the community as well. It turned out she was no recluse, and she soon was attending every village function and event with utmost enthusiasm. Rapidly, she acquired a broad circle of friends.

She was electric, and gradually, most of the folks—who, in the beginning, had spoken degrading rubbish behind her back—came to admire, respect, and genuinely like her. By the time she was pregnant with JJ, she was entirely accepted within the community. She had turned all previous sentiment about her upside down and inside out.

John, on the other hand, remained the same hermit he'd always been, except now people didn't feel as sorry for him or afraid of him. A peculiar little village such as this was used to strange happenings, and in time and in stride, all oddities become accepted realities.

John Mantler Jr. was born in the kitchen of the Mantler shack on a cool midsummer's day with a few little cries and a lot of assistance from a few expert ladies in the neighborhood. Even at birth, it seemed that JJ did not want to be a bother to anyone and wanted to prove that he could be content with whatever was going on around him.

John was more present than anyone would have expected him to be, and by all accounts from the masterful ladies present, "pleased as punch" with the birth of his son. John held him and cried with pride and joy. This was veritably a life from the inside.

The Mantlers lived frugally but comfortably on the monthly

military disability check John received from the Department of National Defense plus whatever extra money John earned selling wood and doing carpentry work. Roxanne worked part-time at the local grocery store for a few hours each week, charming everyone who came in. She took good care of the family money and kept it stocked in a big old shoebox that lived inside another metal box under the floorboards in her bedroom. John had no great interest in money. He believed in being self-sufficient and in not having any obligations to anyone.

The first years of young John Jr.'s life were very good. His mother always made him feel exceptional and loved, and she took extraordinary care of him. Roxanne and JJ were completely contiguous.

In the years that followed the departure of his mother, JJ, subconsciously and out of necessity, took a more active role in his own life. He didn't know it then, but he was learning about independence and survival. He had just turned six when his mother left home, but even at that point, JJ instinctively sensed that his father was not going to be able to play the same role that his mother did. John did not possess the same traits. Prior to becoming a father, he was introspective and withdrawn; after Roxanne's departure, these afflictions slowly returned. He crawled back into the world he had dwelt in before JJ was born and before Roxanne entered the shack.

John looked older and walked sadly again. As the years ensued, JJ took on more and more responsibility. He tended to many of the mundane household duties while John provided backup support, security, and overall logistics. It was easy to live this way in this village, where independence was expected and essential.

The community was inhabited by people who did not complicate life. Even though (at this point in his life) JJ did not have much to measure himself against, most of the actions he undertook worked out for him, so he never feared failure. He would deal with consequences as they came to him, self-assured that he could find a solution.

There were some in his neighborhood with similar habits, but most lacked JJ's conviction. JJ did not have complex demands and never allowed himself to feel that he lacked for anything. He knew who he was, and he accepted his circumstances as he rolled through his day-to-day routines.

His inner security came mostly from Roxanne's abundant love but also from John's stolid independence and indifference to hokey social protocol. JJ learned to ride the balance. His personality, like most people's, was pretty much set by age six. With Roxanne's boundless energy combined with John's stoic predictability, these first six years of life were marvelous.

Roxanne did not do things in the expected conventional ways. For example, she never taught JJ to read using traditional methods. There were no Dick and Jane books in the Mantler home. From the moment JJ could grasp words, his mother read to him from the Compton's Encyclopedia volumes that she had found at the neighboring Butlers. Jim Butler had bought this set of encyclopedias from a fast-talking salesman quite a few years back when his two children were still living at home and attending school. Roxanne would borrow and return one volume at a time. It didn't matter that a lot of the content was of a difficult nature for a child; she found ways to build stories around the subject matter so JJ could connect with it. These volumes had a lot of pictures, but when they were not illustrated, Roxanne and JJ would draw pictures together on a big writing pad to depict the content. It was inspirational, artistic, and fun. The themes and ideas brought forth to ponder were endless.

From the moment JJ was able to interact with her with even a minimal degree of intellect, Roxanne treated him as an equal. She did not understand why most adults assumed children wanted to see books with cute, cuddly animals and silly old aunts in bonnets. She would not subject her son to such dumbed-down nonsense.

There was an unspoken sense of acceptance of one's fate in the community. The people who grew up in the village and stayed there had placed themselves willingly or otherwise remained mute to any alternatives. This meant they did the ascribed work that had to be done to survive, married the person closest to them, raised their children, and interacted with friends and family until such time that death came to reclaim them.

Roxanne did not at all fit into such a state of being. She never consciously planned to be in this village in the first place; she just got lost and trapped there for a while. When she met John on that summer day, she was desperate and had no other options. Her cousin, who it later turned out was really no relation to her at all, had already left the farm where she was staying by the time Roxanne arrived.

Roxanne had nowhere to stay and no means to leave, so she did what she had to do to survive and stay sane. The day she met John, she had been dropped off with her suitcase in the village by a farmworker. She was looking for the post office, thinking that maybe she could call her mother or father back east. However, there was no public phone to use at this small village post office. But it didn't matter; a call would not have provided any help. Roxanne no longer had a relationship with either of her parents.

John Mantler and the shack turned out to be her only lifeline. John never judged or cared how she had gotten herself into such a predicament. He only saw she needed help, and he helped her the best he could. What transpired beyond that was a bit unique, but not without love.

John looked much older than he was due to his disability and sullen nature. But he didn't feel old in those years. Actually, the age difference between them was not that extreme.

For the first time in her life, Roxanne felt safe, valued, and cared for. The years she lived in the shack turned out to be good ones, and she was able to grow. She was a runaway who turned an extremely difficult circumstance into a rather good life. But this would not be her ultimate fate.

JJ would eventually come to know this as well. He realized that the Mantler family into which he was born was indeed different. Neither his mother nor his father was born into this community; both had chosen it. They did not fit into the traditional village mold. John had been something significant in his past life: He was a builder, a leader of men; he had been abroad and in combat. When that life was done, he had consciously chosen this community; it did not choose him, nor did it define who he was. He had lived, loved, and laughed, even if it was only his son who truly knew it. JJ had quite early on come to the conclusion that he was the only one who understood his father.

As the years wound on throughout the time JJ and John lived together in the shack, JJ struggled with one big, unsolvable mystery. He didn't believe his mother was dead. He couldn't be certain of this, of course, but he couldn't bring himself to think of her as dead. At his age, it was difficult for him to understand death; he couldn't relate to the finality of it. His father wasn't much help in this matter either, as he never took any action that would confirm or deny Roxanne's death.

JJ pacified his confusion by determining that his father didn't think Roxanne was deceased either. He thought there must be a reason for what had happened. Someday, he vowed, he would unravel that explanation and understand why his mother had left and where she had gone. But in the meantime, he knew he had to press on with the life that was directly in front of him. The only life he had. While he continued to believe there was an explanation for everything, life was immediate and didn't wait for a person to formulate all their answers.

Years later, JJ would often be challenged for insisting there were reasons for everything that happened. It intrigued him to search for explanations. There were always solutions to problems, and he often found them. Even the best scientists acknowledged that not everything could be explained, at least not yet. JJ focused on the "yet." To him, it meant that you should not stop looking for answers; if something did not have an explanation, it just meant you had to look harder. This was something that would continue to cause him conflict.

CHAPTER 3

TRAIN

His mind was rolling with the wheels of the train;
And rolling again and again.

Nora was in bed when Jon came out of the washroom. He hugged her from behind as he climbed in, and they stayed in that position for the next many hours as the train trundled along the steel rails heading west.

Jon stayed quiet, waiting for Nora to fall asleep. He felt an urge to cry out and tell her what had happened. Not doing so felt like a betrayal, but he kept himself still and let the feeling subside.

Nora soon slept; that was good. Jon did not; that was certain. Nora was an extraordinarily sound sleeper. Once the day was done and her nightly duties had all been accomplished, she could check out like no one on earth. Jon, not so much. His brain would stop; he found no solace in the wee hours. On this particular night, though, he was grateful for the still and silent way that Nora could sleep. He clung to his lover while ruminating on the ordeal of the past evening, feeling completely alone in the world.

Jon had spent the majority of his life alone, and he was mostly fine with that. He had learned to be comfortable within a solitary state. Friends and colleagues didn't notice this because he had become adept at masking his internal nature and at being content. From this day on, though, there would be a very different kind of alone that he would carry with him, one for which he was destined to blame himself.

Growing up, Jon had become skilled at refitting himself to his surroundings. The world around him never intimidated him because he could transform himself to whatever change was required. He was educated, intelligent, and capable. But what had happened to him in these past hours was something he never imagined he would go through.

He was fearful of who he was and what he might become, and this shook him in the most powerful manner. He was disgusted with himself for having run from the scene. More dramatically, he feared he was a killer and would be found out. Luckily, he was also still in shock, preventing him from doing anything rash or foolish. The shock helped him survive.

Jon never slept on trains or planes or boats or very much in general. So, as Nora slept, he lay awake feeling the warmth of her body next to him. There was a sense of safety within the cabin and in holding onto her.

His mind repetitively raced throughout the night, sifting through the episodes of the past evening and tumbling through the sad scenes. He sought a logical explanation for what had transpired. How could such an event have happen to him? How much danger was he in? He wanted to have a plan, a strategy, a base to work from, but for that to happen, he would need much more information. To keep sane, he needed answers, but first, he needed to understand his own questions, and right now, he was a long way from that.

He wondered whether the decision on that bridge to flee rather than report the tragedy to authorities might have been made too quickly; it might have been reckless. How big a mistake this could ultimately become for him, he knew not. As he deconstructed these points and the train continued to roll its way out of Hungary, he ultimately concluded that it had been a good decision to run. It was too late to turn back now, so he committed himself to following through with it.

They merely needed to make it out of Hungary and into Austria to be safe. It was imperative to believe this in order to go forward, so that was what he did. This was his first decision, and once it was made, he felt a bit less nervous. However, the next decision, though quite obvious, would prove to be more difficult and damaging. He again vowed that he could never tell Nora what had transpired.

The role he had played deeply disturbed him. Even now, with his adrenaline still flowing, he was amazed and baffled by the impulsiveness of his own actions. This was not at all a part of his nature, and it was difficult for him to fathom why he reacted the way he did. He felt immense guilt and embarrassment, but told himself there was nothing he could do to reverse or alter what had occurred. He understood it was better to be on this train right now than to be trying to explain what happened on that bridge to the Hungarian authorities. He was, after all, a Western foreigner in an Eastern Bloc nation, traveling on a tourist visa, accompanied by a NATO military employee, and involved in a deadly situation. None of that could be good.

Jon found the incident very complicated to process. He had no idea what the ramifications would be. How could he explain seeing the two men fall from the bridge without implicating himself in some way? What if the third man lived? How would he have explained why he was on that bridge? How many lies would he have to fabricate and deliver? It was too crazy a story to truthfully recreate, and there was no way to predict how it might have turned out. It was a long and risky predicament that his instincts told him not to become immersed in.

There were still too many things that Jon didn't know. Morally, he had not done the right thing; that, he *did* know. However, he had no choice but to deal with the situation as it lay before him. There was no longer a right thing or a wrong thing. From the moment the first body went into the water, there was no more right thing to be done. The right thing was no longer on that bridge; the right thing was now long gone.

Throughout the rest of the night, Jon slowed himself down and visually replayed the scenes as they occurred on the bridge without him in them, as if he were seeing things from an outsider's position. This improved his ability to remember the sequence. It didn't, however, reveal any answer as to why everything got so horribly out of control. How much of this was his fault, Jon continually wondered.

He decided to change tactics and concentrate on what he did know. He knew why he was in Budapest, and he knew why he was on that bridge. He knew why he was meeting Karl Bircher.

Jon had met Karl on a number of occasions in various locations in Europe to exchange information. They even met once on this same bridge in Budapest about a year earlier. These events were not at all unusual during the political climate in Central Europe. Jon knew he would exchange information with Karl and that he was going to take that information back to West Germany and deliver it to his colleague, Peter Otto.

Peter had set up this meeting as well as all of Jon's meetings with others over the years. It was all so simple and routine. Peter had convinced him there was no danger in this game; Peter would have the answers Jon was so in need of.

In the meantime, Jon needed to focus all his efforts on ensuring a safe and problem-free departure from Hungary. Whatever happened after that would have to wait. He lay awake through the early morning, trying not to think about Karl and the third man; instead, he concentrated on what could happen on the rest of this journey back to West Germany.

Jon and Nora had traveled to a few Eastern Bloc countries before, and he knew the border-crossing procedures well enough. They would arrive in the early hours in Vienna, where the train conductor would awaken them and return their passports while he retained their visa documentation to confirm they had left Hungary on this particular train and at this particular time. At the Vienna station, the train would be uncoupled from the Hungarian train and joined to another one that would take them to Munich. They did not have to leave the train here in Vienna, which was a relief to Jon.

There was no reason whatsoever for the conductor not to allow them to pass; he simply had to follow procedure. Even if a body surfaced back in Budapest, it would take far longer than these few hours for anyone to connect the matter to Jon Mantler. He convinced himself that from the moment they had their passports back from the conductor and were uncoupled from the Hungarian train, they would be cleared.

His only physical connections to what had happened on the bridge were his running clothes and the coded note he still held for Peter. He knew he would destroy the running gear as soon as he could safely do so. He thought about destroying the coded note, too, because it didn't feel very important to him anymore. But once in Austria, he changed his mind. He would incinerate the shoes and running gear—but not the note —once he was back home near Heidelberg.

Jon decided to deliver the note to Peter as usual, along with his pressing questions about what had transpired on the bridge. Jon was glad there was no written proof of the information he gave to Karl. So when Karl's remains would be located in the river, which they undoubtedly would be, there wouldn't be any documentation in his possession that could link the man to Jon Mantler. *Never leave a paper trail*, he had often been told, and fortunately, in this case, he would be able to meet that request.

Jon tried to remember everything about the third man on the bridge. It might be important at some point in time. He thought about the man's face; was it clean-shaven? Yes, he thought, but maybe a mustache; he wasn't certain. He wore a long, dark brown coat with a gray scarf and, most notably, a big black toque on his head; it was too wet and dark to see much more than that. Jon never saw his shoes or his pants, but oddly, he remembered that the coat was tailored and that it fit the big man stylishly well. Why would he remember that when most of the other details were obscured?

Jon also recalled his voice. It was hard, heavy, and booming, in an amplified and determined kind of way. It may have been overstated and desperate, but Jon had perceived it as angry and hostile.

He stayed awake, slipping in and out of these conflicting thoughts, until there was a knock on the cabin door, startling him. Jon shook himself to attention, then opened the sliding door to greet the train conductor, who was there to return their documents and inform them that in twenty minutes, the train would be arriving in Vienna. Nora rolled over and sighed but didn't bother to wake herself.

The conductor confirmed they would not need to leave the train or their cabin in the Vienna station, as their car would be connected to a German locomotive. The new train would transport them all the way to Munich. This was good news to Jon's ears. He was most eager to have this train decoupled and connected to the Deutsche Bundesbahn locomotive waiting for them in Vienna.

The rest of the journey through Munich and Frankfurt went tightly on schedule and problem-free. In the early afternoon on Monday, Jon and Nora arrived at their home in a village just outside of Heidelberg as if nothing unusual had occurred. Only Jon Mantler knew otherwise. It was only he who remained overburdened with shock, fear, and guilt.

His mind had steadied somewhat; however, it continued to perplex him how one brief moment of impetuous action could result in so much chaos. It was more than being in the wrong place at the wrong time, more than just bad luck. It was preposterous how, in two minutes, so many lives could be changed forever; how, in mere seconds, futures could be altered and pasts redefined. The world and the way one's place was perceived in it would never be the same again.

Once at home, Jon felt a little better about his immediate circumstances but not at all at ease about what was coming next. He tried to rationalize, conceding that he would forever be unable to change what had happened in Budapest. This was torturous for him as his life was based on being in control. Jon was a builder and a fixer who believed there was a solution for every predicament. He believed in science and that if one looked hard and long enough, answers would be found. At least he believed that until today.

After settling in, one of the first things Jon did was go out to the large garden at the rear of their house and rake up the leaves, grass, and shrubbery. He often did just this when returning from a journey, particularly in the late fall. He then dumped the batch of material into a big barrel and lit it on fire. Once it began to blaze, he added his Budapest running shoes and jogging gear. He watched the inferno burn in a trance. As he traced the black smoke swirling upward from the running shoes, he wondered what he should do next.

Jon was calmer now; watching the burning fire felt like progress. Next, he decided to call Peter. There was no one else for him to confide in, no one else who could help. Surely, Peter would know something that could shed light on why these events transpired.

He did not want to give Peter any details over the phone. All he did was set up a meeting. A meeting within a few days of his return from seeing Karl Bircher would have been the normal procedure, anyway. The call to Peter wasn't much relief, but they scheduled a rendezvous at Jon's office, which was about a fifteen-minute drive north of Heidelberg. The meeting would be on Wednesday morning because Peter was going to be away from his office on Tuesday.

Jon would have to be patient and carry on with his daily life as if Budapest had never happened. He was exhausted physically and emotionally, and by dinnertime, he realized he had hardly spoken to Nora either on the return trip or since they got home. Luckily, she was preoccupied with getting ready to go back to work on Tuesday and didn't seem to notice Jon's odd interest in the household chores. Not yet.

Nora held a highly responsible position at the main NATO headquarters near Heidelberg. It was her promotion to that position that had brought Jon and Nora to West Germany three years ago. Jon had put his life on pause in order to accompany her on what was intended to be a two- to four-year assignment.

Nora was an administrator with the Department of National Defense, and she basically ran the office of General Dangerfield, the top Canadian assigned to the NATO Logistics Centre in Heidelberg. It was common for Jon and Nora to take extended weekend trips like the one to Budapest as tourists to experience European life. Being away from her office for four days meant that she would be up early the next day to catch up on what she had missed. Jon was glad he did not have to do much more than cook pasta for her and was also relieved she did not have time for conversation.

They retired to bed early, and Nora, the efficient sleeper, was immediately out cold, while Jon lay awake, replaying the events of the last day in his mind, then the events of the last months and years, then ultimately most of his still relatively young life thus far. Deep inside, he knew that change was knocking on the door of his shack.

CHAPTER 4

JOHN

If we hear with our hearts, let our souls fly the tram;
Nature's course will convey to the place where I am.

John Mantler Sr. was not anti-community; he was merely noncompliant when it came to routine civic issues and local politics. He rarely left the home he had built, and if he did, it was only to retrieve or deliver his wood. He did not take part in local events, and though he was amiable in one-on-one conversations, he was self-conscious in larger groups due to his physical appearance and the awkward way his legs moved. So he chose to remain inside or near his home, where he could keep his life simple and predictable.

He lived without most modern conveniences. The only newfangled technology he connected to in his home was the electrical grid. This provided the comfort of a refrigerator, a water heater, and a range in his kitchen. Beyond that, there were no contemporary comforts in the Mantler home. There was no telephone, no television, and no running water. Outside information came to the shack when JJ picked it up from the post office two blocks away or from a battery-powered transistor radio that sat on top of the refrigerator.

The Mantlers were amiable and neighborly, however, and had excellent relations with the people living nearby, especially the Butlers next door. The Butlers had a telephone. It was through them that notifications and communiqués were transmitted to the Mantler shack. Mrs. Butler was more than pleased to relay any messages, vital or otherwise, to Roxanne or JJ. No one ever sought to contact John via telephone.

JJ didn't know very much about his father until well after his mother's departure. As a young child, he had been far closer to Roxanne. As he grew older, however, he came to realize that he knew even less about his mother than he did about his father. He knew that she didn't come from this village, and that was about it. Disappointingly, his father also knew very little about her. John Sr. was not one to pry into other people's affairs, so he only recollected what she had told him, and he accepted most of those interpretations, even when he had doubts. John lived his life in a very private way, and he treated others in the same fashion.

According to Roxanne's own information, she had grown up in the East/Central portion of the country in a family with one older sister and one aunt. They lived near the big city of Toronto. Her mother and father had passed when she was still quite young. Her father died in a car accident, which seemed to be the go-to exit for a Martin family member, and her mother succumbed to cancer some short years later. She never spoke about anyone else from her past life.

This didn't provide much of a profile for young JJ. What he would determine in the years to come was that she had come to this village to visit a cousin who had planned to marry a farm boy who lived in the general region. However, by the time Roxanne arrived on the scene, that relationship between the cousin and the farm boy was way over, and the cousin was heading south in a grungy red Camaro with a new guy named Jeff. It was shortly after that fiasco that Roxanne met John Mantler outside his home, and that was about all JJ knew.

JJ tried as hard as he could to unlock the part of his brain that held the memory of his mother. He wanted to relive the times he had shared with her. Emotions often overtook and soothed him when he remembered moments they had together. It also made him quite lonely. He had lived only six years of his life with his mother. It disturbed him that he could only recall the last two or three of those years.

The death thing would become an unpleasant reality and something that he would find difficult to get right with. Death seemed to JJ like something was constantly hanging around and waiting to pounce. His father had tried to explain death to him once, but back then, JJ was still too young to grasp what his father was saying. In his mind's interpretation, death was not final. Despite what he had been told by his father, he continued waiting for his mother to come back. There were different types of death, JJ had decided.

A few months after his mother's blue letter arrived, a neighboring father and husband living in the village had taken his own life. He attached one end of a garden hose to the exhaust pipe of his car and placed the other end through the trunk and rear seat so that the exhaust emptied into the car. Then he sat at the wheel, closed all the doors and windows of the idling vehicle, and went to sleep, never to wake up.

This type of death was the most-used form of suicide in the community. Every few years, there seemed to be such an incident. In this latest case, the car was found by a neighbor the next morning, parked along a tree-lined, dead-end prairie trail leading to a field.

JJ was curious about why someone would go to such lengths to execute themselves. This man was using death as a final solution…a solution to something, but what? How could life be that bad, wondered JJ. In the opinion of most in the village, this man had a normal life. Within a day or so following the event, no one spoke of it again, and the living went on as if nothing had happened. Death for the living was just a pause, a carrying out of rituals, and then getting on with normal things as if death would not be back. But apparently, death would always be back.

Throughout JJ's childhood and especially following the departure of his mother, John Sr. did the best he could to be an effective father. He was genuine in his care and support of JJ's schooling and all aspects connected to his social welfare. He was ever-available and even active in homework. John wished he could be more than that, but he was limited in his parental abilities and could not be someone he was no longer able to be.

They did have many enduring moments together in the shack, though, like the newspaper ritual that they engaged in daily. Each afternoon, JJ would arrive home from school with the capital city newspaper they subscribed to in hand. The two of them would sit in their adjacent chairs and read it, front to back and back to front. They would exchange sections periodically and comment as applicable. The communication was freewheeling on matters relating to national affairs and current world issues in general, but rare on anything related to John's war and Roxanne's departure.

JJ, encouraged by John, also continued the Butler encyclopedia ritual that he and his mother had engaged in. He always had a volume by his bed, but now he would go over to the Butlers himself to exchange it, rotated through them all over and over.

As time traveled forward, John Mantler, perhaps sensing that he needed to do more, opened doors of his past life to his young son. This added warmth and depth to their relationship. One day, John revealed to his ever-curious son that he could speak German, and in so doing, shone a light on his past and his relationship with his own parents. John even began speaking to JJ in German after their newspaper sessions or in the evening when they finished supper.

JJ learned to ask questions in German, motivated by the fact that he could learn more about his father's youth and upbringing. JJ was seven or eight at this time, and his young, receptive brain absorbed the language quickly. He also learned that his father's parents had immigrated from Germany in the early years of the century and taken on a farm homestead in the far northwestern part of the province. This was where John was born and had lived prior to his departure to Europe to fight in WWII. It was also why the know-it-alls in the village knew so little about John Mantler. He had come from even farther away than their vast information network stretched.

JJ was happiest at school. It was a place where he felt valued. He got along well with all his schoolmates and his teachers. He easily adapted to living two distinct lives, one in the community outside and one inside the Mantler shack.

Both lives appealed to him, and as the years rolled by, he became more and more secure within his own life and thought less and less about why and where his mother had gone.

In the weeks and months after she left, he thought a great deal about her and wondered about all sorts of strange things. Because he preferred not to think about death, he imagined her in a far-off place living a life of fantasy and adventure. But after a year or so, this exercise faded, and as his life became busier, he didn't think about her nearly as much.

He eventually graduated from the local elementary school and began attending high school in a small city up the road. One day, after being dropped off from school at the grocery store to pick up the daily newspaper, he entered the shack to find his father asleep on the bed in the living room.

There was nothing unusual about this because John often had a nap after lunch. At first, JJ didn't think anything was out of the ordinary as he dropped the newspaper on the table and tossed his schoolbag into his room. But then it seemed odd that John was not up and making his way over to the newspaper by the time JJ came out of his room.

He looked over at his father, still lying on his bed, and called out to him. There was no reply. JJ walked over to the bed and immediately sensed that something was not right. He cautiously touched John's arm, and that also didn't feel right. John's eyes were closed, but there was no breathing. Everything was too silent and too cold.

JJ did nothing more than sit still on the side of the bed until he actually realized what was happening. For an unusually long time, he waited. He was fourteen and a half years old and had seen death, primarily on farms and in the countryside: dead dogs, cattle, deer, birds, and so on. But this was very different from that, and JJ became frightened and distressed.

A few minutes later, as his protective shock wore off, JJ became emotional. While still sitting on the side of his father's small bed, he began to shake and convulse. He internalized these feelings until he instinctively knew that it was okay to feel this way.

He hummed and did the inner chanting technique he had been taught by his mother. It had been a few years since he had used this method, and for a while, it felt futile and didn't soothe him at all. Eventually, though, he dove to the floor in agony, humming until relief came to him. He remained there for a long time; how long, he couldn't really tell, until later, when he opened the door to leave the shack and saw it was completely dark outside. In that interim, he touched his father once more on the arm and face, but he didn't like the dampness and coldness.

JJ wasn't sure what he should do, so he chose nothing. He didn't want time to stop, and he didn't want time to go on. He didn't want it to go in either direction, so he just sat on the floor beside his father, feeling sick to his stomach. But he didn't just hurt in his stomach; he hurt in just about every other place too.

Once he understood that time was not going to do what he was asking it to, he stepped out into the night air and walked to the Butlers. He knocked on the door inanimately, as if he had too few muscles in his body. It took a second, more focused and forceful tap before Mrs. Butler opened the door.

"JJ, how are you?" was all she could say before she knew that something was very wrong.

"I'm okay, but my father is dead," JJ said with an odd amount of calm.

Mrs. Butler dove into action. She quickly turned around and shouted back into her house. "Jim, come out here, hurry!" she called out into the open space between her kitchen and living room. She grabbed JJ by the shoulder and pulled him to the back porch. "Come in!" she wailed, hauling him through the open door.

Young JJ stumbled over the doorjamb and nearly fell into the kitchen, barely managing to stay upright, as old Jim walked into the room.

"JJ says John has died. We've got to get over there! Come on!" Mrs. Butler headed out the door and into the night. Jim exited behind her and overtook her on the pathway between the two properties, after which Mrs. Butler slowed down to tend to JJ, who was stumbling behind.

Jim stopped before he entered the Mantler shack, then turned and told both of them to wait at the door and allow him to go in first. Mrs. Butler paused to obey before entering the kitchen instead. JJ stood beside her while Jim went alone into the attached living room, where John Mantler lay.

In a few minutes, Jim came back through the door separating the two rooms and respectfully closed it behind him. This symbolically confirmed what JJ had already known and caused Mrs. Butler to sob softly.

"JJ, you don't have to worry. I'll take care of this," Jim said soothingly. "Do you want to come in again and see your dad once more?"

"N-n-n-no, I've made my p-p-p-peace," JJ stuttered. He had no idea where the words came from when he heard them float out into the cold night air coming through the still-open door behind them.

"Well, you will stay with us tonight, and we can talk about this later. Right now, I'm going to get Leonard to help me, and we will take care of things. You just take your time. Go over to our place and try to relax. These things are hard, JJ, but we will get through this together. If you need anything from here, we can get it later."

Mrs. Butler led JJ back down the path to their house.

In this community, most of the men resisted using excessive words in moments of stress. It was expected that participants in a crisis would take action methodically and effectively without a great deal of banter and drama. Jim Butler was one of these men. He walked in the opposite direction, heading off to enlist the services of Leonard, his lifelong friend. Jim had declared that they would take care of it, and that, they would do.

Jim and Leonard were of the same generation as old John Mantler, thus the ideal candidates to handle what needed to be done. It was not their first death. They knew how systems worked and how to bend them when bending was needed. They could cheat and be discreet. In cases such as this, they were the cleanup crew. While Mrs. Butler tried unsuccessfully to get JJ to eat, they had, within a few hours, transported John Mantler's body to an undisclosed location and formulated a plan.

Jim returned to the Butler home before eleven at night. He sat at the kitchen table and explained to JJ that they had taken his father's body to the church, which was across a small street. In two days, on Saturday, they would conduct a small funeral service. Shortly after that, John Mantler would be buried in the cemetery at the back of the village, assuming that this was all okay with JJ, which it was.

"You don't need to go to school tomorrow. You can stay here with us," Mrs. Butler suggested.

"I never miss school. I think I'll go. I've never missed a day of school, ever," JJ proclaimed.

"Well, then maybe that is a good idea. Keep your mind busy and keep things normal. I think your dad would approve of that," old Jim said.

Mrs. Butler aimed one of her scowls at her husband. She did not know the plan yet.

Getting JJ on the bus and going to school that Friday fit far better into Jim and Leonard's scheme. JJ being out of the way meant less explaining was required. Jim knew that John Mantler had heart-related health issues and had long ago suspected that this day might come. The death of John would leave JJ an orphan, and at his age, it meant that he would officially become a ward of the state. Jim and Leonard were determined not to let that happen, so they wanted to get dead John buried as quickly as possible with the least amount of fuss and fanfare.

In these times and in these towns, there was a strong sense of taking care of your own business without outside interference. It was paramount not to bow down to bureaucratic mandates. Here, the older generation lived by a code of doing what they knew was right without reservation or regard to outside convention.

"JJ, you can live here with us as long as you want to, and we'll keep your house next door just as it is now so that you have that home as well," Jim offered.

"Thank you," was all JJ could say because he hadn't thought anywhere near that far ahead yet.

"It's sad about your dad, but you're going to be all right. You have to be!" Jim continued more sternly.

This had the intended effect on JJ. He sat upright as if he had been jolted by a current in his chair. Jim then explained what needed to be done. It was essential that the boy be aware enough of what was taking place around him so Jim and Leonard could proceed. Some of these facts JJ had to be able to deal with right now.

"We'll keep the spirit of your dad alive as long as we can," Jim said. "You need to do that too. Think of what he would want you to do and do that. He would not want you to change anything too much. He would want you to go on and grow up to be the terrific young man that you already are. Maybe don't tell anyone yet about your father; the school doesn't need to know about that yet. Not everyone has to know that your dad is gone."

So, on Friday morning, JJ went off to school as usual and did the best he could to go about his day in a normal fashion. In fact, he didn't think as much about his dad as he expected he would during his school day activities. It was not unusual for JJ to be distant in class, and he buried himself in his books until the day passed slowly but surely. This all changed, however, when he returned to the shack later that Friday afternoon.

Throughout the day, Jim and Leonard had worked on their plan. Leonard built a box and dug a fresh grave on the far edge of the graveyard surrounded by tall trees. Even with the help of two of his sons, it still took the better part of the day. Meanwhile, Jim coordinated with key people in the village, targeting only those who would maintain the essential discretion vital to the plan's success. He clued in the young local pastor, who owed him a favor, and they dutifully arranged a minimal service for Saturday afternoon. There would be no announcements, no invitations, no publicity, and no paperwork involved. Jim wanted to get this low-key ceremony over with as soon as possible and with the least amount of chatter. The expectation was that within a few days, all would be quite forgotten and life after death in the village would resume as it always did. After all, few in the community, or in the surrounding region for that matter, knew that John Mantler was alive while he was alive. Forgetting about him would be relatively easy.

It would not be so easy for JJ, though, and on Friday afternoon when he walked the alleyway from the bus stop back to the shack, he felt a pressure in his head that he couldn't gain control of. He did not want to have to forget his father the way he had to forget his mother. He vowed to himself that he wouldn't.

Trying to forget about his mother over the past few years had resulted in him missing her even more. At this point, JJ had lived more of his life without her than with her, yet his memory of her was still utterly vivid. Most nights before he went to sleep, he would speak to her about what he had done during the day. He did it because it made him feel good and because it kept her alive.

JJ went straight over to the Butlers' house. It was about 4:30 p.m., and the entire cleanup crew was sitting in the kitchen when he entered. Jim stood up, greeted him, and asked him to sit with them at the table so he could explain what they had done and what was scheduled to take place on Saturday.

Inside the kitchen, there were a number of locals. Leonard was there, accompanied by two of his sons; the assistant gravediggers. Mrs. Butler had assembled two of her best friends to assist with the food preparation, and they scurried about the kitchen delivering food and drink to the procedural committee.

JJ was informed that the church service had been reset to 10:00 a.m. so John could be delivered to his resting place under the eyes of the Lord and according to village tradition. Roxanne had been an active member of the church in her last year in the village, and she knew the pastor well, so he was easily convinced by Jim to accommodate the Jim-Leonard plan.

John Mantler was not a believer in God or religion and would not have voluntarily submitted to such a ceremony. Being dead, however, kept him out of the decision-making process. Besides, there were other forces at play here for which the church was being used. JJ realized none of this was within his own scope of influence, so he passively cooperated.

His father had made his religious views clear to young JJ on many occasions. It was one of the rare subjects he readily talked to his son about. "Don't get caught up in the lies that preachers and politicians preach, John." He always called his son John. "They have their own reasons for wanting to twist you into a pretzel they want to eat. Religion is all for control of the population, and nationalism is even worse. Politicians want you to rally around their flag and act like you're better than everyone else. That's how Hitler started everything and came to be such a big power. We're again seeing other countries and their leaders trying to do the same evil things."

Shortly after the service, John would be buried in the corner of the cemetery in the back of town by Leonard and his sons, while the small entourage would slip over to the Butlers' house for sandwiches and pie provided by Mrs. Butler and her conscripts. To JJ, it was all a blur. He didn't feel like he was living in the same world as the adults. To him, it was an obligatory procedure that needed to be done but not one that he had any ability to influence. JJ had no idea what his father would have wanted and guessed that it didn't matter very much now, anyway.

The mini-funeral went off problem-free. Only a handful of people attended, and the whole procedure took less than an hour. At the

Butlers, JJ ate a couple sandwiches, thanked people, and sat quietly pondering his life while Leonard and his sons drank beer and told comical stories about some of the more colorful townsfolk who were not in attendance. JJ was still too young to fully understand how he was supposed to feel about all this, so he didn't feel anything.

By Monday morning, life in the village would go on without John Mantler pretty much in the same fashion as it had gone on with John Mantler in it. He might as well have been still living in the Mantler shack. The fact that he did or didn't was relevant only to JJ.

After the funeral, JJ tried to sleep at the Butlers' house for a few nights and only visited the shack during the daytime to change clothes and connect with his own things. That lasted for only a few days before he was sleeping in his own bed again. He ate with the Butlers most days, to the pleasure of Mrs. Butler. However, as time went on, he stocked his own refrigerator again and ate the way he did when he was living with his father. JJ had been doing more and more of the regular tasks in and around the Mantler home for the last few years, anyway. Based on their uncomplicated existence, it was fairly simple stuff.

John Sr. had tended more to the logistical details in connection with the house and yard, while it was JJ who bought and brought the groceries from the store. JJ managed Roxanne's shoebox and tended to the mandatory paperwork that had to go in and out of the shack. The two of them always discussed these matters, but in the end, it was JJ who wrote the letters, signed the documents, and went to the post office to ensure that what needed to end up in the right place did indeed end up in the right place.

In this village, most everything could be done at the local post office, and if someone needed assistance, there was always the postmaster there to help. JJ cashed the checks by signing John Mantler on the back and turning them over to the postmaster in return for cash. He paid their bills by money order against the cash he handed back to the postmaster. The rest went into the shoebox. It was an effective system.

The two Johns' lives were harmoniously entwined. Every day, JJ knew what he was supposed to do because his father stuck to his routines with few deviations. JJ was content with the way his life had functioned both inside and outside the shack. Now, it would be up to him to find a way to keep it going.

He was aware of the past role his father had played in the community and knew the basics of the story; in fact, now he knew most of the story from what his father had revealed and conversations he had overheard.

No one knew of John Mantler prior to his arrival in the village approximately a year after the war ended. He had purchased a plot of land on King Street and began building his home there. During the construction, he rented and lived in an old house near the cemetery, near where he now lay. He bought out most of the wood from the old town lumberyard that was closing down, and thus, for the rest of his life, he became the unofficial wood supplier to the community.

The most prying of the townsfolk scanned through the provincial networks for information on him, but their investigations did not yield much. It seemed that John Mantler's existence left little of a trail for the gossip crowd. The chin-wag talk around town at the time had labeled him as a good-looking and vibrant young man when he joined the army around 1939. However, he returned six years later looking much older, with a broken hip and bent-up legs.

These stories were loosely sketched together and skimpy on details, but "war hero" was often attached to the John Mantler name when the talk got rowdy down at the Veterans' Club in the little city down the road. John never attended events there; he did, however, receive a military disability pension check from the Veterans' Affairs section of the Department of Defense, which punctually arrived at the village post on the fifth day of every month. He subsidized this income with carpentry and wood supply work, which he orchestrated mostly in his yard and in a woodshed he had constructed behind his small house.

He lived frugally but freely. That his move to the village coincided with the closing of the local lumberyard was fortunate, and John was resourceful enough to make the best of this. From the lumberyard, he salvaged an old truck, a big industrial saw, and a lot of high-quality lumber. This provided him with more than enough material to build his house and kick-start his small carpentry business.

John built his home within a year all by hand, but in truth, he never stopped building on it. There were always refinements to make, especially in the interior. It was a life and love project. Until Roxanne entered the village, he had lived alone, and quite contentedly so.

He was inwardly far more self-conscious about his injuries and broken body than he ever let on publicly. It was frustrating that no one in the village had seen him in the prime of his life before the war usurped much of his usefulness.

As JJ began to live in his shack again, he also took over the life that had filled the place. His native character was probably more Roxanne and less John, though. He did not intend to become the next Mantler hermit. He pressed himself to establish a life outside the shack and be as active as possible. He spent time around town socializing with the folks more than he had in the past. He even occasionally hung out at the gas station, listening to the local small talk. Mainly though, he continued to love school, where he flourished.

As for death, he dealt with it as best he could. He visited his father's grave to connect with his loss and to challenge death's persistent presence. For JJ, death was a weight one had to carry around alone.

CHAPTER 5

TAXMAN

I saw what was served to the masters and what was served below;
Still, I thought I'd be a miner, thought I should let them know.

Jon Mantler first met Peter Otto on a visit to Bonn while he was tending to business there. On that day, Jon awkwardly carried a large cardboard box in one hand and clutched his briefcase in the other as he pushed his way through the big wooden door of the building. A bit clumsily, he managed to wedge it open with his foot and then push his body through, box and case in tow.

A woman, seeing his struggle, came out from behind the reception desk and scurried to assist him as the door pulled closed behind him.

"Thank you," Jon said as she offered to take his cardboard box filled with forms, "but it's not necessary; it's not heavy. I have this under control. I'm Jon Mantler, and I have income tax appointments scheduled here today and tomorrow. I'm from H&R Block tax service."

"Yes, of course. Welcome. We're glad to have you here. I'll call David. I think he has organized everything for you. I'm Natalie."

Jon put his case and box on a small side table along the wall of the reception area. They shook hands politely.

A short time later, a tall, thin man with glasses and a goatee entered from an adjacent door. Jon followed him down a stairwell, lugging the box and the briefcase, to a door. The goateed man attempted to open it, but it was locked. Undeterred, he lunged more aggressively a few times, shoulder to door, until the door relented and dislodged itself. Behind it was a tiny, dusty, green room housing a brown desk, and behind that was what looked like a water tank and a furnace.

"Sorry, but this is about the best we can do right now. We just don't have any free space in the building anymore," the man said.

"It'll be fine."

The time was just after 9:00 a.m., and according to the

prescheduled appointments, he had only about twenty minutes to get his papers organized for his first client meeting. He was in the basement of the Canadian Embassy in Bonn, West Germany.

"Everyone has been informed of their appointment times and this location. If you need anything else, you can call me from the reception."

"Terrific," answered Jon.

The rest of his day was spent meeting with a stream of embassy employees, working through their personal income details and declarations. It was a day full of T4 slips and tax forms, et cetera. Pleasingly, it turned out to be a busy and productive day for Jon and his newly acquired little tax preparation business.

Jon had moved to West Germany only a few months earlier with not much to do and no particular job in his immediate future, so when the opportunity came about to take over an H&R Block tax franchise, he jumped on it.

His main office was located near Heidelberg, but the Canadian Embassy had contacted him a few weeks earlier to have him come to Bonn and provide his services to their staff. Today was the first of two days he had planned for interviewing and gathering each client's personal information and financial records, then starting the form-filing process. He would return in a week with the completed tax declarations for presentation, signing, and submission, followed by the collection of his fee for the service.

Peter was Jon's fifth appointment of the day. Unlike the other clients, he was not a Canadian citizen; he was German but earned most of his income from Canadian sources as a contractor to the embassy thus had to file a Canadian income tax return.

Peter was a dark-haired, well-groomed man of medium build and professionally dressed in a white shirt, jacket, and tie. Jon was also smartly attired but far less flashy or formal than Peter. The two spoke cordially and went through the basic tax format questions with no unusual complications. At the end of the day, as Jon was organizing his desk and files, preparing to leave the makeshift office until the next morning, Peter returned to ask Jon if he wanted to join him for a drink or dinner. Jon made a quick and easy decision to do so, and about thirty minutes later, they were seated in a *Gasthaus* within a few minutes' walk from the nearby hotel where Jon was booked for the night.

Peter was a talker, and he readily revealed his life story to Jon during an evening of beer and intellectual nourishment. Jon was a good listener and interested in learning whatever he could about his new country of residence. Peter had spent most of his childhood and formative years in Rüdesheim am Rhein, not far away from where they were dining. However, he had been born in Karlshorst, a suburb on the edge of Berlin.

Peter's parents had separated when he was four years old, and soon after, his father left Berlin to work for a small manufacturing firm in West Germany. Young Peter remained with his mother, stepfather, and a soon-to-be-born half-brother in the Eastern sector of Berlin. As he got a little older, he would spend summers with his father in Rüdesheim. In those postwar years, despite the fact that the former Germany was split into East and West, it was not difficult to get special permission for children to travel to visit their relatives. Peter was on one of those visits when the terrible event that would define most of the rest of his life occurred.

On August 13, 1961, young Peter woke up on a fine summer day in Rüdesheim, unaware that during the previous night the East German authorities, assisted by the Soviet Army, had deployed soldiers to install barbed wire on the ground to forcibly divide the city of Berlin. Within the next days and weeks, the Soviet and the German Democratic Republic, or GDR, soldiers constructed the Berlin Wall, complete with shoot-to-kill guards in towers across the entire city. Virtually overnight, the free movement of citizens from one part of the city to the other was halted. If you were in, you stayed in; if you were out, you stayed out.

Peter's mother and half-brother lived on the Eastern side of the armed guards and the barriers, and since that day, they had not been allowed to leave for the West. Peter, who on that day was with his father on the western side, could have returned to the East again, but by doing so, it was uncertain and unlikely he would be allowed to leave again to see his father. If he stayed with his father, it was uncertain if and when he would see his mother again.

What was clear, however, was that his life would be safer and hold more opportunities near the Rhein in West Germany than on the communist side of Berlin. Thus, Frederick and Helena Otto, faced with a difficult decision, made the only choice they felt prudent under the circumstances. Peter would stay with his father until they had a better sense of what would happen next. He was eight years old, and from this moment on, he would not see his mother again for many years.

Listening to Peter's story drew Jon closer to Peter, which was the latter's intention. It occurred to Jon that he and his new client had similar lives, albeit on separate continents. Both had been detached from their mothers at a young age and raised by their fathers. Both had been brought up by independent fathers who had lived through extreme hardship and war. Their fathers were of a generation that communicated sparingly. So both boys had to grow up quickly and learn how to care for themselves on a day-to-day basis while still quite young.

Peter's mother was still alive and continued to live in East Berlin; Jon's mother was dead, though he was not totally convinced of that.

As the evening moved along, Jon—usually the listener, not the talker—found himself sharing more information about himself than he normally did. What Jon didn't know then was that Peter was very skilled at making people within his orbit feel a certain way in order to gather information. What people really thought and what they cared most about weren't necessarily reflected in what they said. Peter understood this well. Both men had, in their formative years, become skilled at repressing their inner thoughts and staying wary of fast talkers. What Jon didn't know was that Peter already knew quite a lot about him.

Peter was more than just a business liaison officer promoting Canadian and German business relations. He was also an employee of the West German Ministry of the Interior. He had been assigned to the West German Bundesnachrichtendienst (BND), the foreign intelligence arm of the West German government founded in 1956 when West Germany officially joined NATO. Consequently, Peter had targeted—with the intention of recruiting—Jon shortly after his arrival on German soil with Nora Baker six months earlier.

Peter knew Jon spoke German and had studied it at university. He knew Jon was a highly educated engineer who had been working on a large building project in Canada's capital city, where he met and cohabited with Nora Baker. And he knew that Jon had joined Nora as a common-law spouse when she was assigned to NATO in Heidelberg. It was Peter's job to know these things and to find people like Jon.

Shortly after Jon and Nora landed in West Germany, they visited Berlin and attended a symposium hosted by an educational institute funded by wealthy German businesses. It was run by Dr. Gerhard Mueller, a flamboyant pro-democracy advocate intent on promoting peace and cooperation between Eastern and Western governments. It was common for NATO employees to attend these types of educational events to foster a better understanding of their surrounding circumstances.

Nora was an avid history student, and in her position with the Department of Defense, she was often invited to attend such seminars. Jon was simply tagging along and taking in what was offered. Peter and his team were very interested in the type of people who attended these tours and seminars, and it was during this weekend that Peter first heard about Jon Mantler.

Jon ticked the right boxes for someone who could be of use to Peter and the BND. He was young and well-educated, had German heritage, spoke the language, and, through Nora, was connected to the operations at NATO headquarters in Heidelberg. It would be easy for Peter to paint him as a credible source of information.

The reunification of Germany had become the focal point of Peter's life. He studied business and political science at the University of Heidelberg, where he became affiliated with all the major institutes and political organizations involved in Germany's two-state status. As a result, reuniting the German people, East and West, was what he decided to dedicate most of his time and energy to.

Throughout the rest of the evening, Peter educated Jon profoundly on this topic. It was fascinating for Jon to get such a firsthand and in-depth construction of both the history and the current situation related to post-WWII Germany. He asked questions and received precise and valid answers. Germany was divided, and it shouldn't be, they agreed. They also agreed that this was unlikely to change in their own lifetimes. It would turn out that they were very wrong.

One week later, Jon returned to Bonn to complete the business with his tax clients. He set himself up in the same basement room, and the day went swimmingly. In the evening, he and Peter reconvened at the same restaurant as before. This time, Peter decided to pull a few more colorful cards out of his deck. He planted the seeds that would ultimately lead to Jon working for Peter and the West German government.

It was a dynamic time to be in this line of work. The Soviet leadership was in arrant turmoil following the illnesses and deaths of, in rapid succession, Leonid Brezhnev and Yuri Andropov, and then Konstantin Chernenko. These years of uncertainty, combined with economic mismanagement and geopolitical setbacks throughout the USSR, had induced a shift in Cold War strategies and resulted in an immense increase in activity in the field of espionage and information-gathering.

The BND liaised closely with its NATO partners and other national secret service agencies, including Canada. NATO saw the BND as a valuable asset and capable of gathering information inside East Germany and other Warsaw Pact nations during what was called the Cold War. NATO knew that the BND was well-lodged inside its East German counterpart agency, the infamous Stasi, and by extension, was infiltrating the Russian KGB. This was all part of West Germany's goal to break down and cause the failure of the East German political and economic system.

Causing maximum confusion within the massive East German Stasi network was one of the methods being used by the BND and the one that Peter was taking an instrumental part in. The West Germans wanted reunification of the two Germanies, even though at this time in history it still seemed to be such a faraway dream.

The Stasi system, set up over the past decades by the master manipulator Markus Wolf and now headed by Werner Grossmann, was the main force that kept the East German people under a tight political grip. By employing most of the population to spy on citizens' everyday lives, they thwarted any inkling of free will. It was estimated by the West that one in every fifty citizens of the GDR was an informant. "Government by the people" meant everyone perpetually gathering information on others. Everyone was a rat in some fashion or another. All seeds of dissent were weeded out and destroyed, keeping the East-West divide intact. The communist government, led by Erich Honecker and his aging administration, perpetuated Western misinformation and slander, combined with a heavy dose of fear about who might be watching, in order to hold control. They were experts in this brand of population control.

The mission of the BND division that Peter was part of was to connect with agents from the East who wished to exchange information. Peter was always looking to recruit credible sources who could feed misinformation into the Stasi network. It was a complicated operation, intended mainly to overwhelm and confuse the GDR's systems.

Stasi had a similar plan in place to cripple the West, and until a few years earlier, they were having significant success. Wolf and his network had infiltrated agents within the highest level of Western governments, and the BND was mandated to fight back in this regard. A crescendo intensified when the government of West German Chancellor Willy Brandt was toppled by such an act of espionage. That embarrassment led to a more determined effort on the part of the BND to support the Department of the Interior, which Peter was now involved with. His team was tasked with filling the Stasi network with an abundance of bogus data intended to clog their networks and make their intelligence processing difficult, tedious, and less productive.

It was true that the GDR, though poor and inept by comparison to West Germany, was still economically the strongest nation within the Warsaw Pact. Weakening the GDR would cause economic hardship in the USSR and other satellite nations, making it more difficult for that union to hold. Breaking them up was the ultimate goal of the Western intelligence services cooperating with the BND, like the British Secret Service and the United States CIA. There was still a risk, however, that if government opposition groups took to the streets in Berlin, the Soviets would roll in and squelch the potential uprising as the Stalinists had done in 1953 or in Hungary in 1956 and Czechoslovakia in 1968. Clearly, triggering the Soviet military was to be avoided.

It was upon this backdrop of freedom for all citizens that Jon and Peter built their relationship. Jon was definitely not nationalistic and had never been drawn to politics of any flavor, but he could strongly support individual rights and freedoms. His father had told him never to go to that place where he had been, which Jon still thought was France. Now that he was living near there, something told him that it would be okay to carry on with his father's story in some way.

Peter was very convincing. Jon liked him and thought it worthwhile to help if he could, so he did. Initially, it was not any more complicated than that.

CHAPTER 6

THE SHACK

He minded his business;
And he did what he could to be free.

It was an unusually warm day for early February when JJ was stopped by Geoffrey Jones in the back alley on his daily walk home from the school bus drop-off. February, which in this land could deliver any kind of extreme weather conditions at any given hour, was in a good mood on this day. So was JJ.

He idled along, enjoying the sunshine on his face, until Geoffrey appeared before him in the alleyway. It had been about three years since his father had passed away. JJ had adjusted well to living alone with assistance from the Butlers and occasional behind-the-scenes support from a few community leaders such as Geoffrey Jones.

"Hey, JJ, how are you doing today? It's a great one, isn't it?" the man called out.

"I'm pretty good, Mr. Jones. What's up with you today?" JJ replied, emulating the local banter style.

"Well, I have an idea I want to run by you. Something good to discuss with you, actually. How would you like to come by tonight for supper at our house?"

"I guess so. What time? What's going on?" JJ was not timid about asking people questions. He was curious and enthusiastic about most things and used to not getting answers. However, this rarely deterred him from still asking. It was a trait he would eventually learn to temper when he figured out there were people who did not like to be questioned. That's when silence was an asset.

"I'll fill you in when you come by later. It's all good stuff. See you then. Come over at six," Geoffrey said as he walked back to his house.

"Okay, catch you later."

Geoffrey Jones was the grain elevator agent for the biggest grain-buying company and the largest enterprise in the village, where he lived for longer than JJ could remember. Geoffrey was one of the neighbors who secretly looked out for the boy, whom he genuinely cared for. He knew JJ well because JJ was one of the better athletes in the community.

Geoffrey was a big sports fan, and he organized and coached most of the sports teams in the village. His teams always fared better when JJ was in the lineup. As for JJ, he really liked Geoffrey, but he wasn't a huge sports guy; he played on the teams more as a matter of community duty. He always did the best he could, which was usually very good.

Geoffrey lived with his wife and two young daughters in an old house next door to the post office, and JJ liked visiting them. Mrs. Jones was pretty and friendly, and she always cooked monstrous meals for JJ to devour. She kind of reminded JJ of his own mother, or at least of what he could remember of her, but he never told anyone.

After supper that evening, the Jones' two daughters, who loved to entertain JJ, finished their food and were persuaded to go off to do their homework before they could watch television. Then Geoffrey described his proposal to JJ. Mrs. Jones cleared the table while her husband talked.

"So here is the deal, JJ. My company is planning to build a new house for me here in the village. This one, as you can see, is very old and not too modern. The company doesn't think it's worthwhile to spend money fixing it. They think it makes more sense to unload this one and build something new. So we want to buy your property and build a new house on your lot."

JJ listened but did not speak, and Geoffrey continued, perhaps too abruptly.

"I think this is a good thing for you, JJ. You're going to be leaving to go to university at the end of this summer, right? Have you registered yet? That is going to cost some money, right? You're smart and an excellent student, so of course you'll have to go to university city. That is going to cost money. And you know as well as I do that you aren't likely to ever permanently come back to this little village after you get a proper education. You're going to need money, son, for school and to live in the big city, and this is the only chance you'll ever get to make anything off that piece of land you own."

That was a lot of questions and answers at one time, and JJ didn't know how to deal with them, so he dodged them.

"Why do you want my place?" JJ finally asked. "There are all kinds of free lots lying around in this town." He paused. "I guess…I gotta think about this."

"Sure you do, and we have time to work it all out, okay?" Geoffrey sensed that JJ was overwhelmed and getting emotional. "It's the best location for us. It's a short walk to my work, and it's on the best street in town."

In actuality, Geoffrey was looking out for JJ as much as he was for himself and his company. Most of the people in the village quietly cared about JJ, and a core group of his neighbors, led by Geoffrey and the Butlers, feared that he would not have enough money to go to university. This was the group that had taken care of the delicate circumstances following John's death and had succeeded in ensuring that JJ could remain in his home and in the village. Now they were prepping for the inevitable change to come.

Geoffrey Jones was a kind man with a strong sense of community, and he sought to do the right thing whenever a right-thing situation arose. JJ needed mature guidance at this point in his life. He could use a break or two to get out of this village and on his way to university, a career, and life as an adult. The house sale would provide just that.

JJ and Geoffrey talked about it for another hour, and by the end of it, the boy understood and pretty much accepted the plan.

"You have to consider what you get in contrast to what you need to give," Geoffrey surmised. "And in your case, what you give is something that in reality has no long-term value to you or to anyone else. What you get is a jump-start into the next phase of your life. You're a top student, and you need to carry on with your higher education, and as we've agreed, that'll require money." Geoffrey knew that JJ was a high achiever in school who wanted to continue with his education, but he didn't know about the shoebox.

A switch flipped for JJ. As he walked home later that night, he realized Geoffrey was right. Change was going to be unavoidable; it would always come. He had never actually thought about the Mantler shack as his property. To him, it was just home. It was where he was born, where he felt his mother's love and his father's pain and concern. For seventeen and a half years, it had been his life. So once he got home from the Jones' house, he sat at his tiny kitchen table, and for a good little while, he cried.

Then he started to hum. As he relaxed, he was able to think systematically through what Geoffrey had said. He considered the "give and the get" inference. It struck a nerve because his father had spoken similar words to him, albeit with a slightly different slant.

In recalling those tender moments with John Sr. at this same kitchen table, JJ again felt the magnitude of his father's love. His father's nature was to speak few words; still, it made JJ feel good to remember. Few words are required when they are the right words.

"Wanting and waiting to get things for yourself makes you weak. You must center on the giving!" John Mantler once said. "You need to measure yourself by what you give, not by what you get."

"Wishing makes no sense. Either you can build something, or you can't."

"Focus on what you can do, not on what you can't."

"If you can fix something, then fix it; if you can't, don't waste your energy."

"Hoping that you can do something you can't do serves no purpose. It'll frustrate and weaken you."

What JJ held within him from those special fatherly sessions was indispensable. Fixing the change that was coming was impossible; he did understand that he couldn't build anything here anymore. Things had already changed, and Geoffrey was again correct: JJ had to move on.

He took out a pen and paper from his schoolbag and scratched out a to-do list. At the top, he wrote, "University." He was definitely going to university; this was clear to him since he was a young child and from the time he delved into the encyclopedias. Second, he wrote, "New place to live." Third, he wrote, "Sell," but he couldn't quite bring himself to write the word "Home" next to that. Then he wrote, "Steps?"

Until today, he had not realized how demanding it was to

implement change. He had to formulate a plan and then realized there was mostly no one but himself, and maybe Geoffrey, who could look out for him in the process.

The next morning was Wednesday, and even though JJ had not slept very well, he was up early, ready to move on. He was sort of sorted and felt energized. His love for learning always motivated him, and he was proud that he had never missed a day of school in his life, not even on the day his dad died.

As soon as he arrived at school, he focused on his to-do list. He had a spare period in his schedule just before lunch break, so he went to the guidance office and made an appointment with Miss Roberts. Before today, he had only seen Miss Roberts in the hallways. She was young and quite attractive, so the student gossipers had labeled her "cool." This was about as high a rating a teacher could get in high school. None of this mattered much to JJ, though. He had written a lot of questions on a paper about how to proceed with university enrollment and was seeking advice.

When he met with Miss Roberts, she assured him that with his exceptional grades, he would have no difficulty gaining entry to any university he chose. She was more concerned about what program and subject focus he was intending to pursue. Miss Roberts was pushing him toward medicine, but JJ was not anywhere near making such a specific decision. He just wanted to go and learn all he could.

He knew that both his parents, as opposite as they were, would be proud of whatever he chose as long as he went to school and gave it his all. This was important to him. So Miss Roberts gave him applications to three universities and told him to fill in whatever he could, then bring the documents back so she could proofread and submit them. She also told him that he qualified for a number of scholarships and gave him many more applications to take home and complete. JJ set up a second meeting with Miss Roberts for Friday, stuffed the forms in his schoolbag, and went off to lunch pleased with his progress. By the end of the school day, he had already scratched a number of to-dos off his list.

That evening, JJ sat at his kitchen table again to enter the cumbersome and frustrating adult world of forms. Except for the simple order forms for the Sears or Eaton's catalogs, he had little experience with this kind of paperwork. There were so many tricky and cloudy questions to answer. Worse still, there were verification documents to submit, none of which the Mantlers seemed to have. He did not have a birth certificate, no social insurance card, no driver's license, no bank account, not even a library card. JJ came to realize that up until today, he sort of didn't exist.

The John Mantler who lived in the Mantler shack had been both himself and his father. This had served him well so far, but now the time had come for him to restructure and egress from that coexistence. JJ searched further through the bottom of the shoebox and came up with a crumpled document, a very official, awkward-looking piece of thick paper. It was a baptismal certificate issued by the neighboring church. It was proof of his birth.

Fortunately, young JJ was born at a time when Roxanne was phasing through one of her religious streaks. JJ had no recollection that his mother held any devout beliefs, but she had periodically spent time at the neighboring church, even sitting for a term on the council. This certificate would open the door to acquiring the rest of the documents he needed for his applications.

As JJ worked throughout the evening on the forms, he noted what questions he could answer on a blank page and listed what he could not on a separate page. He also contemplated his entire life thus far. In doing so, he came to a simple conclusion.

Up to this moment, there had been three stages: one with his mother, one with his father, and one by himself. This odd reasoning pleased him, and he became more satisfied with his identity.

While examining the one haggard document that listed his name, birthdate, place of birth, and the names of his parents, he noticed new information. Written there was the date he had been baptized, followed by a stamp and the signature of a Reverend Jon Theiss. There were also two additional names and signatures on the document, witnesses to the holy event: Dorothy Schick and Clarence Lutz. These were two names he had never seen before, and he had no idea who they were. Their signed presence, however, further substantiated his existence and, more importantly, made the document far more official. He could now verify that he was born on August 16 to John Mantler and Roxanne Martin.

He knew he was becoming obsessed with this partly torn and shredded document, and on further examination, it seemed like the handwritten excerpt of his name looked a bit different. He noticed that his name, handwritten by the pastor, was spelled "Jon" Mantler, similar to the Reverend Jon Theiss's name scribbled below it. JJ was intrigued, and it gave him an idea. He decided to alter his identity slightly and step out of his shack and into his next life as Jon instead of John. He had never liked being called Junior, JJ, or any of the other names the village folk had called him. His mother and father had called him John. John would now be Jon.

So, he filled out all the forms as Jon Mantler and packed them into his schoolbag. On Friday, he would bring everything to the eager Miss Roberts; she would review the documents and clarify his next steps. It was late now; it had been a long and deep dive of an evening for him. But there was still one problem.

In the eyes of the law, his father was still considered to be alive. Jon was aware of this because each month for the last few years, he had been signing the back of his father's Veterans' Affairs disability checks to cash at the local post office. That cash, except for what he used for paying the bills and buying food, went into the big shoebox under the floor beside Roxanne's bed. Jon had been doing the same thing while John was alive, so he just continued to do it after his death. He also continued to mail in an income tax return every April, just as he had every previous April.

John Sr. had a social insurance number, and each year, JJ took the one T4 slip that came in the mail and simply filled in the same numbers from the previous year's return, give or take a few dollars, and sent it off to the Tax Department. John declared very little income when he was alive, so Jon declared very little income in the years after his death. He even got a small refund check back, which made the annual exercise well worthwhile. Now, in order for Jon to move on, John would have to move on as well.

Geoffrey Jones was also aware of this, and he already had a

solution. It would be another two days until Geoffrey and Jon would meet again to synchronize their strategies. In the meantime, Jon focused on school.

Miss Roberts had arranged an 11:00 a.m. meeting, and Jon left his history class a bit early to ensure he did not get to her office late. He was eager to learn what her advice would be regarding his half-completed applications. Upon initial review, Miss Roberts confirmed that he did indeed need to have a social insurance number, and in order to get it, he would need to have a registered birth certificate issued by the federal government. This was when the torn and rumpled baptismal certificate came to the rescue. They now had to verify the information on the certificate, which the school principal would take care of. The process would take a few weeks. Miss Roberts would hold the applications and send them out once Jon's birth certificate arrived. From then on, Jon Mantler would officially exist.

Jon was feeling assured and satisfied. After school, he went to see Geoffrey at his office. "Hello, Mr. Jones. I hope you don't mind me coming by."

Geoffrey was alone and didn't seem too busy. "No, it's fine. I'm glad you came by because for sure, we have some more things to discuss. How are you?"

"I'm good, real good. I started to make applications to register for university, so that's pretty all right, I think."

"Yeah, that's good, well done. Look, there are a lot of little things that you and I still have to work out about the house, so can we discuss some of that now?"

There were definite details, all right, not the least of which was that for all recorded purposes and as far as any official agencies knew, his father was still alive. When John Mantler died over three years ago, Jim Butler, assisted by Leonard and his sons, had taken care of it just as promised.

There wasn't a task that Leonard could not complete; he had inconspicuously dug a grave and buried John Mantler while everyone else minded their own business. Minding one's own business in such a small community was rarely done, but for the Mantlers, things had always been looked on differently or not looked on at all.

Geoffrey Jones was also the overseer of this village, which was akin to being a mayor, had the village been big enough to be a town and not a village. After looking away from this matter for three years, he knew the time had come to readdress it. The solution for his company to legally purchase the Mantler shack and for Jon to move on with his life was that John Mantler would have to die again.

Sadly, Jim Butler had passed away a year ago, leaving Mrs. Butler a widow and even more focused on the welfare of young JJ. This did, however, leave the option, should it become necessary, to pin all the blame on Jim for not filing the proper documents at the time of the original death. But that would not be the best outcome for all concerned.

Geoffrey, assisted by Leonard, had now put together a new plan intended to help Jon. They picked a day to publicly declare the death of John Mantler.

Geoffrey had a solid connection to the coroner in the little city down the road, in whose jurisdiction this matter would be registered. He was confident he could get the coroner to sign off on the death certificate based on his word and without the extra need to drive out to witness the body. The cause of death would simply be old age and exhaustion from years of living like a hermit with a disability. Open and shut case, as they said in these parts, died of natural causes.

Geoffrey took his time explaining this to Jon. "We're going to have to work closely together. We'll pay you a few thousand dollars for your lot, and we'll even pay you a few thousand more if you can remove the shack from the property. You can keep and probably sell the wood and anything else you have, so you can make a bit more money. I suspect the wood in that place has a lot of value compared to those high-end new house finishers these days. This could be your summer project to make you extra cash before you head off to university."

"I guess," said Jon. "That shouldn't be too hard. I can take down the house as soon as I finish school in June. It won't take more than a few weeks, you think?"

"Okay, then I'll get things ready, and you think about hiring some more guys to help you with the tear-down. I can help you coordinate that too, if you want. It'll take a month or more, I figure, depending on how much wood you want to save to sell. But basically, it's not a very big place. I'll organize all the paperwork we need to get everything done in the next few weeks. We should talk a bit each day and make sure we know what each of us is doing. What do you think?"

And that was what they did. It was true there was a lot to do, but things were starting to make sense to Jon. He trusted Geoffrey.

At their next meeting, they selected April 4 to be the official date of death for John Mantler. It would be during Easter, and to some degree, public spaces and a lot of government offices would be closed. Geoffrey speculated it would be easier to file the paperwork and slip it through quickly with minimal scrutiny during the holiday period. He spent the better part of the next week preparing paperwork for the sale of the property and the removal of the shack. He also sketched out a plan for the documentation that declared the official death of John Mantler.

Jon would still be a minor in April. Geoffrey knew that signatures would be required for verifying and cosigning many of these documents. Luckily, in his role as overseer of the village, he was also a commissioner of oaths. Therefore, his validation with a fancy ink stamp next to his signature would be accepted without question.

Jon knew that following these declarations, the monthly Veterans' Affairs disability benefits would stop coming to his mailbox. There would be one more, larger death benefit coming, but after that, the young Mantler and the shoebox would have to make it on their own.

Jon left Geoffrey's office again with a head full of thoughts. After school earlier that day, he had felt like everything made sense and he knew what he was doing. Now, after talking to Geoffrey, he had another big list of things to organize. Tearing down the shack would make him a lot of money, but as the evening went on and he pondered it more, he feared it might be a bigger project than they anticipated. Dismantling the shack would take a carefully crafted plan and hard labor. Jon sat at his kitchen table and wrote again.

There was no turning back now. He made a new list of what he would need to do, and in an unusually selfish act for him, he jiggered the list so that acquiring a mode of transportation was first. Even when Jon was still JJ, he was thinking he would need a vehicle by the fall so he could travel back and forth to university. But the task of tearing down the shack was about to take precedence over the need for transportation. He wrote, "Buy a truck," on his pending list, and that made him feel more capable.

CHAPTER 7

NASH RAMBLER

Fly now, fly to tomorrow, with good hope, with no demands;
Let ease be more the master than plots no one understands.

Jon had been driving since he was about twelve years old, which was the custom for any youngster raised in the region. Knowing how to drive was not an issue. The issue was going through the procedure required to receive the official license that deemed you legal to drive. First, there was a written test, which he had passed two weeks earlier. Next was a practical test, which he had scheduled for this upcoming Saturday. The problem was in order to take the practical driving test, he needed to have an actual vehicle to physically conduct the test in.

Mrs. Butler still had one of the two Nash Ramblers that had been her husband's pride and joy for many decades. She didn't know how to drive; however, she kept the car registered and plated, so when she wanted, she could conscript Jon to drive her to the store for shopping or to visit her friend who lived just north of town. Jon had mastered the beastly black Rambler, and Mrs. Butler had no problem letting him take it to the little city of Greyton for the driver's test.

Legally, however, Jon was on a learner's certificate, which meant he could drive the Rambler to the test location only if there were a licensed driver beside him in the vehicle. Luckily for Jon, his neighborhood friend, Harvard Dean, was back in the village this particular weekend. Harvey was a year older than Jon and a university student. He readily agreed to ride shotgun for Jon to and from the test on said Saturday.

On the afternoon of the day before the test, Jon started up the Nash Rambler and drove it over to the local garage to have everything checked out, added oil, pumped up the big tube tires, and filled the big cannonball with gasoline. The car was an immense four-door luxury liner, a veritable tank, with a big, old eight-cylinder engine that sounded like a freight train when you stepped on the gas. It featured a three-on-the-tree standard transmission and a steering wheel as big as a ship's helm. The seats were living-room size. Fortunately, Jon was nearly as tall as Jim Butler was because for many people, reaching the clutch and the brake would require stilts.

Jon and Harvey set off on the thirty-minute drive from their village to Greyton at ten in the morning. This was the first time Jon had driven on the highway, and he really enjoyed the feeling of the big old Rambler rolling down the asphalt. Harvey was having a fun time as well, learning how his half of the big front seat could be unhitched and dropped down between the front and back seats to create a virtual bed.

"If you put both front seatbacks down, you could sleep a family of six in this big bomb," Harvey announced.

The driving instructor evaluating Jon Mantler for the test had never seen a Nash Rambler before. He was also a very short, petite man, and when he sat in the passenger-side seat, he could barely see over the dashboard or out the front windshield. It was difficult for him to assess Jon's driving; he was uncomfortable, but he felt that young Jon was in total control. So within about ten minutes of driving the city streets, the instructor asked Jon to drive back to his office. There, within about fifteen more minutes, Jon had a typed and stamped license in his wallet. One more life step was expunged from his list.

The two boys went to a local café and celebrated this accomplishment with lunch and ice cream, before they headed back down the highway toward home. Jon was glad Harvey was back from university this weekend and that he had agreed to accompany him to this important proceeding. While they had been neighbors and friends all their lives, they were not best friends. Harvey was a year older, and activity-wise, had always been in a different age category. Since he had gone off to university, they rarely saw each other.

Jon did not actually have a best friend. If he could have picked one, though, it would have been Harvey Dean. Harvey had a personality Jon admired. He was sure of himself, always had something cool and appropriate to say, and all the girls liked him. These were traits that Jon thought he lacked.

On the drive home, a few kilometers from the little city and just before a small hill, they saw a large semi-trailer truck ahead of them with its four-way flashing lights engaged. It was stopped almost exactly in the center of the two-lane road. Jon slowed the car down and parked about fifty meters behind it on the right shoulder of the road. The Nash Rambler was of an era before four-way flashing lights, so Jon simply put on the right turn signal and pulled the hand emergency brake while letting the engine continue to run. As he did this, both boys saw a small, smashed-up vehicle that had rolled across the ditch to the right.

What the hell happened here, Harvey wondered.

Jon and Harvey quickly got out of their vehicle and walked forward cautiously. Then they saw an older man at the side of the truck and assumed he was the driver. He was simply standing there, looking out at the crushed car on the far side of the ditch.

"He smashed right into me! I couldn't miss him!" exclaimed the man.

By this time, Harvey was already heading through the ditch to the small car. Jon and the driver filed in behind him. Beside the car stood a woman; lying beside her on the ground was a second woman. The standing woman said something, but it was inaudible.

"Shock," blurted out Harvey.

The woman on the ground was a younger girl, and she was sobbing rhythmically. The boys spurred into action.

"Are you hurt? Can you move? Are you okay?" Harvey asked.

"I don't know!" mumbled the girl between sobs.

"Is there anyone else with you? Anyone in the car?" Harvey questioned.

Jon went over to the older woman and asked roughly the same questions as the semi-trailer driver beside him finally came to life and began being of some use.

"I have a CB radio in the truck. I'll call the police with it," he offered.

"Good idea, do that," said Jon.

The standing woman didn't look well at all, even though she was upright. The girl on the ground was clearly injured, and it seemed like she couldn't move. It was impossible to determine how much was due to shock, and how much was because she was seriously injured.

"We're only a few kilometers from the hospital on the other side of the city. If we load them into the beast, we can have them there in minutes. If we wait here for the police and an ambulance to show, it could take another hour," Harvey said.

"But we can't move the girl over here without something to support her," Jon added.

"You get the Rambler up here. I'll find something." Harvey turned to the two women. "We're going to get you to the hospital. Don't worry, it's going to be okay."

The older woman finally sat on the ground in a daze.

Meanwhile, Jon ran back to the Rambler and drove up as close as he could to the ditch without making it too difficult to get the Nash back up onto the highway. By this time, a few more cars had stopped on either side of the truck, which remained like a monument in the center of the highway. The truck driver was tending to the traffic and leaving all else to the two boys.

Harvey knew that the ditches beside a highway were scattered with junk in the springtime, and in his search, he came up with a thin, old metal highway sign that had been dislodged from its post. "No Littering," it read. It was just long and wide enough to slip under the young girl and allow them to carry her stretcher-like across to the big car.

Harvey used the seat mechanism to drop the backrest on the passenger side. This provided a flatbed for the girl before they carefully placed her through the big back door with her legs onto the front driver's side seat. The other woman walked up on her own, and Harvey assisted her into the driver's side of the back seat.

"There is no more room in the car," Harvey said to his friend. "Drive them to the hospital as fast as you can. You know how to get there, right?"

Jon nodded.

"I'll wait here and help the driver control the traffic."

And just like that, Jon drove back up the embankment and onto the highway, past a row of stopped cars, and aimed the car back toward Greyton. The young girl was constant in her sobbing, while the older woman, who at last seemed to be aware of what was going on, began talking and comforting her. She thanked Jon over and over again for helping them. Both were conscious, and that was good, he thought as he pressed on the gas pedal and rushed the big black Nash Rambler down the highway.

There was hardly any traffic, and in mere minutes, which seemed to Jon like a few hours, he was at the city limits, signaling right to leave the highway and enter the city. Along the way, the older woman introduced herself as Marianne Morris and the younger one, her daughter, as Angela.

"I'm Jon Mantler. Don't worry, ma'am, we're very close to the hospital," he said.

He didn't tell them he had only just received a driver's license an hour or so ago. Angela was still sobbing. He assumed her sobbing was a control mechanism, like his own humming.

"Everybody still okay?" Jon asked. "We'll be there in two minutes, so hang in there, all right?"

He wheeled the Nash Rambler in front of the entrance to the hospital and parked, then pushed the button that shut off the engine.

"Stay where you are, and I'll get some doctors to come and help you right away." Jon ran up the steps to the hospital doors.

This was Jon's first-ever visit to a hospital, so he didn't have a sense of what to do or how to do it as he entered the building. Standing in the middle of the room and yelling seemed to be the quickest and most effective strategy, so that was what he did.

A woman seated behind a small countertop acknowledged him, jumped up from behind her station, ran down a small hallway, and called out to someone in an adjacent room. A man and a woman, both dressed in white, rushed out from the room and followed a fast-moving Jon to his black "ambulance." They examined the two women. A stretcher and two more men arrived, and they took Angela inside. Marianne was able to walk in with minimal assistance from a nurse, though she still looked lost and unwell. Her zombie-like state scared Jon, but he knew he had to brave up.

For a moment, he stayed behind the procession, then walked

through the front doors of the hospital. He waited in the lobby while the other people disappeared down a corridor and through a second set of doors beyond.

After standing there alone for a few minutes, Jon realized he was of no value anymore, so he went back to the Nash Rambler and left. He drove a lot slower this time as he headed back up the highway to the scene of the accident to reunite with Harvey.

Within about a quarter of an hour, he slowed the car and parked behind other cars on the shoulder of the road near the scene. There were now two police cars with their lights flashing, one on each side of the semi-trailer truck still planted in the middle of the road. An ambulance pulled up on the left with no siren but with lights flashing.

Jon walked along the side of the road and spotted Harvey ushering a car around the front of the semi. Otherwise, not much had changed at the accident location.

Harvey was right, he thought as he looked at his wristwatch and calculated it had taken the ambulance about forty minutes to arrive. The black Nash Rambler had completed its mission in under twenty-five minutes. There were two other police officers on the scene now. Jon walked up to Harvey and said he had delivered the women to the hospital without issue.

The two policemen looked at the smashed-up car and took photos of the surroundings as Harvey and Jon approached the wreck, still curious, to get a better look. They thought it was a small Toyota, but it was not easy to tell, because it was so destroyed. It was unimaginable that the two women got out of that car alive, the boys thought.

Jon didn't know it, but the policemen had already spoken to Harvey, and now one of them came over again. Harvey introduced his friend to the officer. Clearly, Harvey was still in control of the scene, at least in their own estimation, despite the arrival of the constables.

"So, this investigation is all going to take some time. We're waiting for more help to arrive from the city. Can you give me your names and telephone numbers on this sheet of paper? We'll call you boys if we need more information since you were the first to arrive at the scene. But you can go home now. We'll contact you if we need to."

"Okay, sir. We just live twenty minutes away," Harvey answered.

He was enjoying the attention and importance he felt in this being-in-charge role. But Jon was confused. He didn't understand why the policeman didn't want to know about the two women he had driven to the hospital. Who did he think was driving the Toyota, and where were they?

It didn't make any sense. He had no experience in such matters, but obviously neither did the policeman. Nonetheless, he wrote "3580" on the paper beside his name, which was Mrs. Butler's number, because there was still no telephone in the Mantler shack.

Jon noticed the semi-trailer truck driver had been sitting in the back of one of the police vehicles all this time. He was alone until the photographing officer went over and sat behind the driver's wheel. The ambulance drivers were standing beside their rig, smoking cigarettes. No one was talking to them.

There was still very little traffic. Only one officer was needed to wave on the sporadic vehicles past the front of the semi-trailer truck, which remained pillar-like atop the slight hill straddling the white line.

Eventually, even Harvey became bored, so the two boys headed back to the Nash Rambler for home, rolling past the left side of the truck cab. As they did, they saw the black tire marks on the highway showing the drivers' unsuccessful efforts to avoid the collision. Both boys marveled at the lack of damage to the front of the truck. Marianne and Angela had been traveling east in the same lane that the Nash Rambler now half-occupied.

"So why did they veer left and cross into the lane that the semi was in?" Harvey asked as they drove away from the scene. "And why was the semi aiming left?"

Jon didn't have an answer to those questions.

"How fast did you get this big hearse going when you were heading for the hospital?"

This was easier to answer, because it was far faster than he had ever driven. "The needle was nearly topping seventy-five," Jon said proudly. "I thought it might explode because of the noise, but I still had about two inches left on the gas pedal."

"That's crazy, J Bird!"

"I think I was at the hospital in ten minutes flat, once I got rolling down that highway."

The young men were excited and felt heroic about their rescue mission. They had done something good today; they had taken action and helped people. They had been of use. They had given. But it was imperative to act cool.

"I thought the mother looked freaky," Harvey noted. "But they were okay when you got to the hospital, right?" This wasn't really a question.

"Her name is Marianne, and the younger one is Angela, her daughter. Yeah, I thought she looked dead too, but she walked into the hospital next to the doctors. I liked her. Angela never said anything on the drive, just kept whimpering, either scared or in pain. Maybe she's gonna be paralyzed, but she did say she could feel her toes. Marianne asked who I was, and we chatted a bit on the drive, but I had to focus on the Rambler and the road."

"I'd sure like to know how they're doing," Harvey said.

Jon agreed.

The Nash Rambler floated to a stop in front of Mrs. Butler's garage as the two continued discussing the condition of the Toyota after the crash.

"There is nothing left of it; it's totally crushed. I wouldn't have wanted to be in that little thing when it clipped that truck. How many times do you think it rolled?" Jon asked.

"I had a pretty good look at it. At least twice, I'd say, and it's lucky they weren't a few feet farther out, or they'd have landed in a lot of water." Harvey said goodbye to Jon and walked across the street to his house.

"Maybe. I'll see you later," Jon called after his friend.

"I think some of us are going over to Willy's tonight. I'll let you know for sure. Say hi to Mrs. B. for me."

"Okay, maybe. See ya."

Jon checked in with Mrs. Butler before heading home. This time, he had a really good story to tell her. He ate supper and bragged about the heroics of Harvey and the big old Nash Rambler. Mrs. Butler was enthralled by the news and pleased that her old car had taken part in a rescue mission. Jon was proud to have an interesting tale to share.

Later at home, he felt tired and decided he didn't want to go out. This was not unusual for young Jon. He was quite happy to take the time to process the day's events in considerably more detail.

The highway accident had overshadowed the satisfaction of getting his driver's license. Quietly, he took the small paper card out of his wallet and set it on the kitchen table. This was the first and only identification he possessed that presented him to the world as Jon Mantler. Below the name were his post office box number and the name of the village he lived in.

He would be JJ no more. Today, Jon Mantler had taken a significant step into his next life.

CHAPTER 8

POLICE

Cops are from the city, it really is a pity, they got no boogie in their bones.
Get their satisfaction cutting other people's action, why can't they just leave it alone?

The next day, Jon was up early, coming out of his outdoor latrine, when he noticed a police car parked in front of the Deans' house about two blocks away. It was unusual to see a police car in the village at all, and even more intriguing to see it outside the Deans' house on a Sunday morning.

It was the weekend, and Jon didn't have to be anywhere in particular, so he headed back into his shack, wondering what the cops were doing in town. About twenty minutes later, he heard a knock on his door and opened it up to see a policeman standing in front of him. It was a warm morning, so Jon stepped out to greet him. The sharp-dressed man asked if he was Jon Mantler, and Jon confirmed that he was.

"Hello, son, I'm Sgt. Morgan. Do you think you could come with me over to the Deans' house? I'm investigating the automobile accident on the highway yesterday that you and Mr. Dean witnessed."

"Ah, sure, just let me get my jacket," Jon replied.

"You can ride over with me," said the sergeant.

"It's only over there." Jon pointed to the Deans' house. "I'll just walk through the alley and meet you there." Only two blocks, thought Jon, why would he have driven?

Jon arrived at the Deans' house before the policeman and entered to see Harvey and his mother sitting solemnly at the kitchen table. Harvey didn't even make any jokes when Jon entered the room. This must have been serious.

The police officer sat in a chair across from Harvey and Jon, beside Mrs. Dean, and toyed with a small notebook and papers in front of him. Then he got ready to ask questions. He was also drinking a coffee, which Mrs. Dean had handed him. The boys just sat and waited for whatever was going to happen next. Jon wanted to know the condition of Angela and Marianne, but he didn't feel comfortable opening the conversation.

"Well, Jon, thanks for coming over. I've already been talking to Harvard," Sgt. Morgan began.

"Harvey," Mrs. Dean interrupted.

"Yes, Harvey, and I think I have a pretty good idea of what you two saw when you arrived behind the semi-trailer truck. We've also spoken to the driver. What I'm not clear on, Jon, is how you transported the two victims to the hospital in Greyton."

"How are they, sir? Marianne and Angela, I mean?" Jon interjected.

"I'm told that they're both still in the hospital but stable and not in serious danger," Sgt. Morgan politely replied. "How did you get them to the hospital?"

"We loaded them into the Nash Rambler, and I drove back to Greyton. They seemed to be in shock, but they both wanted to go to the hospital, so I drove them there as quick as I could."

"And when you got to the hospital, what did you do?"

"I just called for help, and the doctors came out and took them inside."

"Then what did you do?"

"Well, no one asked me anything, and there really wasn't anyone around once they took Angela and Marianne through the doors, so I just stood there for a while. Then I thought I'd go back and help Harvey, or at least I should pick him up again."

Sgt. Morgan wrote in his notebook. "And back at the accident scene, when you got there, what did you see and what did you do?"

"Let me think a bit. I parked the car farther back because I heard and saw the ambulance arriving from behind me. Then I walked up the side of the road to behind the semi. I saw Harvey there with one of the police officers, and I saw the truck driver sitting in one of the cop cars. There were two police cars there, and I think three policemen. Then one of the policemen told us we could go home, so we did. That's about all."

"Did you talk to any of the officers?"

"Not really. Harvey just told me we could take off, and they knew where we lived if they needed anything else from us."

"Okay, I think that is about all I need from you right now. But do you boys know that it's actually illegal to leave the scene of an accident? And it's against the law to move victims from an accident scene. You can comfort victims, but you can't move them. You have to wait for the medics and the police to come and do their jobs."

"I didn't think about that," said Jon half-apologetically.

"That doesn't make any sense," Harvey interjected. "We did what needed to be done! That is just nuts! By the time the ambulance got there, JJ was already back from the hospital!"

"Well, I'm not so concerned with that right now, boys. It's not for me to say what was right and not right. I simply have to report what happened and to inform you of the situation," the sergeant stated, a bit more forcefully as he placed his papers and notebook into his satchel. He thanked Mrs. Dean for the coffee and her kindness.

"So what happens now?" asked Harvey, which was also precisely what Jon wanted to know.

Jon felt confronted and confused. Just a half day ago, he was proud of what he and Harvey had done at the accident scene. Now they were being scolded for their quick thinking and accused of possibly breaking a law.

"Look, I doubt anything, but whenever there is an accident of this nature, we have to compile a report from all the information we can gather. Once that is done, and if everything is clear, we can close the file. People were injured and damage occurred, so there are a lot of factors that need to be considered, especially when the insurance claims come in and need to be processed. They need to have our police reports in order to properly evaluate everything. If we need anything further from you boys, we'll let you know," Sgt. Morgan concluded as he headed for the door.

Once he left, the boys sat around for a few minutes, stunned. The weather was cool, but the sun was still shining, so the boys adjourned to the back doorstep to analyze the conversation and contemplate their situation.

"Do you think we're in some kind of trouble?" Jon asked Harvey.

"I can't see that, but crazy shit does happen."

"Not much we can do, I guess," concluded Jon.

"Well, I don't know about that. I think I'm going to call up Chance and see what he says about all this. This sergeant gives me the creeps, and something seems kind of weird here. Before you came over, he was asking me all sorts of questions about the accident. What I saw at the scene, and what we did when we got there, and what I did until the police showed up. I finally stopped telling him much of anything, then he went and got you. So I think we need to run this by old Chance," urged Harvey.

Chance Lager was not at all old. He had graduated top of the provincial bar just over a year ago and was now working with a law firm in Greyton. He had grown up in this village, and he was the go-to lawyer for everyone and everything in the community. On matters pertaining to the law, politics, or dealing with authority, he was the fixer.

While the boys were considering seeking legal advice from Chance, Harvey's mom came around the corner.

"There is someone on the phone for you, Harvey!" she bellowed. Then she told them she had prepared an early lunch for all of them, and Jon was to return to the kitchen and join the Dean family immediately. It was less of an invitation than an order, so Jon obediently made his way back into the house.

"Okay, Mrs. Dean, thank you," he muttered.

Harvey was in the corner of the kitchen, slowly wrapping up his conversation on the telephone as Jon entered.

"Thank you, I will do that," was about all Jon heard him say.

"Hey, JJ, you're not gonna believe who that was. It was a Mr. Morris. He's the husband of the lady that you took to the hospital. He wanted to thank us, and he asked us to come to the hospital this afternoon to see them. He said both women are going to be okay! And they want to meet us and thank us," Harvey proclaimed.

How did they know where to find them, Jon thought. But before he could ask, pandemonium broke out in the Deans' kitchen because Mrs. Dean had summoned the household for a Sunday brunch kind of thing. Harvey had a younger sister and two much younger brothers, and all were eagerly seated at the table to eat eggs and bacon. The siblings, sensing good news, broke into cheers following his announcement, even though Harvey had not yet told any of them what really happened. They were supportive of him just for the hell of it. It would take the next hour of eating and talking about things before they understood that Harvey and Jon were now indeed local heroes.

Once all the food on the table had been destroyed, Harvey said, "So let's go to Greyton. We'll take my car."

Jon agreed, and within thirty minutes, they were driving back to the city.

Harvey commandeered his older yellow Barracuda down the single-lane highway. "I have to head back to university city tomorrow. I have a few exams coming up in the next few weeks."

"What's that like? University, I mean."

The events of the past two days had drawn the two boys much closer, and Jon felt comfortable asking this. He had always been in awe of Harvey, but now that Jon was about to graduate high school, there didn't seem to be so much air between them anymore.

Harvey had never been in the Mantler shack, and he knew the Mantlers mainly from what he had been told by people in the community. Young Jon Mantler was considered a bit peculiar due to the reclusive nature of his father. It wasn't fair, but what is?

Everyone liked Jon and knew how intelligent and capable he was; still, people kept their distance. Opinions were formed, and once judgments were made, they became embedded in people's minds forever. For Harvey, the past two days had changed all that. He was now very drawn to the wisdom and maturity he saw in his new old friend.

In twenty minutes, they reached the location where the accident took place. Without consulting Jon, Harvey pulled his car onto the shoulder of the road and stopped.

Jon was hoping they would stop there. Both boys had been thinking a lot about the events of the day before. It was about two hours later than that day, and as they arrived from the west, they could see the rise in the road, as it would have looked from the women's perspective.

The light and weather conditions were similar to what they had been on Saturday.

"The top of the truck was much higher than the car, so Marianne would have seen the top of it first, probably before the driver saw her car," Harvey speculated.

"Except the driver sits up higher off the road, so he should have seen the car soon enough," Jon answered.

The boys got out of the car. They were determined to figure out how it all happened. It was more than just an accident now; they felt a part of the drama, and their self-importance was running high. There was usually not much traffic on this highway and even less on this sunny Sunday afternoon, so the boys had time to wander around on the road uninterrupted. First, they stopped to see the skid marks from the truck, still very much present in the middle of the road.

"The trucker, what was his name again? Didn't hit the brakes until about right here, when he was already on this side of the road," Harvey determined.

"His name was Owen, I think. So who wandered into the opposite lane first?"

"When we got here, the truck was still in the middle of the road, but it wasn't as far over this way as the skid marks go. He must have backed the truck after he stopped," Jon added.

"Yeah, because he was about here." Harvey pointed a few feet away from where he was standing. "And I was directing cars by him over here, and there was still a lot of room from the shoulder."

A car was coming from the east, so they crossed the road over to where the small car had started to roll and eventually landed on the far side of the ditch near small shrubs and an adjoining field.

"Marianne must have almost missed the truck, but then she hit the brakes too hard while turning left, and that flipped her. So maybe the truck had to go that far left to miss her," Jon said.

"Or she had to go this far to her left because she saw the truck coming across her lane. If Owen is going that way, then Marianne has to go this way." Harvey demonstrated with his hands and arms.

"The car didn't brake until it was way over here. So she must have thought she could get by the truck, then panicked, maybe. Hard to say."

"The car sure did go flying, though, to end up way on the other side there."

"Yes, but remember, you can't brake anymore when you're airborne," Jon said.

After a few more minutes, they had seen all there was to see, so they returned to the car, mystery unsolved. They continued to discuss the accident scene for the rest of the drive but could not come up with anything more conclusive as to how it had happened.

In about twenty-five minutes, they reached the hospital, and Harvey entered the parking lot.

"I think Owen's big truck wandered so far into the left lane that Marianne was spooked and went left to miss him," Jon offered.

"Based on the skid marks, you could be right," said Harvey.

Walking through the big front doors of the hospital for the second time, Jon was struck by how small it was. It had seemed so much bigger to him the day before. Strange, he thought, how the mind could expand or deflate things based on how you felt at the time.

To Harvey, who had been to this hospital many times before, it was all routine; there was no thinking or feeling required.

As before, there was a lady sitting at the desk at the far side of the room, which was actually not very far at all, and she gave the boys the room number of the Morrises. They went through the next set of doors and down one of the hallways to the wards. This was all new to Jon.

There were two beds in the room. This time, it was Angela who was upright in one of the beds, and Marianne who was vertical in the other. Angela looked alert and was speaking softly to a man seated at the foot of the bed. Angela's mother looked to be asleep, with a plastic hose connected to her nose and mouth. The seated man was big and had a large mustache that twirled upward on both sides. He jumped to his feet when the two boys entered the room. Smiling, he greeted them with an open and ready-to-shake right hand.

"Hi guys, thanks for coming so soon. I'm real happy to see you. I'm Gregg Morris," he declared. "Which one of you is Harvey Dean?"

"That's me! And this is Jon," Harvey confirmed.

It was the first time Jon could recall Harvey calling him by his new preferred name. It felt good.

The boys were just going with the flow in the aftermath of the accident. Had they thought about it a bit more, they would have realized there wasn't really any reason for them to be here at the hospital, except that they were excited by all the attention and liked thinking of themselves as heroes.

Angela smiled and thanked them for getting them to the hospital so quickly. Harvey, always self-assured, moved closer to her and asked how she was, and soon they were deep in conversation. All the girls seemed to like Harvard Dean, Jon thought as he shyly edged his way closer to Marianne's bed. Her eyes were open, but she looked neither dead nor alive.

"They still have her on a lot of medication," Gregg explained when he saw the look on Jon's face.

Just then, two heavyset female nurses came to the room pushing a cart. They declared that they needed the room and asked all three men to please adjourn to the waiting area outside while they tended to vaguely described tasks. Jon was uncomfortable in the room and relieved to get out of it. He had no clue as to what was going on, and it was one rare time when Jon didn't feel the need to know what was happening. He was the first to leave the room.

Gregg Morris was a rancher who lived about an hour outside of the little village. Once he was seated with the boys in the hallway, he revealed that it was not only to thank the boys that he had invited them to the hospital. The police, who were investigating the accident, had visited the Morrises in the hospital on Saturday night, and Gregg had gotten the impression that they were intending to charge his wife with causing the accident. He wanted to know what the boys had seen and what they thought had happened. He had been at the scene twice and was now on a Sherlock Holmes expedition to stay a few steps ahead of the police.

As for the ladies, Marianne and Angela were calmer now, knowing they were going to recover from their injuries, but they were still quite uncertain about how the accident had occurred. Angela only suffered from bruising and muscle strain in her mid and lower back; there were no broken bones or major injuries. This pleasantly surprised the boys, who thought she was the more injured party.

Marianne, on the other hand, had been beaten about quite brutally by the steering wheel of the car as it rolled over multiple times. The result was now worrisome damage to her internal organs, particularly her kidneys. The doctors were reasonably confident she would be fine in time. However, when she had walked into the hospital on her own strength on Saturday, no one was aware that she was bleeding internally.

Two fortunate circumstances probably saved her life. One was her persistence in remaining upright, trying to appear brave and confident for her daughter. She was in shock, but like everyone else, she thought Angela was badly hurt. Being vertical slowed the rate of her internal bleeding and kept it from accumulating in her abdomen. According to Gregg, most people would have lain down and died. The other circumstance was the Nash Rambler boys' swift action to transport the ladies to the hospital. Angela would have been fine either way, but had Marianne not gotten to the hospital as quickly as she did, she might have died by the side of the road.

"What did you guys see when you got there? How do you think it happened?" Gregg pressed on.

Even though both Jon and Harvey had thought about little else but the accident for the past twenty-four hours and had discussed it between themselves, they were not certain as to how or why it happened. They had theories but nothing conclusive to declare.

Harvey gave the shorter version of what he told the police. "Well, first we saw the truck stopped in the middle of the road. It was sunny, but you could still see its flashers on. We didn't see the car in the ditch until we had stopped the Rambler and started to run up to the truck. The car was a long way from the truck. First, we talked to the truck driver near his truck, then we headed for the car and saw Marianne standing there and Angela lying beside her. The driver went to CB the cops. That is exactly what I told Sgt. Morgan."

"Yeah, Morgan came by here Saturday to ask the girls for a report," Gregg said. "He told me you were the first guys at the accident. I told him it's still too soon for them to have to go through all of that, so he buggered off. The girls are still messed up and don't remember much about the accident right now. We're kind of afraid of talking to Morgan; we've had trouble with him before. He's an asshole, and I don't trust him as far as I can throw him."

It was quite common for ranchers and farmers in this region to be wary of the police. Inevitably, everyone would have a run-in with them every few years. Living in a remote rural location many kilometers from their nearest neighbors caused people like Gregg to become vehemently independent. They conjured up their own rules and were resistant to any authority that brought laws manufactured in faraway urban districts that had little or no relevance to people living way out where the Morrises lived.

These districts were policed by the national police force, famously known as the Royal Canadian Mounted Police. They were not locals; they were trained in far-off cities and then assigned to these precincts for a few years before they moved on to new positions and locations. By the time they learned to understand the culture of the community and built the relationships necessary to effectively do their jobs, they were reassigned and off to a new posting.

"So, how does our car cross the road in front of the truck and end up in the trees on the opposite side of the ditch?" Gregg asked. "Marianne is a good driver. She can handle any vehicle as good as anyone."

"Well, I think the truck started crossing into Marianne's lane, and she didn't think she could pass it on the right side, so she tried to miss it on the left," Jon offered. "It's weird, but it's the only scenario that makes sense based on what we saw today. She just clipped the truck, but then she couldn't control the Toyota when she hit the brakes, and she flipped it."

"Yeah, that's what I think too. I think the trucker caused it by wandering into her lane," Morris concurred. "But that doesn't sound like what Morgan was thinking in the little chat that I had with him last night. I think he wants to hang it all on Marianne. And I think that's bullshit."

No one spoke to the bullshit for a few moments until Harvey, who had been unusually quiet and in a pondering state, came up with some advice. "If I was you, I'd call up Chance Lager. You should get a lawyer right now while things are still fresh, instead of waiting until no one remembers what actually happened anymore. Why tell that dipshit Morgan anything until you know what you should and shouldn't be telling him? I didn't like Morgan either. He was grilling me this morning. Like I said before, we should call up Old Chance. He's a wizard."

Just then, the heavyset ladies informed the three seated gentlemen that they could return to the room if they wished. Gregg stood up first and led them back in. Marianne was awake now, and the visit continued for another fifteen minutes, with her taking her turn to thank the boys. She remained in a prone position, but in good spirits. The afternoon ended amiably and on a positive note. Jon and Harvey were glad they had visited and felt proud of themselves. They were no longer boys now; they were men.

When they departed, Gregg followed them out to the hospital exit. "Say, I think I'm going to contact this Chance guy you were talking about. I've heard of him too. Where do I find him?"

"He works at the lawyers' office run by Mayor Ferguson. I'll call him tonight and give him a heads-up. He comes from our town," Harvey proudly declared.

"Okay. Tell him I'll call him tomorrow morning."

The two young men headed back to their homes, satisfied.

CHAPTER 9

AFTERMATH

Once you know what not to do, the moment all else fails,
you'll toss that coin more willingly, and know it won't land tails.

Jon waited until Peter was seated across the desk from him before describing Sunday night's calamity in Budapest. He had spent the previous day trying to decide what parts of the story to reveal to Peter and what parts to keep to himself, but ultimately, he decided to tell all of it.

Jon was eager to find out why his assigned meeting with Karl Bircher had gone so terribly wrong. He expected Peter to know something that would help him understand this torturous misadventure. Jon was shaking inside and hummed to himself. He was angry but kept his voice calm and low.

"Things didn't go well in Budapest. You better listen carefully, because what I'm going to tell you is not good. Karl is dead, and another man probably is too. Do you know anything about any of this?" he blurted out.

Peter sat stunned and frozen. He simply shook his head from side to side in confusion. Jon became even more stressed; he had expected more from Peter. He desperately needed someone to give him answers, and Peter was his only hope. Peter shaking his head in shock was not what Jon wanted to see. This was not the self-assured Peter Otto he knew.

"What happened? What are you saying?" Peter managed.

"What happened? What happened was that I tried to meet Karl each evening for two nights like we planned. Both Friday and Saturday, I searched for him on the bridge, but he didn't show up where we were supposed to meet. I stuck to the plan and just kept going out there every night in the damn rain. Finally, on Sunday evening, he was there on the bridge. We met, we exchanged, and just as we were about to leave, another man came onto the bridge. Karl seemed like he knew him; at least he wasn't that surprised by him. When he saw the man coming, he told me to leave, so I did. But as I was jogging away, I stopped and looked back and saw the man fighting with Karl. I'm not sure why, but I ran back. When I got there, I saw this big man standing over Karl who had fallen down some steps. So I hit him with my shoulder and knocked him farther down the steps. I don't know if he saw me coming. He ended up falling off the bridge and into the river."

Jon stopped talking when he saw Peter holding his hands to his face, cringing. Again, this was not the reaction Jon wanted. He needed reassurance, not fright. Peter's silence made Jon even more anxious, and he started talking much faster than usual. He couldn't stop himself.

"That's crazy… What happened to Karl?" Peter inquired, trying to speak softly.

"After the big guy fell off the bridge, I called for Karl and went to check on him, but he was already dead. I think he hit his head when he fell during the scuffle with the other man. It was hard to tell because it was dark and rainy."

"Are you sure he was dead?" Peter immediately knew this was a dumb question but caught himself too late.

"I've seen dead, and he was completely dead." Jon paused. "That's when I got scared and made a quick decision to get out of there. I didn't want to be there any longer, and I didn't want Karl to be there either, so I pulled him down the last few steps and slid him off the bridge under that stupid chain, through the same gap in the rail that the other man went through."

"Holy shit!"

"Burial by river. Then I jogged back to the hotel and left Budapest with Nora on the midnight train to Vienna, and I've been going nuts ever since. I didn't really think it all through, but I sure didn't want to be in Budapest trying to explain any of this to the Hungarian police. Tell me how something like this could happen? You said there was no danger in any of these interactions, that it was all simple routine stuff, just a game that we needed to play out, you said." Jon was babbling now and looking for someone to blame. "Well, this was not routine, and now I've probably killed a guy, and I don't even really know why or what actually happened."

Peter tightened his brow and inhaled as he struggled to process what Jon was saying. He was sweating. Then he noticed that Jon was so distraught that he was finding it hard to breathe.

"Okay, okay, slow down, Jon. This will all be okay. We'll figure out what this all means and what to do. Let me think. Just slow down. Do that hum thing that you told me about, relax, keep breathing."

For a few long seconds, there was silence. Jon could feel the tears on both his cheeks. Nonetheless, he took the advice and began humming under his breath, trying to channel his subconscious, to connect and manage his emotional energy. He trusted Peter, but he was irritated that Peter could not provide a direct explanation for what transpired on the bridge.

"I can't think of anything we can do now," Jon said.

"What do you say we get out of here and get some air, maybe talk this through outside your office, and if we feel like it in a bit, we can go for lunch. We need to take our time and think things through," Peter suggested. He felt overwhelmed, a rare state for him to be in. Gone was his normally self-assured demeanor.

"I think you're going to have to tell me a lot more about how all this works. I can't make sense of what happened back there, and I have these strange questions popping up in my head every minute of the day since I left that bridge two nights ago," said Jon. "But yeah, let's get out of here for a while."

The two walked out of the office, and Jon told his secretary he would probably not be back until about three. Inga had worked for him for nearly two years, staffing the reception desk and handling the day-to-day workload for Jon's little enterprise. She was trustworthy, efficient, and, most importantly, the customers liked her.

They took Peter's car and drove down the small street that went south. In a few minutes, they were at the entrance to a forest with hiking paths. Peter parked, and they got out and started on a trail that meandered between the trees. Peter had been disturbingly silent for a long time now, pretty much throughout the entire ride. Jon was still frustrated because Peter normally led their conversations. Peter was the talker, not Jon.

"So both men ended up in the river, Karl presumably dead, but what about the other man?"

Peter's question irritated Jon, who wanted answers, not questions. "Karl is definitely dead. I saw my father dead, and I remember every detail of it, so I know Karl is dead. He was dead when he was lying on those steps just above where the other man went through the railing. I just can't believe how crazy it was to have an empty space like that in the railing. Anyway, I guess it was at least a fifteen-meter drop from there into the water. Surviving that fall is unlikely but possible, I suppose."

Jon was thinking rationally and calmly, as if he had not been directly involved in the activity he was describing. He had run through it so many times in his mind now that he was able to describe the details with far less emotion. Subconsciously, he knew that for him to survive, it had to be this way.

"How fast was the river moving, do you think?" Peter continued.

"Fast, I think, because the water level would be higher than usual due to all the rain from the previous weeks," Jon calculated.

"I know Budapest a bit. Where was the bridge that you were on? Which way from the chain bridge?"

"Yeah, that could be a problem. We were north of downtown. The Danube flows south, right back through the center of both Buda and Pest. I suppose it wouldn't take the bodies too long to flow through there if they didn't get caught up in the bends along the way. It was about eight in the evening and very dark and rainy, so not many people were out looking at the river that night."

Peter weighed the situation, trying to understand what might transpire next. "My guess would be that if both of them are dead, the bodies should turn up in a day or two. I just don't know how we could get any information about this without drawing attention to ourselves. Is there anything that could connect you to any of this? Anything on the bridge?"

"Well, I've thought pretty hard about that since," Jon said. "First, with so many bridges, it'll take a lot of time for them to figure out where these bodies actually got into the river from. I'm pretty certain no one else was on the bridge that night. The day before, there was a group of younger people just hanging out. It wasn't raining as much. They'd have seen me, but it didn't matter, because Karl didn't show up. I was just an uninteresting jogger to them, I'm sure. The only thing to consider might be that very few people run for exercise in Budapest, and in the rain, it's even more unusual to see a jogger in the city streets. Most joggers are in some way or other Western, foreigners, embassy people, businessmen, or tourists."

"Did you leave anything on the bridge? Anything that could lead to you?"

"A bit of skin from my knee and my knuckles, Karl left some blood, but not much that I could see. I'm pretty sure the rain that night would have washed away most of it by the next morning. At least to the point where no one would casually notice anything unusual. But it was quite dark, and there may have been something related to Karl or the third man that I'm not aware of. But in my opinion, I don't think there is anything that could connect me to the bridge. The hotel lobby is about the only place that anybody would have seen me in my jogging clothes and maybe known who I was, going out and coming back in every night, but there is nothing suspicious about that in a big Western hotel like that." Jon was relating to the logistics the best he could.

"Well, I don't have any idea why anyone would be chasing down Karl in Budapest. As far as I know, Karl is a pretty simple errand man, one of thousands of collectors of Western information for the Stasi," Peter said. "We set you up as a connection for him, as we've discussed, to be part of our disinformation team, because we thought he had the right connections and was motivated to deliver. If there's one thing the East Germans believe, it's that we in the West love money. They believe this is what drives us, but won't admit they're exactly the same. Karl was not driven by ideology. He liked the perks that came with collecting and delivering the mail to his bosses. I didn't know him very well. Basically, he was a good guy, like the rest of us. I was introduced to him by some of my colleagues in East Berlin a few years ago, and I liked him."

"Then who was the other guy? Karl seemed to know something

was wrong…maybe he even knew him. I sensed it from the minute we met that night that it wasn't just the awful weather upsetting him. Usually, Karl is slow and focused on our meetings. On Sunday night, he was rushed and fidgety. Maybe he recognized this guy. He sure didn't seem so surprised to see him there. So what is the worst thing that could happen to us? To me?"

"To you? Nothing. Even if the Hungarians could connect you to the scene, they probably wouldn't bother to track you down. I'm not worried about the Hungarians. Our problem is Karl being gone." Peter paused. "And not knowing who your third man was, it's hard to make a plan. Are you totally sure that there is nothing else that could connect you to that bridge? Anything else you remember?"

"I remember that the guy was way bigger than me, and I was scared. I don't know exactly, but when he came up the steps on me the second time, he was yelling at me. I don't know what he was saying or what language he was speaking. It couldn't have been German; I didn't understand it. It might have been Hungarian, I guess. It was kind of strange. I just wanted to push him away and try not to get into a fight with him. I didn't really have any idea what I was doing. I didn't want to knock him off the bridge, though. That part should never have happened. There was just this stupid hole in the guardrail down there."

"Hey, it was an accident, Jon. Stop beating yourself up about it. Nothing you can do about it now. Bad luck happens. We need to think forward. I suppose the GDR will want to know what happened to Karl in any case, but especially if this other guy is connected to them somehow," Peter said. "That is possible, I guess, but I don't know why he would be there with Karl. Did somebody get their signals crossed? In any event, someone is going to be missing these two by now."

Peter had made a shift. He was accepting what had occurred and was rationalizing the circumstances as if it were all business as usual.

"But if we're totally sure that there is no way for them to connect you to that bridge, then we're not in any trouble," he continued. "We have to be patient and wait until the bodies surface before we can decide on anything."

"But people are dead here, Peter. I just don't know how

something so strange could've happened."

    "Jon, you still always think that everything has an answer. It just isn't true. You have to realize that not everything can be explained, and there will always be many things that'll remain unexplained. This could well become one of them. We just have to be sure that nothing can connect you to that bridge." Peter added matter-of-factly.

    "I've told you already, I don't think there is any way. Plus, how will they know where the bodies went into the river from? There are a lot of bridges and many other entry points. I mean, as long as the bodies didn't stop close to that bridge."

    "Well, I'm going to go back up to Bonn and contact a colleague who has more experience in these matters than I do. We have a lot of people working for us in Budapest, and he should be able to help us with all of this. All we can do is wait a few days and see what happens next," Peter concluded.

    Jon tried to carry on with his life as best he could. This proved to be extremely difficult, but he tried to behave as normally as possible. He focused on managing his business and tending to as many mundane routines as he could to stay calm. In his spare moments, however, he could not help himself and went back to analyzing the incidents in Budapest.

    In the end, each analysis inevitably found him right back where he started. Jon became most critical of himself. He didn't know why he had reacted so aggressively toward the third man on the bridge. Surely there was an explanation for this. Had he not acted that way, perhaps there could have been some discussion with this third man. At that moment, he didn't yet know that Karl was dead or even injured. Had he read the entire situation wrong, he wondered. What actually caused Karl's death?

    Jon wished he had investigated a bit more. But most of all, he wished so badly that it had not happened at all. He should have kept running once he left Karl, but that seemed wrong too. The more Jon took himself through the events, the more uncertain he was and the more disgusted he became with himself. He felt he was to blame for a tragedy that had resulted in death. It was something he had never imagined could happen.

How could it be that, in mere minutes, one incident could make such an impact on one's life? It altered both the future and the past. Jon thought he knew himself; he was not an impulsive person. How was it possible that he would react the way he did? He was dumbfounded. Now two men were surely dead, and he was likely a killer. Jon felt all alone in what was left of his world.

The week slowly passed. Then one day, as Jon was sitting behind his desk trying unsuccessfully to focus on his job, Peter burst through the door, kicking it closed behind him. He had already stormed by Inga at the reception area and was standing in front of Jon before Jon registered he was there. It was a barge-in, and Jon, immersed in his personal fog, was startled.

"I have news from our guys in Budapest. A body was pulled from the Danube this morning. We don't know who it is yet, but I'm going to keep calling until I find out."

"Shit!" was all Jon could manage to utter. "What does this mean?"

"Nothing until we find out who it is."

"Did you just drive all the way over here to tell me this?"

"This is not news we can deliver over the telephone," Peter told him. "Let's go to lunch, and I'll keep calling my guy. It shouldn't take long for the Hungarian police to identify the body, especially if it's Karl. He'll have all his papers on him."

"I'm not at all hungry, but yeah, let's get out of here."

They left the office, got into Peter's car, drove to the center of town, and parked outside the Schwan Hotel. It was not quite noon when they entered the restaurant and sat at their usual table.

"How did you find this out?" Jon asked.

"My friend in Bonn, Enrico Siemenz, has a lot of people working in Budapest right now. Most are attached to our embassy there, and some of them have sound connections inside the Hungarian police. The Hungarian authorities prefer the West Germans to the Russians and the GDR these days. They know there are substantial advantages in maintaining relations with us. We talked on Wednesday and have been discreetly keeping an eye on the river and the local police. I'm sure we'll know more in due time, meaning soon. Order me a Pils; I'm going to the reception to make a call." Peter got up and left through the restaurant's side doors.

"It's Karl," Peter stated once he returned. "Found near Rákóczi Bridge, hung up on the side of some small boat. Now we need to pay attention!"

There was an element of surprise registered with this news. They maintained an unprompted moment of silence while each of them gave thought to what this meant.

"It depends now on what the Hungarian authorities do. Our guys expect they'll soon turn the body over to the GDR officials. Once that happens, we have enough eyes there too. I'm going to get more information from Budapest by the end of the day," Peter said.

Unbeknownst to Peter and Jon, back in Budapest, the Hungarian police were not intending to do much of anything. Once they identified the body as Karl Bircher based on his soaked GDR passport and the identity card in his pants pocket, they saw no need to investigate further.

There was no other paper trail. They surmised that some drunken German had fallen into the river again, and that was all they needed to do about that. They would simply contact the GDR authorities, inform them of the incident, and deliver the body to them, and from an official Hungarian perspective, that would close the book. It would remain up to the GDR to follow up if they so chose.

"Nothing on the third man?" asked Jon.

"Nothing."

CHAPTER 10

LAWYER

It is a restless game beneath the stars, that keeps no score,
reveals no more, end to fore, reveals no core, ends at four.

Most of what Jon knew about people and how he assessed them was learned from the individuals he encountered back when he was a schoolboy. The wide assortment of independent characters on daily display proved to be educational and entertaining. One such character was Chance Lager.

Whenever there was a legal case to amend and defend or a political issue to debate and defeat, the one person every local resident immediately consulted was Chance Lager. Chance had grown up on his parents' farm next to the village, so technically, he was not a resident of the village. Nonetheless, from the age of ten, he was considered the town's resident genius. Everyone called him "Old Chance" from the time he was a child simply because he had always been wise beyond his years.

He was accelerated through high school and graduated just days after turning sixteen. He went to university after that and came back after a few years with a law degree plus a master's degree in law and philosophy. Now, he worked at a well-known law firm in Greyton.

Chance continued to live on the edge of the village with his parents. Virtually every citizen, and certainly every young person, had at one time or another made use of his services. They trusted Chance and relied on his savvy to reduce their fines or avoid jail time when they were clearly guilty, or to be freed of charges that were questionable. He was the smartest person in any room, the most eccentric, and he always seemed able to determine where the secrets were hiding as he worked his way up the legal and political food chains. In a very short period, he had built a notable reputation in the area, and consequently, everything from speeding tickets to murder charges landed on his desk.

Chance believed in community and loved his native village. He was a prominent initiator of political activities and projects that would enhance the general quality of life within the region. Though still a young man, he was the one who spearheaded all situations pertaining to the long-term welfare of the village and its inhabitants. He was their definition of "the greater good."

His birth certificate name was Charles Konstanz Lager. He had been named after his grandfather and great-grandfather, the largest lake in Western Europe, and a type of beer. His ancestors had immigrated from what was now East Germany. But in a community where everyone had a nickname, Charles Konstanz became Chance, and it stuck. Chance didn't care too much for that name, but he preferred it to Charles, which he considered too common and boring. He likely would have taken any name suggested as long as no one ever called him Charlie. If someone so much as breathed the name Charlie in his presence, he would immediately scold, "It's Chance!"

Truthfully, he would have preferred Konstantin, but try as he did during his high school years, he couldn't get anyone to bite on that appellation. C.K. Lager could have been an option as well. Anything to avoid Charlie. In the end, Chance was all he could get people to commit to, so Chance he was.

To say that Chance was unlike anyone else in this small community would be a huge understatement. Mannerisms and behaviors were passed around from person to person and generation to generation. People tried to act in ways that would fit in and be approved of. This was not Chance Lager. He did not adhere to customs or follow routine procedures, and he did not follow social norms. He spoke oddly, using words correctly but in unusual ways. He also purposefully propelled words and phrases that no one understood, but did it with such confidence and authority that no one would dare to refute him. There was no category one could fit him into and no effort on his part to be so fit.

Chance was not just respected but remarkably well-liked. In a local celebrity way, he was revered and feared. Revered, because everyone in the region had a story to tell or knew of a remarkable tale about him. Feared, because he knew everything, and deep down, you knew that you didn't. People considered themselves inferior in his presence. Consequently, they chose to be his friend and to be on his side, whatever that side was. Fortunately for all concerned, Chance was wired to be on the right side of things once he found out what that was.

It was getting late in the evening on a Sunday, but Harvey still made a telephone call to the Lager home to speak with Chance. Harvey wasn't sure there would be a problem that needed Chance's attention, but the police visit to his home in the morning had him spooked. He wanted the advantage of being first to connect with Chance on this matter. As it was late, Chance himself picked up the telephone.

Chance was a medium-sized man, lean and not muscular but very fit. His face was thin as well, and he had tousled, unkempt hair that cascaded more to one side and less to the other. One would have expected him to wear glasses because he had eyes and a face that one would associate with spectacles; however, his eyesight was remarkably good. His voice was firm and strong but with a variable cadence.

"I'm Chance Lager. You've called the Lager residence."

"Hi, Chance. It's Harvey Dean. Remember me?"

"Certainly, Harvard, I do indeed remember you," came the reply. Then silence.

"Well, ah, I don't know if you've heard about it, but there was this accident yesterday afternoon on the highway just outside of Greyton, and Jon Mantler and I were there just after it happened, and now the cops came and talked to us about it, and because we took two women to the hospital from the accident site, I think they might want to charge us with something. The women are okay but still in the hospital. J and I were there today, but this Sgt. Morgan came to see us this morning…"

"Well aware I am, Mr. Dean. You must not proceed so earnestly. Allow me to direct you onward," Chance said.

At last, Harvey was muted.

"What was the color of the car?"

"Ah, gray or silver, I think."

"Accurate!" Chance retorted.

From there, the conversation was brief and concluded with Chance advising Harvey to assume a fearless wait-and-see position in relation to his role in the event. He also instructed that he and Jon have no further discussions with Sgt. Morgan or any other authority without Chance's presence, and he agreed to speak to the Morrises should they wish to contact him.

"I too have visited the scene of this unfortunate occurrence, envisioned the wreckage and the surrounding parameters," Chance informed Harvey. "I believe you can be at ease."

This satisfied Harvey, and he wanted to call Jon to provide him with the same assuredness, but with no phone connection, that couldn't happen. Harvey was leaving for university the next day, so despite the late hour, he headed around the corner and across the street to the Mantler shack. Like almost everyone else in the town, Harvey had never been fully inside the Mantler home. That was, until this evening.

It was remarkably small. Jon opened the door after Harvey's knock and invited him in to sit at the kitchen table. Most activities in the Mantler shack were conducted there.

Harvey filled Jon in on the details of his conversation with Chance, emphasizing the instruction to not converse with Sgt. Morgan unless Chance Lager was present. Harvey again explained he would be leaving to university the next morning and would be gone for the next three weeks.

The following day, Jon went to high school as usual. Shortly after 4:00 p.m., he was riding the bright yellow school bus as it stopped between the café and the grocery store in the center of the village. Eight students rambunctiously departed the bus onto the adjacent sidewalk. Normally, most of this group would enter one of these shops to mingle, mess around, and buy candy-coated treats, but not today. Today, there was a police cruiser parked at the café, and automatically, without comment, the young students dispersed in various directions away from the scene. This was a conditioned response in the village. It was rare for a police vehicle to enter from the highway that circled past town, but when one did, it operated within a magnetic repulsion field. All the townsfolk retreated and became invisible. They slipped behind a power pole or scurried back into their homes to view what was going on outside from behind a curtain until the cruiser exited the village again. No one engaged.

Police were not disrespected in this village; they were simply deemed unnecessary. The importance of the law was understood, but here it was interpreted based on practical relevance within the community. People living here operated according to their own rules of practicality and commonality. They did not fight each other, kill each other, or steal from each other, so there was no reason for the national police to be in their village. When the police came around, it was assumed they were looking for trouble and likely targeting someone in their community, so the residents were compelled to keep their thoughts and recollections to themselves. The police and the law that they brought came from the city and thus were looked on with skepticism.

Jon Mantler knew the village procedures concerning a police presence and followed the established protocol. He turned away from the store, forgot about picking up his daily newspaper, and headed down the alley in the direction of his shack.

There was also a folkloric aspect of this indifference to the national police that stemmed from the police once arresting Leonard for hunting too many deer. This happened more than a decade ago but was still an oft-recalled event. The community's judgment on this was that it was fine for him to hunt the deer, because he used every morsel of it to feed his family of ten. Times were hard, and food was costly. Quotas on deer were set in the cities so that urban hunters, who did not eat what they killed, would have more game to hunt when they came out to the countryside for sport. This law was not relevant to the population here. Leonard's survival was the law here. The fact that he had been sentenced to six months in jail in the little city down the road for this hunting infraction explained a lot about how the community viewed laws and the national police in general.

Another unjust arrest by the police involved alcohol. Alcohol was controlled by the province and enforced by the national police. It was taxed, sold, and regulated according to the laws of the capital city. There was no alcohol outlet in this small village, so in order to purchase it, one had to travel to the little city down the road and abide by the governmental monopoly's rules. It was expensive and inconvenient. The alternative was to do what older residents here had been doing since before the government and its corporate producers took legal and taxable control of the booze trade. For cost-related and practical purposes, many of the locals made their own moonshine. It was an unspoken and accepted tradition until a zealous police officer, in the mold of Sgt. Morgan, arrested old Albert, one of the town's leading producers of local spirits. Another misappropriation of the law that further tainted the relationship between the community and the police.

When Jon exited the alley to cross the street to his home, the police car turned the corner and stopped in front of the shack. Sgt. Morgan stepped out with a clipboard in his hand, as if impersonating a football coach.

Jon remembered Chance's order not to speak to Sgt. Morgan without his presence. He continued to walk home, passing where the policeman was parked. Of course, there was no one else visibly present in the village at that moment, but all were aware that it was the second time in two days that a police car was parked in the town.

"Hello, are you Jon Mantler?" Sgt. Morgan immediately asked.

The question seemed odd to young Jon, who, just the previous morning, had spent a good amount of time with the sergeant, who clearly knew who he was. Jon thought it was a trick question as he heeded the advice from Harvey and Chance and remained silent. Morgan waited, a bit miffed, before he repeated the question. Still, Jon didn't speak.

The sergeant then produced a folded sheet of paper and handed it over. "Jon Mantler, you're being served with a summons to appear in court under the charge of…"

Jon wasn't hearing everything that was being said.

"All of the information is on this document. Do you understand?" Morgan concluded.

Jon had started humming to himself. He took the paper and the envelope and waited until the sound of talking stopped. He said nothing, and when nothing else happened, he turned and walked toward his little house. He stopped at the entrance door to look back at Sgt. Morgan until the man turned and re-entered his big blue vehicle.

Once inside the shack, Jon sat at the kitchen table and tried to relax while looking at the document he had been served. Within a minute, there was a knock at his door. He opened it to see Mrs. Butler and Geoffrey Jones. The police car had left the village, and the citizens had come back to life.

Geoffrey read through the summons. He took a great deal of the stress away from Jon by candidly determining that it was a bunch of bullshit.

"This is a bunch of bullshit," was exactly what he said. "Let's go call Chance."

The three of them walked next door to Mrs. Butler's to use the telephone.

And this was how a simple, little, rather stupidly issued summons to appear on a misdemeanor charge of leaving the scene of an accident and interfering with police protocol, delivered by Sgt. Morgan, turned into a major community event.

It didn't have to be that way. Initially, Chance Lager didn't foresee it as a problem. But as so often happens when a small force builds momentum and finds itself on the high side of gravity, events take on a power of their own. The documents delivered to Jon requested that he appear in court before a provincial judge in the little city of Greyton on April 14 to offer a plea to the charges listed. If he pleaded guilty, he would be asked to pay a fine determined by the judge at that moment, probably between $60 and $100, and that would be that. But it would turn out that this would not be that.

Under the guidance of Chance Lager, Jon would not be pleading guilty, which normally meant a court date would have to be set. Chance believed that by pointing out the special circumstances pertaining to this specific incident, he could induce the judge to dismiss the charges and void a trial. He knew the local judge and was certain he would understand that Jon and Harvey's actions had been logical and responsible, even heroic. The charges, though perhaps technically applicable, would justifiably be dismissed in this case. So predicted the incomparable Chance Lager.

At the plea hearing in April, the local judge who normally sat on this bench was away on a Mediterranean cruise. A substitute from the big capital city, Judge Eric B. Pendleberry, was now presiding over the local judge's caseload. Immediately after the charges were read to the court, Jon pleaded not guilty. Then Chance requested permission to present the judge with specifics vital to the case, which he was certain would conclude the matter. However, about ten words into his Shakespearean oration, the judge interjected and shut him down.

This judge did not know Chance Lager and straightaway did not like him. With little consideration, he waved off Chance's dissertation and set a court date for the third of May. Chance held in his hand and in his head definitive evidence that he knew would cause the misdemeanor charges to be dropped, but the big-city judge refused to look at it.

Chance was gobsmacked and annoyed. So in the next two days, he went to work and presented a mountain of papers to Judge Pendleberry, intending to educate the city judge on the case before the next court date. Chance knew it was a waste of time and money for the court to take on such an insignificant case. The maximum fine that could be levied on a conviction was less than $250. In his submission, he outlined this and pointed out that the actions of Jon and Harvey were proper under the circumstances.

To pepper the case further, he added a list of requests if the case were to proceed to trial as scheduled. On this list was a request for trial by a small jury, as well as a substantial list of witnesses he would subpoena in defense. Fifteen people were on the list, including Sgt. Morgan, the other two officers who were at the scene, Angela and Marianne Morris, several doctors and nurses, the ambulance drivers, the dispatcher, the truck driver, and, of course, Harvey. Chance wanted to be convincing. There was still ample time for Judge Pendleberry to review and drop the case, but all he did was refuse a jury trial and keep the trial date as is.

Annoyed, Chance formulated an alternate plan. If Pendleberry wasn't going to dismiss the case or allow a jury, then Chance would create his own jury. He made sure everyone in the community knew the details of the case by infiltrating the gossip network and teasing all the local media outlets. He spoke about the upcoming court case at local gatherings where large portions of the citizens were present, such as sporting events, auction sales, and church services. He dramatized the injustice of the police and the courts by bringing such charges against a local hero. One of their own was being wronged in another clear case of the big city vs. us. He even swung the citizens of the little city of Greyton to support his righteous plight.

In mere days, a one-sided public opinion case had been established. Everyone within a hundred-mile radius now knew that Jon Mantler and Harvey Dean had saved the lives of Marianne and Angela Morris by taking swift and clever action. They also knew that the police, led by Sgt. Morgan, had charged Jon Mantler in the case. The local newspaper editorialized the story, and the talk-radio hosts buzzed with excitement about the unjust travesty and the upcoming proceedings.

To the people living in Jon's village, this case had now become substantially bigger than it actually was. It was another example of governments and bureaucrats from outside enforcing their rules and demands on them. Jon, Harvey, and Chance were being treated unfairly, and the community was ready to mobilize to fight in support of their native sons. This was going to be payback for incidents like the deer hunting and home-brewed sagas of years gone by.

CHAPTER 11

COURT

You say you believe in justice, whose justice anyway;
When the bombs hit, what else can you say?

To young Jon Mantler, this all became a blur. At first, after Sgt. Morgan had served him with the papers, Jon was excited about his defense and up for the challenge. He was certain he had done the right thing, and he wanted justice to serve him. But now that it had become such a big circus, he very much wanted it all to be over.

Jon had lived mostly on his own. The key to his survival was learning how to slip in and out of the big world he felt around him. He had always been able to duck into the shade when he needed to save himself. This time, he could find no shade.

Jon functioned in three simple domains: his home, the close community of the village, and the large populace of his high school. He was an exceptional student, but outside of that, he preferred to remain sheltered within the crowd of students. He never sought to attract attention from his peers or his teachers. Until now, his life had been mercifully slow and simple.

In the weeks leading up to his next court appearance, his life was far from simple. Everything had come unglued, and he was humming to himself more frequently. Everyone knew about the court case. Because of his newfound notoriety, school had become awkward. No longer was he able to inconspicuously blend in; he felt on display. When he walked to class or to the cafeteria for lunch, all eyes were on him. The entire school supported his plight; he had saved a woman's life and was now being unjustly persecuted by the law. He was a local hero. A day of this he could have handled, but as it went on for weeks, he came to detest it.

Eventually, his day in court arrived. No one was certain how it would play out, not even Chance Lager. Chance was uncertain about Judge Eric B. Pendleberry, but he was prepared beyond preparation. He had a strategy, and it involved publicity. The lengths he had gone to promote this day within Greyton and his home village were on par with a major sporting championship.

Judge Pendleberry, on the other hand, was not at all prepared for what was to come. He hadn't thought much about it except to affirm that Chance Lager needed to be put in his place and taught a lesson about the law. To him, this was just another little case where the court would levy a fine and collect the related court costs to fund the justice system. A not guilty plea was annoying, but it was obvious to him that if the national police had issued a citation, in the end it would hold up and a fine would be collected plus court costs. By costing his client more than originally levied, this brash young lawyer would learn how the court system really worked and not be so quick to waste court time in the future. He knew best, and he had seen it all hundreds of times before.

However, what he had never seen before was a courtroom so packed with spectators. Every seat in the open gallery was taken, and there were more people standing along the back and side walls. Chance had rallied an enormous amount of support for Jon Mantler and succeeded in making this case a local media spectacle. In practice, he had brought with him a jury of about one hundred local citizens. They were there not to judge Jon, but to judge the judge.

Judge Eric B. Pendleberry wondered about the excessive number of cars parked in and around the courthouse when he arrived earlier, assuming there was an event going on. He was totally unaware that the event was his court case against Jon Mantler.

The proceedings were to start at ten, but many people from surrounding communities were already there at eight thirty, when the judge parked in his spot behind the courthouse. The bigger surprise came when he entered the courtroom from his private side door ninety minutes later.

Everyone in the courtroom on this day knew the details of the case. The local prosecutor assigned to the case was under intense pressure from the community, but he could not drop the charges without the consent of the judge. The only person who didn't know what was going on was Judge Pendleberry, quite simply because he didn't bother to read the paperwork that Chance had submitted to him. Pendleberry expected that his three-week substitute assignment in this hick town would be a simple and problem-free term. He felt he was an esteemed judge and far superior to the locals.

The court read the charges against Jon Mantler from a statement based on the summons originally prepared by Sgt. Morgan. When the time came for Chance Konstantin Lager to speak to the case, he measured his words slowly and deliberately in an effort to not offend the judge. Chance habitually spoke theatrically with distinct emphasis applied to target phrases, but today, he wanted to be sure that every word was recorded in the court transcript, so his speech was akin to a slow-motion replay.

"These proceedings presented hitherto, levied with bona fide intent, notwithstanding, do not pertain to the particular circumstances engaged and present…"

The spectators listened attentively.

"Moreover, if you genuinely delineate the subject matter of this particular complaint imposed upon my client, young Mr. Mantler, you will indisputably resolve that the actions undertaken by he on said day were in absolute conformance with those very determinations."

The judge was in a quandary. He would have liked to throw Chance Lager out of the courtroom and end this oddity, but when he looked out from his perch at the mob before him, he knew he needed to adhere to the law and allow the defense to be heard. So far, he had been given no cause to interject.

"Mr. Mantler emphatically did not depart the scene of this accident as this instance charges, and by no means did he interfere in the accident investigation. The information and the definitions of all matters pertaining distinctly establish otherwise. There was no intent to leave the scene! By transporting the Morrises to the hospital, he was merely extending the scene. One must admittedly determine that he was a real part of the scene. There is no particular boundary established by an accident scene. In truth, the scene is anywhere that elements of the accident exist or are placed. Thus, it was all one scene as all actions related to one and the same accident. The highway was part of the scene;

the vehicles were part of the scene; the ditch was part of the scene. As such, the Nash Rambler, used by Mr. Mantler and Mr. Dean, became a part of the accident the moment Marianne Morris, of free will, entered it. So too, did the hospital the moment Angela Morris and Marianne Morris entered it. Indeed, what constitutes leaving the scene? Surely, leaving a scene requires an intent to leave. Mr. Mantler had no intent to do any such thing. This is further proven by Mr. Mantler himself when he left from the hospital to rejoin Mr. Dean, where there they remained at this portion of the scene to witness the arrival of the ambulance, incidentally a full twenty minutes after the Morrises had been delivered to the hospital. Furthermore, both Mr. Mantler and Mr. Dean were still at the scene when they were told by Officer White that they should go home. Thus, they left the scene only after being requested to do so by the same national police force that has charged them with leaving the scene."

Chance paused briefly for effect.

"As for interference," he continued, "there was no said interference, none whatsoever; there was only adherence. Adherence to common sense and adherence to humanity. Adherence and, may I add, commendable action, bravery, and quick-wit, without which Marianne Morris possibly would not be sitting in this courtroom alive today."

Chance couldn't resist this moment of drama and, in so doing, pointed to the bench where the Morrises were seated. All eyes followed his finger, and a long, loud murmur overtook the courtroom.

The judge interjected rather politely and requested that the spectators remain quiet during the proceedings. Then he asked Chance if he had anything further to offer. This was a big mistake.

From the multitude of people whom Chance had subpoenaed, the first on his list was Dr. Reinhold Senft, the doctor who treated Marianne first in the hospital. His testimony would effectively substantiate that Marianne Morris might very well have died, or at the very least would have suffered long-term organ damage, due to internal bleeding, had she arrived any later at the hospital. This was also the first time that Pendleberry had looked down at the list of fifteen witnesses for the defense that Chance was prepared to call.

Looking out from his bench at the crowded gallery before him, he aptly surmised that every one of these fifteen was likely present. The elder judge had expected a maximum of two hours of court time, and at the pace Chance was speaking, an hour was already gone. Pendleberry was perspiring.

As Dr. Senft made his way to the witness stand, the judge called for a pause in the proceedings. He requested to speak to Chance and the prosecutor outside the courtroom. Judge Pendleberry knew he was beaten, and he had decided to cut and run.

The prosecutor was elated and proposed no objection to a dismissal. This time, Chance Lager said nary a word so as not to interfere with the judge's sentiments. Pendleberry agreed to accept Chance's interpretation argument and find the defendant not guilty. This allowed Pendleberry to go back to the courtroom and look like a kind father ruling favorably on a modest request. The hammer fell, case dismissed, and total victory was boisterously declared by the villagers as the crowd cleared the courtroom.

Somewhat lost in the midst of this was young Jon Mantler. He no longer wanted to be a hero. It was okay for a while, but now he wanted to get away from it. His community was ecstatic with the result of his misdemeanor trial, but Jon didn't see much reason for celebration. It all seemed to be such a waste of time and energy.

Back in the shack, and even in the village, life had, up to this point, made simple sense to him. When you caused an action, you got a rational result. You could determine what would happen based on your intellect and cognitive judgment. Now it seemed that in the life of Jon Mantler, things could happen around you and to you that you could not control. Outside forces could determine your fate, and sometimes you could not do anything to stop them. What if there wasn't a Chance Lager around all the time?

Jon and Harvey rode back home together from the courthouse in Greyton, feeling relieved that the nonsense related to the accident was finally over and that they could get on with their summer.

Harvey was ecstatic and in the mood for celebration. He had been feeling cheated and discomfited that he was not charged along with Jon, but now that all was over, he was revitalized.

Young Chance Lager had masterfully added to his growing reputation in the legal profession. The trouncing of old Judge Pendleberry had gained him enormous press. He had also been retained by the Morrises in their upcoming battle with the insurance company, and all involved were eagerly holding their breath in anticipation of what Chance might be planning in that regard.

Pendleberry was not happy that he had been manipulated and crushed by Chance Lager, but deep down, he knew he hadn't prepared for the case, so he decided to head back to the capital city and forget all about it. He was glad there were only a few days until the local judge would return and prayed that in the interim, there would be nothing on the docket involving Chance Lager.

The actual casualty of this event was Sgt. Morgan, who was transferred from his comfortable Greyton post nine hundred kilometers to the north. Sgt. Moron, as he was now branded, would never return to this area again. He was a victim of the system as well, because in his mind, he was doing his job as it had been outlined to him. Fines kept the justice system fueled; however, there were two systems at play here. The legal system, which could not possibly prescribe a law to fit every case, and the systemic power of public opinion. Morgan was technically on the right side of the law, but he was on the wrong side of the law as conducted by Chance.

The story was top news for about another week until mundane matters returned to occupy people's minds. Life goes on, they say, and so it did for Jon as well. The accident and the theatrical production that followed did, however, change the way he viewed the world and life outside the shack.

Jon's faith in the judicial system and in how the populace determined right from wrong was reshaped. He also lost a degree of respect for people in power based on the actions of Pendleberry and Morgan. There seemed to be a lot of outside interests at play in the decision-making process. He was glad to arrive at his shack later that day, his sanctuary away from the masses, realizing how important it was to be content with one's place in life. He had witnessed how, in the end, a lot of things that were perceived as big deals were actually pointless.

CHAPTER 12

TWO-TONE ONE-TON

When I was a baby tree, so much goodness was waiting all around me,
and planted on every hill; in the air, on the wind, from the rain, with the sun.

Now that Jon had a driver's license, he could start seriously searching for a vehicle of his own. After seeing the crushed condition of the small Toyota that had become tangled up with the semi-trailer truck, he was even more certain he was going to buy a truck.

The Mantlers once owned an old truck. His father purchased it back when he first got to the village from the man who was closing down the lumberyard. The truck hadn't been registered or licensed for as long as anyone could remember. Its purpose had been to move lumber, and it was not driven on public roadways. It was a one-ton truck, which meant that you could safely load a lot more weight onto it than on typical half-ton models that most farmers in the area used.

Jon remembered his father's warnings: "You need to have a one-ton suspension if you want to haul wood," and, "All a half-ton is good for is hauling around a lawn mower."

Jon might have made a mistake by selling the truck a year after his father's death, but in reality, he had no use for it then and little use for it now. Jon was in the market for a truck that would haul wood during his demolition and also haul him to and from university. He decided to do right by his father and scanned the newspapers for a one-ton truck. There were many half-ton trucks advertised, but one-tons were scarce. He made sure everyone in the village knew about his search, and eventually, spreading the word paid off.

"With patience and persistence, you can piss through a rock," one of the locals at the gas station reminded him.

Jon had an abundance of patience. One day, he noticed a newspaper ad for a Ford one-ton scheduled to be auctioned off at an upcoming farm estate sale. Instead of waiting for the sale date, Jon decided to visit the farm to have a look at the truck for himself. This required firing up Mrs. Butler's trusted Nash Rambler again and driving the dusty back roads about fifteen kilometers out to the Walker farm.

Harold Walker was a likable member of the local farming community who had recently passed away from a thing called cancer. He had purchased a Ford one-ton just a year prior to the cancer attaching itself to him. It was Harold's pride and joy, but Mrs. Walker didn't like to drive standard transmissions, and she already had a small automatic car of her own. So the Ford one-ton was designated to be auctioned along with most of the farm equipment and machinery. It took a lot of persistent convincing, but eventually Jon's enthusiasm won the day. He succeeded in persuading Mrs. Walker to sell him the truck in advance of the auction sale.

Jon loved this truck, even the color scheme, which was a kind of blue and white, really more of a cream than a white, but the blue was much more challenging to distinguish. It was easier to describe what it wasn't than what it was. It was not navy, it was not pale blue, it was not sky blue, it wasn't too dark and wasn't too light, and mercifully, it was not turquoise. It was somewhere in between all of that.

It was one of the first trucks of its kind to have what was labeled as an extended cab, meaning there was quite a large space for storage behind the bench seat. It came with a lot of extras, like a removable fiberglass cover, in case one had a load that needed protection from the weather or thieves. Plus an extra gas tank and a metal tool storage unit, both padlocked and bolted to the chassis directly behind the cab. It was actually a pretty serious-looking truck, probably more serious than Jon needed, but for certain it would be able to haul wood.

Jon was positive that John Mantler would have approved of his purchase, and for some reason, that mattered. He paid in cash with the money from the shoebox, and two days later, he drove to Greyton to exchange the license plates and register the one-ton in his name. Jon Mantler was now a vehicle owner.

His new set of wheels was going to be essential to his future in many ways now that he would soon be without a home.

Jon could no longer hide his important belongings in a shoebox under his bedroom floor. With the payments from Geoffrey Jones' company and the benefit payouts from his father's death, he now had a rather heavy shoebox. Cash had always worked well for the Mantlers. Old John didn't want anything to do with banks, and he conducted his life so that he never had to. Banks were bloodsuckers that skimmed money from unsuspecting, hardworking people, according to John. He would have nothing to do with them and encouraged his son to do the same.

Jon decided to make a few alterations to the one-ton to enhance his personal security and logistics. This necessitated taking his truck to a farm friend named Landry, who was handy at welding and, as it turned out, a lot of other creative stuff as well. He commissioned Landry to install a false bottom inside the padlockable toolbox that was bolted to the rear box of his truck. To do so, Landry welded four metal tabs inside the box and attached rubber insulating stoppers to hold up a removable metal slab. Now, what looked like the bottom was not.

Jon then replaced the old cardboard shoebox that Roxanne had left him with a lower and wider wooden box that fit below the slab. He rationalized that if anyone sheared off the lock and broke into the toolbox, they would be doing it to steal the tools on top of the slab and not Jon's stash below. To remove the heavy metal plate and access the false bottom, a person would have to use a magnet, which would be stored in the cab under the front seat. Without the magnet, there was no way to remove the plate. Jon was confident this trick would keep his stash safe, but just in case, his childhood friend Landry had another plan. Innovation was a highly prized trait in these prairie regions.

Landry was a farm kid through and through and a typical young boy becoming a man in this part of the world. They worked long days and nights when work was on the program, which was most of the time, and they played long and hard into the night when work was done or they were rained out. In between, and to tantalize their creative juices, they built stuff.

Landry came up with a more extreme idea designed to keep thieves away from the two-tone one-ton. He installed a second twelve-volt battery behind the seat in the extended cab and live-wired it to the chassis, the cab, and the entire truck box. Landry's theory was that if anyone touched anything metal on the truck, they would get zapped by a powerful shock strong enough to discourage them from further contact. Landry believed that the twelve volts would not be strong enough to seriously injure or kill anyone. But it would serve to send a message. He had done this before with electric fences designed to keep cattle in their pastures.

"No cow has died yet, but they have all, sure as hell, learned to stay away from the fence," he told Jon after installing an on-off switch inside the front wheel well. "The rubber tires will insulate the truck, but if someone touches the metal truck while standing on the ground, *zappo*! They'll ground the live charge. This blue light here at the left of the signal light will be on when the power is on," Landry said. "You can see it easily through the window. So you know not to touch the door handle yourself before you shut off the toggle."

"How do we know it works?" Jon inquired.

"Well, let's try it," offered Landry. He eagerly flipped the insulated, rubber-coated toggle switch and stepped away from the truck. Then he grabbed an iron bar from his garage and jammed it into the ground behind the one-ton. He then took a long piece of wood and tilted the crowbar until it contacted the rear box of the truck. Immediately, sparks flew from the crowbar, similar to the way a battery sparked when misconnected.

"Zappo!" yelled Landry as he used the wood again, this time to push the iron bar to the ground.

Jon wasn't convinced this was all necessary, but he appreciated the ingenuity and enthusiasm the relentless Landry had put into the project.

"Looks like it works!" confirmed Landry as he reached down and flipped off the toggle switch without further incident.

"Do you think this is legal? Can it really hurt someone?" Jon felt compelled to ask.

Landry laughed. "Only assholes that want to mess with your truck."

"What about cats?"

"They jump, so they're safe. Bears could suffer a bit."

"Drunks?"

"They'll sober up real quick."

It seemed that Landry had all the bases covered, so Jon paid him for his work and readied himself to head back down the road, thinking that this was all probably a bit too much. Jon chuckled at Landry's genius and dedication but decided he would probably never actually flip the toggle switch on and risk electrifying an entire neighborhood.

Having a fairly large truck in a big university city might not be all that cool, but clearly, there could be advantages. They must have to haul things in a big city too, he supposed, although he wasn't sure, because he had not yet been in a big city.

He liked the thought of including his father's ideas and advice in his decision-making. It made him feel connected. The one-ton, he was convinced, was the right purchase. He drove down the dirt road feeling grown-up, confident, and alive. When he parked the two-tone one-ton on the edge of his property in front of his house, he felt he had a purpose and an identity. The Ford was now a part of him and a part of the transition that was taking place within. He was no longer the kid in the shack; he was a man, spelled M-A-N-T-L-E-R.

CHAPTER 13

THE THIRD MAN

Magic is the messenger who greets you as a spy.
And warns and warms the ministers who tell you how to lie.

The identity of the third man remained a mystery for nearly another two months. Then, late one evening, Peter Otto had a surprise visit at his home near the Rhein River from his direct superior in the German Ministry. It was more than unusual for a colleague, let alone one of this rank, to visit him at home. Peter deduced that something serious was in play the instant he opened the door. His visitor was Enrico Siemenz.

Peter had known Enrico for over fifteen years. They often worked together on projects and always got along well. They were distinctly different people, however. Peter was passive, calculating, and strategic, while Enrico was impulsive, bold, and action-driven, more sly than strategic, and always on a mission. He had worked in the foreign service of the Federal Republic of Germany, or FRG, a little longer than Peter, but Peter was allocated sixty percent of the time to the international business development department of the ministry and only forty percent to the intelligence service. Enrico was one hundred percent an agent. By the British definition, he would be termed a "spook," but more of a boss spook, not one stationed under a streetlight.

What united Peter and Enrico, and what was paramount to their relationship, was their personal commitment to the cause of freedom, human rights, and dignity for all German citizens. Enrico might bend the rules on dignity, but he was openly and utterly unwavering on the other two criteria. He vehemently detested Adolf Hitler and the Nazi atrocities. He was born only one year after the war ended, and this had a powerful effect on him. He was pro-Europe and loathed imperialism, communism, and authoritarianism, as well as dictators, fascists, and nationalists. He railed against any and all of his own German colleagues who sought to avoid conversation regarding their Nazi past. He deemed it a failure of the German population that they had not taken more responsibility for what was done during the war years.

In his youth, Enrico was influenced by the hippie ideology of the sixties. He was a proponent of freedom. He continued to channel the values of peace, love, and understanding into his adult life. His favorite Beatle was Ringo, not John, Paul, or George, as most of his peers selected. He rated Ringo a puritan and the most true to the cause of peace and love. Ringo didn't have an inflated sense of self and didn't force any expectations on others; he faithfully did his job when it was time to do so and made the people around him better. John and Paul were more ego-driven and less giving, and George was pouty and withdrawn. Ringo was not envious or arrogant; he just delivered the peace and love. In Enrico's estimation, Ringo Starr was THE star. Enrico was all about peace and love, but on steroids.

The discussions he and Peter had were philosophical, political, theoretical, and animated. Their souls and their sentiments were synchronized. However, while Peter functioned in a businesslike manner and followed protocols, Enrico was obsessed with his job and did things in whatever time frame suited him. He took nothing at face value, and he did not operate on trust. Enrico believed there was always a hidden agenda lurking behind anything someone else uttered, so he delved deep into every resource.

"How do we build better systems within our societal structures?" one of them would ask. "In pure theory, communism or some form of it might be the best form of governance, but human nature does not render it functional."

"There needs to be an incentive for cooperation and commonality to exist. Freedom should not be restricted and should also be available to the more vulnerable citizenry," the other would reply.

"But there is no effective way to tax the rich, and even if you could, there is no effective way of ensuring that the tax gleaned would end up distributed in a manner that would result in a more inclusive society."

"Corruption exists in every system that has ever been tried."

The two had undergone countless hours of these types of philosophical conversations over the years, then argued and agreed, and then started up new discussions.

"We need to educate in such a way that the majority of the population understands true happiness comes from within and not from without, not from excess and greed."

"But the populace needs to be incentivized to some capacity!"

"Capitalist values in their best form require production and distribution; economics bind us, trade binds us, but greed divides us."

"Can't save all of the world. Can't solve all of the problems."

"But we have to try something!"

Ultimately, Peter and Enrico agreed on one main purpose: the unification of East and West Germany. They were allies in a quest to attain freedom of determination and freedom of movement for the citizens of all of Germany. One of their tasks in working for the Interior Ministry was spreading confusion and overloading the political system in the East with largely bogus information, thus making it less effective to carry out their propaganda. Speakers periodically blasted propaganda over the wall, and various forms of wireless signals were sent out to educate the public and irritate the authoritarian regime. Yet the wall remained intact. As long as the Berlin Wall stood there imposing and erect where it had been planted since 1961, then the people living in East Germany would remain encamped.

"A wall is better than a war, and we don't want a war," Peter noted.

"We need to find other ways to cause change," Enrico usually responded.

"Maybe we could do with just a little war with no blood spilled. Twenty-five years of the wall is too much."

And this was how most of their discussions concluded.

Today was about to be different, though. Enrico had come to visit Peter to deliver a distinct message. He was concerned that the unfortunate events involving Jon Mantler in Budapest all those weeks ago might have problematic consequences and jeopardize the work that Enrico was involved with in Hungary and the GDR.

"I'm sorry for visiting you here like this, but I have some news that we need to seriously and quietly discuss," Enrico said in German within a minute of entering Peter's apartment. "The Hungarians have today found a body on the south side of Pest. Our guys there think this could be that third man you and Mantler have been going on about."

Peter lived with Sabine, his girlfriend of ten years. They were in bed when Enrico came calling, so it was only Peter who greeted him at the door.

"The description we have so far seems to fit the one provided by Mantler. It's an unusually long time for a body not to show up in a river like that, but sometimes that's how these things go. It seems the high level of water in the Danube back in November whisked the body right through the center of Budapest and out to a flatter and more remote area on the Pest side, where it simply didn't pop up or become noticed until now. If this is your guy, then we have a lot of information to dig into and work to do in order to avoid problems. The reason I'm here is that it turns out this guy works in the government in Hungary; he's connected, and he has been missing since about the time you lost Bircher. This does seem like your guy. In Budapest, it's a story that this guy was missing. But until now, no one knew where this guy went or why. Well, I guess they still don't know why."

"Holy shit!" Peter blurted out.

"Holy shit is right. Now they know where and when he ended up, but they still don't know how, why, or where he got into that river, I guess. We're probably the only ones who have connected the lines between Mantler and Bircher. But it all kind of fits, don't you think?"

"Yes, it kind of fits. So who is he, actually?"

"That is the problem. His name is Igor Tamas Wozneszensky, and he has been an official in the Secretary General's office for quite a few years. He was working in the Kadr government for years, and then during the transition last May, he was one of the many younger department heads who switched over to Grosz's group. I guess he saw the writing on the wall and read it in his own best interest. He has some commie pedigree too. His father was Alexander Wozneszensky, consistently the number two or three man in all of the previous commie regimes, punching for the Soviets ever since the war and until he died in 1982. This Igor is his only son, and he was still a director in the Grosz administration right up until he disappeared. He's a pretty big fish, no pun intended, so he has been missed, though they didn't make a lot of noise about it, probably because they feared he might have defected. The Hungarian police have been quietly but intently investigating and searching for him with a lot of speculative theories on what might have happened to him." Enrico paused.

"Politically, things are getting crazier every day in Budapest right now, and now that they have a body to play with, this all could go down pretty deep and could cause us some serious problems there," he continued.

"What the hell would this guy be doing on that bridge with Jon and Karl? Could he have known Karl?" Peter asked.

"That is a really good question. And we better figure it out fast."

"How close can your guys get to this?" Peter wanted to know.

"We're in there tight enough with the Hungarian police. We have eyes inside; we always know what they do, and sometimes we even know what they're about to do. But the problem right now is that everything's in such political turmoil that we can't predict accurately, because things change from day to day. The government doesn't know what it's doing or which way to pivot, and everyone's fighting with everyone. The old commies are in retreat, and the new commies are acting enlightened, trying not to lose their precious positions. We think Wozneszensky was one of them, a strategically enlightened politician. Probably a modern-day, opportunistic capitalist leftie. There's bound to be speculation that someone threw Wozneszensky in the Danube for some political reason, and that could mean a lot of police investigations going on right now all over Budapest."

"Could this land back on us? What can we do?"

"Budapest is too important in this current situation for us to let this come back on us. I'm sure Hungary will be the first country to break with Moscow. The consensus within the younger leadership there, which seems to have support from the general population, is to move closer to Western Europe. No one expects that Gorbachev will make a move to stop Hungary from seeking more independence from the Soviet Union; he has as much as said so, and as long as he can maintain power in Moscow, this will not be another Khrushchev 1956. If Hungary does open up to the West, then the days are also numbered for the GDR. Peter, we're getting really close to ending communism in Germany, so we can't let this land back on us. We've already been able to get some GDR people out and into Austria through leaks in the Hungarian border controls. So Hungary is the major focal point for us right now."

Peter, a talker by nature, was quiet and listening intently. Most of what Enrico was revealing was new information to him. His role for the past decade had been to flood the GDR with information, to swamp the Stasi network of informants to the point of inefficiency and redundancy. Now he was being awakened to the fact that it all might very well have worked. He did not want Enrico to stop talking.

"Any crazy activity that the hardliners could use to stymie the political reform movement catching on in Hungary is a risk we need to avoid. We've never been this close. All our reports show us that the Soviets don't have the means to suppress these countries anymore, Peter. So I need to go to Budapest on Wednesday and figure out what's happening on the streets there. But first, we need to go see your guy Mantler and make sure we know every bit of what he knows about this bridge fiasco. I'm thinking of taking him with me, actually. We need to end this thing once and for all. What else does Mantler know? What kind of a guy is he, really?" Enrico asked. He continued before Peter could reply.

"If the Hungarians are thinking this is an assassination of some up-and-coming political leader, a son of a former commie regime official, imagined or otherwise, it could mobilize opponents and shift public sentiment back toward the hardliners."

"Mantler's a little rattled right now coming to terms with the bridge incident. But otherwise, he's solid. He's totally trustworthy," Peter affirmed.

"Tell me this, then. You and I have done this for years and years and never has anyone been injured in any of our work, let alone killed, and you bring this Canadian slowpoke onto our roster, and he flips two bodies into the Danube on a casual night's work."

"Well, we put him in that position, Rico!"

"Sure, sure, but I'm just saying the timing and the circumstances couldn't be worse. We've worked decades to get to this point. Russia and the Soviet Unionists aren't able to thwart our moves anymore, and without that military threat, we have a realistic chance to break up the GDR's grip. We can't mess this up now. Mantler's body count isn't helping us here! Call him first thing in the morning and tell him we'll meet him in that restaurant you and I go to, north of Heidelberg at twelve thirty."

"It's not that late, so I can call him now. He doesn't sleep much anyway, especially since Budapest," replied Peter.

"I'm going to take him with me to Budapest, what do you think? He might have some further insight on Karl and this third man that comes to light once he revisits the place. There may be things he knows that he doesn't know he knows. Do you think he'd be of use? You say we can trust him."

"Jon is a good thinker; he's astute; he's logical. He'll be useful. I also think it would be good for him to return and deal with what he has left there."

Peter called Jon and arranged the rendezvous. He also informed Jon he would be bringing a colleague who had information to share with him about Budapest. More he could not share. Enrico, calm now, committed to picking up Peter the next morning for the short drive to Heidelberg. Then he left.

Hungary was indeed well on its way to regime change. The Hungarian political regime, after decades of acting in consort within the house of the USSR, was shifting in response to the perestroika and glasnost programs advanced by Mikhail Gorbachev. Hungary was now making national decisions in Budapest without consulting Moscow. In so doing, they were appeasing the segments of their population whose sentiments and desires leaned more to the West.

In the GDR, however, this was not the case. The old guard in power, led by Erich Honecker, remained determined and brutally committed to maintaining control over their populace. The GDR still had some economic leverage that most of the other Warsaw Pact countries did not, and this gave Honecker confidence that he could maintain authority. Also, he still had the Stasi on his side. This powerful network, led by Werner Grossmann following the quasi-retirement of Markus Wolf, was embedded in every pore of society and could quell democratic aspirations before they could germinate.

They were investigating the death of Karl Bircher in Hungary and were aware of the mysterious disappearance of Igor Wozneszensky. The coincidence was right there, but no one in Berlin, East or West, knew of a connection between Karl and Wozneszensky. Thus, they kept their investigation separate from the Hungarians and watched curiously to see what the Budapest police were doing. The Hungarians knew nothing about Karl, labeling him an accident-prone GDR tourist.

Wozneszensky had been declared missing when, on a Monday morning in November, he did not arrive for work at his government office in central Budapest. His staff did not make too much of his absence at first, but by late afternoon, following a number of unanswered calls to his home telephone, there was concern.

They sent an official to his home, who ascertained that Wozneszensky had not slept in his bed the previous Sunday night. When on the next day there was still no communication from their boss, his assistants turned the case over to the National Police. Initially, their focus was more on who Wozneszensky was and less about what happened to him. Fortunately, this investigation stayed a long way from the bridge where Jon had taken his jogs. It was also a long way from determining how the third man ended up in the Danube.

Peter had pulled Jon from all agency activities immediately after the Budapest incident. Since that fateful day, Jon had felt inept and out of sorts, but he continued his business activities in Heidelberg in as normal a fashion as he could. He was discomfited to be in this predicament.

He never intended to be a secret agent; he had agreed to help Peter because the man was his friend and because he was convinced that uniting the people of Germany was a worthy endeavor. He fundamentally believed the citizens of the GDR should be free to decide their own fate and not be locked behind a wall because of nationalistic ideology. Helping seemed like the right thing to do, particularly as Nora was working for NATO and essentially attached to the same cause. He also liked the money.

Still, the main reason he did the job was the connection he had built with Peter and his willingness to help Peter reunite with his mother. A mother who was not allowed to travel to visit her son because she might not return, might defect, was something Jon thought was worth rallying against.

Jon was anti-nationalist, just like his father, so he didn't feel any passion for German reunification on that level. What he objected to was imprisoning a population of millions under the guise of one political doctrine. He also thought the World War that his father fought in should at last end in a better way for the people living on the other side of the Iron Curtain.

Meanwhile, Enrico was forced to expand his involvement in the Karl Bircher matter now that Igor Wozneszensky was implicated. Enrico assumed—like anyone else looking at this case would—that the connection between Karl and Wozneszensky had to have an espionage link. So far, only he and Peter knew the role that Jon had played in this matter, and Enrico needed it to stay that way.

CHAPTER 14

TEAM MEETING

But who will be the master and who will find the answer
to all the growing cancer in the way of his relief?

Jon Mantler entered the Gasthof Traube north of Heidelberg and sat at a table. He followed the instructions Peter had given him perfectly and arrived early. Jon was nervous but hopeful that this rendezvous would provide him with relief. All he knew from last night's conversation was that they needed to meet immediately and that Peter was bringing along a colleague to help resolve some things.

In these last few weeks, Jon was not functioning well with the anguish of not knowing what might happen next. It negatively affected his ability to run his daily business, and he knew his secretiveness was causing difficulties in his relationship with Nora.

Jon was struggling to deal with the deaths that had occurred within his orbit. His father had said either you can fix it or you can't; if you can fix it, do so; if not, step away. He remembered those words and had used them to guide him in the past. But he couldn't step away from this.

His little secret game with Peter had not been a problem up until now, because it was compartmentalized as just another piece of his businesses. But since Budapest, everything had changed, and it was affecting all aspects of his life. He could sense Nora's irritation with him, but he remained passive because he didn't know what to do about it. Nora knew Peter was a client, an advisor from the embassy, and a friend of Jon's. She had met him and liked him, but she didn't know him well.

Peter had been instrumental in Jon's business success. He introduced Jon to a firm in Frankfurt that paid Jon to run marketing promotions for Japanese televisions and microwave ovens in the tax-free expat outlets in and around Heidelberg. Peter's job at the embassy was to link German firms with Canadian firms, a logical arrangement that provided Jon with legitimate income and a masked way to compensate him for the other work he did.

Nora also knew about the lingering issues from Jon's past, which he kept secret. She surmised that he himself did not understand the issues well enough to dispense with them. She knew that his mother and father were dead and that his mother had left him when he was six. She also knew he had lived in a modest shack largely on his own from the age of fourteen. On the surface, it seemed like he dealt with these tribulations admirably, and, in many ways, it made him stronger. Until these past few weeks, she never expected there might have been any deeper damage. Jon was clearly unable to communicate what was causing his somber solitude. He tried to assure her that he was fine and that it was just related to having difficulties in his businesses, but Nora knew this was not true. Consequently, they each felt bad for the other.

Prior to today, Jon and Enrico had not met; prior to today, there was no need to. Jon was one of hundreds of agents planted throughout West Germany, passing on information to and from a muck of GDR agents. This was a routine that had gone on for decades. Enrico had read Jon's profile from reports that Peter periodically submitted, and until the Budapest kerfuffle, all had been ordinary. Until that moment on the bridge, Jon's work was simply a small cog in the big wheel that Enrico was trying to roll.

The restaurant was one huge room. Jon waited at a table near the farthest windows until he saw two men enter. The first man took a lead position, and Peter Otto followed a few feet behind. They headed straight to the table to greet Jon. The first man was of average height and slim build, with dark hair and handsome features. He was dressed in a sweater and blue jeans, which was in distinct contrast to Peter, who was formally attired in shirt, tie, and jacket. Jon correctly concluded this was Enrico Siemenz, who shot out his arm and hand as Jon rose from the table to catch the handshake as if it were a line drive and he were a shortstop.

"I know you're Jon Mantler. It's so good to finally meet you in person. How are you coping with all these extraordinary circumstances? I'm sure we can resolve things in a good way, so let's go to work on that." Enrico, as usual, cut right to the point.

Peter hugged Jon and mumbled a couple words as Enrico took a chair to the left of Jon.

"Let's order right away so that we can get to our conversation as quickly as possible. Have you ordered anything to drink, Jon?" Then Enrico turned to the waitress, who had just arrived. "Fräulein, could you bring us some water and the menu?"

They were the only guests in the room, and Jon was glad about that.

Peter, who did not get the opportunity to introduce the two men, decided to squeeze himself into the conversation by telling Jon that they had interesting news to report from Budapest and that progress was finally being made. They wanted to share what they expected would happen next.

"How about the Rahmschnitzel? It's good here, if I remember, and I'll have a Pils. How about you two?" Enrico asked.

Peter and Jon took the simplest route on that question and confirmed the same order for all three of them to placate the waitress so the meeting could commence in earnest.

Enrico, as expected, did most of the talking and explained that a dead Igor Wozneszensky had floated up from the Danube just two days earlier and that it was extremely likely he was the third man Jon had encountered on the bridge with Karl Bircher. He had been speaking German up to that point, but now Enrico switched to English as he leaned closer to Jon.

"Now, Jon, listen to me. It's time for you to stop dwelling on what happened on that bridge. What happened was merely a small portion of activity that took place in the universe at that moment in time and space. The fact that you happened to be there is incidental. We human beings, who have developed this smattering of rationality, tend to believe we can control what happens in our world, but we can't. All we can do is choose how we feel and deal with what happens, and in most cases, like in your case, we often choose badly. You're allowing emotions to dictate how you feel and choosing to blame yourself. How you feel about it is entirely irrelevant, and it serves no useful purpose. The past is past; it's gone, and so are Bircher and Wozneszensky. Do you realize that in the ten minutes we've been sitting here, probably a hundred people have died just within a hundred-kilometer radius from here? There's nothing you or I can do about that except choose to feel bad about it if we want to. Either way, it definitely serves no purpose, not to them and not to us. All that actually exists is what you let exist in your mind."

Jon listened, Peter remained in silent agreement, and Enrico continued.

"As I understand the events on that bridge, and correct me if I'm wrong, you went back due to your concern for Bircher. You didn't intend to push Wozneszensky off the bridge. That was an accident, correct?"

Jon nodded timidly, not thinking he was expected to speak.

"You didn't know that Bircher was dead until after Wozneszensky was gone, so it turns out that was also a fate that you could not alter. The fact that you dropped him off the bridge, in retrospect, is an outcome that actually turns out better for everyone concerned. Certainly, it made things simpler for his wife and daughter. His death was not going to be easy for them in any case, but by using the river, you created an accident scenario that uncomplicated their grieving. That is a lot better than having to explain why you and Karl were on the bridge together. You carried out your particular role in this incident in the best way you could, I'd say. That'll not change regardless of how you turn it around in your mind. Now we need to move on and make the best of things."

Peter debated entering the conversation, not accustomed to being silent for long periods of time, but because he was not certain where Enrico was going next, he held back.

"You're correct. I didn't intend for the man to fall from the bridge." Jon felt the silence was waiting for him, so he spoke up. "I've been experiencing strong feelings, it's true, but I do think it's necessary for me to process it this way, emotionally and cerebrally, in order to move on. Up to now, I haven't been able to forget about it, and I don't know if it'll ever be over," he muttered.

"It's over when you say it's over, Jon," Enrico interjected. "And we're going to end it. You and I are going to go to Budapest tomorrow, and we're going to resolve things. That's why we're here today. We want to explain to you what the situation is in Budapest. There are political events playing out there that could affect our overall work in the East. We need to find out more about Wozneszensky. You need to come with me, because you're the last person to have seen him alive. We'll find out what's going on there, I think, once and for all. Who knows what you might remember once you get back to Budapest? For you, it'll be over then." Enrico's confidence was infectious, and both Peter and Jon believed him.

For the next hour, they ate lunch as Enrico and Peter went through the current political situation in the GDR and Hungary and explained the significant role that Hungary was potentially playing in changing the political structure in the Eastern Bloc. They explained to Jon how glasnost and perestroika were energizing a new generation of younger leaders.

Enrico and Peter revealed everything they knew about Jon's November visit to Budapest. They clarified that from their perspective, there was no political or strategic purpose for his meeting with Karl Bircher. The exchange was scheduled with Karl, logistically, because Jon and Nora had a tourist visit to Budapest through their local network in Heidelberg. Karl was often in Budapest on business of his own, so it worked out naturally. Peter knew that Karl often visited Budapest and that it was convenient for him to travel there, so when Jon told him of their cultural trip, he notified Karl through his network and set up the information meeting accordingly. They had done the same a few months earlier, when Jon and Nora had made a tourist visa visit to Prague.

"Why was Wozneszensky, a ranking Hungarian politician, on that bridge with you that night, and did Bircher know him?" Enrico asked no one in particular, because he knew neither of them had the answer.

Enrico then described to Jon the work his office had been undertaking in Hungary over the past two years. This was intended to further ease Jon into understanding that his role in the affair was incidental as well as to prepare him for the upcoming trip to Budapest. Enrico was certain the Soviet Union was about to implode and that Hungary would be the first country to break away from Moscow's grip. Inside Hungary, there was a youthful element of strong, rebellious leadership that had the support of a majority of people leaning to the West. These people were determined to complete the never-forgotten events of 1956. They were emboldened by the messages coming from Gorbachev and were confident that the Soviets would not intervene this time.

He pointed out that the Soviets couldn't afford to take action to stop this momentum for a variety of reasons, not least because their Union was nearly bankrupt. The Hungarians knew this, and so did Honecker in East Germany, but he was choosing to leverage the dilemma to foment more power within the bloc. The GDR was currently a little better off economically than Moscow, but not for long, vowed Enrico.

Peter finally injected. "We've been working with our network inside the GDR in a similar way, but we're not nearly as far advanced there as they are in Hungary. The GDR leadership still has old-school support and control of the army. They're not really listening to Gorbachev. They're scared but not giving up."

Now Jon was listening in stereo.

"If Hungary succeeds and declares some type of autonomy and Russia does not interject on behalf of the Soviet Union, then the GDR will soon fall too, along with most of their neighbors," said Enrico.

"We've already been getting East German citizens out through small leaks in the Hungarian border to Austria. There are crossings where the border guards don't always bother to stop the few people who want to leave for Austria. If they have German citizenship papers, the Hungarian guards don't care anymore where they go. They're only stopping their own Hungarians."

Enrico explained that Hungary was about to sign the 1951 Convention on Refugees at the United Nations in Geneva, even though their reason for doing so was to enable their own ethnic Hungarians to flee Ceausescu's Romania and be granted refugee status, followed by Hungarian citizenship. The consequence would be that they could not detain other citizens from returning to their homelands as long as they could prove their status as citizens of their home country.

There were only a handful of nations in the world, like Israel, Greece, and West Germany, that gave immediate citizenship to nationals returning to their homelands. No other Eastern Bloc country had signed onto this 1951 document. Hungary would be the first, and Enrico and his team were planning to use this legal international convention to their advantage to free as many Germans as they could from the grip of the GDR.

"When we go to Budapest tomorrow, we're going to find out why Wozneszensky was on that bridge. We can't allow his death to become a distorted political affair that revitalizes the hardliners and lets them wrestle back political control! That would set back all the progress that we've made since Gorbachev rolled a different die in Moscow. So describe one more time exactly what you remember about that night on the bridge and specifically about this third man," Enrico requested.

Jon knew it would come to this, and he was ready to share, with only the second person ever, what he had reconstructed in his mind a million times since that fateful day in November. He repeated word for word what he had said to Peter on various occasions. Despite wishing he could deliver more details, there just weren't any more.

The description of the third man was now crucially important, so Jon focused on that. He had not seen him well, but what stood out was that he may have had a mustache; otherwise, he was clean-shaven, and his long brown coat seemed tailored to fit stylishly. He was a big man, but more as in tall and not as in overweight. It was quite dark, and everything happened within seconds. His voice was gruff, but that may have just been due to the language and intensity of the situation.

Jon never understood a word but in retrospect realized it was possible that the man was trying to explain something rather than yelling in a rage. This was what daunted Jon the most about that evening's incident, that he might have misinterpreted the situation. What if there was no reason for him to body-check the man a second time? This was what Jon was having the most difficulty letting go of. It seemed this split-second miscalculation was going to live inside him for the rest of his days on Earth.

"Like I said before, we don't make these decisions. Life makes these decisions for us, Jon," Enrico said. "That is enough for us to go to Budapest with. I don't think that right now anyone else in Budapest knows what we know. We'll need to make sure it stays this way. Our bigger worry is that there are people in Budapest making things up that did not happen. We're near the end of this now, so go home and pack a small bag and meet me at the Frankfurt Airport tomorrow morning at eight. I'll have your ticket and all the documentation you need to accompany me to the German Embassy in Budapest. You'll be an engineer assigned to help us with logistics at the embassy there. You're an engineer, are you not?" These were Enrico's last words to Jon as they concluded their meeting.

Peter left with Enrico and promised to call Jon later in the day with additional information regarding their electronics business. Jon headed to his car for the short ride back to his office. He felt more relieved than he had been since his return from Budapest weeks ago.

Enrico was a very convincing communicator and had succeeded in his quest to rehabilitate Jon from his own afflictions. And Jon wanted to trust that Enrico could and would take care of the situation from here on out. For the first time in a long time, he felt kind of okay.

CHAPTER 15

DISMANTLING

And with that quest came a more able understanding
that without the deepest will to succeed, success would be gone.

Jon had been quite fascinated by his studies relating to time and space over the past weeks at school. He was not yet satisfied with his understanding of the concepts in the textbooks he had assigned himself. What was clear, however, was that his time in his own space was nearing an end.

"Change will come. It's a must; it's constant, and when it comes, you need to make it a good thing. Don't fight it. Lead it," John Sr. had told him.

As he thought about that now, he surmised that the demolition of the shack was probably not the change John Sr. was thinking about when he rendered that nugget of advice. It was relatable more as an emotional change, and that was what Jon had been thinking a lot about. The destruction of the only home he had ever known, the home built by his father, piece by piece, nail and screw, was taking a toll on the young Jon.

"You have to know that you can survive anything, Jon, and you will. I know you well, and you're the most capable person I've ever seen. And believe me when I tell you that I've seen a lot. But when change comes, trust only yourself."

Jon was glad that in the last years before his father passed, they had spent a lot more time talking. His father seemed to catch on to the importance of passing on little bits of knowledge to his son. By the time Jon was in high school, their early evening sessions together had become more and more philosophical in nature. Sadly, John died just as he was opening up to his son about his views on life.

To cope with his personal circumstances, Jon often turned inward to the skill his mother had taught him for reducing his stress: humming and numbing his rampant thought patterns.

Jon suffered from anxiety. The chanting of nonessential guttural sounds stopped his mind from connecting to words and thoughts. Gradually, it quelled the overthinking and overemoting that had ramped up inside his brain. Young Jon didn't exactly understand the reason this helped him any more than he understood Einstein's Theory of Relativity. He just knew it helped him feel better. He implemented the technique most nights to fall asleep. He had not been a good sleeper since the age of six.

Both his mother and father had been gone from his life for quite a few years now. Dismantling the interior of his shack caused him to think more and more about them. Some days, he felt that this change was happening too fast, and he didn't really want to go through with it. Still, he saw no alternative, so he powered himself forward.

It was now the first days of July. More than a week had passed since he had completed high school. Thanks to the extra guidance of Miss Roberts, he was enrolled in university for the fall and would soon be receiving a number of scholarships from various organizations she made him apply to. Miss Roberts was one of the very few who knew anything about Jon's home situation, and she feared he might not have enough money to live in the city. But Miss Roberts did not know about the shoebox.

The physical part of demolishing the shack was not easy, but Jon was diligent. For weeks, he went from room to room dismantling and salvaging the best wood from the interior. His father had meticulously used wood screws to attach all the finishing wood to the beams that held up the walls and the roof, countersinking them and fitting them with wooden dowel pins. Taking these apart was most time-consuming. If he wanted the wood to be sellable, all the screws had to come out so there would be no metal in the wood. Jon had blisters on his palms and fingers from turning the screws with his hands. Eventually, he had to take to wearing heavy leather gloves.

Harder, though, was the emotional part. The destruction of his dear father's lifetime of labor didn't feel fair. As Jon worked through the interior of the house from room to room, he felt like a betrayer. Entering each individual room and detaching the interiors for what he knew would be the last time invoked intense memories. He didn't understand what he was feeling, but he couldn't stop feeling it.

His earliest images in the bedroom were of his mother. This was where she had taught him to read. She was his best teacher. He recalled those hours they spent together with the Butlers' encyclopedias. Roxanne could find an interesting subject and story to build around any topic. It instilled a habitual curiosity for learning that Jon would continue well after his mother's departure and throughout the rest of his life. There had always been one of the Butlers' Compton volumes in the Mantler shack at any given time. There were fifteen volumes, and they had served Jon and presumably the Butler children well.

Recollections of his father came every time he removed wood from the house. His father's love of working with wood and creating useful and beautiful objects with it was a prime source of Jon's education as well. John Sr. taught by example, always showing how things worked and how they were meant to fit together. He taught to take on activities with purpose and to follow logical steps to achieve a planned result.

Geoffrey had been a great help in the demolition, and he was thinking logically when he advised Jon to assemble a crew of young men in the community to assist. Jon was thinking more strategically, however, and decided to employ only one helper. His instincts and experience working on farm crews and construction sites told him that one good worker was more effective than two slackers. One worker with a clear task and an understanding of the project, working in tandem with Jon Mantler, would be his modus. His dismantling project did not require brawn as much as it required precision and consistency.

"More people, more problems," Jon remembered his father telling him. "If you want things to get done right, you're best to do them yourself."

Jon knew exactly what his father meant in relation to group dynamics. He knew all the young people available to him as summer hires, and most of them were immature goof-offs. He surmised that if he were to hire two or more workers, they would spend too much time socializing and showing off to each other and too little time working. Three people on site would also create a hierarchy that would complicate things and lead to petty two-on-one situations and other childlike scenarios. Jon decided to hire only one person to work with him. It was bound to increase understanding and reduce screwups.

So, he only brought on Harvey. His Nash Rambler copilot returned from university at the end of April to work on his mother's farm for the summer. Jon and Harvey had been together on various work crews in the past, and he knew that, given a clear task, Harvey was a strong and tireless worker. It was common throughout the summer for farmers in the region to pull together work crews in seasonal weeks when a lot needed to be accomplished in a short period of time, like stone picking, hay baling, barn construction, or harvesting.

Jon and Harvey were usually the first boys drafted onto these teams because they were both fearless workers. Undistracted, Harvey would be, in effect, a one-man crew. Jon incentivized Harvey by paying him double the going rate and told him he could take off whatever time he needed to work his own farm at the same time that he was demolishing the shack. It was one of Jon's wisest decisions ever.

Jon had had a tidy room laid out for him by Mrs. Butler in the Butlers' home since the day John Sr. died. However, until now, he had rarely stayed there. He preferred to be in his shack, honing his independence. That all changed in the past week when he dragged an old trunk, a suitcase, and a shoebox over to Mrs. Butler's house. The tearing down of the shack had reached the point where he could no longer live there. He had torn out most of the inside walls and stored the salvaged wood in his garage at the end of the property. The electricity was going to be disconnected in a day or two, and though he would run an extension cord from the Butlers' house to assist with the woodwork, it wasn't going to be possible for him to live there anymore. It was another emotion-filled turning point.

Since Jim Butler's death a year earlier, life for Mrs. Butler had become much more solemn. She was aging and lonely. Her method of coping with the change was heaping love on Jon and having him nearby to cook and care for. Jon loved Mrs. Butler too, and he was very pleased for her that Geoffrey and his family would be her new neighbors. Once their house was built, she would have two young girls to cater to and dote on. Time was moving faster now for Jon Mantler.

On a most glorious summer morning, Jon laid out the tools he had gathered to begin the heavier work of dismantling the exterior of the shack. He had already carefully removed all the interior wood and stored it in the garage. He had sold or given away the valued items he no longer needed from the inside. Now, it was time to get serious about the rest of it.

Today, he had run the extension cord from the Butlers' home to the wooden shed behind his house to power the big saw and any other power tools he might need in the deconstruction. He would need the saw to prepare the wood for resale. Jon had been taught well by his father how to use this industrial saw and all related woodworking equipment.

Work would begin on the roof, and Jon gathered the necessary equipment. He had two ladders already propped against the walls of the shack when Harvey Dean ambled up from the alleyway, crossed the street, and walked up to the Mantler shack.

"Hellooo, Mr. Bossman!" he called out.

It was a few minutes after 9:00 a.m., and Jon was lifting two snub-nosed spades and two nail pullers from the back of his Ford two-tone one-ton truck parked beside the single entrance to the shack.

"Good to see you, H." Jon sometimes called Harvey "H" in reaction to his friend's overuse of J-related monikers. Jon realized that it was going to take time and persistence before people in the village would actually call him Jon. The boys joked that it was a pity they didn't know anyone called Ivan, so that they could alphabetically be H, I, and J.

"Besides, they could pick any 'idiot' to be their I," they joked.

"And there is no shortage of 'idiots' in this town!"

H and J had known each other most of their lives. Now, with their friendship developing and Jon enrolled at university, they had decided to find a place to live together. By sharing living quarters, they would reduce costs.

Harvey was a big, strong athlete enrolled in sports and physical education at the university, and Jon was certain he had hired the best worker in the village. When they first met to discuss the details of the job,

Jon had explained that every piece of wood that was stored for sale and reuse had to be free of any metal; therefore, they had to apply the extra effort to pull all the nails and screws out of the planks and boards. The shingles they were ripping off the roof today would be an exception, because they were not reusable. Firewood was all they were worth, so they would be loaded onto the one-ton and transported to a farmyard just north of town that had requested them. But all the boards below needed to be extracted and made nail-free. A tedious task for most, but readily taken on by Harvey.

And so it began, with the two young men scaling the roof via ladder and using the shovels and their gloved hands to tear the sheath-like shingles off the roof. By lunchtime, they had the back of the truck full and about one-third of the roof shingle-free. They felt good about their progress and took a break to eat what Mrs. Butler had punctually prepared and delivered.

They felt a strong sense of purpose and accomplishment looking at the loaded Ford. There was a hard-to-describe pride that came with completing a chore, especially when you could see the results directly in front of you. Jon and Harvey were off to a good start on day one. They felt like tigers.

Being on the roof was Jon's favorite task in the process of tearing down the shack. The prairie on which the village sat was quite flat, and even though the Mantlers' roof was not particularly high, you could still see over or through a lot of the trees. It presented a different perspective. From the top, you could see nearly all of the small village. More importantly, just about everyone in the town could see you, especially the locals who drove down Main Street and then turned on Railway, past the post office to King Street.

Everyone could see them working. Work was a highly valued activity in this village. You didn't just live to work; you lived because you worked. Or so Jon thought. He had grown up thinking that one was put on this earth to work. It was all he saw around him every day.

He felt guilty when he was not working or in the process of planning work. Having people see you shirtless in the hot sun on a roof working was something young men in the village took great pride in. It would take Jon many more years to understand that not working, for example, lying in the sun and relaxing, was not against the laws of nature. Today, however, being on the roof was maximum satisfaction.

After lunch, Jon took the two-ton one-ton and delivered the shingles to his farm client while Harvey got back on the roof to send more shingles flying. They laid a tarpaulin on the ground below, and by the time Jon returned, Harvey had another full quantity of shingles to be loaded. It was a hot day, and they looked like warriors on top of the shack. Harvey wore only a pair of cutoff blue jeans, work boots, and gloves. He was tanned dark brown on his back from earlier days spent on his mother's farm. His front side was still nearly all white, as the type of work he did was the back-bending kind.

Jon spent much less time in the sun, and when he removed his shirt to take on the elements and the rays, he looked sheet-white in comparison. He wore long pants and running shoes and knew he had a long way to go to figure out how to be cool. In Jon's estimation, being cool seemed to come so easily to Harvey.

By the end of the first workday, which they chose to be about 8:00 p.m., they had all the shingles off the roof. The one-ton was full, so they covered the truck back with the tarpaulin and tied it down so that Jon could deliver the shingles first thing the next morning. Then they tended to the daily shutdown tasks Jon had laid out, feeling pleased with their results.

"Let's take the rest of these sandwiches and go down to the well," Jon suggested.

They had transported more of the old wood from inside to the lower end of the lot to be stored dry in the garage. Most times, they used a wheelbarrow; sometimes, they carried the loads by hand. On the lot along the way, just before the garage and adjacent to the big garden, there was an old well. It hadn't been active since John Sr. died, and the village installed a running water and sewage system for most of the households in the community.

The Mantler shack was not a part of this project, as John Mantler was not inclined to become a part of anything communal. Old John stubbornly used his own well and bluntly had no need, nor any inclination, to pay for running water coming to his house by pipe. He got his water from his well and from his roof. He took care of his own waste with a bucket and an outhouse right up until the day he died. His only modern convenience was electricity. He appreciated that form of power and the light it so easily provided. Beyond that, no running water, no gas, no telephone, no need.

In recent years, however, young Jon had determined that it was easier to get his water from the nearby town well than to keep his own well functioning. Therefore, going down to the well tonight would be for another purpose. Jon had never been a drinker of alcohol, but he knew it was an important element of socialization for all his peers. As the leader of this project, he had decided to supply beer as a reward for his crew.

The well no longer had a pump installed, and it no longer served up water; it now served something else. Jon had attached a bucket to a rope and onto a winch so that it could be lowered into the depths of the shaft. He had filled the bucket with a dozen fully loaded brown beer bottles and lowered them into the cool earth below. There they would stay safe and cool until evening, when he would invite his one-man crew to revel in the accomplishments of their first day of labor. He had placed two old lawn chairs there as well, aimed to the west and the late prairie sunset.

The crew sat and shared stories about high school friends and teachers that both had known over the years. In this community, people were evaluated in an odd way. If you were deemed acceptable, you'd be declared "a good shit." This was actually a favorable grade. One could also be classified as a "pretty good shit" or "not a bad shit," the difference of which could only be determined by local experts attuned to the vocal inflection of the evaluator. A good shit was definitely ranked higher than a pretty good shit. What you did not want to be was "a piece of shit," one of the lowest ranks awarded. It was a simple and understandable system. Jon and Harvey had a lot of laughs as they went through people they both knew and ranked them on the shit scale.

They talked about their upcoming trip to the university to secure accommodations and decided to take Jon's truck to make the five-hour one-way journey the following Thursday. It would be the first road trip for the two-tone one-ton, and Jon Mantler was excited about that. Harvey's old Barracuda was in the garage again, so that was not an option. Jon had never been to a university city, or to any city for that matter, other than the little one down the road where he had just graduated from high school.

Jon was not urbanized. The prairies that surrounded his shack and upon which Jon had been born were still very rural in scope and practice. Most of his neighbors had been to one of the bigger cities on numerous occasions and were quite familiar with life there. The Mantlers did not travel. So he looked forward to the road trip to university with real excitement.

Jon and Harvey stayed for the entire setting of the sun, talking and laughing. After consuming a few more drinks, the young men called it a day. They placed the remaining beer back into the bucket and winched it down again into the cool ground. Then they headed to their respective sleeping quarters to regenerate the energy they would need to bring to the worksite at 8:00 a.m.

CHAPTER 16

WILL DENMAN

Sounds of love in our hearts, as our souls relate the signs;
Nature gently tugs at the reins, gently as we cross the line.

As the days rolled by, the tearing down of the shack, which Jon had estimated would take a month to complete, was well ahead of schedule. So it was a fine time for Harvey and Jon to take the journey to the university and seek out accommodations. Harvey's Barracuda was still in the repair shop getting a new exhaust system installed, so, to Jon's pleasure, his two-tone Ford would continue to be their mode of transport.

The demolition was going very well due to the following factors. One, it was a rather small building. Two, Jon had all the details planned and organized well in advance. Three, and most effectively, Harvey was a one-man demolition team and an enthusiastic and indefatigable worker, a fine-tuned machine. Often, Jon would lay out the plan for the day, and Harvey would have it done before lunchtime. Harvey was not burdened by thinking about what to do; he just did, and he did now.

This particular Tuesday in July was a rainy day and, therefore, not a good day to work on the shack. The roof had been totally removed, so there was no productive way to work in the rainy weather. So Jon sent Harvey home and asked him to come back only if the sun began to shine. It was a summer thundershower and difficult to predict what would come next.

In the meantime, Jon planned to go to the garage to take inventory of the wood that he had already sold and try to determine what he currently had ready to offer the public in his next newspaper advertisement. The used-wood sales to date had been terrific, and there seemed to be a solid demand for the rest of the wood that he was salvaging and storing.

As Jon sat in his one-ton watching the rain and preparing to drive around the block to the garage, a big white Cadillac pulled up and parked in front of him. Through the soft, steady drizzle, Jon could see an elderly man sitting in the driver's seat, studiously looking out through the wet window at what remained of the shack. Jon delayed his departure to wait and see what this man would do next. The man noticed Jon sitting in his truck, and despite the rain, exited his car to approach him. Jon rolled down his window.

"Hello, I'm looking for John Mantler's place. I was told he had passed away but that his son still lived around here."

"That's all true. And I'm Jon, his son."

"I'm very pleased to meet you, son. I'm Will Denman, and I knew your dad many years ago."

"Wow, that's interesting, but hey, you're getting wet, why not jump into the truck?"

"Sure." Will quickly passed around the front of the one-ton and entered from the passenger side. Inside, he extended a greeting hand. "Pleasure to meet you, Jon."

"You too, Bill."

"It's Will," the man corrected.

"Oh, I'm sorry. Got it. I really don't know anybody who knew my dad. It's kinda weird."

"I suppose that's true," confirmed Will. "I only knew him for a few years, during our war years, and, well, he was really something. I'm so sorry that he has passed. It's really thanks to him that I can sit here today."

Jon remained silent. He was confused and trying to think of something to say, but mercifully, the man continued to speak.

"I was so sorry. I always intended to find John and connect again, but until I saw the wood for sale advert in the Herald, I didn't know where he lived. And I didn't know until a few minutes ago, when I asked for directions at the store back there, that he had passed on. I'm so sorry, son, to hear that."

Jon saw the sincere emotion and the near tears in this stranger's eyes, and it made him inordinately uncomfortable. He didn't know what to say.

"I don't think I'd ever have survived those years in France without him. Not a chance! Your father took care of us, son."

It seemed like the man forgot Jon was in the car beside him. They both looked straight through the wet windshield as Will continued talking.

"John was a bit older than me, but hell, we were both still pretty much kids, but John, he, he, was way more mature, and bigger, and stronger. Nothing got to him like it did the rest of us. He was the force that kept us alive, our leader, for sure. The one we knew we could depend on when things got too hard to bear."

The rain slowed down. Then the sun came out, and the air changed so abruptly that the windows on the one-ton fogged up from the inside. They both opened their windows at the same time without comment and let the cool, fresh, and fragrant air blow in. It was now one of those rare after-thundershower moments when the rain falls and the sun shines at the same time. It was a bit eerie, but Will didn't seem to notice. He carried on talking.

"There were five of us right from the start who were always together, right from the first training camp. Only three of us came back in the end. Gerry and Cam never got through Caen. Even John couldn't save them there. I was the luckiest of all, I guess…never even got a scratch, even with all the shit we went through. Now it seems like a lifetime ago. Makes me crazy sometimes. Before we shipped out, we actually had a lot of fun trying to act like we knew what we were doing, but we had no idea what was coming at us." Will paused. "Do you know how your dad got hurt?"

Actually, Jon did not, and sensing an opportunity to enter the conversation, he was about to verbalize that when the man carried on and answered for him.

"Probably not, I guess. It was a strange day. We were in a convoy trying to assess the distance between us and the enemy positions near the town where we had established our base. There were about eighteen of us in four vehicles. We were the last in line, just Robbie, your dad, and me. Robbie was driving when we got messed up way too far behind the others. It was late in the afternoon, and the sun was shining low and bright, making it really hard to see. Robbie decided to step on the gas and try to catch up with the rest of the convoy. It wasn't exactly a road we were on; more of an inter-farm trail that suddenly turned into either a soft left or hard right turn. Robbie chose left, and just after that, there was a slope and a ravine in front of us. The actual road was even farther left, but by the time Robbie realized this and turned for it, he hit the side of the slope and it flipped our Jeep. I was on the back and jumped up and left while the Jeep rolled right. Robbie, on the driver's side, did pretty much the same. But your dad didn't have a chance. The Jeep was flipping, and the only place he could go was with it, and then under it, as it rolled over him and down into the ravine."

Will paused, wiped his eyes, and looked at Jon. The sun was in full shine now; the rain had passed, and neither Jon nor the man had any idea what time it was or how much time had passed. It felt like days to Jon, but it was much less than an hour.

"My dad never told me anything about this. He didn't actually talk that much," Jon managed to utter. He was tense and emotional and was now sweating. He was also afraid that the sun would bring Harvey back to the job site, and he wasn't ready for any of that. He wanted to learn more from this stranger.

"I understand that. I've been that same way all my life, just stuffing it all away, trying to leave it somewhere else, kind of ashamed of myself. But for me, eventually, going forward and not backward seemed like the only way to go," Will revealed.

"What happened next?"

"Yeah, well, I saw the Jeep land on its side halfway down the slope and I was sliding down toward it, so I got to my feet and ran to it. I turned off the ignition 'cuz the damn thing was still in gear and running and the wheels were still turning. Kinda crazy, I know, but I didn't think anyone got hurt. The Jeep seemed to be fine, just sitting tilted on its side. I checked it out for a minute or two, and I was trying to figure out if we could get it back on its wheels and moving so we could get the hell out of there. I didn't want us to be stuck, and it was getting late in the day. As I was checking the Jeep, I looked farther down the ravine to the lower road. There were two big German Army trucks parked down there, looking up at us. We weren't much more than three hundred meters away, and within a couple of minutes, they were up on the road above the ravine and on us. In that time, Robbie had come down the slope to get me and tell me that John was hurt and that he couldn't move him. He said, 'He got rolled over by the Jeep. I think his legs are smashed up. He can't get up or walk.'"

"I started to run up the hill to John and got there at about the same time as the Germans got to the top of the ravine. Now I was scared shitless. We had no defense. We were screwed."

"Jeez, that's crazy." Jon was filled with bewilderment. He wanted to cry, but when he looked at Will Denman's sad face, he stopped himself. He felt that he had to be the stronger one in order to help the man with his story.

"I really thought we were done for, and that if we survived this, the best-case scenario was prison camp. But this wasn't a movie, so it didn't play out like people might think. The Germans didn't come in guns a-blazing; they could see that we were no threat. All our shit was strewn between us and the Jeep, and there were about twelve of them and two and a half of us. They sent three people from the truck to speak to us, and the rest stayed on alert at their vehicles. This was when John, lying flat on the ground, took control of the situation. He was on the side slope between Robbie and me, and he began to speak in German to the approaching men. I couldn't understand a damn thing, but it was the craziest thing I ever saw. I went from shitting my pants to smelling like a rose."

At that moment, Harvey sauntered up to the two-tone Ford and greeted his young boss, ready to demolish something. Jon didn't know what to say or do, because he couldn't focus his attention on anything with his head so full of Will's chronicles.

"I think we're just gonna shut it down for today since the wood is still pretty wet. What say you meet me down at the well tonight if it's not raining again?" Jon asked Harvey. "I still gotta meet with this guy some more now, anyway."

"Okay by me. You're the bossman. See you later, Jay!" Harvey turned back down the alley toward his house.

"I hope I'm not taking you away from anything, Jon," Denman

offered.

"Definitely not, sir. I really want to hear about my dad. He never told me any of this. It's like a whole new world to me. Say, do you want to see his grave? I can drive you down there. It's only two minutes from here, on the edge of town." He pointed to the right.

"I'd like that," Will responded. "I should have come to find him years ago. I'm so sorry...I wanted to, but something always got in the way. Time just gets away from us, you know?"

Actually, Jon didn't know this yet.

Jon started up the one-ton Ford, passed by Will's Cadillac, and pulled away from the shack. He turned right at the end of the street and followed the small road about four hundred meters until it ended at the gate of the town cemetery.

This was a place that Jon often walked down to when he needed a change from his regular routine. He used to visit his father's grave and then meander in between an assortment of other deceased townsfolk. It was a sort of connecting thing that he did for himself. Pretty much everyone in this town ended up down here sometime, somewhere down the line, if they didn't move away first.

Jon certainly wanted to know more about what had happened at that ravine in France, but Will seemed to have lost his pace and his place in that tale. So Jon stopped his truck at the gate and decided to prod him.

"Mr. Denman, what happened to you guys after the Jeep rolled and the Germans came up on you?"

"Oh, yes. Well, like I said, your dad was lying on the ground, but he started talking to the Germans as soon as they approached. Robbie and I were surprised that everything was so calm. We just stood there and waited, as we didn't understand a word. Finally, John told us to go down the hill with a couple of the Germans and flip over the Jeep and see if it would still run. The Germans were going to help us, he said. Their leader called for support, and two Germans came with a stretcher and medical equipment to treat John. He was in a lot of pain for sure, but maybe he was still in shock too, I don't know, because he was cool as could be. Robbie and I went down the ravine with five or six Germans, and we pushed the Jeep back on its wheels. We started it up again, and besides a few bends and bruises, it ran pretty fine. Robbie drove it straight up the hill to where John was lying and still talking to the two German commanders."

Jon considered how speaking the same language made such a difference in the way we felt about others.

"Once we got up there, the Germans had John on a stretcher and were splinting his legs. They also gave him medicine for the pain. He looked pretty beat-up, but he was not bleeding or anything. I guess the Jeep went over him pretty quickly and mostly just mangled him into the ground. It seemed to mostly have gotten his hip and legs. Robbie and I still had no clue about what was going to happen, but John had worked it all out with the Germans! It turns out they knew more about what was happening in the war than we did. They told John that we should get in our Jeep and go back to our camp in the village and wait there, because in a day or two, the Germans were going to end the war by surrender. There was no reason for us to be fighting anymore, not them or us. The thing was already done in Berlin, and we were just slow getting the news. So they helped us load John onto the back of the Jeep and sent us on our way. It was the damndest thing. Basically, your dad had saved our asses again. Well, him and the German surrender. When we got back to the camp and told our army unit about this, they didn't believe us at first, but the next day, we got communication from the top that the war was over. Just like that, over! On the day we rolled that Jeep. All that grief for nothing."

Will Denman and Jon Mantler got out of the truck, walked to the far corner of the cemetery, and stared at a lone grave below a small, freshly laid tombstone. It was good that the tombstone was new, thought Jon. He was there just a few weeks ago with Geoffrey Jones to place it. It was minimalistic, respectful, and wholly suited for a man few people knew.

Will said a prayer for his friend and cried for a minute or so. This was both peculiar and distressing for Jon, who had not really cried for his father since that actual day nearly four years ago when he returned to school to find him dead. It seemed so very long ago.

There was a bench near the main cemetery and close to where

they parked the truck. Now that it had turned into a pleasant, sunny day, they sat down beside each other on the bench.

"My dad didn't talk about what happened to him over there. All he told me was to never, ever go to that place. I assumed he meant France," Jon said. "So, I'm happy to meet you and hear these stories."

"Yeah, we were in France, all right, even though for a lot of the war we were in England in the barracks just waiting and dodging bombs. The waiting was hell because we never knew what was going on. I hated it. I can only tell you that your dad was the only reason I didn't kill myself with my own gun over there. Your dad made me believe we'd make it. But then I lost track of him when Robbie and I got sent home first. Your dad was too beat-up to travel right away, even though we knew he was going to eventually be okay. Robbie and I got shipped home, first to England and then on a ship back to Canada. Your dad was still in the hospital back in England, the last I heard. He had a lot of bones to mend before they could move him any farther."

"What did you do when you got back from overseas?"

"Not much for the first year or so. I was pretty lost and a bit of an asshole. I was still young in the head. But then I went to school and studied engineering. It was pretty easy to get good work back then with a university degree. That all went well for me. I worked for a big company for a few years and then went out on my own. I got married and have two grown-up daughters, and that took me far away from those war years. Haven't thought much about it in a long while. I live in university city now, but I come down to the capital city a lot to visit my daughter there."

"What kind of work did you do?" asked Jon.

"Construction, mostly bigger buildings in the city. But I'm not working that much anymore since my wife passed last year," Will replied. "And you, son, what will you do with your life now? Do you have more family in this community? Where are you moving to?"

These were questions Jon Mantler did not often hear and did his best to avoid. It was one of the few subjects that made him feel insecure. He had somewhat of a rehearsed script ready whenever these moments arose, though, and he rolled into that dialogue now. He told Will his mother had passed when he was six, so it was mostly just him and his dad all these years. He chose to use the story that was written in the blue letter because it was quick and easy.

Fundamentally, Jon believed in telling the truth, but in this case, he didn't actually know the truth, so he wasn't telling a lie. Looking at things from this perspective, the blue letter had served its purpose.

Jon explained that he had no other family, only a few really good friends in the village, and that he was already registered at university for the fall to study engineering. He would be moving there in a few weeks. Will Denman was impressed and complimented Jon on his character and his choices.

"Well, I think I should get heading back to the city now," Will said. "But first, maybe I should take a look at some of that old wood you say you have to sell."

"Yes, sir. If you want to see it, I was planning to count up what is ready to sell right now. Anyway, we still have a lot more to do. Most of the walls and the floorboards are still there to tear down."

They drove up to the garage, and Jon showed the remains of John Mantler's life's work to Will.

"The best wood is over here. It's the hardwood from the inside walls," Jon pointed to a stack. "But it's all actually pretty classic stuff. You can't find wood like this anymore. The wood over there on the left wall has already been sold, but all the rest is still for sale."

"Interesting! My son-in-law in the capital city is a pretty big builder, and they do a lot of new house construction. I'm going to see him later tonight. How much are you selling this stuff for?"

"Well, just the going linear rate for hardwood actually, even though it's far better quality than what you'd get from most places."

Jon was not shy as a salesperson. When he knew he was right, he could exude confidence and authority. He did not know this about himself, though, and as a result, his style came off even more honest and professional.

The rest of the conversation was taken up by wood-related details, which Jon was also enthusiastic about. He was proud of his father's wood legacy. It was the root of his existence, his history, and his sense of belonging to something of value. It was a special feeling to meet a friend of his father's and to connect to something from that part of his past.

Will left the village after giving Jon a business card and a promise to return soon with an offer for the wood that he and his son-in-law wanted to buy. Jon returned to the shack to review the next steps in the demolition, feeling pleased with the state of his world.

CHAPTER 17

THE WELL

I remember as a small boy,
when the roads were much shorter.

Harvey Dean was the first to arrive at the well later that evening. He had the chairs already aimed west for the sunset and was on his second beer by the time Jon walked down from Mrs. Butler's house. She was feeding Jon full-time now that the shack was no longer habitable, and Jon didn't feel right eating and running off without attempting to help her with the cleanup and sharing extra chat time. It had truly been a full-throttle day of chatting since Will Denman arrived, but Jon was still keen to sit and talk with Harvey.

"Well-come," Harvey slowly enunciated to Jon once he was within earshot. "How do you think that word came about, Mr. Double J? You think there were just a couple of smart-asses like us sitting beside a well, drinking beer, and it was the closest to a cool greeting they could come up with?"

"Ha-ha, that's pretty clever, Harvard, and probably way better than the real origin of the word."

No one ever called Harvey "Harvard." When his parents discovered the existence of a quite famous university with that same name, they only called him Harvey. This avoided the chuckles that often occurred when the name Harvard Dean was used.

"I see you've been in the well!" Jon sat in the chair and accepted a brown bottle offered by Harvey.

Jon wasn't a beer drinker, but he knew most of his peers considered it an important ritual. It was their way of acting cool and pretending to be grown men. It also often made them a little stupid in the head, which led to a lot of laughing and genuine good fun. Providing beer for one's work crew was an essential aspect of running a jobsite in these parts; it was intended as an after-work bonding and motivating program.

Tonight, it was just Jon and Harvey, but once word got around, a few young men in the village wandered down to the back of Jon's property to hang out and socialize until after the sun went down.

There was no beer parlor, as the older folks called them, in this village, and thus no designated local place for late evening social gatherings. There was only the gas station that closed around 8:00 p.m. or dusk, whichever came last. So during the latter part of the demolition of the shack, the well kind of became the town pub. Jon and Harvey started out with only two lawn chairs and a bucket of beer, but soon about ten more seats and a few fold-out tables appeared.

Jon knew that most people saw him as the kid in the shack. Though he had been outgoing and spent a considerable amount of time outside at school and at community activities, once a label was affixed to your chest, there was no way to shed it. It seemed odd that in his last few days in the village, he was becoming one of the popular kids. All it took to achieve this was to tear down his house and buy beer.

These regular sessions at the well continued for the rest of the summer with pretty much the same five or six regulars plus a wayward guest or two. It became the place to be with friends to tell lies and have some laughs. While the gas station provided a place for the adults to do absolutely nothing, like embellishing tales and pontificating on the events of the day, Jon's well was now furnishing the young folk.

Conversations at the gas station were the same from day to day except when something out of the ordinary took place, like an accident on the highway or a thunderstorm with rain. Daily events were broadcast and editorialized here. When entering, there was a protocol that demanded a certain local savvy. Everyone in the region had a nickname, generally something derogatory or just plain stupid. Still, it was a term of endearment and a mark of acceptance among this exclusively male-dominated collection of misfits. Monikers included Bubbles, Green Bean, Corny, Tiger, Huck, and Tuck. The local banter, in addition to the "shit meter" evaluation system, rendered the gas station an entertainment center. Most conversations regarding a local concluded in the same manner, with slight variations.

"That so and so, he's a good shit, though!" followed by, "Yup, he's a good shit," then onto the next subject.

"So, how goes the war?" was another common term muttered to anyone entering through the door. No answer was required or expected, and there was no specific war being referred to. Only the battle of daily life, of farming in a harsh physical environment under grinding economic circumstances; the fight against the elements and of growing crops. It was the war for survival.

Rainy days were especially rambunctious in the village. Fieldwork was halted, and workers had time off. On these days, the gas station, the local store, and the grain elevators were filled with people from the surrounding area shopping for supplies and generally wasting time socializing. Rain was the leading topic of discussion and was always greeted with enthusiasm. The right combination of sun and rain was the only way to win the war with agriculture.

"Who was that old man you were hanging out with all day?" Harvey asked.

"Ah, he was a friend of my father's from way back. They were in the war together. It was pretty interesting stuff, the stories he told me. And you know what? I think he might buy all of the rest of the wood. He seems wealthy, and his son-in-law owns a construction company in the capital city. They're both going to come back and look at the wood. If they like it, he said they'd probably buy all of it," Jon reported.

This would greatly simplify that portion of the summer project.

Will Denman was the owner of the company that his daughter- and son-in-law operated in the capital city, and he also had a similar business around the university. He became very fond of Jon during his visit to what was left of the Mantler shack. Like almost everyone else, Will thought young Jon Mantler didn't have much to live on and could really use a break. So, even though he didn't come out and say it at the time, he had decided to buy all the remaining wood. It made him feel good doing something to help the son of his deceased friend, plus it was clear to him that the wood was valuable.

"Well, I guess we better get this job done soon so you can cash in big time," Harvey concluded.

The rest of the evening moved along warmly. A few more beers were drunk, letting their imaginations flow wildly as the sun sank and the evening stars sparkled in the sky. Jon, who knew a great deal about everything in theory but very little in practice, was curious about many things that he felt Harvey could enlighten him on. Intriguing things, like girls!

Jon didn't see his life as particularly strange, and he was unaware that others found him complicated. He was remarkably self-confident in almost everything he did; he didn't know any other way to be at this stage of his life. He thought every problem could be solved and anything could be fixed, given the time and equipment required to do so. His exception to this theory was girls.

When he was younger, it was easy to avoid them. His only experience with them was at school. He played on his own or with other boys and hardly acknowledged girls at all. Later in high school, things changed because there was a different expectation. Girls became more playful; they were integrated into classes and events that Jon could not totally avoid. In these situations, he felt awkward and found it difficult to communicate. Luckily for him, the girls in his high school generally hung out in small packs, and he could always find a boy or two on the fringes to shift over to. He became skilled at being alone in a crowd.

This was not a subject Jon had ever taken up with his father. There were discussions that children did not take up with their parents, and for Jon, this was a big one of those. Embarrassed by his lack of knowledge on the subject, he simply chose to let time pass. Privately, he took to researching what he could do to better understand girls. However, both at school and at home, there was a distinct lack of helpful material available.

This was certainly an area where, had his mother stayed, he might have been able to use her help. Instead, he scoured encyclopedias and sales catalogs for pictures and information from which he could learn something more about the female gender. This exercise did not provide him with the breakthrough he so badly needed. It was helpful from an anatomical and biological perspective, but it didn't provide valuable insight into how he should be interacting with females.

There were girls in his school whom he felt aroused by, and he had difficulty adjusting to those feelings. His imagination and personal action gave him powerful satisfaction, but he wanted more than that. He had a strong desire to befriend and spend time in the company of his female classmates. He wished he could be like Harvey, who made the whole boy-girl thing look so easy. Harvey even had a girlfriend.

CHAPTER 18

THE RETURN

No need to conjure or hide what was about;
Then truth changed its color, no longer were we part of each other.

One evening, Jon had to once again lie to Nora. He proclaimed that he had to go with Peter to an electronics fair in Hamburg, and though it was short notice, it was an important opportunity to acquire selected merchandise and meet with new suppliers. He would be back by the end of the week.

Nora thought it a bit peculiar that the usually over-prepared Jon was making last-minute plans; however, she had no reason not to accept his story. A liar he was not. Still, this was far from the only oddity she had detected in the past weeks.

Jon and Enrico landed in Budapest just before noon the next day. On the flight, Enrico briefed Jon about the role he would play. Basically, he was to stick close to Enrico, watch, and be wary. He was there in case something came up where he could provide information based on his dealings with Karl and their altercation with the third man. They traveled on diplomatic status visas, which meant they did not have to apply in advance for entry, but it also meant they would likely be followed and observed by the Hungarian secret police during their time in Budapest.

West-German and Hungarian relations were currently harmonious, especially since Chancellor Helmut Kohl's unusual visit to Budapest in 1984. In many respects, the Hungarians got on better with the FRG than they did with the GDR. Had WWII ended with other geopolitical circumstances, the Hungarians would have much preferred to be aligned with the West Germans rather than the Soviet sphere.

A car from the embassy picked them up from the airport, which, if anyone was watching, would have been the expected procedure. Officially, Enrico Siemenz was in human resources and in charge of transfers and placements of personnel at West German consulates and embassies throughout Europe and northern Africa. Jon would disguise himself as Enrico's engineering assistant, contracted to work on repairs and upgrades to the embassy properties in Budapest. This was a position that Jon would have been pleased to undertake had it been the truth.

Once inside the embassy, however, their attention was focused on sources at the Hungarian police department and trying to determine what was happening in the Wozneszensky case. Enrico and Jon were keen to know what the third man was wearing when his body was found and if he had a mustache. Should ID photos of Wozneszensky become available in the next few days, it would be advantageous to have Jon nearby.

Before the team could tie up potential loose ends resulting from Jon's meeting on the bridge with Karl Bircher, they had to find the strings leading to those loose ends. After two days of focusing on Igor Wozneszensky, they had gathered a significant amount of information, none of which triggered any concern.

His political positioning indicated nothing that would connect him to Karl or the GDR. There was also no evidence that Wozneszensky was involved in any secret service activity. His government work was in finance and business, largely related to energy and resources. Finding nothing amiss in his workplace, their digging brought them to Wozneszensky's personal life, and here they also found nothing unusual. He married young and divorced many years ago. He had remained single since, but a source in his office revealed to an Enrico operative that he had recently been seen with a lady who worked at a foreign embassy. This was the only thing they had to pursue, so pursue it they did.

By evening, the team had scooped information from the Hungarian police that confirmed the corpse of Wozneszensky did indeed have a mustache. It was also revealed that the body fished out of the swamp adjacent to the Danube was clad in a long brown coat.

Igor Tamas Wozneszensky was Jon's third man.

The Hungarian authorities knew nothing about Jon, so Enrico and his team were left to wonder what direction their investigation would take. What cause of death was being sought? Would there be any indication of foul play? Meanwhile, the team focused on the woman Wozneszensky was reportedly romantically involved with. A click came when an informant revealed she was an employee of the East German Embassy. Officially, the West German Embassy and the East German Embassy did not have good relations. Nonetheless, many of the individuals working at either embassy did have personal connections, so dipping into the general gossip pools would likely yield results of any romantic affairs.

Enrico spent the night sleeping on the sofa of an embassy friend who lived within walking distance. If he was being watched, the Hungarians were less apt to surveil him at her apartment than in a city hotel. They would assume a romantic relationship was taking place and thus be more likely to take the night off. He was not worried about any connection being made between Jon the tourist from November and the Jon he had just brought with him on a diplomatic passport. Still, keeping out of sight made sense, so it was arranged for him to stay at the home of another embassy employee. Jon spent the night in the spare room of Georg Benedict, a Hungarian national who had been working at the West German Embassy for nearly a decade.

Work was progressing rapidly the next morning when Jon arrived at the embassy. Wozneszensky's girlfriend had been identified. She was an East German citizen from Berlin named Elke Potzner, employed in the GDR trade and finance department. Enrico was determined to meet with her himself, thinking she might be their best chance for obtaining more information on the third man, and because this was how Enrico operated. The BND had an agent inside Budapest's GDR Embassy, and he was tasked with keeping an eye on Elke.

Enrico wanted to know what she looked like, what she was wearing, and what her role inside the embassy was. He wanted to know everything she did on this day. More specifically, he wanted to be contacted immediately if she left the building and if she was contacted by anyone, particularly the Hungarian police. If his team had learned from the police that Wozneszensky had a girlfriend, it was highly likely the local police would soon be contacting her.

Conveniently, the two buildings were located less than a kilometer from each other, and by noon, Richard Weger, the inside source at the East German Embassy, had compiled and couriered Enrico a detailed profile of Elke Potzner. The crew was moving fast, but she was not. She stayed inside her office all day, never exited for lunch, and had no visitors. Determined to get to her before the Hungarian authorities, Enrico concocted a plan. The portfolio of the girl he received from Weger included interoffice photographs as well as a note from Weger indicating she was far more attractive in person than the photos revealed. He promised she would be easy to identify. It also included her home address. With this information, Enrico and his team mapped out the most likely routes she would take. The plan was to follow, surveil, and intercept her on her journey home. It would be important to the success of this plan if she were actually walking home alone after work. They also knew that you don't always get what you want. All they could do was try based on the most likely assumptions. They rehearsed and waited through the afternoon for the go sign from Richard Weger.

Jon had nothing to do but wait and watch. He was energized by the buzz of activity taking place around him, but stayed cool. He was patient enough to let matters take their course. As instructed, he stuck close to Enrico in case anything materialized with respect to the bodies, and also because everything revolved around Enrico.

Jon liked him. He reminded Jon a bit of his friend Harvey, with whom he had lost contact over the past few years. Both had a natural ability to seem to attract adventure even when not much was actually happening. Their mere presence made you feel alive and engaged.

The call from Weger came at 5:30 p.m. from a café in the city center. The telephone lines at the West German Embassy were clean and tested every day, but Weger could not trust the East German building. He was confident but could not guarantee that Elke Potzner would be on her way home on foot within the next thirty minutes. He couldn't be sure of the route she would take, but realistically, it could only be one of two variations.

Enrico briefed two team members, Andreas (Andi) Dietrich and Jakob Bertsch, who shortly after headed to their assigned locations in the streets of Budapest. Jon was instructed to stay back at the embassy with Benedict and the rest of the staff.

Dietrich and Bertsch hung around the streets separately, waiting and watching until they saw a woman leave the East German Embassy building. From the photos and description, this was unmistakably Elke Potzner. They had prepared for two route options. She turned left onto the main street. About four hundred meters farther, there was a restaurant, and this was where Enrico stepped out in front of her to take his high-risk shot. Obviously, he startled her, but he spoke in a calm and distinct German. He strategically called her by her first name to confuse and shock her.

"Elke, I know you don't know me, but I have some important information for you. You're not in danger. I'm German; I'm not Hungarian. Please believe me that I'm here to help you, and I will not hurt you."

The young lady stopped in a state of bewilderment but did not panic, surprisingly remaining calm.

"You don't need to say anything, but if you'd please come inside this restaurant with me, I'd like to explain everything to you in there. Please know that you're safe." Enrico opened the door accommodatingly, and his gambling paid off when she hesitantly yet willingly entered the restaurant.

Just as Jon had learned two days earlier, Enrico could be extremely convincing. He led her to a table and assisted with her chair.

"You're West German," she said before Enrico took his seat.

At least this made it clear to him she was paying attention. He also noticed that Weger had been absolutely accurate in his assessment: This was a strikingly attractive woman.

"Yes, I'll explain to you why I'm here. I don't know if you're aware that two days ago, your friend Igor Wozneszensky was found dead in a riverbed south of the city. I'm very sorry to have to say this." Enrico noted to himself that Elke did not seem shocked or surprised to hear this news. "He had been working with us on some projects," he added, trying to draw a link. There was no reaction from her side of the table.

A waitress arrived at the table, and Enrico asked Elke what she would like to order. She opted for black tea, and he went with the same to cause the waitress to depart quickly. He had lied about Wozneszensky working for him to make a stronger case for approaching her so abruptly.

Up to this point, he had no idea if that tactic was working.

"I work at the West German Embassy," he said, lying again. "I understand that you were a close friend of Igor and that it must have been hard for you during these many weeks he has been missing."

He could feel the desperation in his statement and knew he was laying it on too thick; these last words dripped off his tongue. He feared running out of moves, and she was not giving him anything to play with. So he stopped speaking and let a little silence hang in the air.

"I was not a friend of Igor Wozneszensky," Elke said quietly but firmly. "In fact, I rather despised him."

This revelation was not at all what Enrico was expecting, and it threw him off-balance for a second. Luckily, the waitress came to deliver the tea, giving him extra time to think.

"Well, I didn't know him personally. I'm just trying to determine what might have happened to him so that I can bring this case to a conclusion." Enrico hoped he could draw her out, but she was being very hard to read. He was getting nowhere and feared losing her entirely, so without giving it much thought, he fired off a wild card. "Have you ever met a Karl Bircher?"

He looked intently at her and saw her close her eyes briefly, then she tightened her face. She didn't need to speak; Enrico immediately knew the answer. It turned out that this question wasn't as wild as he thought. Enrico had been mulling over this connection since he had read that Elke was from Berlin. There had to be a link between Karl and the third man, and in the absence of any other information, it was most likely Elke. When there was nothing else to take, Enrico paused and grabbed onto the something that he had.

"I said I was here to help you, and I promise you that I will," was exactly what he needed to say in that next moment.

He could see she was rattled and afraid now, and he could almost see a tear as she opened her eyes again. "Karl was actually working for us, not Igor Wozneszensky, but I assume you already know that," he said.

"Yes." Elke looked down at her tea as if there was something wrong with it, as another silent moment hung in the room. There were only a few people inside this very big restaurant, and one of them was a member of Enrico's team, who was watching them from a table near the far wall as he drank a coffee and feigned reading a book.

"You knew him from Berlin?" Enrico decided to ask.

"We went to school together. You said you had some information."

"I do, but do you feel comfortable talking here? I interrupted your day. Is there someplace that you need to be or something you should be doing right now?" Enrico wanted to keep the dialogue going. He liked her and wanted to keep her engaged and committed to the conversation. To do that, he felt he needed to get her approval.

"I was just on my way home, so it's okay. I have a dog, but she'll be fine for a while yet," Elke replied more calmly.

Enrico thought quickly, trying to decide what information he should be sharing with her next. He had only been in Budapest for about twenty-four hours and had already figured out the connection to why the third man was on the bridge. In essence, he cracked the case. He didn't have the precise details, but the big picture was there. He decided to tell her all he could in order to reel her in. She seemed lost, and he sensed he should be saving her from something.

"Okay, then, I want to be honest with you. I came to Budapest just yesterday because we thought there was a connection between Karl's death and the disappearance of Igor Wozneszensky. I work with the West German Ministry of the Interior, and Karl helped us from time to time with information. You may have known that." He paused to check her reaction.

There wasn't one.

"It seemed like too much of a coincidence that Karl and Wozneszensky both went missing around the same time. So we investigated, and we got your name from a source inside the Hungarian police. To be honest, we didn't really know anything about Wozneszensky until we saw his name as missing in some police reports around the same day that Karl's body washed up." Enrico took the risk and launched into the whole story. "But actually, the most important information that I can tell you today is that the whole world is about to change. Hungary is most likely to be the first country that'll turn away from Moscow and open its borders to the West, and it'll be soon. I know this because we're working hard to help make that happen. It's crucial for us that the old hardliners and rightists in Hungary are not given any opening to return to power. Right now, the sentiment of the people here is strong for democratic change, and we're worried that the death of a government official, for example, a Wozneszensky, could be used by the old oligarchs and propagandists to change that sentiment."

It was a lot of information for Elke to process, but Enrico was operating on instinct. He stopped trying to read her expression. He saw she was with him and sensed that he should continue his lecture.

"If Hungary succeeds with some form of independence, then the GDR will soon be forced to open its borders as well. Even a hardliner like Honecker will not survive for long in such a scenario, and that is what we're diligently working toward. You work for the East German Embassy, and I don't know where you stand politically on these issues, but the change is coming for sure."

Elke nodded and grimaced in agreement.

Enrico acknowledged her affirmation. He looked her in the eyes with calm assuredness. "It's not more than a year away, and there's actually nothing that you or I can do about it. We've already been getting some German citizens from the East out to the West through leaks in the Hungarian border to Austria, and that scenario is going to continue to grow. We don't believe the Russians will move tanks in here this time, but we do need to watch out for some local crackpot trying to get control of the Hungarian army."

He basically told her the true story as he knew it. For someone who often had to lie, he loved it when he could tell the truth. The truth sometimes even worked. Elke took it all in with no visible surprise. He realized that she wanted to speak.

"I didn't know that Wozneszensky was dead until you told me today," she said. "I thought he may have defected to the West. He had many connections there. But I'm not surprised that he's dead. He was not a good man and probably had a lot of enemies who wouldn't mind if he were dead. I met him at an international diplomatic function hosted by the Hungarian Embassy about a year ago. My superior wanted me to befriend him to learn about how he was able to do so much trade with Austria. The Hungarians are way ahead of us in this realm. I went out with him twice, but I didn't like him. He was arrogant, spoiled, and boisterous. I told my colleagues there was no way I'd have anything to do with him anymore. But he didn't take the rejection well. He visited me and followed me around. He would turn up unannounced almost wherever I went, even showing up at my apartment at late hours. He acted as if we had a relationship, but we didn't. I'm really not sad that he's gone."

Enrico now knew all he needed to know for the moment about what had happened on that bridge. Wozneszensky had followed Karl that night to confront him about Elke Potzner. Karl obviously visited her on the trip to Budapest before he met with Jon. That explained why he was two days late getting to the bridge. Couldn't really blame him for that, Enrico thought. The rest of the details weren't important to him right now. There was no espionage angle at play; there was no danger perpetrated by the Stasi or the BND. The drama that Jon Mantler stepped into on that Budapest bridge last November was all about a woman.

He brainstormed a way to keep the real story of what happened on the bridge silent forever. This move would not only keep Enrico's network out of this mess, it would protect Jon too. Right now, only two people in Budapest could connect Wozneszensky to Karl and Jon. Both were sitting at this table.

He liked Elke, and once he realized how sad and lost she was, he decided to wind her into his new plan. Sensing that she trusted him too, he felt that he could continue to work on her. It was clearly important to keep her safe and away from the Hungarian police, so he decided to pull out another of his high-risk maneuvers, which, if it worked, could resolve everything. If he took her out of Budapest altogether, then there would be no one in Hungary who could ever share the bridge story with any authorities. This would stop it all.

"Do you think he killed Karl?" Enrico asked.

"It's possible. Or there was some kind of accident involving them both," she answered.

"Have the Hungarian police contacted you? Or what about your own Stasi?"

"The Hungarians asked me about Wozneszensky about a week after he disappeared. I told them I hadn't seen him and never wanted to have anything to do with him. I told them I was not in any relationship with him. They said they heard that I was. I told them that was a lie. They haven't come back since."

"Do you think they might come back to you now that he's dead?"

"Yes," she said.

"What about your people in your embassy? Didn't they investigate Karl's death?"

"Of course, but I couldn't get involved in that. Karl is married, with a daughter back in Berlin. I know them both well and wouldn't do anything to hurt them. I had to keep it secret, and I don't think anyone here knows. But I didn't know back then that Wozneszensky was missing too," Elke replied.

"Karl's death has been ruled an accidental drowning, according to the Hungarian police. Did the GDR agree to that too?"

"That is how it still currently stands," she confirmed.

"You're a German citizen. I could get you out of here safely and quickly if you want. I can take you to Bonn, and with your experience and background, I can give you a job with us. You'll be safe and will not have to deal with any of these authorities ever again. And trust me, in a short time, the borders are going to open and all Germans, East and West, will be free to travel as normal human beings, with equal rights and freedoms."

"I have a dog," was Elke's reply. It was a not-no kind of answer.

"We like dogs where I come from. We'll take her with us for sure. She'll be a free German citizen too. But you don't have to decide now. We can talk again tomorrow about this. I know this is a lot to process in a short time. Do you live alone?" He realized he didn't know.

"Yes."

"Do you feel safe tonight?"

"Yes, I think so."

"Well, do you see that man sitting by the window on the other side of the room? He works with me, and if you don't mind, I'm going to have him keep an eye on your apartment tonight and until you enter your embassy tomorrow morning. His name is Andreas Dietrich. When you walk your dog tonight, he'll be watching you. What is your dog's name?" he asked kindly.

Elke felt a relief she had not felt in a long time. It was as if until this moment she had not realized how unhappy she actually was. The voice and the manner of Enrico's conversation had been therapeutic. No one had ever offered to help her before.

"Lilly. She's a big dog," she declared.

"Lilly will love her new home," Enrico encouraged.

They reorganized themselves and left the restaurant, agreeing to meet again at the same place and time the next day. Enrico thanked her for being so open to his suggestion and reiterated that he would keep his word to help her. He truly liked her and was determined to convince her.

Elke headed out the door, turned left, and walked down the street that presumably would lead to her apartment. Enrico spoke briefly outside the restaurant to his shadow friend, Andreas Dietrich, and instructed him to follow her and keep a protective net around her. Dietrich confirmed he had not sensed any sign that they were being watched by anyone. They did not want her in conversation with the Hungarian police on this night.

Enrico was elated with how things had progressed and was starting to allow himself to believe, more and more, that he could actually pull Elke out of Hungary. If he made that happen, the Mantler-Bircher-Wozneszensky problem would go away for good. For Enrico, this was big. If he plucked her right out of the GDR Embassy in Budapest and landed her at the Interior Ministry in Bonn, it would be a major secret service triumph. The information they would be able to mine from her years of service there would have value.

When he got back to the embassy, it was still early evening. Jon had spent the entire day at the embassy with its secretary, Greta Winkler, and was mostly in the dark over what had transpired. Enrico hastily summoned him, Georg Benedict, and the rest of the team into the kitchen and briefed them on his meeting with Elke. They ate sandwiches and drank beer. Enrico was in a celebratory mood.

But they couldn't waste any time in celebration. On the assumption that Elke would ultimately agree to defect, they created a plan for the hopeful extraction. Enrico thought Monday would be the ideal day to execute it, giving her enough time to prepare herself for such a major change in her life. Also, if the Hungarian police didn't approach her by Friday, it was unlikely they would do so on the weekend when their general staffing was reduced and everyone went into lazy mode. That meant that during the next few days, someone had to constantly keep an eye on her.

Enrico didn't want any Hungarian police interference complicating the situation. For this reason, he assigned two other teammates to relieve Dietrich, whom he needed back at the embassy to help with the plan. If they were going to extract her on Monday, they did not have much time to get her, her luggage, and her dog to and through the border.

There was a border crossing into Austria that Dietrich recently had success with in extracting three East German citizens near Bozsok, so that would be the most logical place to try. It was in a rather remote part of Austria, south of Vienna and northeast of Graz. It was a three-and-a-half-hour drive from Budapest, so they had to figure out how to get there and back. Obviously, they could not take one of their own vehicles or borrow one from the embassy, nor could they rent a car.

Enrico was asking for ideas when Georg Benedict proposed that they steal a truck. Well, to sort of steal a truck. First, they would borrow it, then they would steal it. Benedict was a native Hungarian and had farm friends with access to communal work trucks, which, at this time of year, were not really needed for work. He thought he could borrow one of these trucks, a panel delivery-type truck, from one of the farms, but they should make it look like a theft. Therefore, they could protect the farmworkers from any charges of collaboration in case something went wrong. For example, if they were apprehended by the police, the farmer could report the truck stolen in order to avoid any guilt of involvement. Benedict suggested they fake-steal the truck late Sunday night or early Monday morning and pick Elke up in the city directly after that. It could work, Enrico thought.

CHAPTER 19

HOUSE HUNT

Never let your deal go down;
Always take your money to town.

On the Thursday morning of the long journey to university, Jon was up with the first glimmer of sunlight, which came around 5:00 a.m. at this time of year. He had gassed up his one-ton the night before and checked every level, every belt, every wire and tire to be certain that his mostly blue Ford would respond as required to every request on the upcoming trip. Jon wanted to be ready and packed before his copilot arrived to join him. From the Butler house, he brought his new shoebox and a small bag with overnight clothes and secured them inside the toolbox of his truck.

Jon had owned his one-ton for a few weeks now, but so far, had driven no farther than the little city of Greyton and a few nearby villages. The drive to university would take at least four hours and consist of a number of highway changes, so Jon was happy that Harvey, who knew the route better, would be with him.

A few minutes after 6:00 a.m., Harvey walked out of the alleyway with a satchel coolly flipped over his shoulder and greeted Jon, who was already waiting at the wheel of the one-ton. Harvey opened the passenger door, placed his bag in the extended storage area behind the seat, and slid into the passenger seat. It was early for teenagers, so there was little chatter at the onset.

Jon, who had never been to a big city before, felt like this was a turning point in his life. He slowly turned the two-tone Ford around and headed south on King Street toward the highway. Harvey was half asleep, and neither of the boys spoke until they were rolling well on their way. During the last few weeks, Harvey had set up a number of house-viewing appointments in the city, with the first set for 11:00 a.m., so they would have to make good speed. Jon smiled a little as he listened to the purr of the engine, shifted into high gear, and pressed the pedal closer to the floor.

"You need to navigate, and I promise I'll keep it between the fences," Jon told Harvey.

"Sure thing, J man. We change highways about six times, but basically, it's pretty easy to figure out once you have the big map dialed into your mind. We'll turn right in about sixty kilometers. Wake me up when you get to Balderston. You'll see it written on the grain elevator on the right side."

Jon fixed his eyes on every field and farmyard sprinkled along the highway. Eventually, he succumbed to the sameness of the scenery, and that was when the boys began to converse, joke, and make fun of just about everything they could think of. Hours later, Jon spotted the outline of the city far off in the distance. They had joined a major highway now, one where the direction of traffic was separated by a low swath of grass dividing two lanes of traffic on either side.

This was another first for Jon, and there was now much more traffic than he had ever seen. His first look at a big city was ominous, and he marveled at all the tall buildings that got bigger and bigger on the skyline as they neared.

Driving now demanded a great deal of concentration. There were vehicles of various shapes and sizes everywhere around him. He tried to act cool and not let on that he was nervous. As he drove deeper and deeper into the city, he held onto his self-control by just being himself. He knew all the driving rules and held himself tightly in the lane he needed to stay in to keep with the flow of traffic. Everything else he blocked out.

Harvey called out the directions, and Jon signaled, steered, and shifted as if he knew what he was doing, until soon he did. It didn't leave much time for him to marvel at the enormity of this new (to him) city. With Harvey's continued direction and to Jon's great relief, he parked in front of the first apartment viewing they had scheduled. Then he slid out from behind the wheel and onto the sidewalk. Another test passed in the life of Jon Mantler.

Most of the rest of the day was taken up with house and

apartment viewing appointments, where the young men, led by Harvey, saw, asked about, and were rejected by every landlord they encountered. Jon was frustrated by the process of searching for a place to live, but he enjoyed the act of driving between the locations. Driving in traffic was quite fun; the appointments, not at all. He had no idea what he had actually expected on this mission, but constant rejection was not it.

"Is this really how this all works?" Jon asked as they drove to their next stop.

"Market economics, my friend; too many people and not enough beds, so the owner of the bed can charge more and choose who he wants in the bed."

The entrance was not a pretty sight, but once one made it through the creaking gate and the overgrown shrubs surrounding the fence, it opened up to quite a pleasant front yard. There was a concrete sidewalk that connected to the steps leading up to a half-hidden house. The owner, who was waiting on those steps, became awkward once he saw them come through the gate. He wasn't eager to have young men as renters. Harvey had acted and sounded quite a bit older on the telephone, but now that they were there and standing in the front yard, there was little else the man could do but let them in.

The influx of university students to the city each fall created a high demand for short-term housing. Still, many landlords preferred to rent their houses year-round and not by the month to avoid the in-and-out moves. This Mr. Templeman was definitely one of those landlords.

Harvey and Jon liked the small house and its location. It was old, but inside it had good space and two very large bedrooms. It was more accessible from the back lane and had parking there for more than two vehicles. It reminded Jon of Mrs. Butler's home back in the village.

Harvey, who had more experience with city people, did most of the talking with the owner, and that suited Jon just fine. This was the seventh place the boys looked at in what had become a long and trying day. All the places they viewed had waiting lists. You needed to put your details on that list, then hope that in a few weeks, the owner would select you. The chance of an owner picking Harvey and Jon, two young single guys, instead of older students or female students was extremely slim.

Most apartment owners preferred girls, teachers, or graduate students.

The house was expensive compared to the other accommodations they saw. Templeman knew the market, and he was pressing Harvey on a number of rules and restrictions in a manner that indicated he didn't think these two youngsters could afford the rent. There was also a rather high damage deposit equivalent to three months' rent required, plus a utility fee to be paid in advance. Harvey and Mr. Templeman were negotiating for quite some time. Jon was patient for a long time until he wasn't.

"Do you have a contract here and now for us to see?" Jon suddenly interjected. "We can sign a long-term lease for a minimum of one year right now, and we can pay you in cash all up front for the deposit, the utilities, and the first three months of rent as long as you have a contract that we can conclude today. We'll move in on September first," he added.

Templeman had not spoken to Jon Mantler up to this point. In fact, he hardly acknowledged his presence until this very point. "Well, I have a draft in my briefcase by the front door from the last...but it..."

"Okay, I'll get you the cash," Jon interrupted. "Harvey, you can start looking through that contract," he said as he left the house.

Jon went straight out to the one-ton Ford, opened the lock on his toolbox, and removed the wrapped kit of tools that lay inside, then he retrieved the magnet block from under his driver's seat and pulled up the false floor. From inside his new wooden shoebox, he took out a bag of cash and counted out a sum in excess of the amount that he had just promised to Mr. Templeman. Then he put everything back where it came from, locked the toolbox, and walked through the yard and back into the house.

Mr. Templeman had his briefcase open when Jon entered the living room, and Harvey was still standing. It didn't seem as if any of them had spoken much while Jon was outside, but that didn't matter to Jon. He put the stack of cash on the table and counted out the amount he had promised to Templeman. The homeowner became quite nervous as he searched through his documents trying to come up with a draft of a contract, but it was clear that he was looking more at the cash than the contents of his briefcase. Eventually, he pulled out a copy of the contract he had used for the previous renter of the house, who had moved out only a month ago. The only problem was it still showed the old price he had charged the previous tenant, which was significantly less than the inflated amount he had quoted.

"Prices are going up, guys. Sorry, but that's just the way it is," said Templeman.

"Look, all we need is confirmation that we paid you, and then we can use this contract as the basis for the new contract," Jon said. "We know where you live, and we expect that we can trust you and you can trust us. We'll be the best tenants that you've ever rented to. Now, we need to know that we can move in on September first. We'll pay you the rent on the first of every month after that."

After more back and forth, the three men signed the temporary document. Jon and Harvey shook hands with Templeman, and the deal was done. Templeman eagerly took the cash and seemed pleased with his new renters. A meeting of the minds had been struck, and now Jon and Harvey were co-renters of this house on Eastlake Street, just over a mile from the university campus.

The boys played it cool until they started up the two-tone Ford and pulled on down the street. Harvey was particularly excited and jumpy to start asking questions.

"Geez, J, what are you doing with all that money? Normally, you just write these guys a check. That's what I was going to do. And what's with the year lease? We only need the place until the end of April!"

"I didn't think that he was going to rent to us, man," Jon declared. "And I was getting tired of all this runaround. I need a new place to live pretty soon, and I don't think I'll have anything to come back to in the village come next April. We're tearing down my house, remember?"

It wasn't an argument so much as a clarification of the contrasting self-interests of each one. In truth, Jon had not thought this out beforehand at all. The realization had come all at once, and he had gone with his instinct and determination to resolve an uncomfortable circumstance. He felt that this was the right thing to do, the only thing to do, really; he knew he had to move on. His action today was a big step forward for his self-confidence. These were things he would have to take charge of from now on.

Harvey decided to change the subject. "I'm hungry. How about you? What do you say we discuss this over some food? Then we can head over to Jake and Tom's for the night."

It was early evening now. The day had indeed been long.

"Which way to food, then?" Jon was very comfortable wheeling his truck down the big streets of the city now.

Harvey called out directions, and they drove to his favorite burger joint, where they parked, ordered, and ate. Harvey didn't have a lot of money, and like everyone else back home, up until about an hour ago, he assumed Jon Mantler didn't either. He was feeling stressed about the amount of monthly rent he would have to share with Jon, and at the same time, he wanted to be sure Jon knew that he was going to be good for the money and pay his share. It was the "stand tall" way people were expected to be in their community. You weren't supposed to owe anyone anything.

"I'll write you a check as soon as we get back," Harvey vowed.

"No check. Cash only. But it's okay, you can pay me starting in September once you have all your money from the summer. You're aware that I'll owe you more money for the deconstruction work, aren't you? We'll sit down and calculate it out. It'll all work out fine. Also, that house is pretty big. It has an upstairs and a half-finished basement, so we can bring one or two more guys in after September, and that'll cut each of our costs by quite a bit. We should be celebrating. We made a good deal here."

"Yeah, I guess so. We'd probably be going home tomorrow with no digs at all if we hadn't gotten that place. How did you know he was going to go for the cash?"

"Everybody goes for the cash," Jon proclaimed.

"You're becoming a very interesting dude, Mr. Double J. How do you like this big burger? Didn't I tell you they're the best?"

Jon enjoyed the burger. It was unlike anything he had ever eaten. Only on rare occasions in the little city of Greyton had he ever indulged in a similar way, but that was nothing like this big city place, where they were now eating and acting like cool young men. It was new and unique to Jon, but he didn't feel intimidated by it the way he feared he might. He felt invigorated by it all.

The rest of the big city trip was quite unremarkable. They crashed on the floor of two of Harvey's friends from back home who now worked full-time in the city. The next day, they went to the university registrar's office, where they both reviewed and confirmed their program and classes for the fall term. Jon paid all his tuition fees upfront in cash. Harvey showed Jon around the campus and oriented him on student life there.

Later in the afternoon, they aimed the one-ton Ford out of the city and back home. Jon was happy to get home, even though he only had half of a shack waiting for him. He felt grown-up and competent after wheeling his truck problem-free all the way to and from the big city. It was the longest trip he had ever taken and the first night he had ever slept anywhere but in his village. Most importantly, the boys had successfully completed the difficult task of securing accommodations for the fall.

Even though they had arrived late on the previous evening, the two partners were back at the shack demolition site at 8:00 a.m. the next morning. The old shack was a skeleton now. There was still outside wall siding to remove, but essentially all that remained were the frames and the upright bearing walls. They decided to wait on tumbling the roofing frame until all the good wood from the siding was removed intact. Completing the project was now mere days away. More change was coming fast, and Jon Mantler took it in stride.

CHAPTER 20

UNIVERSITY

From alone to the unknown I moved with speed;
And the land of dreams hadn't abandoned me.

Jon loaded the back of his truck with his old bed and a dresser that he had salvaged from the shack, along with a few personal items, then put the truck's fiberglass covering over the back of the storage area. It was the first time he had attached it, and it fit on perfectly. It made the one-ton look much bigger. With the addition of this cover, he could haul things dryly and safely.

Today was September second, the day that he had chosen to leave the village and head off to university. Back when he set that date on his calendar, he hadn't really intended for it to come. It felt sudden and emotional, especially leaving Mrs. Butler, whom he had lived with for most of the past six weeks and lived next door to all his life.

Mrs. Butler had dealt with a lot of loss in her life; it made Jon sad. When he thought about that a bit more, he realized so had he. But he was only eighteen years old, so he never let himself get too deep into that. The deeper thoughts were always there, but they would have to wait.

He needed to make the trip to university alone. His future roommate, Harvey, was still actively working on his mother's farm and wouldn't be heading to university for another two weeks. Most fall classes didn't start until mid-September, but Jon didn't have any reason to stay in the village any longer now that he had completed the demolition and the cleanup of all the wood. He wanted sufficient time to orient himself and prepare for this new life in the city, and he was eager to move into his new house.

The day before, he visited his friend Landry's farm, where they serviced and checked out every piece of Jon's truck one more time to make sure all was ideally functioning. Landry also filled both of Jon's fuel tanks with purple gas to ensure he would not have to stop and fill up at a commercial service station for a long time. Purple gas was a lower cost, because the government levied a lower tax on farm fuel. Legally, Jon was not privileged to this cost reduction, but Landry didn't care a great deal about trivial laws. He simply stuck the nozzle from his big farm tank into Jon's one-ton tanks and each time yelled, "Fill 'er up!"

It was typical of Jon not to leave things to chance, and it was vintage Landry to dispense with laws.

Landry had been a good friend, and Jon was sad that he would not be seeing him very much in the future. It would be some years later that Jon would marvel at how selfishly change operated. He certainly hadn't realized that the moment he said goodbye to his classmates only a few weeks ago, with the standard, "See ya later!" that he would never lay eyes on ninety-eight percent of those friends again. The day you leave school, everything changes.

Riding down the road alone left him with an abundance of time. He thought mostly about what he would do in the big city. As he saw it, there were two big topics to focus on. One was getting the house operating as he felt it should, and the second was reviewing his courses and class schedules. Because of his exceptional grades in his last year of high school, he had been accepted as a direct entry student at the College of Engineering. They accepted only two such students per academic year, and this acceptance came with a one thousand dollar scholarship. His guidance teacher, the young and resourceful Miss Roberts, had done a tremendous job of getting him qualified for scholarships.

Money had never been something Jon thought much about; characteristically, he never spent much money, so there had always been enough of it around to meet his needs. This was a trait he inherited from his father.

Jon didn't do things for money; he did things that made sense. He was wise enough to know his needs were changing, so he tended to his shoebox earnestly.

Driving this road alone also caused him to view the surrounding countryside more intently. It didn't change much throughout the roughly six-hundred-kilometer journey. It was mostly flat farmland as far as his eyes could see, with smatterings of small shrubs, ponds, and trees. There was little traffic on most of the highways he chose, so there was ample opportunity to see how fast the one-ton could go. It had a formidable eight-cylinder engine under the hood, and even with the extra load-bearing suspension, he was awestruck by how smooth the ride was on the freshly paved surfaces.

He had spent most of his driving life on gravel roads with a long trail of dust spewing out behind him, so this was luxurious. The one-ton had become his partner, his trusted companion, connected to his feet and hands with boundless power. Peaceful, easy moments like this one made life worthwhile.

He arrived at the Eastlake Street house in the mid-afternoon and waited patiently for about forty-five minutes until Mr. Templeman arrived at four o'clock. The greeting was amiable, and Jon took possession of the keys to the house. He had never had keys to a house before. The Mantler shack was only ever locked at night with a hook from the inside. No one ever entered the shack uninvited, as far as he knew. What would have been the reason for anyone to enter, anyway? He was warned that things would be different in the city.

On the first night in his new home, Jon adapted to his new surroundings. Templeman had left him a number of papers and instructions, and Jon wrote them all down in a notebook he kept about how life worked in the city. He listed the monthly bills he was told about and given contracts for, and he tried to understand what they all meant. He noticed the banks had placed themselves as intermediaries in virtually everything. It turned out he would have to register with these utility firms in his own name and pay them via bank check. No way, he thought.

When he researched his scholarship programs, he learned that he would need to open a bank account to receive the funds granted to him. Despite his requests, the scholarships would only pay him via check. Apparently, banks here were in control of everything. Banks held your money, collected money for you, and paid out third parties for you, skimming fees every time you made a move. This would have unduly irritated his father.

Jon was reluctant to become the first Mantler to open a personal bank account, so he sought out a post office to cash these checks, as he had been doing back in the village. However, he was informed that this was only possible for small amounts. He tried to cash one of the checks at the bank that issued it, but they wouldn't do it unless he had an account with them. He was annoyed. The banks in this modern world seemed to be able to make up whatever rules suited them, and the general population sheepishly adhered to whatever they proposed. Surely, this would change in the future, he foolishly thought.

His father's friend Will Denman had told Jon to "look him up" when he got to the city. This was a phrase Jon was not familiar with. Will, on behalf of his son-in-law, had indeed purchased the rest of the wood and, in fact, visited the village two more times during the shack's demolition. It had been a most lucrative exchange for Jon and greatly simplified the process of selling off the wood.

Jon liked Will and took him at his word, which was, "If you need anything, just give me a call." Jon didn't have the telephone activated in his house yet, but he did have Will's address and a map. So at noon the next day, he drove across the city to the Denman house. The declared purpose of his visit was to get banking advice. Jon didn't want to enter the banking world…everything his instincts and upbringing told him was that it was a bad idea to become beholden to a bank.

"They pretty much got you by the short and curlies." That was how the folks back in the village would have described it.

Will was true to his word. He was glad to see young Jon again and was not surprised by his drop-by. Helping Jon gave him satisfaction. It was a two-way street, though. Jon couldn't get enough of Will. The stories had given young Jon an insight into his roots and solidified his identity, and he was hungry for more.

It was Sunday, and there was not much for Jon to do, so he agreed to stay for dinner with Will and one of his daughters, who was named Lisa. It gave them a chance to review more stories about John Mantler while Lisa struggled in the kitchen to prepare a roast beef. Will understood Jon's reluctance to become a bank customer, but he assured him that it was the only way to function in today's world. He offered to take Jon to his bank the next day and assist him in opening an account.

"How much do you want to deposit?" Will inquired.

"I don't need to deposit, really. I need to have an account so I can cash some checks."

"Well, that is pretty easily done. We can meet at the bank at ten. That is about as early as they open. It's on Preston Street. I'll write down the address for you."

Jon agreed, and that was that. He adeptly shifted the conversation to his favorite subject, his father.

"Well, we actually spent most of those war years in the south of England, training on equipment and waiting for the day when we'd go across the Channel and into battle. It took years before situations reached the point where we actually went anywhere. There was a lot of lying around and getting bored over there for most of us. But your dad, he was busy all the time, mostly because he spoke German, I guess. There weren't a lot of German speakers at the base we were deployed at, and John was pretty good at the language."

Jon eagerly listened.

"In the two to three years we were there waiting and training, John was gone a lot, and we didn't exactly know where or what he was doing. Usually, he'd get on a big, fat plane with about ten or twelve others, and they'd fly off from our base and head for somewhere in Europe. I asked him a bunch of times what they were doing. They were always gone for many days. Once, it was nearly two months. John never said much about it, just looked tired all the time when they came back. I didn't really know anyone else in that group, so I never got any details. There was no official information ever released about what these flights were or where they went. Most people I knew said they were going behind the lines somewhere, to the Eastern side of the battlefields, connecting with the Russians on the other side of German territory, but no one knew for sure. It would have been pretty risky to be in such a big, slow plane; we all worried about getting shot down. It was hard to hide those big old Hercs in the sky, but they always got back somehow, from somewhere."

"It's so unbelievable to me that he never said much about any of this. I should've asked harder, I guess," Jon reflected.

And it was true; like most young people immersed in their own lives, Jon had not asked a lot about his dad's life. He thought there was plenty of time to learn about his father's past. He never realized that although there was plenty of time for Jon, there was less time left for his father. This made Jon sad.

"Where were they going, and what were they doing on those flights?" he asked.

"After the war, I found out that some of these trips were actually missions orchestrated by the Allies. They'd fly on a far-off northerly route around the actual war zones and meet with the Russians on the other side of the German lines. There was a camp way northeast of Leningrad where the Brits, the Americans, and the French would secretly meet with the Soviets to discuss strategy. The Soviets were holding German prisoners of war there too. And there were also German officers who had defected or been captured and who were determined to help defeat Hitler and the Nazis. Your dad spoke German, and that made him a valuable part of these missions, I assume."

Lisa summoned them to the dinner table.

The remainder of Jon's first week in the city was taken up with more mundane tasks, but he didn't mind. Life in his shack had been full of similar challenges, so he was well prepared for the renovations that he had planned for the Eastlake house.

Jon brought most of his father's tools with him. He intended to alter small portions of the house to suit his individual quirks. He installed simple walls in the basement and prepared a fourth room down there. By the time Harvey arrived, the house they were sharing would be well up and running. It would become a venture as well as an adventure.

Jon left it up to his friend to find the candidates to fill those vacant spaces, because Harvey seemed to know everyone. Consequently, within a few weeks, the house would have two more young, rent-paying lodgers. This greatly reduced the individual monthly costs to the extent that Jon and Harvey could live there quite economically. Harvey was particularly pleased by this. Money was always tight for him; it seemed to flow only outward, and rapidly so.

Jon, against his better judgment and with the assistance of Will, opened a bank account and cashed most of his scholarship checks, the largest portion of which he took with him in cash, and he installed a false wall in the house just inside the door of his bedroom to hide it in. This was where he kept his shoebox whenever he didn't have it locked away in the Ford.

Once Jon knew where everything was on the university campus, he felt a bit more comfortable with his new life. But that didn't last long. His first week in the city was extremely busy, and time seemed to fly by. He had established daily routines that kept him synchronized and balanced as he cleaned and perfected the house. However, as the second week began, he felt tense and rather unwell. Jon became anxious and homesick.

He had never felt anything like this in his previous life. Suddenly, he didn't want to be there. Jon was feeling a different kind of alone, an alone with nothing familiar to console him. He had finished all the work on the house and didn't have anything else to do now. Classes didn't start for another five days, he didn't know anyone in the city except for Will, and with too little to do, he began to detest this new life. He counted down the days until Harvey would arrive.

CHAPTER 21

HOME

My home, home, home, home, home, turned to stone, stone, stone, stone;
I know know know know know, what they show, show, show, show.

Jon decided to buy new clothes. He was anxious about not
knowing how he should dress for his new life. He didn't own many
clothes and had never shopped in an actual clothing store before. All his
clothing was delivered from the Simpson or Eaton's catalogs by box via
the village post office. His mother and later his father had done things
this way, and he continued with that ritual. It was simple: You filled out
the form, paid by money order at the post office, and a week or two later,
your parcel arrived.

His strategy back then was to pay attention to what the coolest of
his classmates were wearing and copy them. Then he would go through
the catalogs to find as near a facsimile of those items and order them.
This worked fine, and he felt comfortable enough within his school
environment, but here at university, he did not feel like he belonged. So
he took his first big steps ever into a department store. It was utterly
stressful, but he managed to purchase the items necessary to look like a
regular college student. He bought a new belt, three new shirts, shoes,
blue jeans, T-shirts, sweaters, socks, and underwear. He paid with a
bundle of cash, and afterward, felt a bit better.

Still, by the first day of classes, for the first time ever, he did not
want to go to school. His shyness filled his head with doubt. He doubted
his decision to enroll in engineering and questioned why he should live in
this city. Everywhere he went, there were people mulling about, and the
traffic noise was blustering. It made it hard for him to breathe. He found
it difficult to sleep at night with the constant swishing and rumbling
noises pressing in on him from outside.

At night, back in the shack, there was only the sound of peace
and quiet. At least that was how he remembered it. The highway that

circled his village had some night traffic, usually a few trucks, but they were far enough away that all you heard was a soothing hum. At night, he would watch the lights of the vehicles proceed through his window and across the ceiling and wall, but he hardly heard a sound.

Jon's first class at the college of engineering building was in a sloped lecture theater. When he entered and took a seat, there were already about two hundred people seated, far more than lived in his village. There were more people here than were packed into the courtroom in Greyton in front of Judge Pendleberry.

He sat in one of the few vacant seats he could find, clutching his bag of books and keeping quiet. There was a pretty girl to his left and a scruffy, long-haired boy-child on his right. Jon smiled nervously at each of them and waited. Soon a tall, middle-aged man came into the theater from the side door and spoke from way down below. He introduced himself and then talked to the crowd about the impact of machines in our world today. He didn't stop talking for the next fifty-five minutes. Then abruptly, he stopped, took his notebook, and left from where he had entered. Jon did not find the lectures uninteresting; however, there was nothing in the information that he did not already know. The point of it all remained a mystery to him.

The rest of the week was much the same, except that the other classes were significantly smaller in number of people. Jon was fine with the impersonal aspect of it all; he valued his independence and was not in a hurry to make new acquaintances. He was enrolled in six classes, and once the last one was over on Friday of his second week, he made an emotional personal decision to load his toolbox and jump in his one-ton Ford to spend the weekend back in his village.

Truthfully, Jon was homesick. Harvey had not arrived in the city yet because his harvest was not completed. He was aware he didn't have a home to go back to in the village, but he was certain Mrs. Butler would take him in for two nights. He made it make sense to him. On Sunday evening, he would return to the city. Besides, he loved driving alone in his one-ton. He also still had a lot of purple Landry gas to burn up. The drive would do him good, he told himself.

Mrs. Butler was surprised and happy to see him when he arrived at about seven in the evening. She cooked for him and was interested in how things were going in the big city. But the rest of his weekend was distinctly less interesting. He hung out at the gas station and the café on Saturday, where he met a lot of his old friends. They laughed and joked about the same mundane nonsense that they had been laughing and joking about for the past five years. Without the shack to go to, though, there was truly no reason for him to be here anymore.

He now understood the wisdom of Geoffrey Jones. Jon walked to the site where his home had been and where they were now preparing the ground to dig the Jones' basement. It was Sunday, not yet noon, when he rolled the Ford out of the village.

It was drizzling rain, and tears rolled down his cheeks as he pushed the road and the kilometers out behind him. He remembered something he had read, probably in an encyclopedia. It said that some cultures believed destruction was necessary for a transition to happen. That was true, he thought; the destruction of the shack had been necessary. In any case, it would be up to him to make it true.

Jon had another four hours of driving and thinking to go. He appreciated what Geoffrey had done for him and vowed to thank him for that at some point. He could feel his past splintering and splattering on the blacktop behind his truck as he pressed the gas pedal away from it. He didn't dare look in the rearview mirror for fear of seeing the remnants. As he drove on, he saw old Jim Butler, Leonard, and his sons, not as they were now, but precisely as they were in the moments when they had helped him survive. Yes, he would try to remember again when it mattered, but for now, he had to leave it behind him on that highway.

He had been thinking often about his father in the last few months while demolishing the shack and while talking to Will Denman. On this drive to his new home, he was ready to feel contentment, acceptance, and unconditional gratitude for old John Mantler. Of course, there were times growing up when young Jon wished his father were more like other fathers in the village, more outgoing, more cool, more active and engaged in the community. None of that mattered to Jon anymore. His relationship with John Sr. was now complete, and he felt only thankful for what his father had given him.

Jon drove the two-tone Ford down the alley and around the back of his city house at about six in the evening. As he parked and shut down the big engine, he slumped his arms on top of the steering wheel and turned his thoughts to his mother.

He had pretty much just hit the pause button on his mother since the age of six. Roxanne was gone in what seemed like a second, and that was about that. Still, he had loved his mother in a way that still gave him shivers and tiny shocks in his arms. Jon had just driven away from most of his important past, but he hadn't moved a meter away from Roxanne.

From this moment on, Jon pretty much knew what to do at university. Over the next weeks and months, he poured himself into his books and began devouring his classes. Harvey arrived a week later, and life in the house on Eastlake became increasingly enjoyable. He started to love school again. His identity issues gradually resolved, except for one big one. Jon still didn't know where his mother had gone or why.

More than that, it bothered him that he didn't know anything else about her. He was still troubled that her departure had not seemed to bother his father a great deal. It was odd how John Mantler had just let things happen. His father seemed to accept her departure in the way he had probably accepted her arrival. Young Jon was the need-to-know type. How and why things happened were important to him, so he researched the life of Roxanne Martin at the university library.

It should not have been an impossible assignment, even though Roxanne originated from a province far away. There were other sister libraries at other universities, and though it was time-consuming, it was feasible to have them carry out specific searches for patrons. It meant sending requests by post and then waiting for an answer weeks down the line.

Jon knew from experience that to actually be dead, there needed to be a death certificate, so he searched for that first. He was not surprised that none could be found for the years listed. This confirmed his skepticism regarding the delivery of the odd blue letter.

He was further puzzled to learn weeks later, through a search of national vital statistics, that there was also no record of a Roxanne Martin in the country within the dates he used. No birth record, no driver's license, no social insurance registration, no library card, nothing that indicated that a Roxanne Martin around her age ever existed.

So who was his mother, he wondered.

Jon was perplexed and disgruntled by these findings. All he could do was put it on his to-do list and investigate these oddities further. In the interim day-to-day, however, he had to live a life. There were so many immediate tasks to carry out. So he tended to what he could while still holding on to his intention to one day find Roxanne Martin.

During his entire time at university, Jon lived in the house on Eastlake owned by Mr. Templeman. Ultimately, he and his landlord formed a solid relationship. Jon increased the rent he paid incrementally each year and paid on time every time. In addition, anything that broke or needed upgrading Jon fixed himself, so Templeman had few maintenance expenses. There were routinely three or four sub-renters living at Jon's Eastlake house and lots of turnover, but Jon quickly learned to effectively manage that.

"Make people feel you," Harvey had once told Jon as they talked about the constant horde of roommates and sub-renters at the house. "Let them know that you care about what they're doing or saying. Beyond that, don't take no shit from anyone."

Jon applied Harvey's concept, and it worked. It was clear to all that Jon was the boss of the place, and even though he was younger than most of his lodgers, his rules were respected. Few problems arose.

Harvey stayed at Eastlake for two more years, but in his fourth year, he married his girlfriend and moved to the other side of the city. They saw a lot less of each other after that; still, their friendship remained solid. Jon was grateful to have it. But Harvey was the only true friend Jon ever had. After he moved, Jon felt all alone again.

CHAPTER 22

ELKE POTZNER

It was in the naked of the night, and on the back side of the wind;
So much danger lurking there.

Elke Potzner was having an emotional evening at home and was being comforted by her loving golden Labrador, Lilly. She was grieving and becoming more encased in a state of unhappiness. She had been in love with Karl Bircher back when they were teenagers in Berlin. But their relationship went off track when they were still in their early twenties.

She couldn't remember exactly why now. She thought they were simply taking a little relationship break, but in that interim, Karl met, impregnated, and married Gudrun, another woman in their general circle of friends.

Elke, who had just begun working in the Trade Department for the state, was dumbfounded and distraught, so when an opportunity came for her to transfer to Budapest, she did.

Karl and Elke kept in contact, however. They became more than friends again when Karl began working for the Stasi in addition to his regular duties as an electrician. This allowed him to visit Budapest whenever he could arrange it.

Karl had always been in love with Elke, but he wasn't willing to break up his marriage. He also had a daughter he loved dearly, so everyone carried on with their lives like most people did.

She was distraught yet thought clearly enough to understand that now, with Karl gone, she should rethink her own survival. Change was plausible. She was an attractive young woman who dressed modestly and was generally understated. She wore little makeup and accessorized with minimalistic jewelry. Her one self-indulgence was her hair. Over the past years, she had ventured into every cut and color change imaginable. She spent more time at the hair salon than anyone in Budapest. Right now, she sported a reddish-brown color with medium shoulder-length waves flowing behind her ear on one side. It was a bit odd but still striking.

It was late in the evening by the time Enrico okayed the truck theft and put the team in motion for the trip to the border. He sensed he should be sharing more of the day's events with Jon and reporting to Peter. He was ready to brag about what he had achieved in just one day in Budapest.

Once most of the team had left for the night, Enrico seated himself adjacent to Jon in two big armchairs in the lounge near the kitchen. He took his time explaining his theory on why Wozneszensky ended up on the bridge that night. He reckoned the man had followed Karl from Elke's house to the bridge, probably with no clear purpose in mind. His actions were likely driven by jealousy, and therefore, one could not apply rationality to them. What Wozneszensky knew about Karl and why he approached the man was unclear, but it most likely had nothing to do with espionage, or so Enrico concluded.

Jon was relieved that Enrico had made such progress, but it didn't resolve the other problems he conjured up in his head. Things were not going well in his business, and his relationship with Nora was being torn apart by his fixation on the Budapest events. Mentally, he remained trapped in Budapest and by the secretive demands of that mission.

Until their move to West Germany, Jon had shared everything with Nora. She knew about his mother leaving, she knew about his father dying, and she knew that Jon lived alone in the shack. This general sense of mystery was part of what attracted her to him in the first place. In recent weeks, however, he had sunk deeper into his hiding place, and she didn't know why. She couldn't help but interpret it as a lack of love. Jon still loved Nora, but he didn't seem to love her enough to fight for her to stay. His inadequacy in their relationship caused him pain that he had never experienced.

But Jon was not thinking about that now. He was thinking about being back on that bridge and whether there was anything else about the third man that could be useful.

Enrico sensed Jon's distress. "Look, what happened on that bridge just happened; there was nothing you could've done about it. You just happened to be there. Remember that! And don't over-interpret it.

We need you with us, Jon." It was the only time Enrico ever called him by his first name.

Jon stayed nearby while Enrico called Peter. It was late and they woke Peter up, but he didn't care.

"We've figured out why the third man was on the bridge, and it was indeed Igor T. Wozneszensky, just as we thought. It also had nothing to do with us or our work, just as we hoped. It turns out it was all just about a woman," Enrico said into the phone. "Turns out sneaky Karl had a girlfriend in Budapest, and Wozneszensky was chasing the same flame. I don't know all the details yet, but I'm pretty certain there is no other link. The fact that Wozneszensky was in government here confuses the issue somewhat, but I think we can handle it and make it all go away for us and for Jon."

"That is a relief and terrific news," Peter replied.

"There are a lot of other things going on here too, but I can't share that with you yet. This could turn out to be really good, though. It has been a hell of a day and a half of work."

The following day came and went without much being siphoned from the Budapest police headquarters. Enrico, who had again spent the night on his friend's sofa to avoid being seen, arrived early at the embassy and prepped his team for Elke's anticipated extraction.

Benedict and Jon entered the embassy just before 8:00 a.m. and waited for Enrico to give them their next tasks. At the East German Embassy, Weger would keep an eye on Elke as she tended through what hopefully would be her next-to-last day of work there. If the Hungarian police were to approach, the expectation was that they would do so through the embassy, but no such visit came. At the end of the day, she left work on schedule and went to the restaurant where Enrico was already waiting for her.

She smiled when he greeted her. It was the first smile he had seen, and it made him feel confident and relaxed. They sat at a different table this time as Enrico wanted to have a better view of the entrance and so Dietrich could station himself in a more strategic position.

"I hope you're well and that you had a good day today," Enrico said.

"It was quite a simple day, very normal," Elke answered.

"I've made all the arrangements for you, if you're in agreement, to come work with us in Bonn. It'll be quite simple to do."

Elke knew that this was a critical moment. She had largely made up her mind on the matter. Still, it was taking longer than she intended to choose and deliver her words. She knew once she uttered them, it would be the point of no return.

"I do have a few little questions."

This was enough for Enrico to inwardly rejoice. He knew he held her in his hands now and that he had to be gentle and patient so as not to drop her.

Elke felt she could trust him, but fear and common sense made her take precautions. She wanted to be certain that she would be employed in the West. The citizenship issue was clear; she knew that an East German was also considered a citizen of West Germany and that it was just a matter of walking into an embassy and proving identification and heritage to automatically become a German citizen. But that was not quite enough for Elke. She felt she should have more concrete proof of work. When she presented this concern to Enrico, he understood and knew exactly what to do.

To totally satisfy Elke's concerns, he suggested that they call the Ministry of the Interior in Bonn together and she could speak directly to the minister himself, or at least his general secretary, to receive confirmation of who Enrico truly was and of her position within the department.

"Let's meet at the Forum Hotel in about thirty minutes. They have a business center there where foreigners can use secure lines out of Hungary to their homelands. I'll connect you directly with my superior, Mr. Hirschmeier, and you can ask anything you want of him and the Ministry. I've explained your work history to him, and he has agreed to give you a minimum two-year contract to work secretarially for us."

So off they went separately on foot to the Forum Hotel. Enrico arrived first and registered to use the business center, where he would alert his boss, the director of the Ministry of the Interior in Bonn, Gerhard Hirschmeier, to the call. Elke joined him a few minutes later.

On the call, Hirschmeier confirmed that she would be given a position in the ministry upon her arrival in Bonn. Once she crossed the border to Austria, she would be met by his staff and taken to the West German Embassy in Vienna, where all further arrangements would be made. "You're a German citizen," he told her. "And we'll welcome you home."

Convinced and committed, Elke was now ready to move west.

All was quiet on the Budapest front this early evening.

Dietrich and Enrico were pleasantly surprised and quite certain that no one was paying any attention to their comings and goings. It was already a different atmosphere in Hungary, even if most citizens didn't realize what was actually happening. The administrative departments that ran the day-to-day activities were confused and in flux. Leadership was in transition with new rules and new people every day. It was unsettling, and as a result, few people bothered to do their jobs at all, assuming they still knew what their jobs were. A wave of Western-style thinking was emerging, but it was ineffective because no one had experience with it.

Still trying to avoid any careless mistakes, Enrico and his staff stuck to established protocols and procedures. He had to keep his team disciplined and avoid triggering local agents to investigate any of their actions. Nothing was allowed to go wrong now.

Monday would be the day of departure, so Elke would have only a few days to pack her life into two suitcases. She was fearful, but deep down, she knew she needed to do this and that she could do this. She knew enough from her own experience at work in the East German Embassy that Enrico's predictions were correct. The world as she knew it was indeed changing, and her role in it needed to change as well. Enrico did his utmost to prepare and educate her on what was going to take place on Monday.

"Did you do anything at work today that could lead one of your colleagues to suspect you will not return to work on Monday?" he had to ask.

"No, I didn't even know myself that I wasn't going to be there Monday," she revealed.

"Good. Is there a way that you can call in to work early Monday morning and tell them you won't be coming in until the afternoon? We should secure some lead time in order to get out of the city."

"I could tell them I'm going to the hairdresser first thing in the morning. I do that sometimes."

"Okay, but then you should actually make a real appointment, say, for ten. Making the appointment is important so it seems legitimate. It's about three to four hours to the border, so if we leave by six or seven in the morning, we can be far enough down the road before anyone will have any reason to suspect you're missing. You need to be ready to leave at six on Monday morning. We want to be at the border before noon. It'll still be dark at six. Either myself or Andreas will be outside your apartment then, about a hundred fifty meters up the street. Two suitcases only, and Lilly," Enrico instructed. "When we see you, come out of your door, we'll come right to you."

For the next hour and a half, Enrico and Elke ate dinner and went through more details relating to her defection from Hungary and the GDR. Enrico kept up the verbal massage and talked about how good her life would be in Bonn. Elke realized she had no more interest in living in Budapest, and after years away from Berlin, no reason to return there either. As the evening continued, she became more content with her decision to leave. The conversation with Enrico helped tremendously. She knew it was her work at the GDR Embassy and her relationship with Karl that had brought her this opportunity, and she was fine with that. It was primarily through Karl that she had some understanding of what life was like in the West. He traveled there often and had confided in her that if he didn't have a wife and daughter in Berlin, he would find a way to move there with her.

She promised to be ready by Monday morning.

"If you need to contact me in case of an emergency, here is a private number in Budapest that you can call and I'll get in touch with you right away," Enrico said. "Otherwise, I'll see you Monday morning. You know that you cannot say goodbye to anyone. Don't take any risks. Remember, you'll be able to contact people again later from West Germany with no risk. You're not going to the moon. Plus, I'm sure travel to and from Hungary will be much easier a year from now. East

Germany too, someday soon."

It was not late when Enrico returned to the embassy to reconvene with his small squad there and work through the extraction plan again and again. Dietrich continued to shadow Elke as they intended to maintain a rotating watch on all activity around her apartment from now until Monday morning. "No risks and no screwups," were Enrico's orders.

Freedom for people like Elke Potzner was at the heart of Enrico's work. For him, true freedom in life was freedom of thought, movement, and expression. Also, he understood that with real freedom comes great responsibility, and he was always up to taking on that responsibility. "Free your mind and your ass will follow," was the motto he was determined to apply to the East German people. He needed her escape to be a success.

Once Dietrich had been replaced on the street and returned to the embassy, they went over the plan another time. Jon retook his position of listening and pondering. He felt responsible and wanted to be more involved; he needed to be of use.

With his calm intellect, Jon was an effective balance to Enrico's impulsive nature. Enrico enjoyed firing ideas at Jon and receiving Jon's astute analysis in return. Enrico now knew why Peter was so confident and protective of Jon Mantler, and he was glad to have brought him on this trip.

First, they laid out the overall plan again, after which they tended to the details of each segment. Then they reviewed each player's role. Georg Benedict, who was Hungarian born and had worked with the West German Embassy longer than anyone in the group, would arrange the fake theft of the truck. Early on Monday, he would bring it to Enrico and Dietrich in the city. Then they would pick up Elke and begin their journey to the Austrian border.

They brought out a number of maps on which they identified telephone stations along the way so they could keep in communication and make periodic contact with the team back at the embassy. Benedict would remain at the embassy throughout the early part of the action, and with the secretary, Greta Winkler, serve as the information conduit in case something went wrong. Meanwhile, Jakob Bertsch would be stationed on the streets near the East German Embassy and in contact with his sources around the Budapest police headquarters to assess activities there. Lastly, there was Weger in the East German Embassy, who would be able to tell just when Elke would be determined missing and what GDR fallout would follow. Everyone would liaise periodically with Benedict and Greta, who would monitor, timeline, and record it all.

They divided the plan into four segments and reviewed the in-depth roles and details once again. The first important part was getting out of the city undetected. Second would be getting to the border within about four hours, while any search for Elke back in Budapest would be monitored and delayed. Third was big: getting Elke through the border and into the safety of the German Interior Ministry authorities waiting on the other side. Last was covering their tracks and getting back to Budapest safely.

They adjourned and scheduled to meet again the next afternoon to work through the script one last time. On Sunday, they would rest and relax and save their energy to carry out the operation the following day.

This was far from the normal routine that went on at this relatively docile embassy, and everyone on the team was excited to be part of it. Most days, the work Enrico's hurried-together team carried out was dull and mundane. It was only in these last tumultuous days that they felt like there was purpose in their assignments. And to think that they unknowingly had Jon to thank for all of that.

The next day, Enrico wanted to brainstorm further about what could go wrong and search for flaws in the planning. Only Andreas Dietrich, Georg Benedict, and Jon were present, and though everything seemed relatively simple and straightforward, Jon, who had been quietly taking in and pondering the plan, had a question.

"I don't think Elke should be carrying two big suitcases with all her personal treasures through this small border checkpoint. If you're presenting her as a West German returning home, she wouldn't have all these belongings with her, let alone a dog. I guess you can spin the dog somehow, but what if they decide to search her luggage, which is realistic, and find souvenirs and pictures of her grandmother in there? Nobody takes this kind of junk with them on a short trip," Jon said.

"That's right. We should only give her one small bag with normal vacation travel stuff and dog treats," Benedict suggested.

"You can take her two big suitcases with you next week when you fly back. As a diplomat, you can take anything you want with you, even women's underwear, and no one will check you," Dietrich told Enrico.

"Yes, I agree; that's a better plan. We can switch that out in the morning after we pick her up. We just need to stop on the way out of the city. Georg, you can meet us in your car at a service stop on the way out, and we'll give you the big suitcases. No one will be around that early in the morning," Enrico decided.

"And what if they don't let her walk through the border? What if you can't get her out as easy as you think? I know you talked a bit about that, but it doesn't seem you're real clear on what to do then," Jon said.

"We do have a plan B for the border crossing in case they don't let her through the controlled gate, but I can't share those details with you. We don't want to confuse and involve everyone with that," Dietrich clarified.

"Andi is right," said Enrico. "Also, maybe we don't get through at all. We can't have this affect everyone here at the embassy. You just carry on as if nothing happened. The problem then is that we have to hide Elke and her dog until we get another chance at it. That'll not be so easy, but that has to be all on us only. I've made arrangements for that in case it happens, but I'm not sharing any of it either. We need to make sure the main plan works. Remember, this embassy knows nothing about Elke Potzner, so the less people actually know, the better. If we don't make it through, then nobody knows anything about Elke Potzner, who she was or where she is. Embassy personnel will be protected under their status as such, so just step away regardless of how you feel. The foreign ministry is aware of what we're doing here, but our people are safer if they know nothing," he added.

Clearly, nervousness was creeping in now that the task was nearing. Everybody was still totally on board, but the difficulty that came from too much thinking was starting to take hold.

Enrico realized he had to push himself into more of a leadership role. They needed to be a tight team to succeed, and they needed to be focused specifically on one plan and not on a series of alternatives. If something went wrong, he didn't want any of the embassy staff to be implicated or face serious consequences. There were limits to how deeply he could involve the embassy and its staff, and he had pretty much stretched that as far as was acceptable. If his plan all went to stink, he could be the only one who went down for it.

Originally, the plan was to give everyone Sunday off so they would be rested and ready for an early Monday start. However, after sensing this tension, he decided to have everyone get together for lunch at the embassy at noon to build morale and have everyone go through their lines one more time before the big performance. Meanwhile, Bertsch, Benedict, and Dietrich would rotate shifts, keeping a watch on Elke's apartment until departure time.

The plan was easy except for one obvious uncertainty. There was no way of knowing if the Hungarian border patrol would let Elke simply walk into Austria, so Enrico had not yet decided whom he should take with him to the border in case things didn't go according to the original plan.

Andreas Dietrich was the only embassy person with experience dealing with border guards, and he had a contact there, so he definitely had to be there. Enrico wanted to have another pair of hands with him for added support in case the border walk didn't happen and they had to improvise. He needed someone able to think on their feet.

Jon very much wanted to be the extra man on this trip. He had been auditioning for a more involved role since he and Enrico had boarded the plane from Frankfurt. One sticking point was that Elke had no idea that Jon knew Karl and that Jon was the one who had thrown his body into the Danube. Enrico didn't want that to get leaked, so he had intended to keep Jon away from Elke. On the other hand, he already had too many embassy personnel involved in his caper, and taking another one of them with him to the border might be more of a risk if anything went wrong.

CHAPTER 23

SNOOKER

It's not what you make, it's what you leave that matters;
The tactic is in the leave.

One day while driving only a few blocks from his Eastlake house, Jon noticed a glass-fronted building with a small sign that read "Pool Hall." It sparked his interest because he had seen only one such establishment before in his life. It caused him to reminisce about a time when he was about five years old. He happily remembered that day because it was the only time that he and his little family had ever traveled anywhere together.

On this particular day, the Butlers had offered to take John and Roxanne with them for what they called a shopping excursion to the little city down the road. The Mantlers never shopped, but on this occasion, five people boarded one of Jim's Nash Ramblers and rolled down the highway to Greyton. Jon never actually knew why Jim Butler owned two Nash Ramblers. It was one of those odd things in life that you never came to understand.

Jon, who was still JJ back then, remembered every segment of this trip because, for him, it was a vast series of firsts. It was the first actual car ride he could remember and the first time he had gone to Greyton. John Sr. rode in the passenger seat next to Jim, and JJ sat between Roxanne and Mrs. Butler in the big back seat. Jon recalled the thrill of seeing so many different things on that day, but especially of spending hours in a pool hall.

Roxanne and Mrs. Butler spent the day together, trampling through the small downtown of Greyton and doing "woman things," as Jim called it. John and Jim spent a short time walking the main street with JJ in tow, but walking wasn't something either of the older men enjoyed or were particularly good at, so they decided to enter the local pool hall. Inside were five big, brown and green velvet-covered tables spread out across a gigantic room. Jim and John walked through to the last open table and looked at long wooden sticks that were attached to the side wall.

"Want to shoot some?" Jim asked John.

"Well, I might be a bit rusty."

It was a good thing JJ was tall for his age, because it allowed his wide eyeballs just enough height to see the multicolored balls lined up in formation at one end of the luxurious table. Jim took a few moments to explain to JJ what the game was called and how it was played.

"All the balls have to go into those side and corner holes. You shoot until you miss," was about all that JJ heard. But he was a smart kid, and as he watched them play, it eventually made sense.

The game was called snooker, and Jim and John played a couple of rounds against each other before two young men came over and started talking. JJ didn't really know what was going on, but soon, the terms of the competition were negotiated, and Jim and John played as partners against the other two. They played for fun and for money. JJ was timid, but he kept his nose as close to the table as he could while still staying out of the way.

The games lasted for hours, but JJ loved watching every bit of it. He welcomed hearing the smack of the balls when they met each other and the *clunk-swoosh* sound that was made when they fell into one of the leather pockets.

Old Jim Butler and crumpled John Mantler didn't look like they should be a challenge for these tall athletic locals, but after taking defeat in the first two matches, they calmly traded shots and gradually pulled even on the scoreboard.

Understanding the details of the game was not a necessity for JJ to become awed by the activity. To get a better view, he stood up on one of the wooden chairs that lined the walls of the big hall. From here, he witnessed, with open jaw, his father transforming from a wounded old man into whatever it was that was knocking ball after ball into the various holes.

As things progressed and the scores continued being tabulated, a crowd of people had gravitated to the table to watch. The room was filled with smoke and smelled awful, which was also something that JJ had never experienced. It was loud and boisterous. Everyone seemed to know everyone else.

JJ understood what was happening in these matches by reading the big sliding numbers on the scoreboard. What he couldn't understand was the cash that old Jim Butler was giving to someone who was standing at the side of the table during a pause in the action. His father was looking tired and took a moment to sit in one of the chairs reserved for the players.

But the rapid action began again, this time with many more people gathered around the table. JJ was the only youngster present, and the crowd let him watch from the top of a wooden box that someone put on top of the chair he had been standing on. From this vantage point, the game was even more mesmerizing.

It wasn't until the ride home that the details were explained to JJ, but even from his perch high up along the side wall, he knew something remarkable was taking place. At the end of the match, John Mantler methodically took control of the table, and whenever his turn came to play, he sank vast numbers of balls in succession. Old Jim didn't seem to put many balls into the holes; he left this job to John, who circled the table, limping and shooting balls until the table was clear of all but the white one as the crowd cheered. After doing this three times in a row, it was suddenly all over. Jim collected a fistful of cash from the man who was standing nearby.

John brought JJ down from his box, and the three of them headed out onto the street to meet Roxanne and Mrs. Butler at a nearby restaurant. This was also the first time JJ had ever eaten at a restaurant. He had a hamburger and chips with ketchup.

"I should learn to play snooker," he said to himself as he drove past the pool hall near his new home on Eastlake.

Throughout the following years at university, Jon functioned in only a few locations: the library, his leased house, his Ford, and occasionally, the snooker parlor. Snooker was all about strategy, and Jon liked that. If you read the table right and played smart, you never actually missed a shot. You had to decide when and how to miss. The "snooker" ensured that you didn't leave an easy shot for your opponent. The strategy and the fact that you could play the game solo made it appealing to Jon, and he quickly became good at it.

What Jon was not good at, and felt thoroughly "snookered" by, was interacting with girls. Around campus, he saw many attractive girls, but he didn't know how to talk to them. He didn't know how to flirt or make small talk. He had seen Harvey do it with ease, but that didn't transfer to him. It was becoming imperative for him to figure it out.

So in the same way that he attended to other must-learn things in his life, he went to the library and studied everything he could dig up on women. He deemed sex to be the most important subject he needed to become an expert at, so that took up a lot of his extra study time. In his high school library, the materials were strictly biological; sex was hidden and forbidden.

If you want to learn what women think, learn what they're reading, he figured. So he read women's magazines. It was a good idea because there was a treasure trove of topics and ideas presented from the women's perspective that Jon had never been aware of.

Through these independent studies, he learned that women were not at all treated equally in society and that corporations and institutions were structured to benefit and cater to men first. He learned about the Women's Liberation Movement and its long fight for equal rights. The women's publications also allowed him to study sex from the woman's perspective. Even though he had no sexual experience, he felt encouraged by what he was learning. He had seen men's magazines like Playboy and Penthouse. They succeeded in getting him aroused but were not nearly as educational as the women's magazines he encountered in the university library. It was the era of sexual revolution, emancipation, and free love. He was in the right place at the right time, and soon, being a student in university began to work out well for him.

Four energetic young men living in a house like the one Jon and Harvey rented from Mr. Templeman attracted a lot of social activity. Soon there were a lot of female students hanging around the house and a lot of parties taking place there. This provided the kind of experiences that Jon needed. Most of these girls were in some way connected to Harvey or one of the other student renters staying at the house, but within a few weeks, everyone became like family. As time went by, Jon learned how to befriend and be accepted within that community.

The women he was now meeting were interesting and concerned about issues like equal rights, feminism, world affairs, and individual freedoms. Jon knew little of the issues they talked about, except for what he had read in the library. The static simplicity of his past life was being uprooted. He thought he understood freedom simply because he had always been free to think and do as he wished. Now he had entered a much bigger world, one where society and politics made the rules. His version of freedom had been a simple freedom to survive, but not at the expense of someone else's freedom to do the same. The definition of freedom in this urban environment where Jon now dwelled seemed to be something quite different. With so many people in such close proximity, personal freedoms had been pressed to conform to societal demands and old traditions.

Jon's first year of university in the big city changed dramatically once he found female friends, or more truthfully, once they found him. Despite being the youngest in the gang that regularly hung around their Eastlake house, he was labeled the most mature and the leader of the house. This role didn't always endear him to his male colleagues, but it did to the girls. By the close of the first semester, he was spending most of his late-evening time with his girlfriends and hardly any time with the guys. He knew he was learning far more from them than he ever could have from his beer-drinking cohorts. Soon his lack of expertise in sex was a thing of the past.

In school, Jon challenged himself by trying to anticipate what the professors were going to present next in his class. When he got it right, it was fun; when he didn't, he was at least learning something more than what was being presented. For the most part, he found the courses interesting and easy. They didn't take up that much of his time, so he spent his extra time in the vast library. This experience was similar to his Compton's encyclopedia days, but with a significant upgrade in material. He loved the fact that he could access just about everything in one building.

Jon was adjusting to this new life. People had told him that the first year was the hardest, and that proved to be true. He also began thinking about the upcoming spring and summer. Harvey would be going back to work on his family's farm and the other two renters would likely be going back home and taking summer jobs, so by the end of April, Jon knew he might very well be alone in the house and thus left with all the costs. He relished the thought of having the house to himself, but not the self-paid part. So Jon did a quick research and determined that far fewer people in the city drove trucks compared to where he had come from. Everyone needed to haul something sometimes, he thought, so why not put the one-ton to work the way he did during the shack demolition?

When the new year hit and it was still very cold outside, he began a marketing campaign. Jon had learned a lot during the months when he masterminded the demolition of his shack. He had been remarkably successful at selling wood simply by putting a series of small ads in the one local and two big city newspapers. Running the ads was quite inexpensive but hugely effective.

Jon decided to apply the same model and strategies to his next venture. He already had a telephone installed in his house, so he would keep that number active and list it in the city's Yellow Pages as A-1 Awesome Trucking. He chose the name so it would appear first in the alphabetical listings, and he used the same name in the ads he ran in the newspapers. University city had three main newspapers, one daily and two weeklies, and Jon had a small repeating ad in each. He began running them three times a week in the daily newspaper and weekly in the others, paying in cash and padding it with a catchy slogan.

"Tall young man with a truck, will haul anything, low hourly rates —call John at A-1 Awesome Trucking!"

He spelled John that way in honor of his dad, but he also thought that there was a subliminal hook to that spelling. He was assuming "honest John" would be inferred, making him look trustworthy to ad readers and potential customers. "Tall" and "young" would send a message of strength and loading power; this, combined with "John" and "truck," would be all people had to remember to call him when they needed something hauled. Whichever hook actually caught on didn't matter in the end because his plan worked. By April, A-1 Awesome

Trucking was in high demand, and Jon was hauling all kinds of items for private citizens throughout the city. It turned out that a lot of people had a lot of something to haul a lot of the time.

Throughout the summer, Jon was busy hauling while he continued to take summer school and night school classes. In the fall and winter, he reduced his trucking hours somewhat and focused on better-paying jobs on the weekends. He earned a lot and collected it all in cash.

The Jon Mantler that most people saw in university city was not the Jon that he himself saw. Jon's self-image was quite contrary to the actual vision that was presented to others. If you didn't know him, your likely first impression would be that this was someone you should want to know. He now looked like a taller, albeit shyer, version of his childhood idol, Harvard Dean.

He could speak skillfully and intelligently on almost any subject, but unlike Harvey, he wouldn't necessarily tell you what you wanted to hear. He didn't have the social experience to enter the superficial rhythm of all that. Jon could copycat the look and characteristics of friends like Harvey, but socially, he was more apt to stay in his shack.

He knew this about himself and that his mind still functioned on a different wavelength, so he tried to avoid social events that would make him uncomfortable. In classes and similar group events, he continued to hang around the edges while appearing present.

Once Jon got used to living in a city, it was easy for him to maneuver his way through the semesters. He ran the house on Eastlake for the whole time he was in university. He continued to play and enjoy the strategy and challenges of snooker. He enjoyed the routines of going to class and running his little trucking business, which became successful to the point where he thought about expanding and getting a second truck and driver. Financially and business-wise it made sense, but Jon's inner wisdom and independence caused him to overrule himself on that point.

Better to do one thing well and be in control of all the aspects of it, he thought. Less people meant less that could go wrong and less potential trouble to have to resolve. It was a similar philosophy to what he had applied to the demolition project a year earlier. Jon was best when there were fewer balls on the table. His real shine came through when things were defined and the game was in progress.

CHAPTER 24

NORA

All the ripples in your waves, like all the ribbons in your hair,
telling tales about the lives we tried to save.

Nora Baker was working in the capital city at the headquarters of the Department of National Defense when Jon Mantler entered the building along with three of his senior colleagues. Jon was in his third week working at TDC, an engineering firm, and in his fourth week of living in the capital.

He was tagging along as a rookie engineer in order to learn the ropes, as his superiors in the department had articulated to him. He wore a new blue suit he had just bought to try to fit into the new corporate world he was recently drafted into. Jon even thought he looked pretty sharp.

The purpose of this visit was for a team of TDC engineers to meet with the DND planning team responsible for managing the renovation and construction of the government-owned properties within its realm. The Department of National Defense was planning an expansion to the headquarters building, and TDC was awarded the contract to carry out the project. It was a big deal.

So far, Jon had nothing to do with this task. He was clearly the youngest on the team and basically along for the ride. The team of four men was ushered into a central conference room. Waiting for them were four other men and Nora Baker. Nora noticed Jon immediately. In particular, she noticed that his suit didn't quite fit his body. She also noticed how he was unlike the other three men. He came in last, looking as if he were entering the room alone, which, in Jon's mind, he was.

Nora was from the east-central portion of the country. She was born to parents who had lived rather privileged lives. Her father, like the fathers before him, had graduated from one of the country's elite universities with a law degree, but he never actually practiced law. Instead, upon graduating law school, he became a political inside operant.

Michael L. Baker worked for the government in power for a few years before he became a diplomat who would take on special government assignments at embassies throughout the world. This caused the Baker family to live for short stints in different countries. It provided an upper-class existence and resulted in Nora having lived most of her life abroad. Nora's mother came from a wealthy background, and she was a renowned author of children's books. Her father was looked upon by business leaders as someone capable of getting things done and by politicians as a person you needed to have on your side. In this part of the country, family connections still meant a lot, and for the Baker family, it delivered opportunity upon opportunity.

Nora was born while the family was living in Sweden, where her father was the legal counsel for the embassy there. Her parents were no longer youngsters when Nora was born. She had a brother who was eight years older. Of course, her brother was also named Michael and was strong-headed like his father. It was expected that Michael, who called himself Mick and wanted to be a rock star, would be the next Baker in the line of lawyers and political influencers. Societal times had changed in the past decade, however, and young Mick rebelled against the male-dominant authoritarian structure that the Baker family functioned in.

A huge wall grew between father and son, which eventually led to Mick entering a world of rock 'n' roll and drugs, leading to his eventual banishment from the family home. This tragic family dynamic resulted in Nora becoming her father's chosen child.

By the time Nora started school, her brother was mostly gone from the house, but the tension remained everywhere. How things had gone so wrong no one remembered, but there was nothing anyone could do about it.

When Nora entered university, she had lived in seven different countries. She rewarded her family by studying political science and business and securing a master's degree in business administration before beginning work with the federal government, where she was assigned to the Department of National Defense. Nora had worked here for a year on the day she met Jon Mantler. Her dedication and the proficient manner with which she managed tasks resulted in her becoming the head administrator of her department within this short time frame.

On the day of their first meeting, there was little opportunity for Nora to converse with Jon. She was managing the agenda and there was no time for her to focus on anything else. Jon had nothing to do but watch, and Nora was by far the best thing to see in this room of stuffed-up men. He was fascinated by the two uniformed military men who acted as if they were in charge of the proceedings but did nothing other than let Nora Baker conduct the conversation and check off the points affecting the project's basic plan.

The men maintained their stern looks to appear knowledgeable about construction, but Jon was certain they had limited knowledge of what was really going on. Clearly, TDC was going to be able to do whatever they desired on this project and probably also its budget. Nora and the bespectacled accountant seated to her right offered their only hope in defending the Department of Defense from the engineers and TDC's billing department.

The meeting was quite short, with no objections or suggestions coming from the generals or the accountant. Nora was able to wrap things up and adjourn within an hour. Once she finally had a chance to relax and take a breath, she tried to make small talk with one of the TDC leaders to get closer to where Jon was standing. She thought the youngest of the delegation had not noticed her at all. But she was very wrong.

While the generals were pursuing the executives near the exit, Nora tried to start a conversation with Jon, but small talk was one of his weakest traits. She came out of the interaction feeling frustrated and invisible, but this made her want to get to know the young man even more. Nora could read and understand spreadsheets, detailed documents, and complicated dissertations, but she could not read people well, and she could not read Jon Mantler at all. Not on this day.

Nora had had many boyfriends in the last few years, most of them during her university days. Physically, she was very attractive to men, and thus, there was no shortage of options for her to pick from. In high school, when hormone-enraged young people interacted and experimented with drugs, alcohol, and sex, Nora stayed outside the fray and did not have even a single relationship. This may have been because she did not live in one place long enough for any significant friendships to develop, or because her fearful, overprotective parents kept her away from most social events.

At university, where she was freer to live her own life, she opened herself to these opportunities and met new people of all persuasions. She learned a lot from these experiences and immersed herself in life outside the restraints imposed by her father and mother. Her encounters with men during this period, however, left her largely dissatisfied. They were boys; they were not men. They were involved in games, not in the pursuit of culture or intellect. The partners she dated were too immature for her to invest in any further.

She resolved to take it slow and remain alone rather than act out of need. She didn't realize that her dedicated, hardworking philosophy and quest for intellect and understanding of what powered the world was a turnoff to the majority of the male university populace. She didn't realize her relationships failed because she was above the level of her paramours.

After that first meeting, Jon was formally assigned to the DND extension and renovation project. A few weeks later, he was visiting the building nearly every day. Initially, he was accompanied by one or two senior engineers on these consultations, but once the details of his work assignment became more clearly defined, he began working there independently.

He remembered Nora Baker, but it never occurred to him that she had an interest in him. Therefore, as was common in the life of Jon Mantler, it would be up to someone else to dictate the basic state of affairs and create a relationship.

Once Nora noticed that Jon was often on the premises, she took care of the next steps. He had needed a security pass to enter the building, which he had, but he didn't have a pass to eat in the cafeteria. This didn't really matter to Jon, but it did to Nora. She promptly secured a cafeteria pass for him. They had lunch together on most days he was at work in the building. That was essentially how they became a couple.

From the outset, their conversations were broad and wide-ranging. Both were in need of an element of intellect included in their flirtation. The lunches expanded to dinners, theater dates, and cultural excursions, while a love grew. Nora was amazed at how naturally it developed, and she was truly happy.

Jon was different from the men she was accustomed to. He was genuinely interested in learning new things and not centered on himself. He didn't know enough about love to know he was in it. But he loved being in her company even more than he wanted to be alone. He planned his days more and more around her than around his own work tasks.

Jon always had a lot of tasks to do. This stemmed from his father's influence and, not unlike his father, he was always busy with something. His father had encouraged him to be a builder, and working with TDC was a move further down this road.

Jon was cultivating a desire to build big buildings. A portion of the DND headquarters project, though not a big building and mostly a renovation, had a new construction addition in the plan that consisted of nearly all glass. He had done his master's thesis on building with glass and, in particular, innovative materials and variations of glass that would allow the construction of taller skyscrapers than those yet built. He wanted to build big and high, not with wood, but with glass.

Nora was the most attractive woman he had ever been around. She was so different from the other girls he knew. Jon had become notably more comfortable with women during his last years at university. He had moved on from the convenient forays with the girls who half-inhabited the Eastlake house in search of more mature city women. As his education and confidence melded, he opened up to new experiences and new relationships. With time, he came to realize he was ready for more serious episodes and for love. Sexually, he thought he was doing all right; he was confident based on what he had learned from his fiery friends back at the house. It was time now to take a shot at love.

So, when, in a few months, Nora suggested that Jon give up the pathetic little room that he had been renting and move into Nora's house, he did so. She had bought a huge house with assistance from her family back when she first attended university in the nation's capital. It was a big house and a big change in lifestyle for him. As far as he could ascertain, he was happy. He had limited knowledge about this type of romance, so it was hard to know what he should be feeling.

It was also Nora's first shot at a serious relationship, but she had a vision of what it should be like. Nora fell in love with the totally honest and curious Jon she had encountered at headquarters. In time, she would learn about the Jon who grew up mostly alone in the Mantler shack. She found his past fascinating and thought she understood it.

Life with Nora was astoundingly different from anything Jon had ever experienced, but he adapted quickly. Luckily, adapting was something he was good at, because in only six months, he had to do it again. Nora was promoted to a new role with the defense department that would assign her to Europe. One of the generals in her sphere was being sent to represent the nation at NATO headquarters in Heidelberg, and Nora was assigned as his lead administrator. She did not want to leave Jon, so she arranged for him to legally become her common-law partner, and in midsummer, they relocated to Europe together. Another change for him that he had not initiated.

The first two years of their time in Europe were ideal. Nora's extensive travel experience and her privileged position allowed them to live well and travel extensively. Jon, being a dependent with an independent mindset, took on projects and tasks that resulted in him developing a variety of business enterprises. Their relationship was terrific until it wasn't. Nora couldn't exactly pinpoint when it all went wrong, but had she thought a bit harder about it, she would have realized that it was shortly after their trip to Budapest.

Nora blamed herself for being so immersed in her own work, and she blamed Jon for not communicating his feelings with her. He seemed to go deeper and deeper into his hiding place, and she didn't know why. She could only interpret this as a lack of love. As a result, she wasn't willing to put in the extra effort required to retrieve him, and she wasn't certain that it was possible anymore. Instead, she decided to give up and end the relationship. In any case, she knew that Jon would not give up; he was not a giver-upper, even in situations where perhaps he should be.

Without consulting Jon, Nora accepted a work transfer back to

Canada. It was a huge promotion, and she would be leaving in three months. It would take Jon much longer than that to dispense with the business interests he had built up in West Germany, so some sort of separation was inevitable.

He thought he still loved her, but under the current circumstances, he wasn't sure of anything. He was hurting a lot and felt like a failure. Once again, change was on its way, a change he thought was caused by his own inadequacy.

It was a classic way for how things end, with love bleeding and everyone in pain, not knowing what happened. Nora channeled herself more intently into her career, while Jon sought the source of the problem. "A temporary separation," was what they officially called it.

CHAPTER 25

EXTRACTION

I stand tall and try to travel through it;
Metal flies all around me.

In the wee hours of Monday morning, Georg Benedict got a ride with a friend to the farm where he had arranged to pick up an old, fat panel van, which was used to transport people and vegetables to the local markets. It was an odd-looking truck-like vehicle, a rare mystery brand, most likely built in Czechoslovakia decades ago. It was a big cream-colored unit with seats for passengers plus an abundance of space for product in the rear. There were two single doors on the passenger side that opened outward, effective for loading people or large objects. There was also a huge hinged loading door at the rear.

If you needed to steal a vehicle, this would be the easiest vehicle on the planet to steal. Why anyone would want to steal such a vehicle was hard to imagine, but easy it would be. It had a standard transmission, so all that was required was to put electricity through the ignition, push it forward with minimal speed, kick it into first gear to turn over the engine, and off you could go. Alternatively, you could adjust the wiring behind the ignition and send an electric spark from the battery to the starter, and that would do the trick as well.

Benedict did none of this, though; he simply took the key from his friend and drove off toward the city. Once he arrived, he took apart the ignition switch so that the ignition could be engaged with a straight penknife. He disconnected and then loosely reattached the wires behind the switch to make it appear it had been tampered with by a thief. Then he drove to meet with Enrico and his crew, who were waiting for him just inside the city in Benedict's own vehicle. They switched vehicles, and then Enrico, Andreas Dietrich, and Jon took control of the panel van.

It was not quite 5:30 a.m. when Elke came out the front door of her apartment, led by Lilly's enthusiastic swagger. Dietrich, Enrico, and

Jon were already there and happy to see her emerge. They were parked about two hundred meters up the street. She walked the dog around a small open space near her apartment. It was still too early for the usual dog walkers to be out, and after Lilly did her duties in the park and sniffed the terrain, they both went back into the building.

"Step one concluded," Dietrich uttered, pleased. "She didn't bail!"

Elke did not have a restful night, but she remained committed to the pursuit of a new life. She dragged her two gigantic suitcases out of her building's entrance at the prescribed time. She had to wait but a minute before the panel van drove up beside her. Enrico greeted her, and the others loaded Lilly and her luggage through the rear door. Seconds later, off they drove.

"Well, here we go. I hope you feel well," Enrico said. "Elke, you might remember Andi from the restaurant, and this is Jon Mantler. He works for me in West Germany and will be assisting us today."

Jon turned around to acknowledge her in the back seat and then quickly turned back again. He had been coached to stay silent and play his role as if he were a bodyguard. No one spoke until Enrico again asked if she was rested and feeling all right. Elke lied affirmatively, after which Enrico explained why they were going to have to repack her luggage. He had arranged for her biggest bags to be delivered separately to her in a few days.

The change was visibly upsetting to Elke, but she didn't overreact to the news. Her mental state was a mystery, especially to herself. This entire experience didn't feel real to her, so she was in a daze and simply let the events take her where they would. She had made her choice, and now she had no choice. In general, people get confused about choices, too often assuming that they have them at their disposal. But this is not true the moment a choice is made. With the making of that choice, all others disappear and are no longer available. They probably leave in search of another chooser.

Elke sat exhausted and quiet in the back seat of the van beside Enrico, with Lilly snoozing between them. She was listening but not hearing what Enrico was saying and didn't seem fazed whatsoever by the presence of this extra person, Jon Mantler. Within a few minutes' drive, she obediently placed some of her items into the smaller suitcase Benedict had brought to a parking lot near the highway.

Elke had chosen to trust Enrico, and whatever actions associated with that choice were now being played out. Soon the four of them, plus Lilly, were on the road again, out of the city and heading west. It was still quite dark outside.

"It'll take us a few hours to get to the border crossing, so try to get some rest," Enrico told her. "If you want to sleep a bit, that is fine. I will wake you once we're closer and explain to you how we think things will work."

"I'm fine, Enrico. You can fill me in now."

She was far more nervous and curious than tired. So Enrico, glad that she was keeping him on a first-name basis, described how they were going to get her out of Hungary and into Austria.

First, he gave Elke a number of new documents that had been created for her over the weekend at the West German Embassy. They had declared her previous passport as stolen or lost and issued her a new FRG passport. She was now officially a citizen and resident of West Germany. They would seek to convince the Hungarian border guards that she needed to get back to West Germany via Austria and that there was no reason for her to go through the normal channels with the Hungarian authorities. The West German Embassy would declare they were in contact with the Hungarian authorities back in Budapest, which was something they had prepared but not done earlier in the day. Dietrich was the key to this strategy, because he knew a border guard at this control who had allowed him to pass through three GDR citizens only two weeks ago. He was hopeful he could get this guard to do the same for Elke.

Their story would include that she was getting married soon in West Germany and they needed to expedite her return to Cologne. A car from the West German Embassy in Vienna would be waiting and visible on the other side of the border, thus further pressuring the border guard to look away as Elke and Lilly walked the two-hundred-meter fenced corridor into the Republic of Austria.

This border was not used for pedestrians; it was exclusively used for importing and exporting produce and related items in and out of Hungary. Only trucks with approved documentation were allowed to enter and exit. There were usually only two or three border guards working this portal, checking and compiling copies of the documents to be sent to the Hungarian finance office in Budapest. It was one of the easiest bureaucratic jobs in the world. If Elke and her dog willingly walked across this border and into Austria, why should anyone really care? Why should people be held in a country against their will?

Enrico conceded, however, that they could not guarantee it would be a slam dunk, so if they were refused at the first border crossing, there was a backup plan that Jon was available for. He would provide assistance as required, or so Enrico told Elke.

This was not actually true, as Jon had no idea what plan B was. Enrico did not go into details so as not to confuse or detract from the confidence he was trying to build in everyone, himself included. He now affirmed that if they weren't allowed to walk Elke through the transport truck portal as they intended, there was a second crossing point only two kilometers away that they could access. Dietrich, who had been silent in Elke's presence for the last four days, outlined what the scene would look like at the first crossing point. He seemed more confident than Enrico that all would go well. This helped Elke's demeanor quite a bit. He made it sound doable by saying that he had done it before.

They would stop two or three times at predetermined locations so Lilly could do what Lilly liked to do and Enrico could access a telephone box and stay in communication with Benedict and the team back in Budapest. Also, Elke telephoned her embassy to inform them that she was going to get her hair done and would therefore not be arriving at her workstation until later in the day.

They timed it to arrive at the border just before noon, because there was generally no traffic going through the border during lunch hours. Truck drivers didn't like to miss meals, and they all had their favorite restaurants mapped out on their routes. In Hungary, everybody stopped for lunch between 12 and 2 p.m.. This would be the ideal time to allow a pedestrian to walk through the border unnoticed.

Once they arrived near the crossing gates, Dietrich pulled the panel van near a small forest along a slight hill that was partially hidden but close enough to see down to the border and across to the other side. They changed drivers, and Enrico took the wheel. Dietrich described the roadways and pointed out where everything important was located. From here, they could see two trucks waiting to cross through the border, one coming into Hungary and one waiting to exit. The distance between the two borders looked to be about two hundred meters.

On the near side, they could see two border guards speaking to the driver of a medium-sized transport truck that was waiting for the barrier to open so it could enter Austria. A similar scene was being played out on the Austrian side. Beyond that and parked on a hill near the small gatehouse, was a large black automobile. This visually confirmed that the pickup crew from the embassy in Vienna was in place.

It was dry and relatively mild on this gray February day in this remote region of Hungary. There were no other trucks intending to access the border. The team waited in their panel van until both trucks had cleared the barriers and driven off on their respective routes, then they drove down to the gatehouse and parked. Dietrich exited the vehicle and entered the office to find his border guard acquaintance. Enrico remained at the wheel with Jon at his shotgun side, with Elke and Lilly in the back. There was a high degree of tension, but no one wanted to deal with it.

Jon, who had hardly spoken throughout the entire trip, decided to break the mood. "Looks like a pretty friendly place."

He wasn't being sarcastic. There was nothing imposing or restrictive-looking in or around the gatehouse; it certainly didn't look like any of the crossings he had seen in Berlin. Elke smiled nervously. Lilly was resting her nose on her owner's leg and looked like she was asleep.

Meanwhile, inside the border office, Dietrich was making no progress whatsoever. His contact, whom he expected would be on shift in this time slot, was not there. The on-duty guards informed him that he had switched his work schedule in order to attend his uncle's funeral. With this advantage lost, Dietrich had to start all over with a brand-new set of guards. It was nearly lunchtime, and only one of the two would be remaining at the post, so Dietrich waited until the older guard left and then went back into the office to work one-on-one with the remaining guard. All he had to do was convince the young man to turn away for a few minutes, maybe go to the bathroom, while Elke and Lilly walked the four hundred or so steps to their new life. It could have been that simple, but it wasn't to be. The young man was sympathetic, but he would not bend to persuasion. He was not a rule-breaker.

Dietrich knew that Enrico would be getting impatient waiting in the truck, so he excused himself and went out to speak to him. "It doesn't look good," he said. "My connection has switched his shift and is not here. Maybe if we bring Elke into the office, she can help us convince him, but I'm not sure it'll work."

"Give it a try. I don't speak Hungarian, so I can't help you much," Enrico instructed.

Dietrich went back into the office to speak to the young guard with Elke and Lilly. He tried to show her passport and documents, but they did not interest the young man at all. This was not a pedestrian crossing, so he didn't care about her documents. He did, however, care about Lilly. He played with the dog, possibly as a diversion from having to deal with Dietrich. Finally, after being certain that they were all foreigners and serious about their circumstances and that he most likely could get them out of his domain once and for all, he suggested that they drive two kilometers north to where there was another crossing point. This crossing was used by local farmers who had unofficial cooperative dealings with farmers on the Austrian side. The crossing was occasionally used for machinery and local visits. There were two wire fences and gates, but they were never locked.

"There is rarely anyone up there, especially this time of year. If I were you, I'd just go up there and drive her to the Austrian side. I can look away from that, but I can't let you cross here."

The guard remained sympathetic, offered a viable solution, and this was going to be the end of the line for him. This was the plan B Dietrich and Enrico had discussed, the same option that they had charted out on a map back at the embassy in Budapest. Odd that the young border patrol officer had suggested it to them. It sounded like an easy solution. They left the office and re-entered the panel van.

"Plan B," Dietrich said to Enrico.

Jon waited patiently to see what plan B was. This day so far had been therapeutic for him. He felt free and alive. The past several weeks were burdened with change and uncertainty. The thought of helping Elke, working with Enrico, and being part of a mission was exhilarating. Even though he didn't specifically know what he was supposed to be doing, he felt that he was of use again. He was cool, and he could feel it. Getting Elke to the other side was symbolic now. It would close the case. It might also conclude his dilemma with Budapest.

Enrico knew plan B, and he wired up the panel van and turned the penknife to engage the ignition. They turned around the big rig and maneuvered it onto the main road heading north. "As far as we know, there is a remote crossing up ahead. It has two gates and a no-man's-land in between. As long as no one is watching, we should be able to drive you through to the other side there," Enrico said.

"I'll tend the gate on this side; Jon, you man the one on the other. Get her through and then get back here as quickly as you can," Dietrich chimed in. "The embassy officials know about this plan. Once they see that we didn't get through the main gate, they will drive up to this one."

That all seemed simple enough. Elke had kept nodding as the explanations were given.

"Slam dunk," Jon said, trying to be a positive team player.

Minutes later, Enrico saw a small exit to the left that he took to be the connector road to the remote crossing. It went through a small forest, which jived with the map they had studied back in Budapest. Approximately two hundred meters further, they came to a very large metal barbed-wire fence.

"Come on, Jon," Dietrich said.

They got out to survey the gate. It had wooden gateposts that Jon thought looked like an old 1950s-style cow fence. There was a provision for a padlock to be attached, but there was no lock. Dietrich unhooked the metal clasp that coupled the two posts and then the one attached to the stretched wire gate, and the whole thing fell to the ground. There was a good amount of barbed wire attached to the upper part of the gate, but it conveniently fell as well.

"Too easy," Dietrich uttered with a smile.

The panel van had big old truck tires, so Jon and Dietrich were not worried about the barbs if the wheels had to cross any of them. Nonetheless, they pulled the gate as far to the right side as they could to make plenty of room for the truck to exit.

Jon jumped back into the passenger side. Dietrich stayed at the gatepost to be ready for the return while Enrico hit the gas hard. They drove quickly through the gate and the three hundred meters or so of buffer zone until they reached the gate for Austria. They were fifty meters from freedom for Elke Potzner. She quietly waited and watched as Jon jumped from the vehicle, crossed in front of it, and headed to the gate.

"Padlocked!" he called back to Enrico. Otherwise, the gate looked similar to the one on the Hungarian side. Both were probably built back in the fifties by the same Hungarian Warsaw Pact soldiers, Jon thought.

Enrico kept the engine running and left the vehicle to join Jon at the gate. Jon was good at thinking on his feet, Peter had once told him. This was the time to apply that skill.

He looked north and south, and now all they had to do was get Elke and Lilly and Elke's one bag to the other side. But the fence was about eight feet high with barbed wire tied tight all the way to the ground. Jon looked for weaknesses and flaws, but none were apparent. The gate was meant to open, so how to break the lock?

Jon was back at the van, opening the back two doors to search for something that could be used as leverage. He found a tire iron and a sledgehammer where the spare tire was housed, and he ran to the gate.

"These two posts are wood. We need to see how solid they are. It doesn't look like we can do much with that chain and the lock. I assume we don't have much time to waste," Jon said to Enrico, who was not as calm; he could see freedom through the fence.

He could also see a big black Mercedes parked higher up on the main road on the Austrian side. The forest had ended when they entered the no-man's-land, and they were now quite exposed. If they couldn't get Elke to the other side now, this whole operation would be for nothing.

Jon used the hammer and the tire iron to test the condition of the wooden posts. He wanted to see how deeply they were set into the ground and how weathered they might be. He was primarily looking for rot just below the ground. He dug around the two posts that were the gate's main source of strength.

"It's somewhat rotted, probably not enough, though still worth a shot. When I push on it, it gives a little. The posts are not very thick, so that's good." Jon assumed that Enrico knew what he was talking about, even though he didn't. "You wind that van up to about thirty or forty and you aim your left wheel right here," Jon ordered as he pointed to a specific spot on the left post. "That old truck has a real bumper, heavy chrome, and it's attached to the chassis. It's made for pushing things, not for collapsing in accidents like cars today. Now, hit it!" Jon yelled to Enrico.

Enrico was supposed to be the action guy, but at the moment, he was stunned. It took him a couple of seconds to understand the instruction, then he slid into the panel truck and backed up about fifty meters. He ordered Elke and Lilly out of the van, then geared and revved the truck to high speed. Jon stepped a few meters to the left for safety, and wham!

It almost worked. Jon jumped back in front of the truck to assess the damage. There was only a little damage to the van, as the chrome bumper was a brute. Unfortunately, there was not much damage to the fence post either, but according to Jon, just enough to warrant a second assault. The fence post was bent but not completely broken. It was rotten enough below the surface to have pulled upward and partially out of the ground. Jon kept hitting it with the sledgehammer and prying at the earth below it.

"This time, keep your left wheel inside the post. If you bounce off of it, just keep going. You might take out most of the fence, but you could be through enough, at least far enough to get out on the other side. The wire is going to stretch, and the gate might come down. Can't be totally sure. Take Elke and keep going if you can."

Enrico backed up again. This time, he ordered Elke and her pooch back into the van and had them get down on the floor behind the front seats. Elke was obedient, Lilly less so, but she was certain to stay near Elke regardless of what the game was. Enrico applied much more force this time, now that he understood what was required.

The cream-colored van lifted in the air as the left wheel went over the collapsing fence posts. After being airborne for what seemed to Elke like several minutes, they landed in Austria. Jon had a ringside view of this stunt and watched as wood, metal, and a lot of wire went flying over and under the screeching vehicle.

Once on the other side, Enrico drove on for another one-hundred meters until he saw the small road that led up to the main one, toward the black Mercedes. As he stopped and exited his vehicle, he waved to it. He helped Elke and Lilly out of the van and carried out Elke's bag. This was it. All she needed to do now was walk toward the two men who were coming down the hill to assist them.

Jon studied the damaged fence in detail to determine the best way to get back through it from the Austrian side. The entire wire gate was now ripped out and lay flat on the ground. He carefully pulled part of the largest debris to one side. The rest of the mess, which was most of the upper barbed wire, they could drive over and through.

He looked back over to Austria and saw Enrico hug Elke and then usher her toward the two men. Enrico waved at them and then got back into the idling, grunting beast of a van. Jon ran to him and soon both were in the van, aiming for the gate.

"Straight down the middle of that gap this time," Jon instructed Enrico.

They bounced up and down, but this time they sailed through the rubble that used to be a locked gate with more ease. A minute later, they were through the corridor and crossing the second flattened gate into Hungary.

Dietrich pulled the gate back up behind them and fastened it, trying to disguise any tampering before he jumped back into the van. Enrico turned left and headed farther north, intent on leaving both border crossings behind them as quickly as possible. Jon paused to smile to himself as the roar of the van engine reminded him of a big black Nash Rambler he had once known.

CHAPTER 26

RESOLUTION

Fly now, fly to tomorrow with good hope;
Fly now while the wind is still, and in a conforming sphere.

It was not nearly as easy as they told themselves it would be…not exactly a walk through the meadow. But it was done, and Enrico was elated. Elke was now in the safety of Enrico's German colleagues from the embassy in Vienna.

Jon Mantler was feeling an energy he had not felt in a long time. It came as a relief.

The excitement of success was blooming as the truck lumbered down the road. No one in the car made a sound for what felt like an unusually long period of time. Jon smiled in the silence, waiting for someone else to break the mood and speak. But for the next two kilometers, no one did. It was as if they feared that if someone broke the silence, their spell of good fortune might also break. No one wanted to be responsible for that.

Andreas Dietrich and Georg Benedict were tasked with organizing this last part of the journey. Initially, there was no great expectation that they would be apprehended on their return; however, the planners wanted to be safe. They were aware that the old farm van was not an inconspicuous instrument and would be unable to elude anyone, so a procedural wrinkle had been added to this part of the plan.

"We need to drive about fifteen kilometers, then turn east onto a small roadway. If that odometer works, have a look and tell me when we've gone twelve. There is an old agricultural installation, and we need to get there to wait for Georg. He should be well on his way from Budapest by now," Dietrich said.

"You got it," Enrico confirmed. "Andi, did you see anything or anyone on the roadway while we were busting through that fence? My guess is that the only person watching us would be maybe the young border guard with his field glasses, but he wouldn't be reporting us to anyone. He will just pretend he didn't know anything or see anything. That's his smartest play."

"No, I didn't see anyone," Dietrich answered. "I'd say it only took you guys ten minutes to get through and less than five to get back. It probably felt like more to you, but that's not much time out here, because nothing really ever happens. I didn't see any trucks heading to the border crossing either. It's still lunchtime."

"This old whatever-it-is of a truck has come through like a lion!" said Enrico. "But it must be a bit beat-up looking now. We'll have to figure out a way to fix that. It'll be worth it, though. Guys, we really did a fantastic job today. Excellent work on the gate crash, Jon."

Enrico was on a first-name basis with everyone now. A momentous bond had been built among these three comrades out in a little field between two old countries, between West and East, and in the cold of a war.

"We were really lucky that the first gate wasn't locked," Jon added.

"Yeah, I don't know if we'd have tried to run that gate on the Hungarian side. Too risky. That might have awakened the guards," Enrico said. "We can secretly arrange to repair the Austrian side from Vienna, and the Hungarians won't have to do anything. They don't need to investigate because nothing happened on their side. We need to hope they take the lazy route."

Enrico declared that they were nearing the turnoff to the farm. They drove into a large yard and parked by a toolshed. There was no one on site; only Benedict actually knew where they were.

Benedict, with his local farm knowledge, had arranged for them to store the panel van here. It was a precaution. Enrico first wished they had chosen a location farther from the border, but keeping the farm van on the road too long could trigger an incident. It was better to switch vehicles just in case things went badly, as they almost did.

It was an old Habsburg villa site. They didn't have a key to the main house, but it only took Dietrich a minute to open a window and crawl in, then open the back door. Enrico went straight for the telephone on the wall, and with Dietrich's help, was able to get a call through to Budapest. There were no trackers on these old telephone lines, so there was no need for extra precautions.

Greta, the secretary, and Jakob Bertsch were at the embassy now, waiting for Enrico to call in. They learned there was no alarming news coming out of Budapest yet. Nothing new had been reported by Weger at the East German Embassy, but it was still early in the afternoon on a Monday in Budapest.

Things crawled forward slowly after the weekend. Enrico confirmed that the main mission was complete and a success. They were now waiting at this contact point for Georg Benedict to arrive.

Greta informed Enrico that Benedict was on his way in his uncle's big new automobile. He had left well before noon on the assumption that he would be on site about 3:00 p.m. Most likely, they would not have to wait very long.

Enrico asked Greta to arrange flights for him and Jon to Frankfurt for the following day. There was nothing more Enrico needed to do in Budapest now. The situation was resolved, and it would be best if they were gone from Hungary as soon as possible. With Elke Potzner and Jon Mantler out of the country, no one was ever going to link Igor Wozneszensky to Karl Bircher.

In retrospect, it was beneficial that it took so much longer for Wozneszensky's body to be found. The police would eventually close the file. Enrico now wanted to get back to Bonn as soon as possible. He would be a bit of a hero in his department back home, and he was eager to feel the energy of that and to be there before Elke arrived. She would be at the embassy in Vienna for a few days getting processed and oriented.

The three adventurers were in high spirits as they sat around discussing their current circumstances. Jon was jovial and feeling self-satisfied for the first time in a very long time, especially because he was able to contribute to the cause.

There was still a clean getaway to execute, but Enrico clarified that whatever happened now that Elke had been delivered to the other side wouldn't really matter, because it could be dealt with diplomatically.

The consequences would be minimal and manageable. They weren't particularly worried about having to deal with Hungarian authorities, but avoiding them completely until they were back in the Budapest Embassy was still the best practice.

Benedict arrived nearly on schedule with keys to all the doors. He was driving a big silver sedan. They parked the trusty panel van in one of the sheds near the barns and locked the doors behind it. Surprisingly, the cream-colored vehicle, though scratched and bruised, showed no visible sign of structural damage. Still, Enrico was glad they had decided to stash it away and switch to a less conspicuous sedan for the remainder of the trip. The scratched-up truck would have been much more likely to attract attention on the highway back to Budapest.

Benedict would come up with a plan to get it repaired, cleaned, and returned to the farm in due course. All remained calm at the farmyard, and they didn't waste any time getting back on the road once everything was locked up. Soon they were cruising east on the main road back to the big city. They arrived at the embassy at about 6:00 p.m., tired and hungry.

Enrico made calls to everyone necessary to report what he could about what had happened. He talked to Elke, who was now safely lodged and hosted by the German Embassy staff in Vienna. She was dazed but relieved, and she thanked Enrico for facilitating her escape. He was in a glorious mood.

Jon's mess had been converted into a victory. Enrico vowed to acknowledge that properly once the excitement settled down. For now, those still on the team decided to go to a nearby restaurant for drinks and nourishment.

It was there a few hours later that Jon and Enrico spoke in more depth. When Enrico recapped the day's events, he acknowledged that there were moments where, without the courage and determination of both Jon and Dietrich, he would not have succeeded. "This is how good teams function," he said. "When one is weakened by doubt, the other steps forward and pushes them all through."

Enrico realized that he may not have gotten Elke into Austria without Jon's quick and precise actions at the last border gate. Time would have been a factor if they hadn't been able to get through as quickly as they did. The Hungarian guards could only ignore them for so long before they would have had to take action.

"Jon, I really want to thank you for all your help. I don't think we'd have gotten through that last gate without you." Enrico lifted his beer glass to salute his colleague.

Benedict and Dietrich left for home, leaving only Jon and Enrico at the restaurant.

"Things got pretty tense there at that last fence. Good thing you knew where and how to hit the gate. How do you feel about things now? Now that we know what happened and how things stand here, can you move on from Budapest? We're going to be out of here tomorrow," Enrico said.

"Yes, I'm fine with everything. And thanks for your investigation and for getting to the bottom of how things came about, and who knows what else," Jon answered.

"Ready to leave Budapest tomorrow, then? Probably a long time until you vacation here again," Enrico joked.

"I'm ready to go, all right. Now that I know what happened was an unfortunate situation and an accident and that it's over, I do feel better. I'd kind of like to go back to that bridge one more time, though, if that's all right with you," Jon proposed.

"Sure. We don't fly out until later in the afternoon. We can go there before lunch. I get it. I'd like to see it too, actually."

The next morning, they got Benedict to drive them north along the river and up to the bridge where Jon's life, and consequently the lives of a few others, were forever altered on that rainy night in November. To Jon, it seemed like such a long time ago, even though it had only been about three months. It also still felt like it happened to someone else and not him. It happened to a different Jon Mantler, and this made it easier to feel removed from that reality.

Benedict parked the car on the street adjacent to the bridge and waited while Jon and Enrico left on foot to cross onto the bridge. Jon replayed a vision of jogging up toward the other side. It all looked so different in the bright sunlight. He stopped when he was about one hundred meters from the stairs near the forested side. This was the spot, he reckoned, where he had stopped to look back on that dark night to see Karl in conflict with the third man.

He couldn't remember anything else significant from that moment, so they walked the rest of the way to the stairs. He couldn't actually remember running back along this path either. It wasn't until he looked down the steps to the bottom that his memory kicked in. The third man was tall and wore that long brown coat, and Jon saw him lean over Karl near the bottom of the last set of stairs. In the bright sunlight, he could now see the entire surrounding area of the steps and down to the water below.

It looked totally different from what he had remembered. It didn't look imposing or dangerous at all. He could see how the steps adjoined the gangway that connected the lower portion of the bridge and the forest near the riverbank. The water was much closer to the bridge than he recalled, and he could now clearly see the break in the guardrail where the knee-high chain was attached. There was also an extension ladder connected to the base of the bridge that would allow a person to climb down to a boat if there were one in the water below.

It all made more sense in the light of day. The bridge made sense, but what happened on that Sunday night still didn't.

Nowadays, the old bridge was only used for foot transportation, and they watched people walking across it in both directions. Jon now understood what Enrico had told him about time and space. The moments don't repeat; they just leave, never to return again. Jon recollected that over the centuries, much had taken place on this bridge over this portion of the Danube, many moments in time and probably more than a few deaths that no one would ever know about. He decided to try to live in the next moments, understanding they would come and go with or without him.

"What do you see?" Enrico asked.

"Not too much, actually."

Just as Jon delivered his words, they looked down from the top of the stairs and saw two birds flying below, landing on the guardrail beside the chain. One of the birds skipped from the rail and sat on the base below. The birds chirped and waddled as if they were staking out new territory. Jon and Enrico watched silently as the birds flapped their wings to take off, flying high across the water. Then they followed the river away from the bridge.

"I guess we can go now," Jon said.

They joined Benedict and drove to the airport to leave Budapest. Jon and Enrico were anxious to board their flight. They were ready to get on and move on.

"What now, Jon? Are you going to get back to running your operations in Heidelberg?" Enrico queried. "I think that we can find a new role for you."

"I guess, but things need to get better all the way around. It hasn't been easy these last weeks to hold it all together, but maybe now things will be different."

He hoped.

CHAPTER 27

THE WALL

Walls hanging from the ceiling, closing the door on a greater feeling,
and changing all the cards in the game.

On one cold, gray, late evening in mid-November, Jon received an unusual and highly spirited telephone call from Peter Otto. Over the last several months, the governing bodies and structures of the Eastern European nations were in flux.

One by one, old rules and the leaders were being taken out. The "dominoes," as the media called them, were falling. Hungary, as Enrico had long been predicting, was one of the first countries to liberalize and try to embrace a form of democracy.

"Jon, it's happening. We have to go to Berlin right now! I talked to my brother just a few minutes ago, and the Berlin authorities have scheduled a press conference for tomorrow afternoon. I'm thinking this is it for the Eastern regime. They're going to have to make significant reforms now. With so many people in the streets, the Communist leader Egon Krenz and the rest of the GDR leadership are going to have to do something soon. They can't hold out any longer. Pack some stuff, and I'll pick you up at your place in two hours. We can be there by morning. We have to be there, Jon. This could be it, a once-in-a-lifetime moment." It was more of an order than an invitation.

Jon was rattled by the hurriedness of Peter's words but not surprised by the announcement. For weeks now, thousands of people had been demonstrating in Alexanderplatz, and the number of participants was growing every day. The Soviets had clearly shown that they would not intervene in their satellite nations' affairs. Poland was making decisions internally and installing democratic reforms, and Hungary had completely opened its border with Austria in September. East Germans could now freely leave their country via Hungary, and many of them did. In Berlin, however, they were still being blocked by the wall.

Jon agreed it was a once-in-a-lifetime moment and thus readily consented to travel with Peter to Berlin to witness history in the making. The plight of the divided German people had become a determinant part of his life in these past years. It was the basis of his relationship with Peter, so being in Berlin with him now to feel the winds of change seemed like the right thing to do.

In about two hours, Peter arrived in his large Mercedes. They revved out onto the autobahn, heading north toward Braunschweig, then east to Helmstadt.

It turned out to be quite a ride. They were not the only Germans heading to Berlin to experience history in the making. At the checkpoint near Helmstadt, there was a significant traffic jam. Paperwork had to be checked, and even though it was the middle of the night, many vehicles were backed up, waiting to enter the one-hundred-kilometer, fence-lined corridor known as "the death strip."

Once they were through the checkpoint, it became an impatient free-for-all. There was slow-moving traffic consisting of trucks and Trabants in the right lane that caused many periodic stops, while powerful Western cars, like Mercedes and BMWs, took to the outside lane to race past. Frequent and dangerous death-defying maneuvers were required to overtake and escape the backlog of traffic. It was peculiar to some degree to see Westerners risking their lives to get into East Berlin after thirty years of watching East Berliners risking their lives to get out.

Peter and Jon talked about the past year leading up to this moment and listened to the news on the radio to learn what awaited them in Berlin. Radio reports estimated that four hundred people had gathered on the Eastern side of the wall. It was easy to monitor this from the Western side, because many buildings in West Berlin were built tall and near the wall, allowing people to see down into Alexanderplatz. For decades, the West had been looking into the East just as the East had been surveilling the West from a tall TV tower built by the GDR in the late sixties.

Peter was not totally convinced that the Soviets would not intervene to stop Berlin from acceding entirely to the West. Russia's interpretation of history was that it had won the Second World War by defeating Hitler and taking the capital in 1945. They were the true defeaters of the Nazis and the winners of the war, so it was their right to hold Berlin. In the view of the Russians, the Western Allies had simply waited outside the city and then later came in to divide up the spoils. There was some truth in this. It had been a costly victory for Russia, with an estimated twenty million lives lost in the war with Germany. Berlin would be a hard prize for them to give back to the Germans, thought Peter.

It was still early in the morning when they arrived in Berlin. Despite the rather cold and damp weather, pedestrians were everywhere. Peter knew the city well and, even with the constant flow of people, found his way to a tall building housing a number of West German state offices. This was where the Interior Ministry of the FGR operated in Berlin.

Peter and Jon joined a number of colleagues already at their workstations, eager to see what would transpire. There was little news coming from the other side of the wall. The ministry's regular sources were dry of information. Like everyone else, they had no idea what was going to happen. It was a tense and awkward moment in the long history of the Second World War.

The rest of the day dragged on with only one report from the East stating that there would be a press conference held later, when GDR officials would announce new travel regulations. As no time was given for this conference, Peter and Jon took to sleeping the rest of the morning on two big sofas in the ministry lounge. They were awakened later in the day to view the press conference and witness a confused Günter Schabowski accidentally bring down the Berlin Wall.

The news was inevitable, because for weeks, many citizens had been leaving for the West via Hungary. Few expected it to play out in such a blundering way. Schabowski was reading from a prepared statement that he had not properly previewed and didn't seem to understand. When he was asked by reporters for details about what it meant, he had no actual answer, and so, by default, the wall was soon to be no more.

In the early evening, the staff at the ministry watched again as

Schabowski told the Western media NBC's Tom Brokaw that East Germans could now go through the border. Confusion, already supreme, took on a new energy. There was no official notification or instruction given to the police or the border guards. Confounded citizens gathered on both sides of the wall, sensing that something had happened, but it was unclear what that was. Initially, the checkpoint gates remained armed and manned, and the wall remained stark and intact.

At about eight in the evening, Peter and Jon ventured onto the streets to have dinner. They entered a packed restaurant where all the patrons were engaged in the same intense conversation and asking the same questions. "What is going on? What is going to happen now?"

When they left the restaurant before midnight, the streets were even more packed than before. At the Bornholmer Strasse checkpoint, the crossing guards in charge, after hours of intense pressure from hundreds of East German citizens directly in front of them, panicked and left their posts. Frustrated and receiving no directives from their superiors in the ensuing hours, they had given up.

When one young civilian jokingly walked up to them and asked if he could proceed through the checkpoint, they didn't stop him. This one young man then walked through, and hundreds and eventually thousands followed him. So began one of the biggest parties in world history.

News spread fast. The Bornholmer Strasse gate was just a kilometer north of where Jon and Peter were dining. As they walked back toward the ministry office, they heard cheering, followed by a wave of enthusiasm coming toward them.

"It has happened!" Peter exclaimed. "Finally! I knew it!"

"Unbelievable," Jon replied. "Now what?"

"We go to the wall," said Peter.

Within what seemed like mere minutes, the streets totally filled with people. For the first few hours, it was all Easterners coming to the West. Once it became clear that there were no longer guards on duty, Westerners ventured curiously into East Berlin as well. Soon people were literally climbing the wall. German citizens from either side were meeting on top, sharing beer and Sekt. Drinking on top of the wall was the newest national sport.

The two German states were no longer divided. For the East German authorities, there was now no way back. Once a few are free, all will be free.

Peter and Jon, along with ministry officers who had joined them for dinner, were now at the wall. Like magic, every bar and gasthaus that had just closed down was now open again. If a proprietor thought a guest was from the East, the beer was free. The night was cold, but no one noticed. The city was full and alive.

Jon's group made its way along the wall from the north down to the Brandenburg Gate in about an hour, and within that time, more people continued to stream in. People with hammers and other utensils chiseled away at the structure behind the Brandenburg Gate. Within the hour, the gate was passable on foot, and the Westerners stumbled into the East while the Easterners wandered West.

Eventually, Peter, Jon, and their group ended up in a small bar nearer to where they had begun the evening. It was warmer inside, and they watched the mayhem until the wee hours of the morning from this vantage point. No one was going home anytime soon. It was a cold and windy evening, but it was no longer a cold war.

"No more people getting shot trying to get over that damn thing!" Peter proclaimed.

"Remember, it was just last February they shot and killed that gymnast kid," Jon replied.

"Yeah, Chris Gueffroy, only twenty years old, dead trying to get out. If only he had known today was coming."

"What was it...over one hundred forty people killed trying to escape to the western side of Berlin? This better be over now."

The next day, following two days of very little sleep, Peter and Jon did not move from the safe confines of the ministry office until well past noon. Outside, the party continued unabated. No one in either Berlins was going to work. It was basically an undeclared national holiday. The ministry decided the same and made plans to organize celebratory events in the next few days. The party would continue, but perhaps in a calmer and more structured manner.

Peter's colleagues in Berlin had waited decades for this day to come. There was an understanding in the department that they should be commemorated for their efforts. Jon was again hanging onto the edge, partaking in something that he felt he did not belong to. Aside from Peter, the people in this group did not know about Budapest, and Jon was grateful for it to stay that way. Who he was and why he was there didn't matter to anyone else.

With great speed, the events of the next days became formalized. The Interior Ministry organized dinners, luncheons, and functions designed to reward its Berlin staff for their dedicated and successful work, the goal of which had always been to bring down the wall and reunite the two Germanies. That was quite certain to happen now, as one could witness the wall coming down piece by piece as each hour passed. It was announced that more officials of the department would be arriving from Bonn to join the festivities. Jon was happy to learn that Enrico Siemenz was one of them.

Jon had not seen Enrico since February, when they had flown back from Budapest. They were supposed to meet for an official debrief after their activities there, but it never happened. Life turned hectic for both men, and the months quickly ticked away.

Jon's connection to Enrico had always been through Peter, who kept Jon in the loop about how things were going at the ministry in Bonn. Jon knew Enrico had been promoted to director of the agency at the beginning of the year. The recruitment and extraction of Elke from Hungary had sent him up the ladder.

This pleased Jon. He liked Enrico and appreciated his help in solving the Budapest bridge incident. Peter saw things a bit differently, however, and felt that Enrico should have been much more grateful for Jon's help and the role he played in his recent good fortune. If Jon hadn't tossed two bodies into the Danube the previous November, Enrico wouldn't have had this unique case to grandstand on. Jon didn't think about things that way; he didn't envy the success of others.

The real prize, however, in all these events, was Elke Potzner. It turned out she did have an abundance of valuable information relating to GDR operations in Budapest that the agency was able to mine and exploit. During her many years of moving papers around in the embassy, she had seen a lot of names come across her desk. She was very surprised to learn that so many simple things she knew and thought to be trivial were of interest to her new colleagues in Bonn.

Elke's memory was stellar. The names she knew verified key GDR manipulators, not just in Budapest, but in many other locations within the Soviet bloc. This helped their department focus its resources on the most effective targets.

A lot had happened since Jon and Enrico flew out of Budapest, not the least interesting of which was that Elke and Enrico were now romantically entwined and living together in Bonn. Jon was not surprised when Peter told him. He knew that Enrico was seriously smitten with Elke, and he sensed how impatient he was to get back to Bonn from Budapest to catch up with her again. Jon was happy the way things worked out for both of them; he thought about things like that.

The first event on the Interior Ministry's "Fall of the Wall" celebration was a dinner at a neighborhood gasthaus. Enrico and his entourage, including Elke and Dietrich, had flown in from Bonn in the afternoon and were the first to arrive. Jon and Peter came a bit later, because Peter was on the telephone with his mother and half-brother, Joachim, to arrange a meeting with them the following day. Uncertainty was still abundant throughout the city.

People from the Eastern side who had missed the previous night's events were walking all about on the western side of the wall as if they were tourists. There was still a festival atmosphere about, but inside that, a kind of odd normalcy was evolving. Most of the previous night's revelers eventually returned to their own beds for rest and recovery. As the day progressed, word continued to spread. The borders remained unmanned, and many more people ventured into West Berlin. Peter was monitoring the situation and eager to reunite with his family as soon as it was safe.

CHAPTER 28

REUNIFICATION

Happy in our colors, happy in our skin,
happy with the people, happy from within.

Early the next evening, Jon Mantler, feeling content, sat at a big round table in the corner of a massive beer hall and watched Peter's mother, Helga, as she sat with a shy smile and glistening eyes, watching her two sons laughing and reconnecting. She was certainly happy with the events of the day, albeit a bit reserved.

Jon could see Helga's apprehension. She had long been waiting for a day like today, but for older citizens like her, it also came with reluctance and fear.

Jon looked out the window to the street and saw endless streams of young people stumbling up and down the asphalt, beer and Sekt in hand. For the youth, this was a wonderful game. The future was wide open. History was being made, and the whole city felt it.

Helga Otto was trying not to think too much beyond this day, but she couldn't stop her emotions that caused trembling inside. She understood her sons needed this freedom to connect and build their own lives in a unified land and in the context of other European nations. It was difficult to know what would be coming next to her homeland, as the past few decades had been punishing. Having her two sons together, however, was a tremendous feeling, and it was enough for now.

As for Jon, he was pleased to see this family reunited. It made the difficult instances of the past year almost worthwhile. He tried to imagine what a reunion with his mother might feel like. There must be scary aspects to that as well, he surmised.

What would he actually talk about, he wondered. What would he say after so much time apart? Just as these thoughts weighed down on him, he saw the front doors of the beer hall open and familiar people briskly walk through.

Enrico and his team from Bonn had arrived in the new Berlin. Jon had heard at the ministry that his colleague was on his way, so he was not surprised to see him burst through the door. He was a bit surprised to see Elke and Dietrich walk in behind him, though. There were six of them in all, and they had flown in to celebrate the end of the occupation, as Enrico preferred to call it. A lot had happened since Budapest. The reunion was growing, and Jon was happy to see these friends again.

For the team at the Interior Ministry, this was the day they had been working toward for most of their careers. Jon did not have that level of passion for the cause, but he was happy to have been of use in the outcome. He was not German, he was not nationalistic, and he had not been a Cold War fanatic.

Jon was a need-to-know kind of guy. He still had unresolved questions percolating in his head about the circumstances leading up to the bridge incident. Jon thought Elke could help him. He was uncomfortable around her because he felt responsible for what had happened to Karl. He didn't know Elke very well, but he wanted to know what she knew about him and the bridge.

Months passed since they had all left Budapest, and in all that time, there were no conclusive discussions between Enrico, Peter, and Jon. The Soviet bloc had rapidly continued to disintegrate, keeping Enrico and Peter very busy, with Jon keeping to himself.

Today, Enrico was back on top of the world; his energy was boundless and the beer flowed. As before, he became the leader of the party. He was aware he had neglected some of his duties with respect to the Budapest caper and Jon Mantler, though. Jon didn't see this as a problem or hold any ill feelings in this regard; he just wanted the rest of his answers.

"Jon, Peter, everyone—it's so fantastic to see you all here in Berlin!" Enrico shouted. "Let me introduce everyone. And Frau Otto, what a pleasure to meet you at long last."

He carried on in that vein, introducing and warming up the crowd until everyone was connected in one big group. After a while, once the party was spinning along swimmingly, he steered Elke, Jon, and Dietrich to a corner of the big table to engage in a special toast.

"To the extraction team from Budapest!" he proclaimed as they all raised their beer glasses. Then Enrico reeled off again, thanking everyone for what he boastfully declared to be the turning point in the breaking of the GDR. "I know it's just the first days, but they'll be finished now, for sure. And you all contributed to the freedom of the people of East Germany. Reunification can't be stopped now."

They all conversed warmly and reminisced about the escape from Hungary. Dietrich was particularly jovial and happy to see Jon after all this time; Jon did his best to reciprocate. He was uncertain of his status with Elke, so he was content to talk with Dietrich.

"It's okay now, Jon, Elke knows who you are," Enrico said in a moment when only he and Jon were engaged. "And yes, Elke and I are together now. Everything has turned out in the best way. I really love her, Jon. It's crazy, I know, but this all just happened in the past few months."

Jon knew Enrico and Elke were together, and he was happy for them. "Does she know that I was there on the bridge with Karl?"

"Yes. I've told her pretty much everything I know, but you should talk openly to her. Or not. Whatever is good for you. I'd like us all to understand what happened, accept it, and be well with it. Especially you, Jon. Things happen for a reason, but sometimes, as in this case, there were choices that had to be made by all of us. It's over now, and we all have to make the best of it. Elke and I sure have. I think if you talk to her directly, it'll help both of you. She wants to talk to you too, and to thank you."

"Thank me?"

Elke Potzner was finally living a happy life. Escaping from Budapest was the best thing that could have happened to her. It was not just because she had fallen for Enrico, although that was a significant part of it. She loved everything about living in the West. Her life had been on hold for too many years. Her messed-up relationship with Karl had caused her to leave Berlin to try and start life over in Budapest, but Budapest was even darker and drearier for her than East Berlin.

Elke had a lust for life that she was never able to express. In Bonn, she was finally around like-minded people she could flourish with. It was as if she had gone from a black-and-white movie into one filled with living color. But the fact that two people had died for her exfiltration caused her guilt, even though there was nothing she could have done about it.

The trip back to Berlin was important for her. She eagerly began planning to visit her mother and father and introduce them to Enrico. She also very much wanted to have time to speak alone with Jon Mantler. Enrico had told her about the events on the bridge that triggered the sequences that led to her leaving Budapest, but she wanted more than Enrico's third-party colored dissertation of the story.

The celebration carried on, making it difficult to converse one-on-one. By now, it was nearing midnight. Elke smiled at Jon to make him feel more comfortable. Jon thought he was smiling back, but he wasn't sure. He did notice she looked even more beautiful than when he had seen her in Budapest. And she was a full-blown blonde now.

"This is such an amazing evening," she finally said to him.

"Yes. But I'd really like to talk to you about Budapest, if that's okay," Jon dove in.

"Yes, of course, but we should do it tomorrow when we can actually speak without this noise. Perhaps we can meet and talk before the lunch tomorrow," Elke suggested.

"That would be ideal. The restaurant is beside the ministry, so I will come by there a bit earlier, say eleven thirty," Jon said.

There were no hotel rooms to be had in central Berlin, so everyone partied all night and then crashed for a few hours of sleep at the homes of some ministry colleagues, or, in the case of Jon and Dietrich, back on the couches at the ministry offices.

The next afternoon allowed for a quieter time. Everyone had agreed to meet for lunch at a restaurant often frequented by the ministry staff in Berlin. A large table had been reserved. Jon was the first one to arrive. Peter had gone to get his mother and brother from their home in the East, which was proving to be not as easy as he had expected.

Not every border crossing was open, and there was a lot of traffic of all sorts, going in conflicting directions. Many border guards were back at their posts, largely out of habit, and operating seemingly with no actual instructions. On their own initiative, they tried to direct traffic as best they could, which was to freely wave cars, trucks, and cycles through the open checkpoints. Peter's arrival at the restaurant was greatly delayed, but today, when the times really were changing, time didn't matter. People felt that from now on, they would have all the time in the world.

At the restaurant, Jon selected a table near the door, away from the large table reserved for the ministry staff. He usually stayed out of the center of gatherings, especially when he did not really feel part of the group. But in this case, he was preparing for Elke's arrival.

Gradually, the bulk of the revelers from the previous night's party straggled in and take up the vacant seats around the big table. Enrico and Elke soon arrived. Elke took the one seat near the wall directly across from Jon while Enrico hurried off to converse with other friends.

Jon needed Elke to know how he felt about what had happened to both men on the bridge that night. He cared about how it might have affected her. He still felt guilty, and this meeting was necessary for him to ultimately deal with that.

Both were clearly more relaxed today, and Jon decided to start the conversation.

"I didn't know Karl so well, but I had met with him one other time in Budapest, in Berlin, Prague, and even in Italy once. He told me a bit about himself, that he had a daughter. But generally, he was kind of a quiet guy, and I thought he was tough. I liked him, though. I feel bad for his wife and daughter, and for you, of course."

"Yes, Karl was basically a quiet guy, but he was the smartest man I ever knew," Elke said. "We grew up together, went to school together. When we were young, we did everything together. We lived in a small community where everyone knew everyone and had lots of friends. It was in East Berlin, but it was a good place to grow up and be a kid. But we split up later for a while, a stupid thing, and he got together with one of our friends in the group. When she got pregnant, he married her. He felt he had done the honorable thing. I guess I still loved him, but I decided to work in Budapest when I had the chance. He would visit me when he came to town. It wasn't that often, though. That went on for a few years until, well, you know, until…"

"I think Karl died immediately when he hit his head on the metal steps that led down to the bottom of the bridge," Jon explained. "But I don't know how it happened. I didn't see what happened between him and Wozneszensky. I left Karl earlier when he told me to go. We could see someone coming, and it did seem like he knew who it was. He told me to leave. I was already on the other side of the bridge when they had their altercation. I ran back when I thought Karl was in trouble, but I couldn't see much in the dark and the rain. By the time I got there, Igor was standing over Karl. I thought Karl was in danger, but now I think Karl was already dead. I'm not sure, really. I may have made a mistake. Maybe Igor was trying to revive Karl when I hit him. I just don't know for sure. But I'm sure he was dead. He wouldn't have suffered," soothed Jon.

"Igor was not a good man," Elke said. "He thought he was better than everyone else. He was angry with Karl because of the night before. But I didn't think he was violent. He was more lost and didn't know how to talk to or deal with women. Who really knows anything about someone like that?" Elke puzzled.

She told Jon all she knew about Igor Wozneszensky. They had had two dates, and she didn't like him at all. He was stalking her and trying to start up a relationship. However, the night before the meeting on the bridge, when Elke and Karl were returning to her apartment, Igor was there.

"Karl was a tough guy, much tougher than Igor," Elke said. "Igor was just big. Karl told Igor to stay away from me or he would have trouble. They had a bit of a verbal fight. It didn't last long. It's already a year ago now, but I remember it like yesterday. It scared me. I don't know how it can still be so clear when so much has happened since." She paused. "What I think is that Igor came by my apartment again on Sunday night and followed Karl to the bridge. Igor was compulsive. Karl told me that he had to go out for a few hours, and he left my apartment at about seven in the evening. I knew he was going to do something that he couldn't tell me about, and I expected him to return around nine. When he didn't return, I thought something strange might have happened, but I couldn't call anyone because he was not supposed to be there. I knew Karl was working for the Stasi, so I had to keep my mouth shut. When Karl's body was found a few days later and Igor stopped contacting me, I thought that was quite a big coincidence. But again, I couldn't speak to anyone. I was afraid."

"But you know they both ended up in the river because of me?" Jon asked. "Igor was an accident. I body-checked him once. Well, twice. The second time, I'm not totally sure how it happened. He fell backward over a small chain-link barrier and into the river. And then I dragged Karl down there too and shoved him off the bridge," Jon confessed.

They both got very quiet.

"I know. Rico told me," Elke said. "It's hard, sure, but it was better that way than what may have happened if you called in the Hungarian authorities. Not just for you, but for Igor and Karl too, and for me, I think, and the families," Elke stuttered. "Our embassy was handling Karl's death, so that was a bit hard to deal with, but I had to stay silent about it. The Hungarians didn't want much to do with it. They just sent us Karl's body and ruled it an accidental death by drowning. There was no investigation to speak of. If you had reported what actually happened, it would have been a huge drama and much more horrible for everyone. Just as well, I suppose, even for Karl's wife, who is actually still a friend of mine, and his daughter. I will probably see them soon. It'll be the first time since Karl died. She doesn't know what really happened, and she doesn't know about me and Karl. Never would be the best time for her to find out. She will only know what the GDR police will have told her. I'm not sure what that is, but whatever it is, I don't think we want to change anything now. No reason. She doesn't need to know he was working for the Stasi and how he ended up in the river."

"I suppose," was all Jon said.

"Really, your quick thinking worked well. And don't forget, they wouldn't have gotten me out of Hungary if you hadn't figured out how to get us through those last gates. Without you, Jon, I wouldn't be here today. I don't know what would have happened to me. I didn't know how stuck I was until the day Enrico stopped me on the street in Budapest. He was so kind and spoke so softly that I felt I had to listen. Now I feel as if deep down, I knew I was being saved. I wanted to hear everything he had to say. I think I actually fell in love with him that day, right there. His eyes were so vivid and clear that I felt I could see my life shining in there. Karl was dead, and I felt terrible about that, but at the same time, I too was dying."

"But you must have been afraid when we were running the border," Jon interjected.

"I was afraid, of course, but it was all a bit foggy at the time. I didn't actually believe we'd get through the border, but I didn't care so much. I'd have gone anywhere with Enrico. I never thought about the consequences of getting caught. I never let that into my head. So I was more dumb and numb than afraid. It was only once I was safe on the other side that I panicked and kind of broke down. That was when the fear actually kicked in. I started to think, 'What if.' But the embassy crew was really terrific at getting me through that. I was so worried about you guys making it back to Budapest safely. My mind was a big mess. The next hours were another blur until I heard the good news."

They decided to end their conversation, satisfied that there was nothing more to say. They joined the bigger group at the table for the celebratory lunch and took the next night and day to be a part of the historic German end to the Second World War. Tomorrow, Elke would reunite with her parents for the first time in over two years, and Jon Mantler would continue on with his life.

"I'm going to see my mother tomorrow for the first time in two years," Elke exclaimed.

Jon thought, two years!

"Reunification."

He was closer to acceptance now. He understood that he was never truly in control of everything that happened in his life. The best he could do was to do the best he could do.

CHAPTER 29

ABBY

So I peel the skin from the apple,
I cut through the noose with my knife.

These days, Abby often stretched out and comforted herself in her favorite lounge chair. She would lie back and relax while watching the evening sun slide down behind the tall forest out on the far side of the lake. It was a ritual she loved, particularly at this time of year, when the daylight stayed longer in this part of the northern hemisphere.

Abby bought this wood cabin more than a year ago, and with the exception of cold weeks in the winter months, had spent every weekend there since. This particular view was a big reason she had chosen the cabin. Here she could peacefully pursue her deep-rooted thoughts. Inside the cozy solitude that the wall-to-wall wood provided, she felt content and able to contemplate.

A pause and a place for analysis had come into her life. Abby was fifty years of age now, and her accomplishments in the second half of her life had been remarkable. She was Dr. Abigail R. Norton, a practicing psychologist and part-time lecturer at a respected university.

Owning the majestic cabin on this tranquil northern lake was another significant accomplishment. Having raised a capable and independent daughter, who would soon be graduating from university, was also an accomplishment. When she added the joy of sharing the past two decades of her life with a loving, nurturing partner, she felt enormously grateful. On recent evenings, however, she found herself thinking more about an earlier life. A time when she had timidly returned here, near where she was born. A time that was indisputably the worst of times.

Suppressing that past was something Dr. Norton knew a great deal about. It was a topic she had studied in detail at university and often lectured on. The fact she knew how the psychological intricacies of this affliction functioned did not, however, cause her to change her behavior regarding her own suppression. As any bad habit will tell you, knowing what you should do rarely results in the actual doing.

Abby felt true remorse at how easily she had let time slip away. The first few years she could forgive, because, as she now understood it, she had not been well in the past. In the decade that followed, however, she had no excuse or explanation. Once a certain amount of time went by with no consequences, it became progressively easier to continue to put off doing what she knew she should have done. Time went by and she let it, almost pushing it on, all while telling herself that she would do something soon, until that soon was long gone.

There may be something to the midlife crisis we analyze, Abby thought as the night of reflection turned painful. Turning fifty years of age is an awkward awakening for most people. It may be the first time the idea of being "old" crawls into one's consciousness and pervades their conversations. Acknowledging that a large part of one's life is over is quite humbling. You will never have these years back, and as the song says, you will never pass this way again. You can only check the scoreboard and recalibrate your successes and failures. A time, perhaps, for honesty and reckoning.

This was precisely where Abby found herself on this particular night. She had been near this point before. The different this time was that she knew, in order to move forward with the rest of her life, she had to go back.

Today, her pushback began while recalling the three-day bus ride that returned her to this province. She recalled the horrible reality of being all alone in this big world with virtually nowhere to go. It was not the first time she was in a dire predicament, but this felt so much worse. For the second time in her life, she was pregnant. Though it was somewhat of a blur, she remembered how she had become pregnant. It made her feel weak and ashamed, back then and now. Her relationship with the young neighboring pastor should not have gone this far.

Now that she had more than just her own life to think about, she dug deep. She had previous experience in the grocery industry and thus was able to get a job at a local food store. She hid her pregnancy for as long as she could, and through pure hard work and a positive attitude, she managed to endear herself to her colleagues on a human level.

This effort paid off for her once the pregnancy became apparent. The store managers liked her enough to bend a few rules to help her. They considered her a valued employee and juggled dates so she could receive full benefits from their group insurance program and qualify for maternity leave. This meant she had health insurance that provided income benefits during the last part of her pregnancy and also time off after the birth. Her baby, whom she named Raquel, was born in the small city hospital with the tender professional care of a local nursing staff.

Sitting in her cabin now, she was content remembering those moments of her life, the moments when things shifted for the better. Abby fondly recalled first meeting Janice. It was about a week after she started working. She was stocking shelves with canned goods when Janice approached and asked for directions. They both smiled at a soon-forgotten joke, and from that mini-encounter, a life of friendship and love grew.

Janice was a regular shopper at this grocery store and lived only a city block away. Abby was in desperate need of a friend and was happy whenever Janice came by the store to talk. Soon they were meeting after work and hanging out together at neighborhood events. For quite some time, Abby didn't really understand what was happening. She had never considered being in a relationship with a woman and wasn't sure how to feel about it. For Janice, it was love at first sight, and the situation felt as natural as rain.

The rapid changes taking place at this stage of Abby's life were largely outside her realm of control. Her emotional state, ingrained into her by the pregnancy and the poverty, had rendered her in need of security. Again, she had to rely on her survival instincts. Accepting Janice's sincere friendship was integral to that survival.

They became inseparable, and it felt good. Janice relentlessly stayed by Abby's side throughout the pregnancy. After Raquel was born, they moved in together and became a little family. The relationship developed fast, but early on and deep down, Abby sensed it was right. As she came to better understand herself, she understood it was more than just safe; she was genuinely happy. Janice was able to provide a home on a level that Abby had never experienced. She could breathe now, and she didn't have to run anymore.

Same-sex relationships were not embraced or acknowledged in the small-town society where Janice and Abby lived, not in those times. Practically, though, people were more apt to look the other way. Especially in the case of two females sharing a home together. Abby was considered a single mom with a roommate, and that helped.

Most importantly, Janice brought a calm solidity to Abby's life. Prior to this moment, the only luck Abby had was the Booker T. Jones/ Albert King kind. The kind where if it weren't for bad luck, you wouldn't have any luck at all. Now she had a totally different attitude toward luck. It was more in the vein of Hemingway's *The Old Man and the Sea*, which says that when luck comes, you have to be ready to do something with it. Luck is always spinning somewhere around you, she decided, and you need to put yourself in a position where it can hit you. From then on, she would be ready the next time luck came to town.

Caring for Raquel in those early years gave her a renewed determination to make something more of her life; with Janice's limitless support, she was able to do so. She remembered how much joy it gave her to interact with a child again. She knew she had been a good mother before things went wrong. This time, she would make sure that nothing would go wrong.

Cohabitation with Janice provided opportunities she had not expected. Janice loved Raquel as if she were her own child, and she actively engaged in being a parent. Two decades later, they were still a happy family.

Abby was able to fulfill some of her secret dreams and enroll in university classes while still working shifts at the grocery store. Janice worked as a realtor and had a flexible work schedule, so she was easily able to assist in caring for Raquel. It took several years for Abby to achieve her first degree at university, but she moved on quickly with her studies after that. At first, she took mainly night and summer school courses to make up for the limited time she was able to attend university. She continued to work shifts at the grocery store to make ends meet and to be able to mother Raquel. It was through these studies that her healing really began. Entering the world of academia was the best therapy. She became a researcher in the field of psychology and was soon profoundly immersed in it.

She carried on and on with her studies, eventually achieving a doctorate in psychology. Through the process, she developed a better understanding of her own life. Life today was tranquil and idyllic, and it was nearly unimaginable that there had been such a tumultuous other side to it. Her second life, as she secretly referred to it, was filled with success, while her first life was splattered with pain and unrest. Coming to terms with those early years became manageable through her study of mental illness and the various personality disorders that had dominated her younger life.

There had been happy times, too, when she was raising her son in that far-off place in the center of the country. She often thought of those good times, but it was so much different from the life she had now with Janice and Raquel.

It took a doctorate degree in psychology to effectively bring the earliest years of her life to the surface. The abuse, the alcohol, and the mental illness that had afflicted her parents were real. Her numerous attempts at suicide were too. She had lived many of the lives that she was now analyzing in cases and textbooks. Remembering always made her body tremble, but understanding and accepting it eventually made it okay.

Abby had spent the first half of her life running away from herself and the second half of her life running toward herself. She agreed that those worlds needed to collide and find a way to coexist. She knew it was up to her to initiate it. There would be consequences to manage, but she would no longer avoid them.

Her story began in a small town in the province of Ontario, not far from where she now lived. She was born to Dan and Mary Norton. Her earliest memories were of living on the outskirts of a town in a big house with a big yard. It could have been a rather paradisiacal existence, but it was not that at all whenever Dan Norton was nearby.

Dan was a long-haul trucker who was away from home most of the time. Abby remembered when she was very young how excited she would become when the big maroon semi-trailer her father commandeered would gear down and smoke its way up the long, wooded lane to their house.

The first day of his return was usually joyous. Her mother would dress up and cook something special. Abby would get to eat cake, and her father would usually bring her a present. That was about as good as it ever got. The rest of Dan's days at home with the family were taken up primarily with drinking and carousing with his male friends in the neighborhood. Abby and her mother would lie low and out of the way as much as they could on those days, because Dan was not a happy or fun drunk. He was a mean, abrasive man when under the sway of alcohol.

Abby had long ago decided not to remember many details of her early life, even though she actually did. What she recalled the most was the feeling that her father didn't want her. She wished she had been born a little boy, because she thought Dan would have loved her more. He loved hunting, fishing, and football—things Abby was not designed for.

Initially, Dan took most of his anger out on his wife, but as Abby got older, she became a target as well. She was not sexually abused by her father, at least not that she could remember, but she did remember being belittled and beaten. Defensively, she drew closer to her mother, and they supported each other while waiting for Dan to hit the road again on his next trucking assignment.

Life was more tolerable as long as Dan was on the road, but when Abigail was about eight years old, Dan left the big rig permanently and ceased being a long-haul truck driver. This was going to be the change that the family needed, he declared, but of course it didn't turn out that way.

Dan parked the truck and took a sales job at a nearby automobile dealership. He parked the truck, but he didn't park the drinking. As time went by and with Dan near home, everyday life became worse for Abby and her mother, not better.

Abby's mother had grown up in a secluded part of Ontario as an only, not necessarily wanted, child. Both her parents were acutely self-centered and severely religious, so Mary grew up under staunch social restrictions. Her life was tragically defined forever at age nineteen, when both of Mary's parents were killed in an automobile accident. God's will, she called it when sharing the traumatic story with Abby.

Mary was away studying in the big city and becoming more self-reliant when the accident occurred. This terrible event destroyed her ability to continue that pursuit. At nineteen years of age, she inherited the country house and surrounding property where they now lived and where she would live for the rest of her life. It was too much responsibility for Mary, and she managed her responsibilities poorly. Her parents' devout religion and the consequences of a strict upbringing left her incapable of fully understanding the circumstances she found herself in.

To cope, Mary tended to rely on the dominating presence of people around her, like Dan Norton. Abby understood this now, but not back then. Looking at it later, she realized that her mother had been unwell for most of her life. Having studied personalities and associated disorders over the past decades helped her to make sense of it. It was clear that her mother suffered from a mental condition characterized by excessive apprehension. This triggered defense mechanisms to distance her from stressful situations.

Abby believed that, had Mary been correctly diagnosed at that time and treated effectively, life for the two of them might have been quite different. However, in those times, mental disorders and mental health in general were rarely diagnosed and treated in small communities like where the Nortons lived.

Abby turned ten on the same day her mother gave birth to a son. A special day no longer hers and one she would now forever share with her brother, Randy. Dan and Mary had convinced themselves that this family-building exercise was just what the Norton family needed, and that from this birth onward, life for the Nortons would be joyous.

In reality, Abby would feel even more isolated, only now from her father and her mother. More and more, she purposefully distanced herself from both of them. Neither one provided the love and support she needed. She loved school, though, and that became her prime sanctuary. Most days, she was sad when the 3:30 p.m. bell rang and she had to leave school to return to the country house to Mary and Dan. Whenever possible, she stayed at school to help her teachers with whatever task or activity they would allow her to do, so she did not have to spend more time than necessary at home. She cleaned a lot of chalkboards and stacked a lot of library books.

It was around this time that the suicidal thoughts emerged. At night, she often wished that she would simply fall asleep and not wake up the next day. Never a good sleeper, these urges were the strongest in the middle of the night. How terrible, she now thought, to be so young and to feel so fraught. Most likely, she was alive today, because back then, she was too young to know how to kill herself. Her thoughts of suicide continued as the years crawled by, but her fear of the unknown and an instinct to survive always pulled her back from that brink. Instead of committing suicide, she became a runner, someone who habitually ran away.

Abigail Norton began running away at a very young age. As a small child, she found special hiding places in the forest near her home where she spent as many hours as she could away from her house whenever her father was home. By the age of twelve, she was leaving home entirely for longer periods of time. The first few times, she ran away from her father. She was sure he hated her because she was not a boy, and seeing daily how much he cared for little Randy significantly enhanced that feeling.

Most times, Abby left to stay with her aunt, Dan's sister, in a small town near Toronto. The first few days with her aunt were always good fun, but ultimately, things waned, and they were unable to build a solid relationship.

It turned out the only thing Abby and her aunt had in common was their abhorrence of Dan. Beyond that, they were total opposites. Eventually, she would feel strong enough to come back and try to live with her mother again, and the cycle would play out again. She employed a strategy to stay out of her father's crosshairs, but eventually, there wasn't much left of her mother to come back to. Her mother decided to stand by the madman she married rather than support the tender needs of her daughter. The last time Abby ran away, it was not just away from her father. Mary's mental illness had become more serious, but no one in their circle of acquaintances recognized it.

Back again at Dan's sister's house, Abby avoided conflict by spending as little time in the home as possible. She contributed to the living costs by working at a number of jobs, primarily in the service industry, and excelled in high school. Academically, she was one of the highest achievers in her school, but she was never able to make genuine friends there. She struggled socially and exhibited severe signs of low self-esteem. Most of the time, she preferred to be alone. It was not what she wanted, but it was safer than any of the alternatives she saw around her.

It was here at her aunt's house one summer that Abby met Tracy, a girl Abby thought was her cousin but was actually the niece of one of her aunt's boyfriends. Tracy was a few years older, and in Abby's estimation, the coolest and most self-assured person she had ever encountered.

Abby desperately wanted Tracy as a best friend, like a big sister. They spent a wonderful summer together, and for Abby, it was the most memorable period of her life thus far. So when it came time to run away again, which was immediately upon graduating, it was to reunite with Tracy. Running halfway across the country on a series of buses on a mission to find her was completely irrational, but it made sense at the time. It was a desperate cry for help.

Tracy had made the journey west a few months earlier after meeting a young farm boy who was visiting Toronto for an event. Tommy lived with his family on a big farm in the general vicinity of Greyton. Tracy planned to marry him and live happily ever after in the land of big skies and plenty.

By the time Abby arrived at the remote family farm to meet her friend and mentor, Tracy had grown bored with both Tommy and with life on the prairies. She was snuggled up in a Camaro with a mechanic named Jeff, heading south. Tracy was gone like a summer dust storm, and Abby felt rejected again. This time, there was the added trauma of being displaced in a far-off land with no money and no place to live. Tommy's farming family was puzzled at what she was doing there and not at all interested in having another mouth to feed.

Today, looking out the window of her cabin, Abby tried with

limited success to understand how she had felt on that day all those years ago. She could not suppress her emotions any longer, and cried.

"There will not be a perfectly right time and no absolutely wrong time. We can only act and do when time decides," Janice had once told her when they were discussing her dilemma. It had been a life lesson in psychology.

Time was now deciding.

Abby wished Janice, who was back in the city working this week, were there with her now. Janice was the only person she had ever been able to truly confide in. Janice was compassionate and wise; the one Abby had always needed in her life.

CHAPTER 30

THE BEACH

Pummel the tin with an anvil,
as the water washes away at my life.

One late morning, as Jon sauntered out of the shack to the beach cot he had been inhabiting each day for the past twenty days or so, he noticed a knapsack and a big towel lying out on the sand a few meters away. There was no one nearby as he stepped past it on his way to his station. The weather was already warm, and the sun was working its way across the bluest of skies. Jon lay back on the cot and opened his novel for his morning read.

Jon had spent most of his days in this same spot, reading, thinking, sleeping, or simply looking inquisitively at the Mediterranean Sea. He had never spent time on the water or near the sea before; he had always lived on dry land. Now he was trying to become a friend of the sea. It was something that interested him and that he knew little about.

Three weeks had passed quickly since he had arrived at this relatively quiet spot near St. Maxime, and he expected that it would be many more weeks before he would move on. The weather was pleasantly warm for this early in the spring, and he relished the sunshine while his thoughts sliced through the recent years of his life.

It had taken a few months and a good deal of expense to make the changes he deemed necessary and to sell or give away all he owned. Jon had decided not to be part of the new united Germany he had played a small role in bringing about. Enrico offered him work with the ministry he was now heading up, but Jon didn't feel a strong enough connection to this new world order manifesting around him. He knew there was much more change to come, but his time in this particular part of the world was over.

Once he had officially checked out of Germany, he was still left with a fairly substantial shoebox. When spring finally sprung, he loaded up a rental car and headed for the French Riviera. He moved into a small wooden hut up a hill from a somewhat remote beach with the intention of evaluating and recovering from the past few years of his life. A change needed to come, but he had only a few vague ideas as to what that should entail.

First, he needed to come to terms with recent issues and incidents. He had compiled quite a long list that included Nora, Peter, Enrico, Karl Bircher, Igor Wozneszensky, and Roxanne Martin. Jon wanted to better understand his role in these individuals' lives and what he should do next. But first, he simply wanted to be alone; he had always mostly been okay with being alone.

Each day as he watched the ships sitting high on top of the water inching their way near predetermined destination, he thought about what it might be like to be a captain of such a ship. Steering it far out on the sea would be an exacting and formidable task. It would demand high degrees of precision and dedication. These were skills Jon knew he had. He wondered if he had applied enough of those qualities to his life so far.

"Change will come," John Mantler Sr. had forewarned. "You can't stop it, so don't fight it."

Society had led Jon to believe that change was a necessary progression, and that change made things better. Reflecting now, he measured things differently. He was not certain that all the changes in his life had been for the better. He felt like he had been living from the outside in and not from his own inside out. So much had come to him externally and were predetermined by outside forces. He needed to build a new relationship with change.

As a notion, that was easy. It made sense as a noble objective. He would have to become a different Jon Mantler; however, to command such change would require an altered attitude and mindset. There would be new skills he would have to learn. He was trying to take the first step, which was to figure himself out; this was why he had come alone to this place by the sea at this very point in his life. To get ahead of change.

The split with Nora still burned fresh and raw in his psyche. It caused him pain and consternation. He was pretty sure that he loved

Nora, but if that was so, why did he not fight for her to stay? What did he really know about love, anyway? Why did he not really let her into his world? To understand one's own love, one needs to understand one's own self, he surmised. Was this where he had broken down?

What if he had confessed the Budapest events to her? It would have been a betrayal of his German colleagues to do so, but they were all on the same side of the war. There was no NATO breach, just different factions working on different aspects of the same thing. Still, it would have put Nora in a difficult situation. She would have been duty-bound to report the event to her superiors. What would have happened was a big guess, but not much of it would have been good. There would be substantial risks of leaks as well. Could he and Nora have kept the secret together? Would that have kept their relationship alive? What would have changed?

Delving deeper, he realized that most of the changes in his life were due to age, and as such, were largely unavoidable. Beyond that, the major decisions in his life had been dictated by others: "I was just going along for the ride."

It was Nora who was attracted to Jon; she initiated the relationship. She made the decisions about how their time together would be constructed. She owned the home where they first lived, and she took him abroad. In Europe, it was Peter who targeted Jon to work for the German government. Before that, he had been recruited out of university by the engineering firm TDC, and that was how he ended up in the capital city. Even back in his village, Geoffrey Jones had initiated the demolition of Jon's shack. Jon went to university because almost everyone else did, and because Miss Roberts orchestrated it. In the past, he had always thought of himself as independent and in control of his life, but today, on this beach, he was feeling like the only things he had done of his own volition were to toss two bodies off a bridge. But not all the steps in his life were bad.

It would of course take more time to recover from Nora's departure. They were together for nearly five years, and Jon had not intended to end the relationship. Subconsciously, perhaps he did, but it was not a Mantler type of thing to do. Nora brought a maturity and quality to his life at a time he certainly needed it. She was intelligent and sophisticated, which appealed to him. With Nora, he was no longer alone inside his own mind, although if you had asked Nora, she might have disputed that.

Jon had never felt alone with Nora. He was content to share her company, and their years together were good. Still, when she announced she was taking a new position back in the capital city and effectively leaving him, he was not shocked. He concluded that things between them could not be repaired. They had reached a stage in their lives where being together was not their only priority. Jon had become too distant, and Nora didn't believe he would ever break out from inside himself. He always went back to the shack, she thought.

Later that morning, Jon paused to look out to the sea, where he saw, far off in the distance, a man emerging from the lapping waves, walking directly toward him. As he squinted through his sunglasses, Jon felt an electric shock bolt through his body. For a moment, he thought it was his father walking out of the sea across the sand. It was an intense and unearthly feeling.

The man continued, and with each awkward step, Jon became more and more astounded at the resemblance. As the man approached, Jon noted he was taller and walked straighter than John Mantler would have. He looked older, too, but so would his father if he were actually walking toward him now. Jon couldn't steer his eyes away.

"Bonjour, monsieur," the man said once he realized Jon was looking at him.

Jon replied with the same phrase, whereupon the man on the beach immediately realized his new acquaintance was an English speaker and switched languages.

"I declare that it could not be a finer morning to enjoy this sea. Is it acceptable to you if I occupy this space?"

"Of course, certainly. It would be a pleasure," Jon answered politely.

"Thank you, kind sir." The man nimbly stretched out on his towel to absorb the sunshine.

The older man quietly read from a paperback while Jon did the same while continuing to observe the man from behind, occasionally glancing over and feeling awestruck by how much he reminded him of his father. If John were alive today, he would be this man's twin.

A few minutes later, the man rose to his feet and talked about the weather and the ocean until a chord was struck. "I have a hunger," the man ultimately declared. "Would you do me the courtesy of joining me for an early lunch, or a *petit déjeuner*, whatever you choose to call it? It would be a great pleasure for me."

"That is a good idea. Let's do it," Jon said.

"I'm Charles Sapriel. I live just down the road from this beach. I've seen you here the past few days. How do you do? I like to practice my speaking of English."

"I'm Jon Mantler, and I'm sorry that I cannot speak French."

They continued their chatter as they walked for about five minutes up the beach. Sapriel limped along, guiding Jon across the boardwalk to a café. The old gentleman ordered for both of them while explaining that the establishment was owned and run by his daughter, Monique. She was the reason he had returned to St. Maxime since retiring from his work in Lyon.

This was the first local Jon had met during his brief residency here, and he was very much enjoying the experience. In the ensuing days, they met on the beach every day, and Sapriel eagerly outlined the main events of his life. The conversation flowed freely. Besides being the spitting image of John Mantler, Charles Sapriel could tell stories in the league of Will Denman. Jon loved war stories, and Sapriel provided a different perspective because he was fighting in the French resistance near where John and Will had been when the war abruptly ended for them.

Life after the war was even harsher for Sapriel and what was left of his family compared to John Mantler Sr. in Canada. Jon was intrigued and keen to better understand what had transpired in Europe between the end of the war and when he arrived in West Germany.

As the days rolled by and with their daily conversations, Jon could feel a change taking place. A messenger had come to deliver Jon's unfinished business with his father.

CHAPTER 31

ROXANNE

The tools we acquired will be the perfect fit.
This time, the door will open and stay.

John Mantler was outside repairing the front window of his house when she came around the corner of the street that connected to the post office. Despite the passage of so much time, Abby's recollection of that day was still remarkably vivid. She recalled stopping beside him on the street without saying anything. She wanted to speak but couldn't; all she could do was cry.

John's voice was soothing. "Oh, come on now, nothing can be that bad that it can't be resolved. Can I help you?"

"I'm just having a terrible day again," she said, sobbing.

There was a bench beside the entrance to his house, next to a big fir tree. They sat beside each other on that bench as he tried to calm and console her. It was there on that bench, in what can only be interpreted as a bold and desperate act of self-preservation, that Abigail Norton became Roxanne Martin.

"I'm so lost. I have no place to go. I just don't know what to do," she bawled. With that, she released selected parts of her life to a shocked and empathetic John Mantler.

Some of what she told him was true. Abby was more surprised than John at the words coming from her mouth, and the more words flew out, the more she believed them. Once she started, she couldn't stop.

Getting as far away from Abigail Norton as possible felt like her only chance of surviving. It had taken her a long time to ultimately understand what had happened to her on that day. Oddly, now she was even a bit proud of herself for being able to carry out such a bold action. She was desperate, acting on instinct. Abby also understood how unwell she had been back then. She had been running without success for such a long time and had reached the end of her line.

She detested who she was back then so much that, right on the spot, she reinvented herself and became Roxanne Martin. The name just fell out of nowhere, and once it did, that was who she was.

John Mantler heard her story and sincerely felt sorry for her. He believed that only some of what she told him was the truth, but it didn't matter. He sensed no one else in the world was going to help her, and that was true.

John provided her with refuge and a brief chance to stop running. A shelter from her storm. It was the first time that someone was actually willing to be there for her.

"If you wish to, you can stay here until you can get yourself together. I have a second room inside you can use. Maybe we can even get you some work around here so you can earn a bit of money while you figure out what to do next," John offered. "But it seems like you need to rest up before you can decide anything."

The relationship began with this simple act of kindness. There was no intention that it would be anything other than that. Abigail Norton was now Roxanne Martin, and immediately, that gave her hope for a future, whereas Abigail had none.

John was easy to be with, and on this day of reflection, she felt the same love for him as before. He was quite a good-looking man when Roxanne arrived in the village. His physical disability was not as pronounced, and he had not yet been labeled "old John Mantler" by the locals. That all came later. Abby still remembered the handsome man on the bench. We see what we want to see.

Their relationship began as a friendship, but the friendship evolved into something more. Roxanne trusted John from the outset. A lot of what she told him was accurate, like how she ended up where she was.

After graduating from high school, she told him she had decided to bus out to the prairies to connect with Tracy, the woman she assumed was her cousin. It was an act of utter desperation. But by the time she arrived, Tracy had deserted the area. The Tracy and Tommy part was already common knowledge in the community, but no one knew anything about any Roxanne, and those dots would never be connected.

John was pretty much smart enough to know what was true and what wasn't, as well as what did and didn't matter. John didn't care about gossip; he was fine helping Roxanne by letting her stay for a few days until she could sort things out in her life.

Roxanne didn't like the lies she told, but it turned out that she was good at it. It wasn't a big stretch to go from Norton to Martin, or to go from Abigail, a name she used to hate, to Roxanne, a name she preferred to Rachel, which was actually her second name. Had she been thinking, rather than quickly reacting, she would have become Raquel, a name she very much liked. But as life would turn out, she would find use for that one later.

John never expected to fall so in love with Roxanne or that she would stay with him for six years. He also never knew he would be such a good father. On that first day, he was the perfect gentleman with no agenda other than being of use to her. He fixed up a cot for her to sleep on in the second of the three rooms in his small house. John was also a good cook, with a big garden of fresh produce, and he cooked meals for his rare guest. Roxanne couldn't cook at all, which was one of many things that she had not yet been given the opportunity to learn in her short and difficult life.

From the outside, a nearly twenty-year age difference may have been hard for some people to comprehend. For most people, anything that is not their own shoe size is hard to comprehend. But right now, neither John nor Roxanne cared much about what other people thought. Roxanne saw the kindness in John's eyes the day she walked past the Mantler shack. She felt secure in his presence on a day when she so needed to be saved. Her experiences with men up to that point had been beyond horrific.

Abby, now a psychologist, knew that when she arrived at the Mantler shack, she was suffering from a form of mental illness similar to what had afflicted her own mother. Heredity and genetics were at play here.

Roxanne had no long-term plan other than to keep breathing and take it moment by moment. She had made a lot of mistakes in her few years. Traveling thousands of kilometers across Canada, the slim hope that she would find a better life was likely to be her biggest mistake yet. It was a stretch to think she would connect with her assumed cousin, whom she had only met once. Desperate people have fewer options and are forced to believe in impossible outcomes.

Roxanne felt comfortable at the shack. Days went by, then weeks, and progressively she made friends with neighbors. With no other place to go, she tried to relax and enjoy the peace. Then she became pregnant with JJ, and that changed everything, remarkably for the better. She embraced all aspects of motherhood as if she had been given a restart on life. It was like a drug, as if all facets of her past were wiped clean from her slate. She vowed that Roxanne Martin would be the best mother imaginable, and for six years, that was exactly what she was.

Abby fondly reflected on those years she had spent raising young JJ in the village. John and Roxanne focused all their attention on their son. Raising him in the village created wonderful memories. It was hard to believe how quickly those years passed until the inevitable change came.

The way it happened was never totally clear to her, and it remained largely a blur even now. She never intended to have a relationship with the young pastor of the neighboring church, but something happened. He had been young, charming, and convincing. Up to that point, her experience with religion was based on the influence of her mother and had left her riddled and confused. She had no specific faith or conviction and was just a mother living in a small community where the church played a prominent role.

Becoming part of the congregation was an expected neighborly and social thing to do. Roxanne lived near the church, so it was a convenient activity to take on. She even became a member of the church board for a time, which brought her in close contact with the young Reverend Theiss.

Becoming pregnant again broke the relatively peaceful and contented life she had built in the village. Again, she felt she had to run. A lot of life is decided for you and not by you. She could count on half of one hand the number of times she had had sexual contact with a man, so it seemed unfair that from that she would get pregnant twice.

What in that part of her life back then had ever been fair, she now thought. So similar to how she came was how she went. She had run away from Abigail Norton to become Roxanne Martin, and now she would run from Roxanne Martin to again become Abigail Norton.

She hated herself for leaving young JJ but didn't see any other options. She knew he would be well taken care of by John and the people in the village. She never intended it to be a forever thing.

Over the years, she kept in contact with a confidante in the village who reported to her on the life of JJ. She knew about John's death, she knew about the dismantling of the shack, she knew about the court case and the many scholarships. Harvey's mother at the post office had secretly kept her up to speed with the life of Jon Mantler.

Abby kept track with the intention of defining the ideal time to make contact. The university years certainly could have been an option; Jon was probably mature enough to welcome such a reunion then. Another opportune time would have been when he moved east to join TDC as an engineer; she was pondering that just as Jon and Nora were relocated to Europe by the DND. Keeping track of Jon in Europe was a bit more difficult, but because Nora worked for the Department of National Defense in a high-profile role, her whereabouts were quite transparent.

The truth was that until now, Abby hadn't had the courage to take the action she should have. She always found odd reason to justify postponing her many intended contacts.

Abby knew this had to change, especially now that she did not know where in the world her son was. She knew Nora had returned to the nation's capital and that Jon Mantler had not returned with her. This was the first time in all these years she did not know where he was.

She needed to find him. This was her big "river to cross" moment that could not be put off any longer. The next day, she scheduled two weeks off work, packed her bags, and headed to the airport.

CHAPTER 32

LIVING UP

When you get back home, we will build it.
Once you are well, I will show you the way.

Jon was entertained by the narratives and interpretations of life that Sapriel related to him. There were war stories that reconnected him to his father and the conversations with Will Denman he had treasured so much. But Charles Sapriel was not a mere orator; he was a skilled listener as well, and within a few days, the topic of discussion centered on Jon Mantler.

Jon found he talked more about himself than ever before. He laid out the events of his life to this man, who could have been his father's twin. This charming man had triggered an awakening in him.

He had never been able to go so deeply into how things affected him. There was always something else that needed tending to. Before he could close his feelings about whatever had just happened, he would become engaged with something else, so his feelings never reached a conclusion. Jon's anger and disgust had changed the relationship he had with himself. The conversations with Sapriel were invaluable for this reason.

Sapriel had acted similarly in his youth, particularly in the years after the *"guerre horrible,"* as he referred to it. "Jon, you're still so very young, yet you're acting as if you're an old man, afraid of what truth might do to you."

Jon knew that was so. He was becoming his father. In the days that followed, he opened up and told Charles Sapriel almost everything that had happened in his life. He talked about his parents, about growing up in the village and the tearing down of the shack, then all about his university days and his move east into Europe. He even talked about the relationship with Nora.

Notably, for the first time ever, he talked about what happened in

Budapest. Sapriel's wisdom and life experience allowed him to listen with a unique consciousness. Once Jon sensed that someone understood him, he felt relieved. He had never disclosed to anyone outside of the small circle what he had done on that bridge. He admitted to a stranger that he had killed someone.

Trusting someone with his true feelings at this point in his life was therapeutic. A point had come where he understood he could not do everything alone. Alone, he could not go deep enough. The self-induced aloneness he had been clinging to had served him, but in the last two years, he had suffered. Sapriel provided a channel through which Jon could rerun his life, bringing great insight into the most critical aspects of his existence.

Jon had never intended to completely forgive himself for the impulsive actions he had taken on that night in Budapest. The talks with Sapriel changed that. It was time to accept things.

"Merely a brief bit of history that, in the grand scheme of things, you were witness to," was how Sapriel described it. "Be grateful that you could experience such a fascinating episode. More important than what you do in your life is how you feel about what you're doing in your life."

Jon listened intently and tried to register his new mentor's words. With the fall of the Berlin Wall and the end of authoritarian rule in Hungary and the GDR, the incident on that bridge would never come to light. Even if there existed paperwork from an investigation, there was no one in any position to care about it now.

Jon began to understand that the dilemma lived on only in his own mind. He vowed he would no longer allow even thirty seconds of his time on earth to inhabit such a powerful space in his life. Sapriel had put it all in clear perspective for him.

"You have already let this shatter you. What more is there for you to do but stop it and get on with your life? You must now do what is most important and appealing to you."

It was Sapriel who drew their conversation to the questions surrounding Jon's mother. An unresolved issue he had left dragging behind him. The one that kept him mostly okay with being alone.

"This business of not being certain if she's alive or dead needs to be attended to. Someone will have knowledge of this. What are you still waiting for?"

These impromptu social sessions went on for two more weeks until the time came when they both knew it had to end. Jon had said all he could, and now he was certain about what to do next. Sapriel delivered one last push.

"You need real people in your life, Jon. You need friends and people for you to care about. I know this, and this is why I live close to my daughter, and here, back near the people I started my life with. You need to go and find these people, and you need to learn how to be their friend."

Jon had to admit that, outside of his colleague Peter, who cared a great deal for Jon, the only friend he had ever had in his life was Harvey Dean. He decided that, although he knew how time changed people and that a history with someone could never be relived, he would reconnect with Harvey. That would be good, he thought.

"I'm not your father, Jon, but if you think you need fatherly advice, here it is. Start living it up; stop living it down. Your father was a good man, but you're not him. Respect him, but don't become him. Go and build things, yes, but not for your father. Build things for yourself. Go and find new people and give them a place in your life. Open doors; don't close them behind you. And you must go and find your mother. At a minimum, you must find out exactly what happened to her," Sapriel said.

Four days later, Jon Mantler walked out of the shack on the hill above the beach with two big bags. Then Sapriel drove him to the airport in Nice.

* * * * *

ABOUT THE AUTHOR

R G Schmidt writes fiction, poetry, and songs. A world-medaled athlete and five-time Olympic Coach in curling, he has coauthored *The Five Elements of Curling Technique*, published his poetry in *Poetic Expanse - A Compilation*, and released the acclaimed music album *Bridges From Both Sides* as Slyd Blvd. He was born in Canada and lives in Switzerland and in Greece.